Winifred placed her hand on Quinn's cheek and ran her fingers across his lips. It didn't surprise Quinn to find that though his own throat was near closed with unfamiliar emotions, Winifred had no trouble talking. "Yeah, I remember," he said.

"As you might recall, I was really more asleep than awake at the time . . ." She moved her fingers gently through his hair.

"Uh-huh."

"What I wanted to know was, would you kiss me again?"

"I'd be pleased to," he whispered and dipped his head.

The Bandit's Lady

⚒ MAUREEN CHILD ⚒

HarperPaperbacks
A Division of HarperCollinsPublishers

This is a work of fiction. The characters, incidents, and
dialogues are products of the author's imagination and are
not to be construed as real. Any resemblance to actual events
or persons, living or dead, is entirely coincidental.

HarperPaperbacks   *A Division of* HarperCollins*Publishers*
10 East 53rd Street, New York, N.Y. 10022

Copyright © 1995 by Maureen Child
All rights reserved. No part of this book may be used or
reproduced in any manner whatsoever without written
permission of the publisher, except in the case of brief
quotations embodied in critical articles and reviews. For
information address HarperCollins*Publishers*,
10 East 53rd Street, New York, N.Y. 10022.

Cover illustration by R. A. Maguire

First printing: December 1995

Printed in the United States of America

HarperPaperbacks, HarperMonogram, and colophon are
trademarks of HarperCollins*Publishers*

❖ 10 9 8 7 6 5 4 3 2 1

The Bandit's Lady

1

Yellow Dog, Texas, 1870

"Keep your hands up!" The gunman tightened his grip on the money bag in his left hand and motioned with his gun hand. Roughening up his voice so they wouldn't recognize it, he added, "And don't nobody try to follow me, neither!"

Quinn Hawkins backed up a step or two, his gaze constantly moving over the faces of the four people in front of him. Four people he'd known most of his life. A sharp stab of uncertainty speared through him but as his gaze locked on the paunchy, sweating face of the banker, Charles Bentley, Quinn ignored his pang of conscience.

He had no choice.

Three customers were lined up right alongside the bank president, their hands held high. Quinn's gaze swept across the familiar features of his friends and neighbors. He wasn't surprised to see that Old Man

McDonough and his son Dusty looked fit to bust at being prisoners. And if given half a chance, Quinn knew that Dusty would jump him—gun or no gun. Mrs. Hightower, a middle-aged lady twice the size of most men in town and the only woman in the bank, looked as though she was about to keel over in one of her "spells."

Even as he thought it, the woman started to sway. Hell, Quinn thought. Just what he needed. If she fell over, she'd hit her head and maybe get hurt bad.

Beneath the red bandana covering the lower half of his face, Quinn frowned. "You there," he jabbed the barrel of his pistol toward the bank president. Briefly, he enjoyed the sharp look of panic that settled on Charles Bentley's overfed, doughy features. "Help her sit down 'for she falls down."

Bentley grumbled something under his breath and Quinn bit back a smile. It was almost worth robbing a bank and risking jail or worse just to watch old fancy-pants Bentley staggering under the considerable bulk of Erma Hightower in one of her legendary faints.

Still, Quinn's chance of getting caught got better the longer he stayed around. He had no time to be wasting. Sheriff Bruner might get back to town early and then where would Quinn Hawkins be?

In jail, that's where.

Once Bentley had Erma safe on the floor, Quinn took another step back toward the door behind him. Then he played his last card. "My partner's watchin' this place and he won't look kindly on the first face that pokes out that door, y'hear?"

"You got no call to go threatenin' a lady, boy."

Quinn snapped Old Man McDonough a quick look. The man's gnarled fingers were curled into helpless fists over his head.

"Ain't it bad enough you takin' honest folks' hard earned money?" the older man snapped.

Honest folks.

Quinn's jaw clenched tightly. Until that morning, he too was "honest folks." The whole idea for a holdup had come on him suddenlike the night before and at the time, it had seemed like a damned fine idea. Now though, looking into that old man's eyes made Quinn Hawkins ashamed.

But there was no turning back now.

"Hush you," Erma warned the old farmer. "You want that devil to start shootin'?"

Devil?

Dusty took a half step forward and Quinn moved the barrel of his pistol until it was aimed at the center of his friend's chest. He hoped to hell Dusty stood still, because if he didn't, Quinn was in trouble. There was just no way in hell he could shoot Dusty McDonough.

"No son," the farmer muttered quickly. "Money ain't worth dyin' over."

Nor killing over neither, Quinn silently added.

"You won't get away with this," the banker said in a voice strangled by the weight of Erma Hightower's huge body laying across his chest. "You'll be caught. I'll see to it."

"Maybe," Quinn acknowledged, "but for now, you just remember my partner and his rifle waitin' outside."

One by one, each of the four nodded. Mrs. Hightower clutched at Bentley's pant leg and the banker did his best to shake her free.

"You bunch stay put . . . and *quiet* in here for ten whole minutes, then you can go. Understand?"

They understood. He saw it in their faces. And all it took was a pretend partner with a rifle to get the job done.

Slick as ice, he told himself. For his first effort at being a criminal, he thought everything'd gone real well. Nothing had gone wrong. No one was hurt.

Bright sunshine lay across his back as he stepped clear of the bank onto the wide boardwalk. Just a few more steps then a quick dash to the back of the building and he'd be free and clear. Didn't matter if they raised a posse. Once on that horse of his, no one could catch him. Hadn't his gray won every race in these parts the last three years running? Another smile curved his lips and his moustache brushed against the bandana. He'd be real glad to get shut of *that,* too. Surprising how irritating a scarf across a body's face could be.

Winifred Matthews staggered slightly under the unwieldy weight of her overstuffed carpetbag. She should have left it at the stage stop, she supposed, but truth to tell, she'd been so excited, she hadn't even thought of it.

Shifting the carpetbag's handle from her right to her left hand, she squared her shoulders and continued down the narrow, dusty street. Imagine! She, Winifred Matthews, spinster schoolteacher from Maine, was standing in the middle of Yellow Dog, Texas.

It was just like a page out of one of her dime novels.

She stood in the middle of the one and only street— or *road,* if she were to be completely honest. Just wide enough for two wagons to pass each other, the dusty track wandered and curved a bit as if it had been laid out by a drunk. And at either end of the town, that road stretched off into what appeared to be miles of unbroken wilderness.

Winifred smiled to herself and pulled in a deep breath of the still cool, sage-scented early morning air. Her gaze slipped over her surroundings eagerly. Stalwart, weather-beaten buildings crouched behind uneven, wooden boardwalks. Some of the buildings boasted two-story false fronts that leaned precariously toward each other as if for support. There were no sturdy, brick houses built a century ago here. *Here,* there was no past. Only the present—and the future.

A future Winifred Matthews would now be a part of.

"Miss Matthews!"

Winifred turned around to face the couple who'd shared her stagecoach ride.

"Supper is at six now, don't forget!" Adelaide Simpson called out as she snatched her parasol from her husband. "A lady such as yourself shouldn't be alone on her first night in Texas."

Alone is exactly what Winifred had been hoping for. She wanted to sit and stare and think. She wanted to enjoy the new sights and sounds around her. She wanted to become one with the Wild West.

Besides, during the last few days, Winifred had learned that Adelaide Simpson *loathed* the west. She had nothing but complaints about the dirt, the heat, the lack of "society." All the woman wanted to talk about was New York, Boston and the refinements of civilized living.

Everything that Winifred was trying to leave behind.

However, she'd already learned that it was nearly impossible to say "no" to Adelaide Simpson. Actually, it was nearly impossible to get any word in at all.

"Henry!" Adelaide shouted to the mousey little man at her side.

Henry jumped.

"Henry, you will call for Miss Matthews at a quarter of six, isn't that right?"

"Of course, my dear."

It was the longest sentence Winifred had heard Adelaide's poor husband utter in the last two days of travel.

"I'll be ready," Winifred answered quickly. It was, she was sure, the only way to escape and continue her tour of Yellow Dog. Clutching the handle of her carpet-bag tightly, she turned and started walking again.

"The hotel is at the other end of town," Adelaide shouted and Winifred winced.

"I just want to look around a bit before I get settled," she called back and never slowed her step.

"Well I never!" Adelaide's voice thundered into the still, morning air. "Henry! Have you ever?"

Winifred didn't wait to see if Henry had ever. She hurried her step and followed the road around a slight curve. She'd disappointed Adelaide, Winifred knew. She recognized that tone of voice. She'd heard it most of her life.

Winifred shook her head in an attempt to dislodge memories of past failures. After all, she told herself, this was the adventure she'd waited years for. And by heaven, she was going to enjoy every minute of it.

Her footsteps were muffled by the dirt road and but for the rattle of the trace chains on the stagecoach horses, the town seemed unusually quiet.

Apparently, it was too early in the morning for people to be about. Most of the stores were still closed, the shades drawn down over the locked doors. The board-walks were nearly deserted, except, Winifred noticed, for the two men planted in chairs outside the saloon at the far end of town. Their booted feet propped up on the hitching rail in front of them, they looked comfortable enough to have spent the night there.

As she rounded the edge of a closed and shuttered barbershop though, Winifred stopped. She stared open-mouthed at the man not ten feet away from her. Tucked away by the curve of the road, she hadn't seen him at all until that moment.

How exciting! And what a beginning to her new, adventurous life! Not five minutes off the stagecoach from Maine and she stumbles into an actual bank robbery!

Oh, if only her mother could see her now, Winifred thought. Wouldn't she be proud?

Quickly passing her too heavy, overstuffed carpetbag from one hand to the other, Winifred stole even closer to the man backing out of the bank. Intent on his crime, he didn't notice her approach. Eagerly, her gaze swept over him, from his worn, denim jeans to the empty holster riding his hip to the red scarf pulled over the lower half of his face.

How thrilling! she told herself as she moved in even closer. Just like the stories she'd been reading to her pupils for the last two years.

He didn't notice her as she crept up behind him. No doubt it was a serious business, being a criminal required all of one's concentration. Carefully, quietly, she stepped up behind him on the wooden boardwalk and leaned to one side to peer around him into the bank.

Four people inside. Thankfully, they appeared to be unhurt. However, they did look uncomfortable, holding their arms high over their heads. Winifred glanced at the rather large woman, her legs stretched out across the floor and her upper body propped against a well-dressed, portly gentleman. The woman opened her eyes, saw Winifred and promptly moaned just before throwing herself into a faint. The back of the woman's head clipped the portly man's chin and he jerked back, slamming his head into the teller's cage behind him.

Winifred began to make mental notes for the entries she would make in her journal at the first opportunity. She noted the slash of light across the bank floor and the dust bits drifting in the sunshine. She glanced around her and observed the play of shadows on the weather-beaten buildings. She took note of the horses at the hitching rail behind her, stamping their feet with the steady rhythm of a heartbeat.

But especially, she noticed *him*.

As close as she was to him, he was even taller than he'd appeared at first. Of course, most men of her acquaintance didn't wear boots with heels, either. With his back to her, it would have been impossible to see his face even had he not been wearing that scarf. But no matter, she told herself, her imagination could take care of that.

She would make him hard and angry looking in her journal. Perhaps with a scar that sliced across his cheek and forehead. All good villains—or heroes, for that matter, had scars.

His obviously new black hat was pulled down over sun-blond hair that lay just across the frayed collar of his white shirt. As for the rest of him, she took an instinctive step closer. He looked just as she'd expected the men in the Wild West to look.

Tall, leanly muscled and just a bit . . . dangerous. Well, perhaps more than a bit, considering he *was* holding a gun. As that thought flitted through her mind, the robber slid his gun back into its holster and took a quick step backward.

She wasn't prepared. His bootheel came down hard on the tip of her shoe and Winifred grunted.

What the hell?

Quinn jumped, lost his balance and took another step back before he could stop himself. Something big and soft slapped against the back of his knee and he felt his leg give out beneath him.

Keeping a firm grip on the money bag, he threw his right hand back to steady himself and caught a handful of a woman's skirt. Before he could let go, he'd pulled her down on top of him and together, they fell to the boardwalk.

A sharp pain shot through his hip and her elbow speared into his chest. His breath rushed out of his lungs and as he gasped for air, he looked up into a contrite pair of forest green eyes.

"I beg your pardon," she managed to say as she shoved her hat back into place. "I only wanted to watch."

Dammit. A near perfect holdup spoiled because of some nosey female!

Holdup!

Immediately, he dragged his right arm free of her body and pulled his pistol from its holster. Shoving himself into a sitting position, Quinn pulled the woman face down across his lap until she lay like a child waiting for a paddling, which he was sorely tempted to give her.

Inside the bank, Dusty McDonough had indeed taken a few steps in the hopes of catching Quinn with his guard down.

"Don't do nothin' stupid," Quinn told him deepening his voice and urged the man back with the barrel of his gun.

Dusty swallowed, gritted his teeth and moved back to stand beside his father.

"You must be forgettin' that partner of mine, huh?"

Dusty blanched a bit.

"Thought so." The woman on his lap began shoving and pushing at him, trying to get free, but Quinn laid the money bag and his left hand flat against the small of her back. "Set still," he ordered then turned back to the people in the bank. "And you . . . just don't do nothin' for ten minutes. Y'hear?"

Disgusted, Quinn then turned his attention to the squirming female on his lap. Her hat had fallen over her forehead and the hem of her skirt was tossed up, revealing what looked to him like a dozen petticoats.

She turned her head, pushed her hat up out of her eyes and glared at him.

"Have you quite finished?"

Quinn blinked. Most women he knew would have been screaming and carrying on by now. The others would have punched him dead in the face. A smile tugged at the corner of his mouth but he fought it back. He didn't have time for none of this nonsense.

"Hell no, I ain't finished," he snapped and just barely remembered to deepen his voice again. "But if you'll haul yourself outa the way, I'll get on with it."

She frowned at him and her hat, a yellow contraption with a big orange bow on one side, slid down over her eyes again. Gamely, she once more pushed it back into place.

"I'd be delighted to 'haul myself' up sir," she said, "just as soon as you remove your booty from my person."

"Booty?"

"Your ill-gotten gains."

"What?"

"The bag of stolen money."

"Oh!" Well why the hell didn't she say so? he asked himself. Still keeping one eye on the folks in the bank, Quinn released her and she immediately started moving. She scooted around for what seemed forever, like she was trying to build a nest, not get up. Her backside shot straight up as she wiggled her knees onto the boardwalk and Quinn's gaze, despite his best efforts, shot to her petticoat-covered behind.

Almost more than a man could bear, he told himself and reached up with his gun hand to pull the hem of her skirt down over the yards of white lace.

"What are you doing?" she asked, turning her head to look at him.

"Coverin' you up, lady," he grumbled.

"Oh. Well, thank you very much."

"Will you get off me?"

"I am *trying* to do just that," she assured him.

Quinn groaned, tried to ignore her movements and kept his gun trained on Dusty.

But she wasn't finished. Muttering under her breath, she curled the fingers of her left hand around a handful of cotton and gave herself a yank upright.

As she rose up, blocking the line of sight between him and the people in the bank, she inadvertently jerked the bandana from his face.

It happened so fast, he didn't have time to stop it. Before he knew it, Quinn was staring into the woman's surprised features as she studied his undisguised face.

"You're not right at all," she told him and shook her head while he quickly grabbed the bandana and tugged it back into place.

"Dammit lady," he mumbled and gently but firmly shoved her off his lap.

Winifred plopped down onto the boardwalk and stared up at him. He clambered to his feet and she was still sitting there, shaking her head. This was all wrong, she told herself. For heaven's sake. *Everyone* knew outlaws were ugly, scarred creatures, shunned by society.

He glanced down at her and even though his bandana was once again shielding his features, she thought she saw him frown. Well what in heaven did *he* have to be upset about? *He* hadn't had one of his illusions shattered, had he? Oh, and she'd been so excited, too. Coming face-to-face with her first rough, hardened criminal and discovering that he was actually handsome was most disconcerting.

Imagine. Not only did he have a strong jawline and a straight, well-shaped nose, but he also boasted a sweet blond moustache and his lightly-tanned flesh was unblemished. Not a single pockmark or scar to be seen.

He'd even *shaved* recently.

Winifred shook her head again in disgust. It was all very disappointing.

"Get up, lady."

"Hmmm?" She cocked her head and squinted against the sunlight to stare up at him.

"I said, get up." He sucked in a gulp of air and blew it out on a sigh. "You're comin' with me."

"Oh, thank you, but I couldn't possibly."

"I ain't askin' ya, lady. I'm *tellin'* ya."

"Well, I must tell you, I don't respond well to being ordered about."

He muttered something unintelligible.

"What was that?"

"Nothing." He sidestepped closer to her, tossed the money bag into her lap and said, "Hold it."

Instinctively, Winifred's fingers closed over the tightly-knotted cloth bag. She quickly snatched the handle of her carpetbag just as the robber grabbed her upper arm and yanked her to her feet.

"Here now!" the young man inside the bank shouted. "You got no call to be takin' her anywhere!"

"You hush," her captor answered, "and just remember to stay in there 'til ten minutes after I'm gone."

He started walking backwards again, dragging Winifred along with him. Burdened as she was by the money bag in one hand and her own baggage in the other, Winifred's movements were clumsy. Her right foot caught up in the hem of her dress and she felt a sharp tug just before she heard the sound of fabric ripping. They'd only taken a few steps when the villain stopped, looked up to the roof on the right and waved. Winifred glanced in that direction, but saw no one. She shook her head, dismissing her curiosity. Heaven knew, she had more than enough at the moment to occupy her thoughts.

They were moving again and her carpetbag slapped against the back of Quinn's knee, making him lurch ungainly. He grumbled and told her to drop the bag.

"I'll do no such thing."

"Then keep it outa my way."

"If you would be so good as to carry your *own* plunder," Winifred pointed out, "it would be much easier for me to manage my bag."

"Plunder?"

She held up the money sack.

"Oh." He dragged her closer to the hitching rail and quickly slipped one of the horses's reins free. Holding onto the leather strap in his gun hand, he said "Can't very well carry the bag, hold my gun, pull a horse *and* hold onto you, now can I?"

He had a point, though as far as she was concerned, it was hardly necessary to maintain such a firm grip on her person.

"What are you planning to do, sir?"

"Escape."

Of course he was going to escape, she thought and tried unsuccessfully to snatch her arm free of his grasp. "I *meant* what are you planning to do with me?"

He paused a moment, looked down at her and his eyes narrowed thoughtfully before he said "Damned if *I* know."

He led her to the back of the bank where a big, gray horse stood waiting. Throwing his black hat aside, he grabbed the dirt colored Stetson hanging from the saddle horn.

"If you'll just release me," she told him, "I'll be out of your way in a moment and you can get about your . . . *business.*"

"Can you ride?" He stashed his rifle in the scabbard and secured the money bag to the saddle.

"I beg your pardon?"

"Horses," he snapped. "Can you ride horses?"

"Certainly," Winifred started "back in Maine, I—"

"Good." He interrupted her, bent down and scooped

her up in his arms. Her carpetbag swung wide and slammed into his hip. He grunted. "Drop the bag."

"No."

He inhaled sharply, lifted her high and set her down in the saddle astride the brown horse's back. Her eyes wide, she clutched at the saddle horn with one hand and tried desperately to hold on to her carpetbag with the other. But her position was too precarious. Weighed down as she was by her baggage, she slowly started to slide off the side of the big animal.

"Hang on!" the Quinn snapped.

Apparently, Winifred thought as she felt the last of her balance dissolve, he couldn't see that that was precisely what she was trying to do.

"Thought you said you could ride," the outlaw muttered.

He pushed her back into place and snatched her bag from her hand. "Hell, the damn thing feels like you got rocks in it." Dropping it to the dirt, he told her again, "Hang on to the saddle horn."

"What about my bag?"

"Forget your bag."

He walked around her animal to the bigger, gray beast beside it. As he slid one foot into the stirrup, Winifred leaned to one side and allowed herself to drop off the horse. She hit the ground, staggered and bumped into the horse before she could catch herself.

"What in the *hell* are you doin'?" he said, his voice low but not nearly as deep as it had been earlier. "I told you to hang on."

"I didn't fall off," she told him as she bent down to retrieve her property. "I dismounted."

"Ain't what it looked like to me," he muttered. Hurriedly, he came back around the beast and grabbed her. But before he could pick her up, Winifred kicked him in the shin.

"Cut that out."

"Unhand me this instant."

"Ain't no time for this, lady."

He would have to make time, she told herself. She absolutely refused to take another step until he told her exactly what he had in mind for her.

"I am the new school teacher here in Yellow Dog, sir and I demand to know what you are going to do with me."

The tall man opposite her paused for a long moment and stared down at her. His hat shaded his eyes making it impossible for Winifred to read whatever emotion was there. Still, she suspected it was anger. Even the rigid way he held himself veritably screamed with bad temper.

"You ain't the teacher now, lady," he finally said.

"Really?" she asked. "Then what exactly am I?"

"My hostage."

Hostage? So stunned that she was unable to fight him, the villain easily lifted her to her saddle again. But when he started for his own horse, Winifred snapped out of her state and immediately said "I'll *need* my bag, if you please."

"Dammit, lady . . ."

"Sir, I can hardly be a proper hostage without my luggage, can I?"

2

A *"proper"* hostage? Quinn stared up at her and even the bandana hiding most of his face couldn't disguise the open surprise on his features. After a long moment, he bent down, swept up her bag and carried it to his own horse. He stepped easily into the saddle, shoving the carpetbag's handles down over the pommel, then leaned to the side to snatch up her horse's reins. Still grumbling, he ordered, "Hang on this time," just before he urged the horses into a run.

Quinn threw her a quick look over his shoulder as soon as they were clear of town. She was bobbing up and down in the damned saddle like a cork on the end of a fishing line. Blast it. He should've known better than to believe her when she said she could ride. Quinn frowned slightly as he realized that his horse was running only at half speed.

Of course, dragging that female along was bound to slow him down. But he couldn't very well leave her behind, now could he? She'd seen his face. She could tell folks in town what he looked like. And it wouldn't have taken them any time at all to figure out who their bank robber was.

But dammit all to hell . . . she was ruining *everything!*

"Excuse me?"

Plus, he complained silently, she talked too damn much.

"What?" he shouted back, not bothering to turn and look at her.

"Could we slow down just a bit now, do you think?"

"No."

"I seem to be having some sort of difficulty here," she called back and her voice wobbled with the horse's every step.

Difficulty? That didn't half cover it, he thought with disgust. He glanced back at her and felt his jaw drop.

Quickly, he yanked back on the reins and his horse drew up sharply, twisting its head in protest. The woman's horse skidded to a stop too, all four feet digging into the hard earth.

"Oooooohh . . ."

He didn't look at her again. He didn't need to. He knew damn well what was happening from that first glance. Quickly, Quinn tried to get off his blasted horse. "Dammit!" Her blamed bag was in the way and his left leg was trapped between its overstuffed contours and the hard edge of his saddle. As he worked himself free, his left foot got caught in the stirrup. He swung his right foot over the gray's back and hopped on one leg, cursing viciously under his breath at the trouble one small woman could cause.

Then he heard her hit the ground.

As if on cue, his bootheel slipped free of the stirrup and he slowly turned around to look at his hostage. Her damned hat hanging down over her eyes, she sat on the dirt, hands braced behind her. Her black skirt had billowed up around her waist and Quinn got a good long look at her shapely, stocking-clad legs before she pulled her skirt down over them.

She shoved her hat back onto her head and stared up at him. He wasn't quite sure what kind of reaction he'd expected from her, but the grin she gave him wasn't it.

"My goodness!" she said and lifted one hip to reach beneath her. A moment later, she was holding a rock the size of her fist in her palm. Just before she tossed it to one side, she added "You certainly have hard ground in Texas."

Quinn shook his head, stepped closer and picked up the fallen saddle blanket beside her. Giving it a quick shake, he threw it across the skittish horse, then stroked the animal's neck gently. "Ground's hard everywhere, lady."

"I suppose that's so," she conceded and began to push herself to her feet. Every inch of her body hurt and Winifred knew she would soon have a painful bruise on her backside thanks to that rock. But at least, she told herself with determined optimism, she'd managed to make her outlaw stop riding for a moment.

"Thought you said you could ride," he grumbled and bent down to lift the saddle off the ground.

"I can."

He snorted.

"Of course, I'm more accustomed to riding sidesaddle," she pointed out. And, she added silently, the horses she was accustomed to riding were too old and worn out to even entertain the notion of running.

Instantly, memories of Sunday afternoons spent in the park came rushing back at her. How she'd loved dressing in her riding costume and guiding her mount around the circular riding track. Every week, she and her steed of the moment would meander across the well-worn trail and she would imagine all sorts of adventures.

One week, she was an outlaw queen, leading her band of ruffians through treacherous canyons. The next, she might be a female bounty hunter, trailing after a criminal too wily to be caught by a mere man.

Winifred shifted position and pain shot along her thighs. Immediately, her memories faded. It seemed reality had very little to do with her imagination. As she watched her outlaw saddling the horse she would soon be expected to ride again, she rubbed her backside in a futile effort to ease the ache there.

He was grumbling again. As he reached beneath the horse's belly for the cinch strap, Winifred asked, "Why did the saddle fall off?"

He didn't look at her, just threaded the leather strap through the buckle and began to fasten it. Grudgingly it seemed, he answered, "This is Dusty's horse. That younger fella in the bank?"

"Yes . . ."

"Well, I forgot ol' Dusty's got a soft spot for his animals. Whenever he climbs down, he loosens the cinch strap, so the horse can rest better."

"How thoughtful of him."

The outlaw turned his head slightly and stared at her for a moment. With a small shake of his head, he turned back to his task.

"Yeah," he grunted. "Real thoughtful. And it also keeps a horse thief from gettin' very far if he tries to steal Dusty's mount."

Winifred chuckled. "Apparently, that safeguard works very well indeed."

"Yeah." He dropped the strap, flipped the stirrup down into place, then stopped dead.

"What is it?"

He didn't answer.

Winifred stepped closer. The poor man looked as though he'd been hit with something. His blue eyes were wide and blindly staring and his mouth hung open. Carefully, she reached out and laid one hand on his arm. He didn't glance at her.

"Excuse me," she said and paused. She had no idea what to call him. There'd hardly been time for an introduction. And she certainly couldn't refer to him aloud as "her outlaw." "Sir" seemed a bit ridiculous, considering the circumstances, but then again, she asked herself, what choice did she have? "Sir? What is it? Is something wrong?"

Moments passed before he finally swiveled his head around to look at her. Shaking his head slowly, he said softly, "You are somethin' else, lady."

"I beg your pardon?"

"I just robbed a bank. Got tripped by a nosey female." He spun completely about to face her, hands at his hips. "She pulls my bandana down and sees my face so's I have to drag her along when I leave."

Winifred straightened up and lifted her chin. Accidents happened to everyone.

"And *now*," he threw his hands high then let them drop to his sides again. "*Now* I realize not only am I a bank robber—I'm a *horse thief!*"

"Oh."

"Yeah, *oh.*" He snatched his hat off, slapped it against his jean-clad thigh, then shoved it back on his head. "Y'know, they *hang* horse thieves around these parts."

"Hang?" Good heavens.

"Sonofabitch," he muttered as he snaked out one hand to grab her.

"Well, I'm sure they won't hang you," Winifred said, for some reason wanting to reassure him.

"And why's that?" His hand around her upper arm, he pulled her over to the horse's side.

"Because it wasn't your fault, of course." Winifred knew exactly what she was talking about. She'd read enough about the Wild West to know that justice was all important. An innocent man would never be hanged for a crime that he'd had no intention of committing. "You were forced to borrow this animal for my sake."

He snorted.

"Naturally," she continued, "when you're caught, you will have to spend quite some time in prison. Robbing a bank is a serious matter, after all."

"Is that right?"

She heard the sarcasm and chose to ignore it.

"Yes. But I shall be happy to testify in your defense about the horse stealing."

"Oh, and you think that'll take care of everything, do you?"

Winifred stared up into his eyes and was struck again by the clarity and depth of their color. A lock of blond hair lay across one dark-blond eyebrow and she had the ridiculous urge to reach up and brush it away. He was only inches from her. She could see a few golden strands of hair peeking out from the vee of his unbuttoned collar.

Suddenly quite warm, she inhaled sharply and waved her fingers in front of her face like a makeshift fan. It did no good at all.

"Of course it would," she started and cleared her throat when her voice sounded unmistakably shaky, "I possess a sterling reputation and as a character witness, I'm sure I could convince the court of your innocence. In the matter of horse stealing, I mean."

"Uh-huh." He nodded and one corner of his mouth lifted in what she was sure would have been a mocking smile if he'd allowed it to blossom. "Lady," he continued and bent to scoop her up into his arms, "there's one thing you're not considerin' here."

"What's that?" Winifred asked and tried not to think about how she was being cuddled close to a handsome man's chest.

"Why would they listen to you at all?" he asked.

"I've already told you . . ."

"Yeah, but lady, you can't be no character witness."

"Whyever not?"

"You'll be on trial too."

"What?"

He grinned and Winifred blinked.

In seconds though, the smile was gone again. Swinging her high in the air, he practically tossed her into the saddle. Grabbing onto the pommel with both hands. Winifred stared down at him when he began to speak.

"Yes ma'am," he said softly. "You forget. *You're* the one ridin' that stolen horse."

"Get *off* me, woman!" Charles Bentley pushed at Erma Hightower's broad shoulders but he might as well have been trying to pull a stump from the ground one-handed. Erma was not about to be moved before she was good and ready. And apparently, she wasn't quite finished with her spell yet.

She mumbled something and fluttered her eyelashes.

Bentley's eyes rolled and he pulled in several shallow breaths. Erma's weight across his ribs prevented anything else.

"That sonofabitch took my horse!" Dusty's arms dropped to his sides and began to tingle as the blood rushed back into his fingertips. Staring out the open bank door, he shook his head in disgust.

"Just a horse, son," his father told him and began to swing his arms in circles, hoping to stimulate the circulation. "We'll get it and the money too. Soon's Bruner gets back to town."

"I ain't about to sit around and wait for the Sheriff to raise a posse, pa," Dusty told him. "I'm goin' after my horse and by God, I'm gonna get that mare back or die tryin'."

"Talkin' like a fool ain't about to help," his father said quickly. "No horse is worth dyin' over."

"Maybe she ain't," Dusty acknowledged "but that foal she's carryin' just might be."

The older man sighed. His son had a point. He knew Dusty'd been tryin' for years to get himself a good stable full of breeding stock. Now that he'd finally saved up the money to have his mare bred to one of the finest studs in the territory—some no good steals her.

But still, George McDonough wasn't about to lose his only son over a damned horse.

"The horse is immaterial," Bentley pointed out in a gasping wheeze.

"What's that?" George turned, wrinkled his brow, looked down at the still-trapped banker and didn't bother to hide a small smirk. It did George's heart good to see the uppity dandy having to grunt and shove his way out from under Erma.

Grimacing, the banker mumbled, "Madam, some assistance if you please," and wriggled sideways until he was free of the woman's determinedly prostrate form. He laid her head down, none too gently, on the plank floor, then struggled to his feet. Tugging his bottle-green waistcoat back into place over his thickening belly, Bentley then smoothed one long strand of hair from a deep side part across a bald dome to the other side. Only when he was satisfied that he was once again presentable, did he speak.

"I *said*," he began and stretched both chins up from his too-tight collar, "your missing animal is hardly what should be considered the vital matter in all this."

"So *you* say!"

Bentley hardly spared Dusty a glance. Instead, he turned and hurried to the bank vault. The big iron door was hanging open as the villain had left it. His thick, sausage-like fingers thumbed through the stacks of cash, coin and papers inside in a matter of moments. Straightening up, he spun around and looked at George.

"Fifteen hundred dollars missing."

George blinked and rubbed one hand over his stubbly jaw. "How the hell can you tell that so quick? You hardly even looked through anything."

"It is my business to know," Bentley assured him and looked down the considerable length of his nose at the farmer.

George watched the prissy fellow with disgust. Clearly, Bentley made it a habit to run his fingers through the bank's assets. Probably liked to play with all the money after hours, George thought. How else could he have known down to the penny just what was missing?

"Fifteen hundred?" Dusty asked and took a half step toward the teller cage. "Is that all?"

"*All?*" Bentley's face flushed a dark, blood red. "Surely that's sufficient! Would you have felt better if the outlaw had taken *everything?*"

"Well, why didn't he?" Erma asked from her position on the floor.

All three men looked down at her. Laid out across the wood floor, patches of sunlight dotting her faded, gray cotton dress, Erma looked as comfortable as if she was home in bed.

The big woman had lived through Indian raids, border wars, cholera attacks and smallpox epidemics. One little bank robbery sure wasn't enough to upset her. Though George McDonough had known Erma long enough to know that she'd milk the situation for all it was worth.

Why, by the time she got finished telling the tale of this holdup, she'd have herself firing two six-guns and holding a shotgun in her teeth.

Erma crossed her stretched-out legs at the ankle, threw one arm behind her head and looked from one to the other of the men before speaking slowly. "I asked why would a fella go to all the trouble of robbin' a bank and only take a *piece* of the pie? Why not the whole damned thing?"

"Y'know," George said on a low whistle, "she *does* have a point."

Dusty chewed his bottom lip thoughtfully.

Bentley's forehead wrinkled all the way back to the center of his shining scalp.

"It don't make sense," Erma said, more to herself than the others. "Not a lick of sense."

Even in spring, sunshine in Texas was a thing to be reckoned with.

Winifred's fingers were cramped around the pommel of the saddle, but she didn't dare let go. Drops of perspiration rolled down from her hairline and left long, jagged clean streaks in the dust covering her face. She blinked her eyes against the sun and the dirt and clenched her teeth as she bounced down hard into the saddle. The pain in her behind had long since passed from an annoying ache to shrieking agony, but she was determined not to complain again.

She'd tried that already, *hours* ago. He'd hardly glanced at her. Then in that gruff voice she was beginning to know too well, he'd said, "Ya shoulda thought of that before ya went bargin' in where ya had no business bein'."

Well, Winifred told herself, there was no rational retort for that. Of course, she might have pointed out that simply because she'd been curious about criminal activity, didn't mean that she'd had any interest in being a participant! But then again, she thought, answering him would have required her to talk and hold on to the racing beast beneath her at the same time and that was proving to be a more than formidable task.

Every bone in her body felt as though it had been taken out for a good shaking. Now she knew exactly what a parlor rug went through every spring and fall. There were aches and pains in places she'd never allowed herself to acknowledge before today.

And too, riding a horse astride seemed to lead to all sorts of . . . *peculiar* sensations in her nether region.

Winifred's mouth felt as dry as the earth beneath the horses's feet. Dirt and grit had imbedded themselves in her teeth and she knew she'd never be able to wash all of the dust out of her hair.

She couldn't even occupy herself with looking at the scenery as they rode. That ended after the first fifteen minutes or so. After all, they'd been travelling for hours and the landscape looked exactly the same. They might have stood in one place for all the change there'd been in the flora and fauna.

Dirt, wide patches of grass, a few bushes, and what seemed to be some species of dwarf oak trees were the only sights to see. And the land ahead of them appeared to stretch out forever in all directions in an unbroken series of rolling hills. Even when the land appeared to be completely flat, Winifred had learned that there were deep gullies hidden from sight from which an animal occasionally leaped into view.

"We'll stop at that wallow for a bit," her captor said suddenly. "Let you catch your breath."

"Thank Heaven!" Winifred muttered.

On the lee side of a small hill, her outlaw brought his horse to a stop and Winifred's mount halted alongside. Immediately, she pushed her hat out of her eyes and took a good look around her.

There was a small pool of water, surrounded by thick, lush grass and Winifred knew she'd never seen anything half as lovely. It made her feel better just to look at the peaceful, pastoral scene.

Beside her, her captor was obviously unmoved by the beauty of the place. The villain pried the handles of her carpetbag from his saddle horn and tossed the bag to the ground. Then he swung down off his horse and glanced up at her. "You best get on down and walk awhile. We'll be leavin' again directly."

After that short speech, he turned back to his animal and began to strip the saddle from it. Her eyebrows lifted and her mouth twitched with the impulse to tell him just what she thought of his cavalier attitude, but she resisted. Watching him, Winifred realized that he had no intention of helping her dismount. Any complaint she might have made died unuttered as she recalled the slapdash way in which he'd thrown her into the saddle earlier. Perhaps, she decided, it was for the best that he left her to her own devices.

Laboriously, Winifred kicked her right foot free of the stirrup and slowly swung her leg over the horse's broad back. As she moved, she whispered words of encouragement to the beast. "Hold still now, horse. I'm not accustomed to you yet and I would appreciate all the help you can offer."

"Who are you talkin' to?" he said shortly and set his saddle off to one side.

"My horse," Winifred replied, never taking her eyes from the animal's head as it twitched and snorted.

"Naturally."

Winifred ignored him. If he wasn't going to assist her, he was really in no position to criticize. Her right foot hit the ground and her leg seemed to turn to rubber. Gritting her teeth, she determinedly pulled her left foot free, wincing as her muscles screamed in protest.

Both feet firmly on the ground, Winifred only wasted a moment wishing she could actually *feel* the good earth.

But beyond pain, there didn't seem to be any feeling at all in her lower limbs. She tried to take a step, but her right leg folded as what seemed like hundreds of tiny needles poked at the sole of her foot. If not for the firm grip she had on the worn, leather saddle, she would have crumpled into a heap.

Her outlaw finished his task of rubbing down his animal with its own saddle blanket and turned to look at her. Across the mare's back, their eyes met.

He stared at her silently for what seemed forever. She felt his gaze move over her dusty, worn out appearance and instinctively she straightened just a bit under his appraisal.

"Tired?" he finally asked and Winifred was surprised at the note of concern in his deep, rumbling voice.

She was so tired, she felt as though she could fall asleep standing up, if she could only trust her limbs to support her long enough. But for some reason, when she answered him, Winifred heard herself say, "I suppose I am a bit weary."

A smile tugged at one corner of his mouth again and disappeared just as quickly as it had come. He reached up and pushed the brim of his hat back higher on his head. His deep blue eyes shone with an inner humor he refused to acknowledge.

"It'll help if ya walk around some. Get the blood movin' in your legs again."

She told herself that she surely shouldn't be discussing the condition of her legs with a perfect stranger. She even briefly entertained the notion of being brave, stoic. But, as she shifted slightly and felt her left leg tremble, Winifred gave in to the inevitable and admitted, "I would be happy to do as you suggest and walk around for awhile, sir." She sucked in a great gulp of air and finished lamely, "But, I'm afraid my limbs won't support me."

"Limbs?" He frowned slightly, wrinkling his brow, then realization dawned. "Oh. Your legs're wobbly." He nodded and stepped around her horse to her side. Peeling her fingers from the cantle, he draped her right arm around his shoulders and encircled her waist with his left arm. "Why didn't ya say so?"

Winifred tilted her head back to look up at him. She'd never been held so familiarly by any man. Even her father, God rest him, had kept an affectionate, yet proper distance between them.

"Let go," her outlaw told her.

"Hmmm?" The warmth of his hand at her waist sent tingles of awareness all throughout her body.

"The saddle horn," he said and nodded at the still clenched fingers of her left hand. "Let it go."

"Oh. Of course."

Shaking his head, he started walking slowly, absorbing her unsteadiness with his strength. Winifred's fingers tightened on his shoulder and she tried to ignore the heat she felt where his side pressed against hers.

Every step sent new pin prickles of discomfort shooting up from the soles of her feet, but Winifred had stopped noticing. It didn't matter that her legs had the strength of wet feathers. It didn't matter that she was in the middle of nowhere with a man she'd never seen until a few hours ago.

All that mattered at the moment, she told herself, was one thing. Slanting him a look from the corner of her eye, she asked, "Would you mind telling me your name?"

3

Those eyes of hers had taken on a look that Quinn didn't recognize. All soft and dewy, that unfocused look might have been caused by the pain in her legs she was no doubt suffering. But somehow, he didn't think so.

Her voice was kinda breathy too, and he wondered if he really had ridden her too hard. Hell, maybe she was gonna pass out. Well that would be dandy, wouldn't it? Kinda put a real stamp on a day that was turning out to be quite a test.

Still, he looked down into those eyes again and thought briefly that if he'd *had* to be stuck with a hostage, he could've done worse.

Grass green eyes, a short, straight nose and her skin, when it wasn't covered in trail dust, was the color of fresh cream. Her hair was mostly covered by that god-awful hat she was wearing, but what he could see of it was real pretty. About the rust red color of clouds hit by the rays of the sun just before it drops out of sight.

She wasn't very tall, he thought, noticing that the top of her head—without that hat—would hit him right about chin high. Although, since he stood just at six-foot-four, not many people seemed tall to him. He held her waist a little tighter and felt her lean into him a bit. However tall she was, his brain noted, she had plenty of curves in all the right places.

Immediately, he quashed the thought. That was the *last* thing he needed to be thinking about now. Besides, he had no right to touch the woman at all. It was only pure chance that she was here with him. And as soon as he could, he would be leaving her in some town or other. Deliberately, he ignored the sensation of warmth that crept through him from the spot where their bodies met. He was an outlaw now, he reminded himself. And she was his school teacher hostage.

Nothing more.

"Well?" she said and he shook his head free of rambling thoughts.

"Well what?" Hell, he'd forgotten her question.

"Are you going to tell me your name?" She inhaled sharply and sighed it out again. "I can't very well call you 'sir', now can I? And, since it appears that we're going to be in each other's company for some time, I feel it's only right for us to introduce each other properly."

Properly? She's worried about *proper*?

"After all," she continued, apparently warming to her subject, "it's not every day that I'm carried away by a ruthless outlaw."

Ruthless? Quinn's brow furrowed and he opened his mouth to argue that point. But she cut him off.

"Of course, I'm terribly ignorant of the rules in a situation like this, you understand." Her left leg buckled and she fell against him. "Sorry. You see, I've never had the opportunity to meet a villainous desperado before and I'm quite at a loss as to how to proceed."

Now Quinn stumbled. Villainous Desperado?
Him?

Oh, Lordy, what had he got himself into?

"My name," she went on and gave him a smile "is Winifred Matthews."

"Winifred?" He didn't realize he'd repeated it out loud until she remarked on it.

"Yes, I'm afraid that's it. Dreadful I know, but . . ." She lifted her shoulders in a small shrug. "I would have much preferred something elegant, like Deirdre. Or perhaps, Charlotte. Unfortunately, my opinion wasn't asked for at my Christening."

"Uh-huh," Hells bells, how that woman could talk.

"And yours?"

"My what?" He was fast losing track of this whole conversation.

"Name. Your name," she said slowly as if to a dim-witted child. "After all, I've already seen your face, what more harm could it do for me to know your name as well?"

She had a point. "Hawkins, ma'am. Quinn Hawkins."

"Quinn?" she closed her eyes briefly and said his name again soundlessly.

He watched her ripe, kissable lips pucker over the saying of his name and found himself wondering what her mouth tasted like.

Lord! Quinn gave himself a shake and a stern, silent warning.

"I like it," Winifred announced and opened her eyes again to look up at him.

He liked that shine in her eyes, but wasn't about to say so.

"It's very . . . *romantic,*" she finished.

Romantic. He frowned to himself. "Nothin' romantic about it," he assured her. "Just my ma's last name before she got married, that's all."

"*I* think it's romantic." She nodded abruptly. "And it suits you, too."

"It better. It's all the name I've got." Enough of this, he told himself. Pretty soon, he'd start listening to her nonsense and then where would he be?

Pulling her arm down from around his shoulders, Quinn took a half step back from her. "Legs all right now?"

"Hmmm?"

Her eyes had gone all fuzzy again, but he ignored it. "Can you walk on your own now?"

"Oh!" She flexed her knees gingerly, then smiling, clasped her hands in front of her. "Yes, thank you. I seem to be much better."

"Good." He turned for the horses, leaving her at the side of the small pool of water. "Keep walkin'."

She watched him walk to her mount, flip the stirrup up and begin to undo the cinch strap. Apparently, he wanted the horses to have a good rest too. Winifred rubbed her backside thoughtfully for a moment, then began a slow walk around the perimeter of the shallow pool.

Long and narrow, the tiny body of water looked too refreshing to be ignored any longer. Winifred retrieved her carpetbag, opened it and rummaged through her clothes until she found what she was looking for. Then sighing gently, she sank to the ground, dipped her lace-edged handkerchief into the cool water then squeezed out the excess before wiping the fabric across her face. It was heaven. Quickly, she took off her hat, smoothed her hair back and leaned down to splash some of the water directly onto her still-flushed cheeks.

Though grateful beyond words for the miniature lake, she couldn't help wondering about it.

"Mr. Hawkins," she started.

"Quinn. I don't respond to Mr."

"Very well, Quinn. I was just wondering. Why would anyone dig a waterhole out here?" She waved both arms as if to indicate the vast openness surrounding them. "In the middle of nowhere?"

"Nobody dug it," he said as he set a huge rock atop both horses's reins to insure they wouldn't wander off. Slowly, he walked to the water's edge and dropped to his knees in the soft, grassy dirt. Cupping one hand, he lifted some of the water to his mouth, then ran his wet hand across his features before continuing. "It's a wallow."

"You said that before. What exactly is a wallow?"

"Buffalo wallow."

"Buffalo?" The magic in that one little word. She'd read so many wonderful stories in which the authors described thundering herds of the magnificent beasts. How the sound of their hooves pounding against the earth could be heard for miles. How the very air trembled with their passing. How the Noble Savage had revered the hairy beasts for their hides as well as their meat.

"Buffalo," she repeated, drawing the word out and letting her tongue savor the saying of it. How she would love to see a herd of buffalo.

"Yeah," Quinn's eyes were wary as he went on "they, uh, like to have a good scratch now and again and when they roll over onto their backs and scoot around, it leaves the ground like this. Kinda hollowed out."

Her eyes widened and her voice dropped to a hush. How powerful they must be! "One beast left an impression like this?"

"Hell no! Not one. Prob'ly hundreds of 'em have rolled around right here." He shook his head slowly. "Hell, if one of the damned things could do this to the ground, a body wouldn't be able to walk the country for all the holes!"

She hadn't thought of that.

"Are there any of the beasts in this area, do you suppose?"

"Hope not," he countered and bent over the water to splash water in his face.

"Whyever not?" she countered quickly. "Oh, I would dearly love to see a herd of 'Magnificent specimens of God's greatness' thundering across the plain."

"What?" The bridge of his nose wrinkled as he narrowed his gaze to stare at her. "Magnificent Beasts?" he repeated. "Where in thunder did you ever hear 'em talked about like that?"

"Oh, all of the books I've read have made quite a point of saying just how important those animals are to this land."

"Figures," he said on a choked off laugh. "Books."

"And just what is wrong with books?" Why, Winifred had learned everything there was to know about the Wild West from her books. They'd entertained her during the day and filled the loneliness of her nights. In her armchair adventures, she'd locked horns with outlaws, outwitted Indians and saved entire cavalry outposts from all sorts of dire plagues.

How dare he mock her books.

"Nothin' wrong with 'em, I guess," Quinn acknowledged. "But I got to wonder how many of them writer fellas've ever been west of St. Louis!"

Hmmm.

He yanked his hat off, pushed his fingers through his pale blond hair and grinned at her. "Buffalo ain't 'magnificent beasts,' lady," he said with a shake of his head. "They're some of the dumbest critters the Good Lord ever made."

Her features must have shown her disbelief because he drew in a long breath and went on.

"Why, a man could stand upwind of a herd of 'em and shoot most of 'em stone dead and the others don't have the sense to run. They just beller and wander around, steppin' over the bodies, waitin' their turn for a bullet."

It was an ugly image he'd painted. Unfortunately, she suspected it might be true. After all, she reasoned. Who would know better about the West's creatures? A man who lived among them—or her? Still, she felt obligated to defend the great shaggy beasts.

Winifred frowned and straightened her shoulders. Hands clasped primly in her lap, she looked across the waterhole that Quinn Hawkins owned to a buffalo and said "And are there many Buffalo left now, do you think?" She knew the answer very well, she just wanted him to say it.

"Nah," he sighed and pulled up a handful of grass. "Hardly any of 'em around these days."

"And why is that, do you suppose?"

"Them damn easterners. Called themselves hunters!" He sneered at the thought. "That's like callin' a skunk a house-cat. Just 'cause it's got fur and a cute little stripe, don't make it the same thing at all." Quinn shook his head and stared off into the distance. "Come in by the trainful, they did. Them big, brave, so-called hunters didn't even bother to climb down off the train to do their shootin'. Just stood on the platforms and damned near killed all the buffalo before they got tired of their 'good time.'"

"So," Winifred said softly, still watching the disgusted expression on his face, "who do you consider 'dumber,' the poor animals simply living their lives—or the fools who killed wantonly until they very nearly wiped out every living buffalo?"

Quinn cocked his head and stared at her. For several long, silent minutes, he simply looked at her. Winifred wanted to blink. To look away. To *say* something. But she didn't. Instead, she waited. And at last, she was rewarded.

"Reckon you're right, lady," Quinn said quietly. "I guess there *are* some things dumber than a buffalo after all."

Inordinately pleased, Winifred lifted her chin and smiled at him. When he smiled back, she felt a strange, swirling sensation in the pit of her stomach.

She must be hungry.

*   *   *

"If y'all would quit tryin' to talk at once," Tom Bruner said for the third time, "maybe we could get somewhere."

The four people across from his cluttered desk glared at each other briefly, then one by one, turned back to him and started talking again. Their voices got louder and louder as each tried to outshout the other, until Tom thought his already pounding head might just bust right in two.

Wasn't it bad enough that he'd spent most of the day riding alongside the most cantankerous, foul-mouthed, evil-smelling prisoner he'd ever encountered? Tom stifled the groan building in his throat as he thought back over that long ride to Austin and home again.

Once he'd finished delivering his prisoner to the Marshal in Austin, all Tom had been able to think about was getting back to Yellow Dog where nothing much ever happened, beyond a Saturday night brawl in the saloon. All he'd wanted to do was get something to eat and then stretch out on a lumpy cot in an empty cell and sleep 'till Judgment Day.

Wouldn't you know some sonofabitch outlaw would pick *today* to rob the bank?

He rubbed his eyes with the fingertips of one hand and held his other palm up for silence.

It took a few seconds, but everyone seemed to wind down at once. Silence. At last.

"Erma," Tom said with a nod at the big, raw boned rugged-looking woman, "you first."

"Sheriff," Bentley shouted. "I protest!"

Tom winced and glanced at the banker sourly. "It ain't your turn to protest, Bentley. Now hush."

The man looked fit to strangle, but he quieted.

"Go on, Erma."

She sniffed at the men beside her, then turned to the Sheriff. "Well Tom," she began and planted both hands on her wide hips, "you coulda knocked me over with a stiff breeze, I was that surprised. Nobody ever robbed our bank before!"

"I know."

"And him such a young fella, too," Erma shook her head. "A real shame to see the young ones wanderin' off the Path."

"How do you know he was young?" Tom asked. "Did you see his face?"

"No, but he moved real easy and quick." She jerked her head at the youngest of the men surrounding her, "Kinda like Dusty does when he's on his way to Martha Sue's house?"

Tom swallowed a smile and Dusty's feet shuffled against the gritty, plank floorboards.

Bentley frowned and shifted from foot to foot.

"Anyhow," Erma ignored the banker, "he had blond hair and he was tall. I'd say a touch taller than Dusty, wouldn't you say, George?"

"If you'll just—" Bentley tried but George cut him off.

"Yeah, I reckon so." McDonough rubbed his chin and added "His voice was scratchy rough too, Tom. Like he was havin' a hard time talkin'."

"He was trying to—" the banker was interrupted by Dusty this time.

"An' he stole my mare, Tom."

The Sheriff's eyebrows lifted. "Sadie?"

"Uh-huh." Dusty stuffed his hands in his pockets and kicked Tom's desk. "And she's about to foal any damned minute."

"Will you stop whining about that horse?" Bentley managed to say. "We have other—"

"Course," Erma tossed in, "the fella *did* kinda need that extra horse at the last minute, so to speak."

"Guess we shoulda told ya about that right off," George said quietly as his eyes rolled up to inspect the ceiling.

"Told me about what?" Tom's gaze slipped from one familiar face to the next. Excepting the banker, Tom Bruner had known those people all his life.

Old George McDonough had switched Tom right along with Dusty the time or two he'd managed to catch the boys up to no good. For the last thirty years or so, he'd also taught every kid in town how to fish.

And Erma saved the world by way of her cookstove. Tom still remembered the year he was ten and his mother died of fever. For six solid months, Erma had brought him and his pa a hot meal every night. And at the end of the six months, she'd helped the elder Bruner figure out how to live again while at the same time teaching a boy that even a man had a right to cry sometimes.

As for Dusty, Tom bit back a smile. He and Dusty and Quinn Hawkins had shared everything. From their first cigar to their first drink of hard liquor to their first visit to a cathouse. In fact, he didn't have a single memory that wasn't tied somehow to the people in his office that minute.

Except for Bentley, that is.

Even for a banker, Bentley didn't have much of a heart. He'd moved into Yellow Dog and promptly offended everyone in sight. He'd made more enemies in one day than General Sherman had in Atlanta.

In the last few months, the new banker in town had foreclosed on three farms and ranches and bought up the notes on four or five others. And in every case, as the sheriff, it was Tom's duty to see that the foreclosures and the evictions were carried out. He frowned and clenched his teeth tight together.

Like everybody else for miles around, he had no reason to care for Charles Bentley.

Tom looked back at the other three faces across from him and was surprised to see that his old friends were tryin' to avoid his gaze.

"What?" he pushed himself to his feet. There was something else wrong. He felt it. "What's goin' on?"

"*I* can tell you that, Sheriff," Bentley said, and stepped to the front of the small group. He pointedly ignored the others in the room and focused solely on Tom. "After stealing my . . . I mean, of course, the *bank's* money, the villain kidnapped a young woman right off the street."

"What?" Tom fairly leaped around his desk and didn't stop until he was leaning over Bentley, forcing the shorter man to tilt his head back uncomfortably.

"She bumped into him," Bentley quickly continued and tried not to sound as nervous as he looked, "and knocked him down."

"True, true," Erma muttered.

"And when she got up," Dusty added "I think she pulled his bandana down. Got a look at him."

"You *think?*"

"Hard to tell," Dusty admitted slowly. "She was blockin' my line of sight."

"Must have seen him," George said. "He latched onto her like the last flapjack at a free feed."

"Why didn't you tell me this right off?" Tom couldn't believe it. Someone kidnapped? By a bank robber? In *Yellow Dog?* Things like this just didn't happen. And when they did, he reminded himself as he frowned at his friends and neighbors, folks were supposed to tell the sheriff!

"Well now, suppose it slipped my mind," George muttered. "Gettin' old, y'know."

"Now calm down, Tom" Erma put in, obviously intending to brazen it out. "Nothin's lost here. You still got to go after him anyway. It's not like you woulda let him go if it was just the money he took."

"Yeah, but a young woman's safety is a bit more important than money, don't you think?"

"'Course it is, Tom," Dusty tried to defend all of them, but his arguments were weak. "We was just . . . upset is all."

"Not too upset to tell me about your damned mare!"

Dusty's gaze dropped.

"Look out, Bentley," Tom said and tried to push past the banker. "I got to get goin'."

"For a posse?" George asked.

"No posse," Tom shot back. "Just me and maybe one or two others."

"Why?"

He hardly glanced at Erma. "If this fella's holdin' a hostage, I don't want him gettin' nervous, seein' a bunch of armed men chasin' after him." Snatching his rifle and belt gun down from the pegs on the wall, he muttered "We don't know what kind of fella this man is. What he might do."

"Yes we do."

Slowly, Tom and the others turned to look at Bentley. "What do you mean?"

"I mean," he sneered at the three people on his right before turning back to the Sheriff "I've been trying to tell you for several minutes that I believe I know exactly who your thief was."

Tom took two short steps and stopped in front of the man. Bentley looked as puffed up with himself as a Christmas turkey. The banker had a way about him that really grated on Tom's nerves. Right now, he'd like nothing better than to grab Bentley by that tiny swatch of hair he had stretched across the top of his bald head and shake him like a rat.

The how and the what and the why could wait for later, Tom told himself. Right now, he only wanted the answer to one question. He leaned over the banker, letting his sheer size intimidate the other man until his smug smile disappeared.

"Who?" he asked, in a voice deep with barely contained anger.

Beads of sweat broke out on the banker's forehead and he swallowed heavily a time or two before saying simply, "Quinn Hawkins."

"Quinn?" Winifred watched him straighten up from dunking his face in the pool and couldn't help noticing the droplets of water that clung to his dark blond eyelashes. He blinked them away as she stared at him. Rivulets of water rolled down the length of his throat and disappeared under the collar of his shirt. Dampened, the soft fabric hugged his flesh and he reached up to pluck it loose.

Big hands, she thought idly, with long, slender fingers. Even at a distance of two or three feet, Winifred could see the calluses dotting his fingertips and palms. A mental image of those hands smoothing over her flesh shot through her brain and Winifred's breath caught in her throat. The backs of his hands were brown from days spent in the sun and a dusting of pale blond hair peeked from beneath the frayed cuffs of his shirt.

Suddenly, he snapped the fingers of his right hand and she started. Blinking furiously, she gave herself an inward shake and forced herself to meet his curious gaze. She didn't blame him for wondering what was wrong with her. She was wondering the same thing.

Winifred had never experienced such a thing before. Even the imagined touch of his hands was enough to start her blood racing and her heart pounding. Great Heavens! No wonder her father had always discouraged her mother's longing for adventure.

All *sorts* of things could happen if one weren't very careful.

He snapped his fingers again.

This time Winifred forced her mind back from its nonsensical wanderings.

"You all right?" he asked, his gaze narrowed as he watched her warily.

"Certainly." Her voice broke and Winifred delicately cleared her throat. He really was much too handsome to be an outlaw.

"All right then," he said, but he didn't seem very sure of her answer.

Reaching deep into her brain for one rational thought, Winifred remembered what it was she'd wanted to ask him before those hands of his had sent her off down another path.

"There's something I need to know," she said.

"What's that?"

"You said earlier that I am your 'hostage.' Is that right?"

He inhaled slowly, deeply and kept his jaw locked. Jerking her a nod, he remained quiet, waiting.

It was true, then. She hadn't really believed it, earlier. And somehow it made everything much more exciting to know that she was officially a hostage. Oh, if only her mother had lived to see this, Winifred thought with regret.

Jane Matthews was the only other person in the world that Winifred was sure would have enjoyed the situation as much as she was. From the time she was old enough to understand, Winifred's mother had told her tales of pirates and knights and cowboys. She'd woven wonderful stories about faraway places and the people who lived there.

Every night, from the safety of Winifred's tiny bedroom at the top of the stairs, mother and daughter would sail off together, searching for adventure. Winifred still remembered the longing that colored her mother's voice when she spoke about England or Spain or dastardly, one-eyed pirates on the high seas. Jane had spun tales of cowboys and Indians, of brave young men and beautiful women, of fortunes and treasures, of hearts, won and lost.

She'd instilled a love and thirst for adventure into her young daughter's heart that rivaled her own. And every evening, when storytime was over, Jane would go downstairs and sit in her chair opposite her husband and knit quietly until it was time for bed.

But Winifred knew something that her professor father did not. She knew that although Jane's body and mind were there, in the little town in Maine—her heart and soul were somewhere else. *Anywhere* else, finding adventure.

"Lady," Quinn spoke and shattered Winifred's memories. "Did you want somethin'?"

"Hmmm?" She stared at him blankly for a moment then recovered herself once again. Really, she must try to get a firm grip on her wandering thoughts. "Yes. Yes, I did. If I am indeed your hostage, there is something I'd like to know." Pulling in a great gulp of air, she rushed out, "What exactly does a proper hostage do? I'm afraid I haven't the slightest idea. Since this is my first time, I really would appreciate your advice, as I would hate to do something wrong."

Quinn shoved one hand through his hair and welcomed the cold feel of his fingers against his scalp. If she wasn't the beatinest woman he'd ever met, he didn't know who would be.

He snorted and shook his head. Looking at her, he could see the eagerness in her eyes and wondered what kind of woman she was to accept so easily. There weren't many *men* who would have been able to just roll along with today's strange happenings. And he would've bet that any other woman he'd ever met would have spent most of her time either tryin' to escape or kill him. But not Winifred.

Winifred. Hell of an ugly name for a woman like her. She was too pretty and too damned tiny for such a big, old-fashioned name. Made him think of maiden aunts and cats.

And she was no maiden aunt. A spinster, he figured, but not a damned thing prissish about her. She was pretty, he admitted. And Lord knew, she was clumsier than any *two* people had a right to be. But Jesus, he told himself, there was a lot more to her than her beauty or her clumsiness.

His body tightened and he grumbled softly to himself. That'd be enough of *that!* Shoving himself to his feet, Quinn somehow managed to keep his back to her as he walked over to where the saddles lay in the shade of an ancient oak.

"Quinn?" She called, obviously not ready to let him ignore her. "Have you any advice?"

"Yeah," he shot back and anger colored his voice. That he was angry at his own lack of control, she didn't have to know. In fact, it would be better for both of them if Winifred just figured he was mad at her for pestering him. "I'll give ya some advice, lady," he continued and bent down to snatch up his saddlebags. He didn't even look at her as he shoved one hand into the deep, leather pocket. "All you got to remember is to do everything I say—every time I say it."

"Oh. Is that all?"

"Yeah."

"Well, that certainly sounds easy enough, doesn't it?"

Dammit, she still sounded cheerful. It appeared that it was goin' to take a helluva lot more than him snapping at her to ruin her good time. Solemnly, he shook his head. Somehow, Quinn didn't think anything about riding with Winifred was going to be easy.

4

"Here," *Quinn said* as he tossed her a strip of jerky from his saddlebag. "That's all we got time for now. Won't be stoppin' again 'till late." He dropped to the ground beside her and pretended to stare at the still pool of water. Instead, he covertly watched her.

She picked the dried up piece of meat off her lap and touched it to the tip of her tongue. A quick shudder rolled through her body and she looked at him. "It's quite salty."

Quinn nodded as his teeth bit down on his own leathery strip of meat and tore off a bite. "Gotta salt it to cure it," he shrugged. "It'll hold ya though. And ya get used to the taste of jerked meat." He chewed silently and watched her from the corner of his eye. Her straight white teeth clamped down gingerly on the edge of the meat. When she bit into the jerky like she was tucking into a slice of chocolate cake, he hid a smile. She frowned then pulled the meat back and looked at it as if trying to figure out how to eat it. To give her a little hint, he took another bite of his own jerky, pulling and ripping at the leathery texture.

This time, when she bit down, she grabbed the other end of the jerky in both hands and tugged at it. At last, a small piece of meat ripped off and her head snapped back with her prize.

That silly hat of hers flopped around on top of her head and now lay over one ear. Sunlight caught the fiery strands of her red hair and lit them up like a Roman candle. One long lock of curly hair had fallen loose from the knot at the back of her head and lay across her bosom. Quinn's gaze dropped to the swell of her breasts, hidden beneath the simple blue blouse she wore. With each breath she took, the middle button strained and pulled against the fabric and he found himself staring at the tiny pearl button, hoping it would pop free. With a guilty start, he looked away and told himself that he ought to be ashamed, taking advantage of a woman he'd abducted. Why, she was probably scared to death of him and only trying to hide it to protect herself.

He chanced a quick look into her green eyes and saw open pleasure shining in their depths. If she really was trying to hide how scared she was, she was doing a helluva good job, he told himself. To look at her, anybody would think she was having the time of her life.

She hadn't complained hardly at all and he knew damn well she had to be stiff and sore all over. This wild run across open country was a lot different than riding sidesaddle on a quiet little city horse for an hour or two. He swallowed back a smile. The way she'd been bouncing and flying all over the mare, Quinn knew that she wasn't used to riding. He had to give her credit though, she'd managed to hang on *and* keep up. Hell, except for the fact that her legs had given out on her when she tried to stand, he'd have never guessed that she was hurting.

Instantly, memories of holding her close, helping her walk off the pain, raced back into his mind. Her warmth, her curves resting against him. The easy way she accepted his hand at her waist and the urge he'd had to let his fingers move up to caress her breast.

Quinn blinked, shifted position to ease his sudden discomfort and tried not to think about that. He had to remember she was his prisoner. His hostage.

He glanced at her again. Of course, it would be much easier to think of her as a prisoner if *she* thought of herself as such.

She looked so damned pleased with herself as she tried to chew the jerky, Quinn shifted his gaze to the buffalo wallow.

How had things gone so badly so quickly? And how the hell had he ended up with a hostage? But most importantly—what was he going to do with her? Oh, he knew what he'd like to do with her . . . but that was out of the question.

"Thish ish akshually quite tashty," she said around a mouthful of beef.

Quinn shook his head slowly. Even chewing didn't stop her. She was without a doubt, the talkin'est woman he'd ever run across.

"Mishter Hawkinsh," she said.

He sighed. "Quinn."

"Quinn." She swallowed heavily, pushing the meat down her throat with an act of will.

"What?"

"This is all very exciting," she began and pushed her hat back into place. Immediately, it dipped down over her eyes. "And I don't want you to misunderstand." She inhaled sharply, pushed at her hat again, then sighed. "I'm having a wonderful time."

"I'm real relieved to hear it."

"But," she added on a more somber note "I *am* the new school teacher in Yellow Dog and I simply must report for duty sometime soon."

Well, that about beat anything he'd ever heard.

Quinn was new to this kidnapping thing, but he was willing to bet that not many hostages up and told their captors when it was time to go home.

"You can't." He got up quickly, walked to where he'd picketed the horses and grabbed up both sets of reins. Now that they'd had time to cool off, he led the animals to the small water hole and let them drink their fill.

"But I've signed a contract," she pointed out, and staggered to her feet, still clutching her half-eaten piece of jerky. "I've given my word in good faith."

"Lady," he sighed and patted his horse's neck gently, "didn't I just tell you that you're to do what I say when I say it?"

"Yes," Winifred answered calmly, "but I was sure you hadn't considered what my absence will do to the children of Yellow Dog."

"They'll survive awhile without schoolin'," he assured her.

"Perhaps, but . . ."

"Lady," he let his head fall back on his neck as he fought for patience. No matter the brave front she was putting up, he figured she was probably a bit scared of what he might be planning for her. Hmmph. She'd probably be surprised if she knew he didn't have a plan. "I just robbed a bank." Lord those words sounded strange coming out of his own mouth. "I got a few other things on my mind besides the schoolin' of children."

"I've already given you my solemn promise that I won't tell anyone where you've gone." She began to walk to him, then stopped suddenly. "Botheration," she whispered and bent down. He watched her pull a piece of her torn hem from the toe of her shoe before straightening up and walking toward him again.

"Lady—"

"And please do stop calling me 'lady'," she interrupted. He grumbled something that only his horse could hear and the beast lifted its head as if surprised at the tone.

"Lady," he repeated deliberately, "you don't get a vote in what we do or where we go."

"I don't see why not," she pointed out and took another step. "We're traveling together after all. Shouldn't our destination be a mutual decision?"

Quinn rubbed one hand across his face and fought to hold the curses springing to his lips inside. Anybody else's hostage would probably be crying, and praying for salvation. His wanted a say-so in how things're done. It figured.

It also figured that the first time in his life he did something dishonest, nothing was going as it should have.

Lordy, how'd he get himself into this?

"We ain't 'travelin' together, lady," he pointed out, with all the patience he'd been able to summon. "I'm travelin' and draggin' you along with me."

"Exactly." She took another step or two toward him and stopped suddenly. "What on earth?" she muttered and bent down. "Oh dear."

"Oh, dear, what?" he said, warned by the odd note in her voice.

She straightened up and held out his hat to him. His crumpled, dented hat with the dainty footprint on the crown.

Quinn sighed heavily, leaned forward and snatched the hat from her hands. Mumbling, he pushed and shoved at the old felt hat, trying to get it back into its original shape. Wind and rain and sweat had worked on the felt over the years until it had finally frozen into just the right shape. It fit his head perfectly. But that one step of hers had managed to destroy the last of his hat's strength. No matter how he tried, the crown and brim stayed permanently dipped and broken.

Wonderful, he thought and slammed the hat down on his head. It didn't even *feel* right now.

"Ah," she said with a pleased smile, "as good as new."

Quinn glared at her and noted that he could now see the brim of his hat where it dipped low on one side. He closed his eyes.

It shouldn't have surprised him when she changed the course of their conversation abruptly.

"Doesn't my horse seem exceptionally . . . well, *fat*," she asked after a respectful moment of silence.

"She ain't fat," Quinn said slowly, his eyes opening again and shifting to stare at Dusty's prize mare. "She's pregnant."

"Oh!" A slight flush of color swept up his prisoner's cheeks and Quinn fought down a half smile. All alone with a 'villainous desperado' like she'd called him, miles from help, her reputation would be good and ruined, he told himself and it didn't seem to bother her any. But she blushed over a pregnant horse.

Carefully, tenderly, Winifred laid one palm on the mare's distended belly. As a ripple of movement crossed her palm, she looked up at him, delighted. "Come and feel this, Quinn!"

"Lady, it's just the foal movin' around."

"Well, I know that, but I've never really . . ." she grinned as the foal shifted position again. "Oh, isn't that marvelous!" Then she stepped up to the mare's head and gently rubbed the animal's cheek. "How excited you must be—" Winifred broke off and looked up at Quinn. "Does she have a name?"

Oh, he thought dismally, she has a name. And half a barn all to herself. And the best oats Dusty could find. And her own stable boy. Hell, Dusty did everything for that horse just short of bringing her inside and tucking her into his own bed.

His inner smile at the thought faded abruptly. Ah Jesus, Dusty was gonna be madder than a whore at a preacher's party about losing the mare.

And he was probably already on the trail coming after her.

With that notion firmly in mind, Quinn moved to snatch up the saddle blankets. "Her name's Sadie."

"Sadie." Winifred sighed it out. "Isn't that nice? Are you happy about your baby, Sadie?"

The mare's big head twitched and jerked up and down almost as if she were nodding.

Winifred laughed, then stopped suddenly as she saw Quinn beginning to saddle his horse. "Are we leaving already?"

"Yes'm."

"But is it safe for Sadie, do you suppose?"

"Lady, that horse is used to movin'. And with as slow as we're ridin', she'll be a lot safer than I will."

"Do you think there are people coming after us? So soon?"

"Bet on it." He tightened the saddle cinch strap on his gray, then moved to throw a blanket over Sadie's back.

Winifred looked over her shoulder back the way they'd come. In her mind's eye, she imagined a crowd of Texas Rangers, guns drawn, riding at a full charge. And when her rescuers finally caught up to them, she asked herself, what would they do to Quinn Hawkins?

Shoot him?

Her gaze shot to the handsome man who was her captor.

Hang him as a horse thief?

Horse thief.

"Quinn," she said quickly as their earlier conversation leaped to the forefront of her mind.

"What?"

She ignored his sharp tone and asked "What you said

earlier? About my being a horse thief?" He glanced up at her momentarily then looked back to his task. "Were you being serious?"

"Yes ma'am," he muttered and tossed the stirrup high onto Sadie's back so he could reach the cinch strap. "I surely was."

"You mean, that if I were to stay behind with Sadie, the posse might very well hang me?"

"Uh-huh."

She frowned and glanced back to the open country behind them. Even though he said it was true, Winifred couldn't really bring herself to believe it. Why everyone knew Western justice was fair. No one would hang a woman without first giving her a trial.

Would they?

Of course not.

"Quinn," she said and heard him sigh "I think it would be for the best if I stayed here with Sadie and waited for the posse to arrive."

He braced his forearms on Sadie's saddle and stared at her. His expression was unreadable.

Resolutely, she went on "I don't think a Western posse would teach a woman a 'hemp dance' out of hand and—"

"What did you just say?"

"Which part?"

"About a . . . dance?"

"Oh. A hemp dance."

"What's that?"

Winifred frowned slightly. Really, he was living in Texas. Shouldn't he know even better than she, the expressions used most often in the Wild West?

"A hanging, of course," she said.

A gust of wind shot across the open plain and tugged at her hat. Winifred blinked against the dirt flying into her eyes then reached up and tied the ribbon beneath her chin a bit tighter.

"You ain't stayin'."

"I appreciate your concern, of course," she started.

He cut her off. "Lady, even if that posse don't hang ya," he waved one arm in a wide arc, indicating the land around them. "You can't stay here alone. Hell, there's coyotes and wolves and snakes and all manner of other critters—four *and* two legged—wanderin' around out there. And most of 'em would dearly love to come across some crazy woman all alone except for a pregnant horse."

She glanced again at her surroundings and looked at them with a new eye. The shadows were lengthening. Patches of darkness lay across the open land like pockets. And in those pockets rested dangers that she hadn't even considered until that very moment.

A shiver quaked through her body and she wrapped her arms about herself. The adventure she'd always dreamed of seemed much bigger suddenly than it ever had before. In a few hours, the sun would set and night would swallow up everything. She'd never been alone in the darkness before. Oh, in the city, no one was really alone. There were neighbors within reach. There were the police officers strolling the sidewalks. Even the occasional stranger out for a moonlight walk.

And in Maine, she had a house. With lamps. With doors. With locks—not that she'd ever used them in the small town where she'd lived.

Here, her gaze moved over the open sky and dropped to the land stretching out forever in front of her. Here, there was nothing between her and the elements. There was nothing to protect her from assault, whether it be from nature or man.

She was well and truly alone. For the first time in her life, she had nothing and no one.

Except Quinn.

"Storm's comin'," he said quietly.

Winifred looked at him and he pointed off to his left.

She glanced in that direction and saw rolling gray clouds huddled together on the horizon. A distant rumble of thunder reached out for her and in the mass of clouds, she saw a dim flash of lightning.

"We best get goin'," Quinn said, "find shelter for the night."

Winifred tossed one last glance back over her shoulder at the way they'd come. The way a posse would be coming. Then she looked back at Quinn and nodded. He was right.

She had no choice.

Quinn Hawkins? A thief? A kidnapper?

Tom Bruner shook his head and turned up the collar of his coat. He still didn't believe it. And he wouldn't until he faced his old friend and Quinn himself admitted it.

Although a treacherous voice in the back of his mind whispered that what the banker said did make some sense. Tom stared blankly into the small, square shaving mirror hanging on his office wall. Looking back at him, he saw the stamp of weariness etched into the fine squint lines around his brown eyes. He reached up and touched the tip of his index finger to the slash of white streaking across the dark brown hair at his left temple. It stood out in stark contrast and served as a constant reminder of just how close he'd come to dying a few years back.

If Quinn hadn't called out a warning, if Tom himself hadn't reacted quickly, that gunfighter's bullet would have punched a hole right between Tom's eyes. Instead, it had scraped along his scalp, hurtling him into unconsciousness. But Quinn was there to look out for him. It had been Quinn who'd shot that gunfighter. Quinn who'd carried Tom to a doctor and Quinn who'd stayed by his side until he was sure Tom would wake up.

When that long, bloody gash had healed, the hair along Tom's temple had grown back snowy white. And everytime he looked into a mirror, Tom was reminded that he owed his life to Quinn Hawkins.

And now, it was his job to hunt Quinn down.

Sighing heavily, he reached to his left, plucked his dusty black hat from the hall tree and shoved it down onto his head. Turning away from the mirror, he opened the door and went outside.

Closing his office door behind him, Tom walked across the boardwalk and stepped down into the street. He slid his rifle into its hand-tooled leather scabbard and plucked the saddle bags off his shoulder. Quickly, he tied them into place behind his saddle and looked across his horse's back at the other man preparing for the journey.

Dusty looked grim, determined. Not that Tom blamed him for that. He knew how much that mare and her foal meant to Dusty and the future of his ranch. But Tom would have felt a lot better if he'd been able to convince someone else to go along with them. Dusty's temper wasn't an easy thing to deal with in the best of times. On this trip, it was going to be the very devil.

Lord help them all if it turned out that Quinn was the man behind the holdup. Old friends or not, Dusty was just liable to shoot Hawkins out of hand without bothering to hear an explanation.

Under his breath, Tom muttered an oath that was half-curse and half-prayer. There was no way he could keep Dusty from coming with him. Even if he tried, the man would simply follow after. And nobody else wanted to leave the comfort of their homes with a storm brewing. He tossed a quick glance at the sky and frowned.

Clouds were moving in fast. At best they had another hour or so before they'd have to hole up and wait it out. But at least, he told himself as he swung aboard his mouse-colored gelding, they'd have a chance to pick up the trail before the rain washed it away. If nothing else, they'd have the direction the thief took when he left Yellow Dog with his prisoner.

Tom tugged on the reins and urged his horse into a slow trot toward the edge of town. He didn't turn and look behind him. He could hear Dusty's mount hurrying to catch up. The wind pushed at his hat brim and Tom lowered his head a bit, burrowing his chin into the warmth of his coat collar. As he settled into the rocking rhythm of his horse's movements, his mind wandered back to the running thief and his prisoner.

Jesus. *Prisoner.* He'd done some asking around and from what he could tell, Tom figured the woman who'd been taken was the new school teacher everybody'd been waiting for. He could only imagine what a spinster lady from Maine was going through. Kidnapped, on the run, terrified. Hell, for her sake, he almost hoped it *was* Quinn who'd taken her. At least then, she'd be safe. Hawkins had never hurt a woman in his life. Of course, she couldn't know that. Right now, Tom told himself, she was probably crying her eyes out, begging her captor to let her go.

"Dammit lady," Quinn shouted, "let me go!"

He turned in a slow circle, trying like hell to pull the woman's clinging hands off his face and eyes. She'd already smashed what was left of his hat down over his forehead and now her frantic palms were adding to his sudden blindness.

Quinn felt her feet as she tried to climb up his back to his shoulders. Her bootheels dug into his hipbones and the toes of her hard, black shoes scraped along his spine. Her short, rapid breathing rasped in his ear and the fall of her skirt, whipped by the rising wind, snapped around the two of them, entangling his arms.

"Lady, calm down!"

"S . . . s . . . sn . . . snake!" she stuttered and with each new try on the word her voice rose until she finished on a scream that pierced his left ear like a spike had been driven through his head.

"It's *dead,* dammit!"

Her right foot slipped, glancing off his hip. He felt her balance dissolve and tried to brace his legs to hold them both up. Her left arm wrapped around his throat and the crook of her elbow closed over his Adam's apple. Quinn stretched his neck and raised both hands to the arm choking him. Her black skirt billowed out around them again and her left foot still dug into his hipbone. She was stuck to him like a tick on a dog and suddenly, he had a lot more sympathy for that old hound of his.

Her right foot, swinging free, smacked into the back of his knee and Quinn only had time to instinctively turn a bit before they fell. His right shoulder took the brunt of the impact and he groaned when a new pain roared through him. He heard her breath rush from her lungs, but she still had enough wind left to shoot off the ground and climb atop his prostrate body.

Gathering the folds of her skirt up, Winifred's gaze moved over the rock strewn dirt frantically. She knew the snake was dead. She'd watched him shoot it and could swear she still heard the echo of the pistol shot. But where there was one snake, there was probably two. Didn't most creatures travel in pairs?

And if the other one was nearby, wouldn't it be furious at the two humans who'd killed its mate? Winifred drew her feet up under her, Indian style and hugged her knees to her chest. Rapid, shallow breaths shot from her throat and she wiggled around on Quinn's body until she was sure she was safely out of reach of any deadly fangs that happened to be close by.

The man beneath her groaned and slammed his hands onto her hips, holding her steady. "Jesus lady," he moaned softly, "you're killin' me."

"I'm sorry if I'm too heavy for you, Quinn," she said, her gaze still shooting around their campsite. She couldn't see into the makeshift tent he'd put together with a few branches and his rainslicker. For all she knew, anything could be hiding beneath the cover of his bedroll.

Deliberately, she kept her gaze from lighting on the headless body of the snake Quinn had killed moments ago. Later, perhaps, she would remember the speed with which he'd drawn his pistol. The accuracy of the shot that had severed the snake's head. Later. When she could pick and choose her memories. When she could avoid seeing the snake's lifeless body snap and twist. When she could ignore the memory of her own scream or the frantic, terrified way she'd climbed up Quinn's body as if he were a tree.

"Lady, get off me," he said in a none too gentle voice.

"No," she told him. "There may be more of them."

"Snakes don't travel in packs, lady!"

A mental image of a herd of snakes, slithering across the plains rose up in Winifred's mind and she shuddered. Instinctively, she moved around on Quinn's body, reassuring herself that she was well off the dangerous ground.

"Stop doin' that," he warned through clenched teeth.

"What?"

"Wigglin'."

"I'm sorry if I'm hurting you."

She didn't sound sorry, Quinn told himself as she rocked her behind over his throbbing groin. But if she didn't stop moving soon, she damn well might be.

5

"Get up!" Quinn ordered and as he said it, he rolled out from under her. Not even bothering to grab his hat, he stumbled to his feet, then bit back the groan that accompanied the movement. Jesus, his body was reacting to her like she was the first woman he'd ever seen.

He sucked in a deep breath and told himself to calm down. To regain control of the situation, though truth to tell, he didn't really think he'd ever had control of it. As he watched her, Winifred moved in closer to him, holding the hem of her skirt up around her knees. Unwillingly, his gaze dropped to her shapely legs, covered in plain, black cotton stockings. He had to force himself to look away.

Then his gaze met hers and he could see the fear in her eyes. Desire faded away, to be replaced by an almost overwhelming urge to protect her. Reassure her.

He laid one hand on her shoulder and she jumped. Quinn shook his head.

"The snake's dead, lady."

"That one," she agreed. "But what about its wife?"

"Wife?"

"Or husband," she shrugged. "I don't know how to tell them apart."

A smile tugged at the corners of his mouth. He gave her shoulder a gentle squeeze. "This ain't Noah's ark, lady. Snakes mostly travel alone."

"Are you sure?" her eyes were wide and even in the growing dimness, Quinn was caught again by the deep, rich shade of green staring at him.

"Yeah." He let his hand drop away from her reluctantly. He had no business noticing if her eyes were pretty or not. "Yeah, I'm sure." Looking for a way to change the subject and to get her mind off the snake he'd shot, he said, "Do you know how to lay a fire?"

Her gaze slid to the body of the snake, but she nodded.

Quinn reached out, took her chin between his thumb and forefinger and turned her face back to him.

"That storm's gonna be right on top of us before long." He tossed a quick glance at the sky. "We might have enough time to brew up some coffee and maybe fry some bacon before it hits."

She nodded.

"Really shouldn't be riskin' no fire," he added, more to himself than to her. "But I reckon whoever's comin' after us'll have to hole up too, 'cause of the storm." He smiled at her in an attempt to chase away the lingering traces of fear in her eyes. "So, we'll chance a hatful of fire, all right?"

She frowned slightly, then nodded.

"All right." He turned her around toward the hastily built lean-to he'd constructed and gave her a gentle push. "There's dry wood enough layin' around. You get the fire started and I'll cook. Matches and such are in the saddlebags."

Slowly, carefully, she began to pick her way across the clearing toward their shelter. Her skirt hem still clutched high above her knees, Winifred looked carefully at the ground before she took each step.

Shaking his head, Quinn added "I'll just see to the horses."

He wasn't sure if she'd heard him or not, but he wouldn't be gone long in any case. They'd been lucky, he knew, stumbling onto the outcropping of rock on the side of a low hill. It wasn't much, but it should provide the animals with enough shelter from the storm. And there was plenty of grass around for them to eat.

Soon he knew, there'd be more than enough water, too. Quinn shot one more anxious look at the dark, heavy looking clouds scuttling in from the east. From the looks of it and, he added as another clap of thunder rolled down around them, the sound of it—they were in for a real gully washer. And that, Quinn told himself, was the only thing that had gone in his favor since the minute he'd backed out of that bank.

Deliberately, he turned and looked back at the way they'd come. Somewhere behind them, a posse was riding. Tom Bruner would be leading it and that fact gave Quinn a low, sinking feeling in the pit of his stomach. He was damned sorry it had come to this.

He was sorry too about lying to Winifred about folks considering her a horse thief. Quinn's jaw clenched and he tipped his face up into the cold, driving wind. For an honest man, he'd sure as hell been lying and stealing a lot lately. Hell, he knew as well as anybody that not a lawman in the country would see her as stealing that horse. How could they? *She* was stolen, too! And he probably shouldn't have scared her so much about the dangers of being on her own in this country.

But hell. If she wasn't half-sure the posse would be looking for her—or too scared to go off on her own— she could just take off. And he couldn't have that. Not with Tom Bruner and the rest of 'em closing in.

Jesus, maybe that's what he was most sorry about. Being hunted by a friend.

But there was nothing to be done about it now.

Dark clouds scuttled across the sky, bumping into each other in time with the thunder. Even the air smelled like rain. A small smile touched Quinn's features briefly, then faded.

Tom Bruner was a good tracker. In fact, he was one of the best. But even ol' Tom couldn't follow a trail that had been washed away by a spring storm. Quinn knew good and well that once the rain stopped, every trace of him and Winifred would be gone. It wouldn't hold the man chasing him off forever, he knew. But at least it would slow Tom down several days if he had to scout around to find new tracks.

And those few days would be all Quinn would need to find a town big enough to leave Winifred in before he headed out of the territory for good.

Deliberately, he turned away from his back trail and the men chasing him. Instead, he walked over to where the horses were picketed.

The animals were restive, uneasy with the approaching storm. As Quinn stepped up alongside his gray, he whispered "Easy, Reb," and rubbed the flat of his hand over the animal's long, graceful neck. Reb's eyes rolled nervously and he threw his big head back, tugging at the picket rope.

"C'mon now, boy," Quinn told the animal. "You don't want to look scared in front of a lady, now do ya?"

Sadie seemed to know that he was talking about her. The mare lifted her head and blew out a soft greeting. Then she bent her neck again and began to crop at the grass.

"Lookit there," Quinn whispered to his own animal, "ain't you ashamed?" The gray shook its head. "A big ol' boy like you carryin' on so while a pregnant lady just eats her supper and minds her own business."

Reb dipped his head and took a mouthful of grass, soothed by the man's hands and voice. Thunder crashed again and this time, the big gray ignored it. Quinn smiled and moved around his horse to check Sadie's picket and give her a friendly pat.

While he was there, he let his hand slide down along Sadie's flesh until he reached her swollen belly. The foal within rolled and shivered, tickling Quinn's palm with the movement. He grinned. Winifred was right. It *was* wonderful.

He walked up to the mare's head and ran his hand down the length of her nose. Quietly, he said "You're about ready to pop that baby right out, aren't ya, Sadie?" She ignored him and pulled another clump of grass from the ground. "Well," he continued whispering, "you do ol' Quinn a favor, will ya girl? You hold that baby in just as long as ya can, all right?"

Quinn snorted a laugh. It had been a helluva day all the way around. It was only right that it end up with him trying to make a deal with a horse.

A sharp, sudden wind shot past him and carried the faint odor of smoke. Good. He smiled and nodded. At least she hadn't lied about knowing how to light a fire. Nothing he'd like better than a hot cup of coffee before all the cold and wet started down on them.

If he was at home right now, he thought, he'd have the animals all tucked into the barn, warm and dry. And he'd be in the house in front of the stone fireplace his father had built. His mother would be there, drinking coffee while she hunched over the ranch books, trying to make the numbers come up different.

Mercy Hawkins was a woman who didn't know the meaning of the word quit. At least, she hadn't. Until Bentley'd arrived in town and ripped the ranch she'd built nearly single-handedly right out from under her.

The day the banker had ridden out to the ranch to let

them know that he had bought their loan, was the first time Quinn could remember seeing defeat in his mother's eyes. She'd known right from the first that Bentley wasn't interested in them paying off their indebtedness. All he wanted was the ranch and the water rights that went with it.

A different smell mingled with the scent of wood smoke and drew Quinn from his memories. He wrinkled his nose and paused, trying to identify the odor. Shaking his head, he took another whiff as he started walking toward the lean-to a few feet away. As it finally dawned on him that the strange odor was burning cloth, he was already at a run, imagining that Winifred had somehow plopped herself down in the flames.

He came around the edge of the shelter and skidded to a stop. Then cussing a blue streak, he snatched up his smoking hat and tipped it over, spilling the burning twigs and sticks onto the ground.

Winifred stared at him. He was furious. Curses she'd never heard before came pouring out of his mouth as he stood there, slapping his still-smoldering hat against his thigh.

Tiny pieces of burning felt flew off and landed at his feet before being lifted and tossed by the wind until their glowing edges were darkened again. She glanced down at the ground and saw that her carefully laid fire was quickly dying. Using one of the sturdier sticks she'd found, she pushed the still flickering pieces of kindling together into a haphazard pile and carefully added thin twigs to the small blaze when it began to catch. Only then did she look up at Quinn again.

He was glowering at her. His right hand in the bowl of his hat, two fingers stuck up through the crown. She frowned but continued to meet his gaze bravely. She'd done nothing wrong. In fact, she'd done exactly what he'd told her to do, no matter how foolish it had seemed to her at the time.

Imagine wanting someone to build a fire in your hat!

"What in the livin' hell were you doin'?" he demanded and his shout came on the heels of another crash of thunder.

Winifred winced, blinked when the streak of lightning briefly lit his features into a mask of light and shadow, then answered him as calmly as possible.

"I was only doing what you expressly told me to do."

"When did I say to build a fire in my *hat*?"

Wood smoke twisted and danced in the wind, stinging her eyes and burning her nose with each breath she took. Instinctively, she waved one hand in front of her face before she added another small stick to the brightly burning fire.

Really, she told herself, he might have shown a little appreciation for her efforts. It had taken her three times just to strike a match without the rising wind blowing it out. And finding twigs and sticks small enough to nest in the bowl of his hat hadn't been an easy chore either!

A sense of righteous indignation swelled in her breast and Winifred glared right back at him. "Did you or did you not tell me that we should have a 'hatful of fire'?"

His jaw dropped and his eyes rolled skyward before centering on her again.

"That's just a sayin'," he told her, and from the sound of his voice, she knew he was clenching his jaw. "A 'hatful' of fire means a *small* fire." He shook his right hand in front of her face and all she could see were his fingers, jutting up from the jagged, blackened hole in the crown of his hat. "It don't mean to build a fire in my hat!"

The edges of the hole were curled up and still smoking. His fingers pointed at her accusingly and Winifred couldn't seem to tear her eyes away from them. Still though, she managed to say "You might have said so, Mr. Hawkins."

"Quinn," he grumbled and pulled his hat free with his left hand.

"Quinn, then. I didn't think it made much sense at the time, but I assumed you knew what you were talking about."

He mumbled something under his breath and Winifred didn't even want to know what it was. After all the curse words he'd shouted at her, if there was something so dreadful he felt he had to whisper it . . . well, she was better off not knowing that kind of language.

"It didn't make much sense," he repeated, slowly shaking his head as he inspected the gaping hole in his crushed hat.

"Of course not."

"Then why'd ya *do* it?" the question came softly and was almost lost in the sudden roar of the gusting wind.

She shrugged helplessly. "You did tell me to do what you said, when you said," she reminded him.

He sighed heavily. "True enough."

"And I thought perhaps," Winifred added, "that building a fire in a hat somehow would make the cooking fire . . . movable."

"Movable?"

"Yes." She crossed her arms over her chest and met his gaze squarely. "I thought perhaps you wanted to be able to move the fire in out of the rain."

"You didn't figure that a fire would burn clean through it?"

"Well, no." She hadn't stopped to think about it at all, actually.

Quinn nodded and she could see that most of his anger was already gone. Happily enough, her outlaw seemed to have the kind of temper that though it blew up quickly, was just as easily dismissed.

He was silent for several minutes. His long-fingered hands curled and uncurled the crumpled brim of his hat as he watched her. Winifred looked back at him until her eyes were stinging as much from the unblinking stare as from the smoking fire.

Finally though, he reached some sort of inner decision. Slapping his hat down onto his head, he ducked beneath the rain slicker roof of their shelter and took a seat beside her on the blanket.

Winifred swiveled her head to look at him. He gave her a brief, lopsided smile and a shrug of his broad shoulders. "No point worryin' over what's done," he said softly. "Anyways," he added on a sigh, "it's just a hat. What say we get that coffee and bacon cookin' before the storm puts our fire out?"

As he rummaged through the saddlebags, drawing out a battered tin coffee pot and a small skillet, Winifred watched him. She didn't think it would be prudent of her to comment on the fact that the curled, blackened edges of his hat made it look as though he had two tiny horns jutting up from the top of his head.

"Will you set still?" Tom complained and gave Dusty a hard shove that almost tore the slicker off the both of them.

"Hell, you're hoggin' the damn blanket and the damned rain slicker and I'm gettin' soaked over here." To prove his point, Dusty scooted around on the edge of the blanket and tugged again at the waterproof covering.

"Next time you go on a damned manhunt, bring your outfit with you!" Tom grumbled, reached up and tugged the brim of his hat down low over his eyes. Rain sluiced off the sides of his hat to the ground under his shoulder and formed a small puddle of mud.

Nothing he could do about it, he knew. But all the same, he'd like nothing better than to push Dusty

McDonough out from under his slicker and get a little sleep. It would serve the hotheaded fool right. He'd never met anybody who didn't have the sense to travel with a rain slicker.

But then, Dusty'd been too busy planning on what he'd do to a horse thief to care much about a coming storm.

When that thought entered his brain, others crowded in after it. Tom found himself wondering what Quinn was doing at that moment. If he'd found a place to hole up in. And where he'd be headed when the rain quit.

It was gonna be hard as hell trying to pick up a trail after a rain. He had no idea which way to start looking. Quinn Hawkins wasn't a stupid man and Tom had no doubt that once the storm was over, Quinn would be heading in a different direction from the one he'd taken before the rain.

Tom sighed and lifted his right shoulder out of the mud slightly. Him and Dusty would have to split up and ride in a wide circle scouting for new signs. It could take them hours—or even days.

He opened his eyes and stared up at the blackness of the inside of his hat. The hard driving rain pelted him and landed with loud snaps and pops against his hat. It didn't feel right, he told himself. He shouldn't be having to chase down Quinn Hawkins. And Quinn shouldn't be having to run from the law and his friends and everything he knew and held dear.

But it was happening. And Tom knew deep in his bones that it *was* Quinn he was chasing. Everything Bentley had said kept running through Tom's brain.

Tall.

Blond.

Young.

Hell, Tom thought with a grimace, he was the same age as Quinn and right now, thirty-two didn't seem so damned young. But, compared to Bentley, he supposed it was.

Those weren't the only clues pointing to Quinn though, Tom admitted silently. Actually, it was the last thing Bentley'd said that had convinced Tom that his friend had indeed robbed the bank. The amount of money stolen, fifteen hundred dollars.

There had been a few thousand in that vault but all the robber took was fifteen hundred.

And fifteen hundred dollars was the amount of the Hawkins loan that Bentley had bought up from Henry Simpson.

Mercy Hawkins stood on the wide front porch and shielded her eyes as she stared into the distance. The long line of thunderheads moving in closer every minute looked more threatening to her than they normally would have. She bit her lip and let her right hand drop to her side.

Wind grabbed at her, pulling at the collar of her plain white shirt and tugging the pins from her still dark brown hair. She leaned against the porch post and tried to tell herself that her son would be home soon.

But deep inside, she knew better. She'd been to town that afternoon. She'd heard the talk. The whispers started up by the story banker Bentley was spreading. She'd heard them and laughed in the faces of her friends when they came to her with sympathy.

"Not Quinn," she'd told them. "My son's no thief. Bentley's the thief!"

But no one wanted to talk about the new banker. He was a miserable enough fella, but he wasn't news. Quinn Hawkins robbing a bank. Now *that* was news.

So Mercy had defended him, proclaimed his innocence and then left town as quickly as possible. She'd needed to be home. Where she could think.

But she didn't like the thoughts spiraling through her brain. She drew no comfort from her own arguments to the townsfolk. Because she knew in her heart that they were right.

Her son *had* robbed that bank.

The dang fool.

And now he was out there, running from the man who'd been his friend most of his life. Worst of all, Mercy admitted silently, was knowing there wasn't a damned thing she could do to help.

"What're you writin'?" Quinn asked her and leaned a bit closer.

"I keep a journal," Winifred told him and lifted one edge of the book higher in an effort to keep him from reading what she'd written.

"'Bout what?" He told himself he didn't care. After all, what did it matter to him what kind of nonsense a female wrote down in a little blue book? Still, his curiosity was aroused and Lord knew there was nothing else to do but wait out the storm.

Not entirely true, a small voice in the back of his mind whispered. There were a few other things they could be doing. And just the notion of 'em was enough to have Quinn's body hard, tight and uncomfortable.

He winced and told himself that if he didn't stop thinking such things, he wasn't going to live long enough to find a new ranch somewhere. Shifting slightly, Quinn pulled off his battered hat and stuck his face out from under their makeshift roof. Eyes closed, he tilted his face up and let the cold, hard rain pound some sense into his brain.

After a moment, he drew back inside and pushed the water from his face and hair with the palms of his hands. The cold water hadn't helped any. More than just his curiosity was still aroused.

"Why did you do that?"

"Huh?" he looked into her wide, green eyes and knew she didn't have a clue as to the effect she had on a man. He gave her the first lame excuse he could think of. "Washin' my face."

"Oh."

It was near pitch dark. He didn't know how the hell she could see well enough to write anything. But after looking at him briefly, she turned back to her task. He studied the long fall of her hair tumbling down her back and before he could stop himself, he reached out and gently lifted one of the springy curls. Quinn wrapped it around his finger and smoothed his thumb over the silky softness of it.

Unaware of his touch, Winifred kept writing. He wondered what she might do to him if he was to just pull her into his arms and kiss her until her ears started ringing. With his next breath, he told himself he was acting foolish and let the dark red curl slip from his finger. Obviously, he thought, his only hope of ignoring her lay in getting to sleep as quickly as he could.

Even before he'd finished the thought, Quinn had stretched out and tipped his ruined hat over his eyes. "We'll be leavin' at first light," he reminded her gruffly.

"I understand. Good night."

Nothing good about it, he told himself and crossed his arms over his chest.

Winifred glanced back at him, then looked again at the wobbly lines of writing in front of her. The night was nearly black, but she could see just well enough to keep one line from running into the next and so she continued.

As outlaws go, she wrote thoughtfully, *Quinn Hawkins seems to be a pleasant enough fellow. Though as I believe I remarked earlier, he's much too handsome to be an outlaw. From everything*

I've read, there should be an evil glint in his eye and he should definitely be sporting a scar. His eyes are blue. A clear, deep blue that makes me think of a cold, clear winter sky. Though I haven't as yet seen an evil glint in them, I have seen sparkles of a temper that is quite something to behold. However no matter how angry he gets, it is quickly done and forgotten. Hardly criminal behavior, one would think. On the other hand, he did kidnap me and carry me away. Oh, it was so exciting. Like the stories mother told me about knights and princesses. And he's held me very close to his person more than once since this adventure began. I can't tell you what it was like, feeling a man's heart beat in time with my own. And when he touches me, I get the most peculiar sensations that begin low in my stomach then spread to my limbs and—other portions of my person. Right now, he is sleeping beside me and I have only to reach out to touch him. Of course, I wouldn't, but still the opportunity is mine for the taking. Did I mention that he also has a moustache? It is very handsome for it is the same golden color as his hair. I wonder what it would feel like to have that moustache brush across my skin? Oh. I can hardly believe that I was shameless enough to put that in writing. But then, who else can I tell besides you, dear journal, about my experiences on my grand adventure? There is no one else. Oh—I must tell you too that Quinn Hawkins shot a snake for me today. Quite possibly saving my life. It was a hideous monster, with fangs and an enormous rattle which sounded out threateningly just before Quinn shot it. Just like mother's knights, he rescued me.

   A snake is really somewhat like a dragon. Isn't it?

6

She snuggled in closer and Quinn moved his right hand up and down her back slowly in a lazy caress. She sighed and her breath puffed against his throat. A satisfied smile curved his lips as he rolled to his side. Eyes closed and caught in that dreamlike state that hovers just beyond wakefulness, Quinn lowered his head and kissed the woman in his arms.

Her lips were soft, inviting. He teased her mouth with the tip of his tongue until she opened to him, welcoming him into her warmth. Quinn groaned in the back of his throat and held her even tighter. He moved his mouth over hers with slow deliberation until her breathing quickened and her hands moved to encircle his neck. She arched against him and he shifted slightly, letting his lips slide from her mouth to the tender, sensitive flesh of her neck. He trailed a long line of kisses down the length of her throat and felt the rapid rush of her pulse beneath his lips. With his left hand, he reached for the uppermost button of her shirt and pushed it free.

The woman beneath him twisted slightly and bent her head back further, silently demanding more of his kisses. He smiled to himself and gave her what she seemed to want as badly as he did. The second button was dispensed with as easily as the first. Quinn opened his eyes to slits and caught a brief glimpse of the white lace edging her chemise before he heard it.

A soft voice, breathy with passion and surprise.

"Great Heavens!"

He paused, his breath caught in his throat, his heart-beat thundering in his ears. Cautiously, Quinn opened his eyes. Winifred Matthews's throat was bared to his gaze and immediately, he squeezed his eyes shut again.

Shit!

He heard her breath, coming in short, harsh gasps and mentally called himself every foul name he could think of. Fumbling, suddenly clumsy, Quinn's fingers tugged the open vee of her shirt together before he chanced a quick look at her through slitted eyes.

Her eyes wide and glazed with desire, her lips puffy and red from his kisses, the little schoolteacher looked—all too tempting for comfort.

Quinn pushed himself away from her and sat up. Shoving one hand through his sleep rumpled hair, he stared out blankly at the rain washed land in front of him. Wildly, frantically, he tried to make excuses for himself. He was tired. He'd been too long without a woman. He was half-asleep and so didn't even realize what he'd been doing.

None of them were any good. First off, he was never *that* tired. And hell, he'd gone longer periods without a woman and hadn't stooped to forcing himself on the first one he came across. As for not realizing what he was doing . . . hell, why lie to himself?

Ever since the moment she'd tripped him up outside the bank then fell across his lap, Quinn's body had been reacting to her. Even if his brain hadn't been paying attention—his hands and mouth knew just what he was doing.

He sucked in a gulp of cool morning air and told himself that he was surely on the road to hell. In the last couple of days, not only had he become a common thief, he'd taken to molesting sleeping women!

Quinn groaned and rubbed one hand over his eyes.

"Mr. Hawkins—Quinn," she said and he felt her sit up beside him.

He stifled another groan and forced himself to say "Lady, before you climb up on your high horse and start callin' me every kind of a so and so—"

"But . . ."

"I want to say I'm uh . . . *sorry.*" That last word was hard. It wasn't often Quinn put himself in the position to apologize. And Lord knew, having to ask pardon for damn near undressing a sleeping woman was a humbling experience.

"Oh."

He glanced at her and watched her chew her bottom lip thoughtfully. Quinn tried not to notice just how thick and long her curly red hair was. While he was at it, he also tried not to remember that she smelled like lilacs.

After several long minutes passed in an uncomfortable silence, Winifred finally spoke "Is kissing considered to be a part of the usual kidnapper-hostage situation?"

He frowned and looked away from her. Somehow, Quinn thought, he doubted it. But then, he'd be willing to bet that not many kidnappers grabbed a woman like Winifred Matthews off the street, either. "No," he told her and hoped she'd let the whole thing end. He should have known better.

"Well, I'm relieved to hear it," she said on a half-laugh and scooted closer to him.

"I reckon you are at that," he agreed and understood that she'd just told him to keep his damned hands off. In a nice, ladylike way of course. But then, she had no way of knowing that he'd already planned to do just that.

"Oh my yes," she said and patted his shoulder before wrapping her arms around her upraised knees. "I simply cannot imagine Dastardly Dan doing to someone what you were doing to me."

"Dastardly Dan?"

She nodded, turned her face toward him and rested her cheek on her hands. "A notorious outlaw from whom even Texas Rangers ran in fear."

Texas Rangers? Running in fear? It was all Quinn could do to keep a straight face. The only place he'd ever heard of a Ranger running, was *to* a fight. Not from it.

But her calm, direct stare was almost hypnotizing and despite the fact that they should be getting ready to pull out, Quinn heard himself ask "Why is it you don't think ol' Dan would be kissin' a woman?"

"Well," Winifred started and paused a moment to think about her words. "He's cruel and not at all interested in the welfare of others."

"Ah . . ."

"He doesn't appear to be much taken with the sins of the flesh either, now that I think about it."

Now *there* was a man not worth knowing, Quinn thought.

"And of course, the hideous scar he carries as a constant reminder of his previous encounters with Marshal Travis, would quite naturally frighten a hostage." Winifred nodded to herself, "Yes, I should think that any woman would be entirely appalled at the idea of Dastardly Dan nibbling at her neck."

Quinn cleared his throat.

Winifred was warming to her subject. "Of course, Dan's only real friend is his horse, Black Wing."

Black Wing?

"So naturally, his social circle is quite small."

"Oh, naturally."

She nodded.

"Who's Marshal Travis?" He didn't give a hang who Travis was. But, the more wrapped up she became in talking, the less likely it was the conversation would get back around to that kiss. And that's just the way he wanted it. Besides, he was beginning to enjoy the look in her eyes when she told a story.

Those same green eyes took on a dreamy, shining look as she said "Marshal Travis is the bravest lawman in the Wild West. He is the only man capable of capturing Dastardly Dan, you know." Winifred straightened up as if taking credit for the fictional capture herself. "He's done it many times."

A ridiculous spear of jealousy lanced through him when he saw how much she admired this Travis fella. Quinn couldn't help himself. He had to say it. "If he's so all fired good, why don't Dan stay caught? Any Marshal worth his salt ought to have to catch a man only once."

Offended on behalf of her hero, Winifred snapped Quinn a heated look. "Dan is a wily fellow. No prison can hold him. And when he's free once more, the authorities look to Travis for help."

"Hmmph!" Quinn shook his head, suddenly very tired of the wonderful Marshal. "If Travis had a brain in his head, he'd just shoot the bastard dead and stop all that runnin' around."

Winifred clambored to her feet, tripping on the length of ripped hem as she moved. Staring down at her captor, she set her fists at her hips and told him "Marshal Travis is an honorable man and doesn't believe in violence if it isn't absolutely necessary."

"Sounds to me like it's plenty necessary." Quinn stood up too, glanced at the cloud dotted sky then looked back at her. "Sounds too, like he ought to put rocks on the man's grave once he's six feet under, just to make sure he don't come crawlin' out."

Winifred frowned.

"Lady," he asked and was interrupted.

"Will you please stop referring to me as 'lady'?" Her fists dropped to her sides. "Can't you call me Winifred?"

Quinn swallowed and took a good, long look at her. All his adult life, he'd pretty much moved from one woman to the next. He'd never found anything like the kind of feelings he'd seen between his parents. And if he was to admit the truth, he really hadn't been looking for it, either. Quinn had never really thought of himself as the husband kind.

Loving one woman for your whole damned life just seemed like too much to ask of anybody. Hell, he'd never met a woman he could *like* for his whole life.

Until he'd stepped on Winifred Matthew's foot while he was robbing a bank. Oh, he didn't love her. Hell, he didn't know her well enough for that. But he was sure enough beginning to *like* her—a lot. And that could be just as dangerous for a man like him.

So no. He wouldn't be calling her Winifred. Besides not caring for the name, using her Christian name would just lead to more closeness between them. Something he didn't need at all.

But she was right. Even *he* was tired of calling her "lady." So he compromised.

"I'll call ya . . . *Fred,*" he finally said.

"Fred?"

"Yeah. It's a helluva lot shorter to say than Winifred," he told her. Silently, he added, if he kept calling her by a man's name, maybe he'd fool himself into leaving her the hell alone. But, as he'd watched her cock her head and smile at him, he doubted it.

"Fred," she repeated. "I like it." She'd never had a

nickname before. And the fact that her outlaw had given
it to her made it all the more special. She'd read enough
books about the West to know that most people had
nicknames bestowed on them by their friends or enemies. Names like Shorty or Whitey or Digger. It was
part and parcel of the romance of the West. And now
she, Winifred Matthews, truly belonged.

Winifred could hardly wait to write about this in her
journal. And the *kiss*. Oh, my heavens, she thought as
she relived each detail. How would she ever be able to
describe her feelings accurately on paper? How could
she explain the warm, liquid sensation that had gripped
her while Quinn's mouth and hands moved over her
body? And how could she get him to kiss her again?

She smiled softly. Oh, how her mother would have
enjoyed hearing about all of this! Not the kiss, of course,
she told herself sternly. But everything else about this
experience would have pleased Jane Matthews to no end.

"I stuffed some dry wood at the back of the shelter
last night." Quinn told her suddenly and she blinked
away her wandering thoughts. "Why don't you make a
small fire? On the *ground*," he added pointedly and she
frowned at him, "while I pack up camp. We'll have some
coffee then get ridin'."

"Already?" Winifred couldn't keep the whining tone
out of her voice despite her efforts. Her entire body was a
mass of aches and pains. Her legs felt as though they could
barely support her and her behind was still throbbing.

"Yeah." He jerked his head in the direction they'd
come the day before. "Whoever's trailin' us will be gettin' an early start, so we will too."

Quinn took a single step back and fell over her carpetbag. He hit the ground hard, but the mud absorbed
most of the shock. Lifting his palms, he stared at the
muck covering his hands, then tilted his head back to
look up at her.

"Are you all right?" She asked, even though she could see that he was. Except of course, for the mud soaking into the seat of his jeans.

"Fine." A single word forced out from between clenched teeth.

"Well," she said, keeping her voice light as she tugged her carpetbag out from beneath his knees "I think I'll just go and change clothes."

"Yeah." He nodded. "Me too."

"Of course," Winifred sensed she was about to start babbling, so she started moving for the small stand of oaks to her right. "I'll uh . . . it will only take me a moment," she promised.

"Fine." He pushed himself to his feet, grumbling under his breath all the while.

Winifred didn't wait around. Instead, she clamped both hands around the handle of her overstuffed bag and started walking. The weight of the bag was enough to pull her over so she had to lean far to the opposite side while the tapestry bag slammed into her knees with every step.

Perhaps she should simply have pulled out a fresh shirt, she told herself as she struggled with the heavy bag. But then, she risked one glance over her shoulder and saw Quinn tugging his boots off so he could remove his wet pants. Yes, she sighed, it was probably better that she'd left right away.

As she neared the oaks with their low hanging, sheltering black branches, she began to smile. This adventure was fast becoming everything she'd ever hoped it would be.

Dusty sneezed for the umpteenth time and muttered a vicious curse.

Tom hardly glanced at his riding companion. He didn't much care if Dusty'd come down with pneumonia during the night. Whatever happened, it was his own damned fault. And because the man hadn't come prepared, Tom himself was more wet than dry and it was his slicker they'd huddled under most of the night.

The sky still looked threatening, too. Though there were small patches of blue to be seen here and there, they were no match for the thunderheads still scuttling across the sky. With any luck though, the next storm wouldn't hit for a few hours. And though that probably wasn't enough time to find Quinn's new direction, it might be enough to at least figure where he didn't go.

"Here."

Tom shifted his gaze to Dusty, standing right in front of him. The man's almost black eyes looked watery, unfocused and he sniffed as he handed Tom a misshapen tin cup with steaming coffee in it.

"You look like hell," Tom told him and took a small sip.

"Good." Dusty sniffed again and swallowed a gulp of the near boiling coffee. "I'd hate to feel this bad and not look it."

"Why don't you go back home? I'll go after Quinn on my own."

"Not a chance." Dusty shook his head and winced. "I'm gonna find that mare myself and I ain't goin' home without her."

"What about Quinn?"

"What about him?"

Tom studied his friend carefully but couldn't read a thing from his carefully guarded expression. Dusty's deeply tanned, sharp planed features were blank. Looked like that touch of Comanche blood Dusty'd inherited from his great-grandmother had affected more than his long, straight black hair and dark eyes.

But he could save that stoic Indian crap for someone who didn't know him as well as Tom did.

"You gonna help me bring him in or not?"

Dusty took a long drink, looked at Tom over the rim of his cup and shoved one hand into his damp jeans pocket. "We don't even know for sure if it *is* Quinn."

"Yeah we do."

Dusty shrugged, narrowed his gaze and stared out at the wide Texas land spreading out in front of them. "What if it is?" He flicked a glance at the man beside him. "You really want to bring Quinn Hawkins back so he can go to jail?"

"He robbed the bank."

"Yeah, and only took what Bentley stole from him in the first place."

"Don't matter."

"Sure it matters, *Sheriff!*"

Tom bit down on the inside of his cheek and kept his gaze away from Dusty's.

"It's been the three of us since we was boys together." Dusty stepped in front of Tom, forcing the other man to look at him. "Hell Tom, he's closer to us than a brother!"

"He robbed the bank," Tom said stiffly and tried to fight against the old loyalties Dusty was stirring up.

"All right. He robbed the bank." Dusty spilled the rest of his coffee into the mud, pushed his long hair back out of his face and went on, "He took that money so's he could get another ranch goin' somewhere for him and his ma. And you want to put him in jail for that?"

"No I don't *want* to!" Tom shouted and gave up all pretense of calmness. "Goddammit, do you think I like havin' to chase down Quinn like he was some no account? Do you think I like bein' on Bentley's side?" He pulled in a long, shuddering breath. "Quinn broke the law, damn his hide anyway. There's nothin' I can do about it."

"Sure there is," Dusty said, his voice low and even. "Once we find my mare, you can forget you ever saw Quinn."

Long, thoughtful minutes passed. Tom heard the

wind in the grass and smelled the scent of rain in the air. He tilted his face into the cool breeze rushing across the plains and closed his eyes against what he had to say. Opening his eyes again, he looked directly into Dusty's gaze and said quietly, "No, I can't."

"Dammit!" Quinn spun about, staring off toward the trees where Winifred had gone to change clothes. He'd already gotten himself into some dry pants, packed up the camp, and had gone to saddle the horses.

No, he told himself angrily. Not *horses . . . horse.* Sadie was missing.

"Fred!" he shouted, and started for the trees just as she stepped into the clearing.

Winifred smiled to herself. Fred. Shaking her head slightly, she finished buttoning her rose colored shirt, then bent down to pick up her carpetbag again. Stumbling across the wide, mudhole covered clearing, she called back "I'm hurrying."

Apparently not fast enough, she thought as she watched Quinn running to her. His long legs carried him quickly and she barely had time to notice how nimbly he avoided all of the mudholes before he was at her side, snatching her bag from her hands.

Holding her luggage with his left hand, his right cupped her elbow and began dragging her back to camp.

"Great Heavens," she muttered, trying to hold her skirt hem up out of the muck. "I wasn't *that* long! Surely we don't need to run!"

He went right past the campsite and rushed to the overhang where they'd left the horses the night before. Quinn's big gray was saddled and waiting.

Winifred frowned, leaned forward and looked first one way, then the other. Finally, she tilted her head back and asked, "Where is Sadie?"

"That's what *I* want to know," he snapped.

"And you're asking me?"

"When I picketed those horses last night, they were tight. There's no way Sadie could have pulled free." He dropped her arm suddenly and shrugged. "Hell, she wouldn't have tried. A horse that well trained doesn't try to get away from a picket rope."

"Really?" she hadn't realized that. But of course, her books never really went into much detail on things like a campsite or what did Quinn call them? . . . picket ropes.

But if what he was saying was true, then she was doubly confused. Tapping her index finger against her chin, she said aloud "Then I don't understand at all."

"What?" he said on a sigh and the word almost sounded like a groan.

"Well," Winifred started, "after you'd fallen asleep. I finished my journal entries and I felt a need to . . ." she broke off, glanced at him then quickly looked away again. "I had to uh . . ." she paused, hoping to heaven he would understand what she was trying desperately not to have to say.

Her prayers were answered. After a moment's thought, Quinn inhaled sharply and said "Oh. All right then, you," he waved one hand, "uh . . . *then* what?"

Pleased to have that part of the conversation finished, Winifred fought down the embarassed flush in her cheeks and continued.

"Afterwards, I stopped by to check on the horses." She risked another brief glance at him. "The rain had stopped—momentarily as it turned out—and well, I simply couldn't sleep." She shrugged. "The excitement, I suppose."

Quinn bit his lip to keep from interrupting her. Lord knew it was taking her long enough as it was. Couldn't sleep for the excitement, she said. Huh. Most women would have been terrified, being alone with a man who'd kidnapped 'em. At the very least, scared.

But Fred was excited.

Lord help him.

"And . . ." he prodded when she took too long to start talking again.

"And Sadie had eaten all of the grass near her." Winifred's hands lifted in a helpless gesture. "She seemed hungry, and as you well know, she *is* eating for two."

"What did you do?" he whispered and silently congratulated himself on not shouting.

"Nothing, really," Winifred insisted.

"What, *exactly?*"

"I moved her."

"You did *what?*"

Inhaling sharply, Winifred lifted her chin and faced him. Her gaze was steady, if a little worried. Quinn looked into her green eyes and fought down the urge to pick her up and shake some sense into her. He settled for asking "Where did you put her?"

"Right there," she pointed to a small patch of grass just off to Quinn's right.

A small patch of *empty* grass.

There wasn't a sign of Sadie anywhere.

"She seemed very contented when I left her to retire for the night."

"I'll bet." In fact, the little mare probably thought she'd been let loose in heaven. Until the rain started again during the night. Hell, she probably wandered so far off, she'd gotten lost and couldn't find her way back to camp what with the rain wiping out any scents she might follow.

"Will she be all right, do you suppose?" Winifred bit down hard on her bottom lip and Quinn had the ridiculous urge to comfort her. *Comfort* her! And it was *her* fault!

"She'd better be," he mumbled in response, mentally imagining Dusty's face if Quinn ever had to explain that his friend's horse had gotten "lost." "C'mon Fred," he said and took her arm again to lead her over to Reb.

"C'mon where?"

"To find Sadie of course," he shot back then stumbled slightly as her bag slammed against his knee. "Damn this thing anyway," he muttered and tossed the garishly colored bag under the overhang where the horses had been stabled for the night.

"My bag!" she cried and bent to retrieve it.

"It'll be here when we come back," he assured her with one last glance at the bag lying atop his bedroll and supplies.

"What if someone comes along and steals it?" she demanded. "Everything I own is in that bag."

"Heavy enough to be carryin' your damn house along with ya."

"If someone steals it, I won't even have a change of clothes," she argued fiercely as he swung aboard the big gray horse.

"If somebody's dumb enough to steal that damned thing, they'll be easy enough to find," Quinn told her and reached down to grab her upper arm.

"How do you mean?" Winifred asked and gasped as he yanked her up and plopped her down in front of him on the saddle.

Quinn groaned and tried to inch back in the saddle, but it was no use. Her behind was going to stay pressed firmly against his already responding groin. This woman was going to be the death of him.

"I *asked,*" she reminded him and looked over her shoulder at him "how do you know that we could find the thief that easily?"

"Fred . . ." he sighed and snaked his arms around her waist to pick up the reins "as heavy as that damned thing is, no thief'd get a hundred feet before collapsin'."

Reb started out slow, picking his way through the

mudholes covering the ground as if afraid to get his hooves dirty. The rocking motion of the horse's steps did little to ease the growing ache in Quinn's body.

"If you're sure . . ." Winifred said uncertainly and turned back for one last look at the bag containing all her earthly possessions.

"I'm sure," he snapped, then groaned plaintively, "and for God's sake, Fred. Set *still!*"

7

Mercy Hawkins sat on the wide front porch of her ranch house and took a swallow from her fourth cup of coffee. But all the coffee in the world wasn't going to make up for the fact that she'd been awake all night long.

She'd lain in the big double bed in her room, staring at the ceiling and listening to the rain on the roof covering the house she and her son had built. And when she couldn't bear to be still a moment longer, she'd risen and wandered through the big house. From room to room she went, sliding her palm across the polished wood furniture and silently admiring the sturdy walls and oak floorboards.

Everything on the Hawkins ranch had been built to last. From the smallest peg on the wall of the barn to the hand carved newel posts on the freshly painted white front porch. She and Quinn had worked together from dawn to dusk for years to create a ranch to be proud of. And they'd succeeded.

The Hawkins place was finally starting to turn a profit and in a few years would probably be one of the most prosperous ranches in Texas.

Which was the reason Bentley had wanted it bad enough to steal it.

Oh, he'd been slick about it, Mercy told herself as she propped her booted feet up on the handrail in front of her. Even legal, she supposed. But it was stealing, pure and simple. No matter what he wanted to call it.

She set her flower-sprigged china coffee cup down on the small table to her left and let her feet drop to the floor with a thud. Standing up, she walked to the farthest corner of the porch and stared off into the distance.

At forty-eight, Mercy Hawkins knew she was still a handsome woman. She wasn't blind. She'd seen the looks men tossed her way when they thought she couldn't see them. Hard work had kept her figure trim and the sun had darkened her skin to the color of a ripe peach. Her long, dark brown hair showed very little gray and she still insisted on wearing it in a single braid that fell down the middle of her back to just above her hips. Like every other morning for the last few years, she wore a plain white shirt tucked into a split, deerhide skirt she'd designed and made herself that was bleached to a pale ivory color. In the first rough years on the ranch, she'd simply worn a pair of her late husband's trousers. But as she got older, and the work got easier, she'd begun to favor something that at least looked like a normal skirt. Even though the hem stopped just at the top of her knee-high, calfskin boots.

The early morning air was still, but for a slight breeze blowing in off the plains. The wind carried the promise of more rain and when a coyote howled suddenly, Mercy's thoughts centered on her only child.

Quinn Hawkins was no thief.

Her son was a good, honorable man pushed beyond his limits by a greedy, grasping bastard with no sense of honor.

"Bentley," she muttered and even the man's name

tasted bitter on her tongue. This was all Bentley's fault. Damned banker.

The man had only been in town a few months and already, he was helping himself to the best ranches in the country. Why, Bentley was snapping up land and water rights so fast that soon, he could be king of this little corner of Texas. She slapped her palm down on the narrow railing. Mercy knew as well as anyone—whoever controlled the water rights, controlled the land.

Well, Mercy didn't care if he *had* bought up their loan from the storekeeper. She and Quinn had built that ranch up from nothing and by damn, she'd burn the buildings down and salt the waterhole before she'd hand the title over to that bastard.

Just who the hell was he, anyway? And what was a man like him doing in Texas? He'd made no secret of the fact that he hated the country and the people. All he could talk about was New York City. Well, if it was such a damned fine place, then why did he leave it?

Even as that thought entered her mind, a sly smile played on her lips. Maybe it was time she did a little checking up on Mr. Charles Banker Bentley. Maybe there was a good reason he'd left the East.

And maybe it was good enough that the Sheriff might be interested to learn it.

Turning around quickly, Mercy raced back down the length of the porch for the front door. She'd stop just long enough to get her coat. Then she'd go see Erma Hightower.

Quinn bit back another groan as Winifred wiggled around in the saddle, trying to find a comfortable position. Beads of sweat broke out on his forehead and his fingers clenched around the horse's reins.

He told himself that any other woman would have

noticed the hard knot she'd been sitting on for a half-hour or more. But not Fred. Blissfully unaware of the torture she was inflicting on her captor, Winifred ignored his orders to be still.

Deliberately, Quinn tried to push his brain into other directions. Think of something else, he told himself. *Anything* else. Reaching, grasping for mental straws, his brain dredged up an image of the Hawkins ranch. As if he'd been doused with a bucket of cold water, all of his lustful daydreams dissolved.

He could almost hear the wind whispering through the papery cottonwoods surrounding the place. In his mind's eye, he saw the two-story ranch house with its wide, wraparound front porch. Quinn smiled to himself at the image of the round, turretlike room at one end of the house. It had been hard as hell to figure out how to build that tower, but worth it when he saw his mother's delight in it. From the time he was a boy, she'd told him about how one day she'd have herself a real "castle" room, as she called it. Round, with windows ringing the walls so she could see everything all at once if she wanted to.

Now, he imagined Mercy Hawkins sitting at the table in her castle room, wondering what in the hell she'd done wrong to make her only son a thief.

Quinn frowned and squinted off into the distance. All right, maybe robbing the bank hadn't been his best idea ever. Maybe it was stupid.

But he'd about wore himself out the last couple of months trying to find a way to keep their ranch legally. And he was almost out of time. There was only three weeks left until Bentley foreclosed on the Hawkins ranch.

Then what was Quinn supposed to do? Rent a room above the saloon for his mother? Was he supposed to just walk away from the years of work and planning and sacrifice that had gone into building the Hawkins ranch? Was he supposed to just hand the title over to Bentley and say "Here, hope you're happy"?

Well, he couldn't do it. And if that made Quinn Hawkins a bad man, he'd just have to live with it. He wasn't gonna stand aside for some fast talking, know nothing from back East and watch his mother have to scrounge for a place to live.

"Quinn?"

"Hmmm?"

"Will we find her, do you think?"

"Huh? Oh, yeah. Yeah, we'll find her." He tried to push himself further back in the saddle again and failed. Again. Frowning, he added "She's around here somewhere."

Winifred shifted again and Quinn's hard won control over his body ended.

"This isn't a very comfortable way to travel, I must say."

"Can't be helped." Except by maybe a long soak in a frozen-over lake.

"When we find Sadie," Winifred continued, "where will we go?"

"North and east, I s'pose."

Giving up her efforts to hold herself rigid in the saddle, Winifred leaned back against him. Quinn closed his eyes briefly. Lilacs.

"Are we going to a town?"

He sure as hell hadn't planned on going to a town. It'd be a lot safer for him if he stayed shut of people altogether for a few months. But now, with Winifred Matthews along, he'd have to stop somewhere long enough to leave her in a safe place. Quinn knew he couldn't keep traveling with her for much longer. He'd go right out of his mind.

"Guess so," was all he said though. Then added, "why?"

"I only wanted to let you know that if you should stop at a town, I wouldn't betray you."

"Huh?"

Still leaning against his chest, she tilted her head back until she could look up at him. "I remember reading once where Dastardly Dan abducted a woman . . ."

"Yeah . . ."

"And to keep her from telling anyone, when he went to town, he left her, bound hand and foot, in a dark, damp cave." Winifred shuddered slightly. "It was dreadful. There were rats and bats in that cave and she was simply terrified."

Quinn's lips twisted. Dastardly Dan sounded like a helluva nice fella.

"So I wanted you to be sure that I would never betray you. Your evil secret is safe with me."

He rolled his eyes heavenward. Evil secrets. Caves. Bats. What kind of stuff did this little schoolteacher read, anyhow?

Aloud, he assured her "There's no caves around here that I know of, Fred. And there's sure nothin' damp, exceptin' for the rain."

"Well, that's good."

"And if I go to a town, I'll take you in with me." He glanced down at her and saw the relief in her eyes. She believed him. Trusted him. For God's sake, she'd just admitted he had an "evil" secret, and she trusted him! Oh, Lord. "Now look for that damned mare, will ya, Fred?"

"Certainly."

Another long, uncomfortable hour passed before they finally found Sadie, knee-deep in a small patch of bluebonnets. Trying to convince the mare to leave her delicious breakfast proved to be a difficult task though and it was nearly two hours before they were back where they'd started that morning.

As they rode into camp, a soft rain started and Quinn

pulled his slicker free of the bedroll, shook it out then draped it over Winifred's shoulders.

"What about you?" she asked even as she snuggled deeper into the protective shield of the slicker.

"Won't be the first time I got wet." Quinn hurriedly tossed the saddle onto Sadie's back and began to cinch it up. He glanced over at Winifred and saw his knee length duster was hanging down around her ankles. Something inside him twisted. She looked kinda . . . lost, somehow. They'd left camp in such a hurry, she hadn't had time to put on that silly looking hat of hers. Now, the misting rain settled on her hair and the deep red curls began to droop about her face.

Quinn sighed heavily, grabbed up his bedroll and tied it behind Sadie's saddle. Then he crossed the open ground to Winifred's side, curled his fingers around her upper arm and pulled her toward the mare.

"I put the blankets behind your saddle. Since you got the slicker, we can cover 'em up and hopefully keep 'em dry, all right?"

She nodded, then reached up to push a sodden lock of hair out of her eyes. It immediately dropped back down and before he could stop himself, Quinn reached out, tucked that hair out of her way, then let his hand drop to his side.

"It still doesn't seem at all right," she said with a small shake of her head, "Me wearing your raincoat and leaving you to be soaked."

"I told you. Won't be the first time."

"Still," she nodded thoughtfully as if agreeing with herself as she spoke "I think it would be best if we simply went on riding together. It was a bit uncomfortable, but we could manage. Then we could share your, what did you call it? Your slicker?"

Quinn had started shaking his head the moment she began speaking. By the time she was finished, he blurted out "No ma'am. Uh-uh. Not goin' to do that." If he spent one more hour with her sitting on his lap, he'd go out of his head. There was only so much a man could take.

Dammit, weren't hostages supposed to be afraid of their kidnappers? So how come *he* gets one who wants to take care of him? And why did it bother him that she looked so—disappointed that he wouldn't let her?

As he studied her, another lock of sodden hair slipped from the messy knot at the back of her head and lay like a wet red ribbon against her cheek.

Dammit.

Grumbling under his breath, Quinn yanked his hat off and plopped it down on her head. He felt the misting rain settling on his hair and face and told himself it would be good for him. Right then, he needed all the cold water he could get.

She was dwarfed by his hat and slicker. Her delicate features were lost in the oversized clothing. Winifred Matthews should have looked funny. Silly. Instead, she looked so damned—cute.

Then she started talking again.

Winifred reached up to pull his hat off. "I insist you wear this," she said. "I have a perfectly good hat I can wear."

"Fred," Quinn retorted as he lifted her to the saddle, "that hat of yours ain't even good decoration." Her skirt hitched up, exposing her stocking-clad leg. Quinn closed his eyes and swallowed a groan.

"But it's . . ."

"Didn't we talk about this already?"

"About what?" she asked.

"About what hostages are s'posed to do?"

"Oh."

"Yeah, oh." He frowned up at her before reminding her "You're s'posed to do what I say, when I say. That right?"

"Yes, but . . ."

"Just hush and hold on, will ya?" he snapped. He'd never met such a talking woman in his life. Quinn stepped around the mare, climbed up on Reb's back then leaned down and snatched up the mare's reins with his left hand.

As they started out again, Fred was suspiciously silent.

Quinn pushed one hand through his hair, sweeping the damp, blond mass back from his forehead. Blinking into the steadily building rain, he ignored the urge to turn around and look at her.

All he'd wanted to do was rob a bank, he told himself helplessly. It had seemed simple enough. Quinn muttered a curse. He was willing to bet nothing like Winifred Matthews had ever happened to Dastardly Dan.

"Quinn!"

He tugged at the picket ropes to secure them then turned on his heel and sprinted toward the sound of her voice. What now? he asked himself silently.

"Quinn!"

She shouted again and this time, he heard the terror in her voice. Then he saw her and felt the first stab of fear slice through his own chest.

Winifred lay stretched out along the bank of the rain-swollen creek, her right arm thrust into the rushing water. The muddy bank shifted beneath her body with her movements and she felt the cold begin to seep through her clothing. She blew at the grass tickling her nose and tried to ignore the clammy, clinging discomfort of the thick, black mud embracing her. Frantically, she brushed her hand through the clear, cold water, hoping to find some trace of their supplies.

Where *was* he? Why wouldn't he come? She stared down into the water, afraid to turn her head and look for him.

"Quinn!" she called again, but her voice was muffled this time as she slid down closer to the water's surface. Droplets of water splattered up into her face but she ignored them and tried to stare down into the swirling depths of the creek. But the water was too deep and too swift. The narrow creek bed was filled to its capacity by the recent rains and Winifred was surprised at just how strong the stream's current was.

The water pulled and tugged at her arm, like a playmate urging her into a game. She felt its strength drawing her further into the powerful water and fought against it. But the mud beneath her shifted again and she dug the toes of her shoes into the too soft earth looking for purchase.

"Quinn!"

It was forever. It had been hours since she'd first called to him. And he wasn't coming. Perhaps he'd decided that the easiest way for him to be free of her was simply to let her drown. Perhaps he was more like Dastardly Dan than she'd wanted to believe. Perhaps not all bad men had scars after all.

She bit her lip and grabbed at the grass with the fingers of her left hand. But the rain had soaked the earth so completely that she yanked the grass free and continued her slow slide into the surging water.

Winifred squeezed her eyes shut, determined not to watch the water rush up at her. Her right leg fell off the bank into the stream and the piercing cold stabbed at her. She gasped and braced herself for her tumble into eternity.

"Goddammit!"

As if from out of a dream, Quinn's voice reached her just before he snatched her from the creek and dragged her backwards to safety.

Winifred pulled in a long, shuddering breath and leaned into his warmth and strength. She concentrated on the feel of his hands as they moved slowly up and down her spine. Her cheek pillowed against his chest, she listened to the erratic pounding of his heart and thought it the most wonderful sound she'd ever heard.

"What the hell were you tryin' to do, lady?" he whispered and tightened his hold on her.

She tried to answer him but her teeth began to chatter instead.

He sighed, cupped the back of her head with one hand and drew her back so that he could look down into her eyes. "You all right?"

Winifred jerked him a nod and tried desperately to keep from shivering. It was no use though. The thick mud had seeped into the fabric of her clothes. Her skirt was wet and clingy from the icy water and her right hand felt numb from her futile attempts to salvage their supplies.

"No," he muttered more to himself than to her, "you ain't all right at all, are ya?"

He didn't wait for an answer. Instead, he swept her up into his arms and cradled her close against him. Winifred instinctively burrowed even closer to his warmth, letting his strength wrap itself around her like a comfortable blanket.

Hurrying, Quinn walked back to where he'd left the horses tied to a live oak. "I'm gonna set you down right here," he told her as he plopped her onto a thick, fallen branch. "As soon as I get a fire goin', you'll feel better."

Winifred didn't care about a fire. All she knew was that she'd been much warmer when she was huddled next to his body. Through the haze of cold and weariness that was washing through her, Winifred watched as Quinn quickly laid a small fire. Just the sight of the first, tiny flames was comforting. As her outlaw fed more and more sticks into the fire, the blaze grew brighter, stronger. Only when he was satisfied with the size of the fire did Quinn turn for his bedroll.

He untied the rawhide strings, shook the blankets out and came back to her. Effortlessly, it seemed, he lifted her again and sat her on his lap. A soft smile curved her lips until she felt his fingers tugging at the top buttons of her shirt.

Immediately, she batted them away, straightened up and tried to push off his lap.

He only tightened his grip on her.

"*Mr.* Hawkins!"

Quinn sighed. "Lady, if we don't get you out of them mud soaked clothes, you're gonna get good and sick."

"If I get out of these clothes," she said in her haughtiest manner, which was ruined by the chattering of her teeth, "something far worse might happen."

Eyes innocently wide, he tightened his grip on her waist to hold her in place and asked "Like what?"

Winifred licked her lips and spit at the taste of river mud that accompanied the action. Quinn grinned.

"Lady," he said then started over. "*Fred,* you're the hostage, I'm the outlaw. Right?"

She nodded and shivered at the same time.

"Right." Moving one of his hands up to the collar of her shirt, he deliberately began to work at the buttons. "Then since we both say *I'm* in charge here, you're gettin' out of these clothes. Now."

Winifred was much too cold to argue the point any further. She would simply have to trust in the fact that up until now he hadn't made any untoward advances. Except of course for that one kiss which surely didn't count since she'd slept through most of it. Deliberately, she ignored the fact that she could still feel his lips against her flesh. Inhaling sharply, she decided that just in case, she would take a small precaution.

Pushing herself from his lap, Winifred stood in front

of him. "Please hold the blanket up and turn your head," she stammered.

"Jesus!"

"I really am very cold, Quinn. Please hurry."

That simple statement, uttered in such a small, shaky voice, seemed to touch him. Without another word, he leapt to his feet and held the gray wool blanket up in front of him.

"Now turn your head," she said.

He grumbled, but turned to his left. Quinn heard her muttering and for a moment, he was almost sure he could also hear the sound of buttons sliding free of fabric. In his mind's eye, he saw the edges of her simple white shirt fall open. He saw a white cotton chemise and the shadows of her nipples, hard and erect straining against the material.

Another whisper of cloth and he imagined her skirt, followed by her petticoats, drop to the ground. His mind painted a too real image of Winifred, clad only in chemise and pantaloons, stepping into his embrace. Mentally, he held her close, smoothing the palms of his hands up and down her back and around to caress her breasts. He could almost feel her nipples beneath his palms. He could almost taste her kiss and feel her breath, warm and sweet on his face.

Quinn's body tightened uncomfortably and he groaned softly as he shifted position, hoping to ease the discomfort. But there was no ease for him. He was trapped with his tormentor. And the worst of it was, she had no idea what it was she was doing to him.

"I'm finished," she said and tugged at the blanket until he released it. Wrapping the wool around her, she moved up close to him and laid her head on his chest again. "Hold me please," she said. "I'm still very cold."

Quinn swallowed, let his arms slide around the woman he was itching to hold and said "I'm warm enough for both of us."

8

Mercy leaned on the tabletop and stared out the none too clean front window. In a wash of afternoon sun, Yellow Dog looked just what it was—a small, lazy town where no one hurried what had to be done and ignored what ought to be done.

Not that the folks in Yellow Dog didn't care, but mainly they went along with the notion that a man's business was his own. Win or lose. In this country, a man was expected to saddle his own bronc and solve his own problems.

Mercy's gaze shifted to the curve in the street where the bank lay hidden from her sight. Inside that bank, she knew Charles Bentley would be standing behind his teller cage. Not a trustful man by any means, Bentley hadn't hired anyone to work for him. He preferred to personally take charge of the hard earned money being handed over for safekeeping.

Not like any banker Mercy'd ever heard of. Mostly, they liked sitting behind a big desk looking as important as they felt themselves to be. But Bentley was different. *How* different, she wasn't quite sure yet.

"For God's sake, Mercy!" Erma snapped as she came into the room "Starin' out that window ain't gonna make things happen any faster. Set down and have some tea."

Straightening up, Mercy sighed and turned away from the window. She stepped back and noticed that she'd left distinct handprints on the dusty tabletop. One corner of her mouth lifted. No one had ever accused Erma Hightower of being too fussy.

Brushing her palms against the sides of her split skirt, Mercy walked to her friend's side and took a seat on the settee. She reached for the plain white cup and saucer Erma offered her and took a long sip of the steaming tea. As an afterthought, Mercy snatched a sugar cookie from the plate on the table. Taking a bite, she acknowledged that though Erma didn't care if a desert's worth of dust piled up, the woman could sure bake.

"So, what're you gonna do if you don't hear back from that fella in New York?" Erma asked around a mouthful of cookie.

Mercy shrugged. "Send a wire to someone else, I guess."

A long moment passed before Erma said thoughtfully, "You know, don't ya . . . none of this is gonna do Quinn a damn sight of good."

Mercy's gaze shot to the other woman.

"When Tom catches up to him—and he will," Erma met Mercy's gaze evenly, "Quinn'll have to serve his time."

"No one knows for sure that Quinn is responsible for that holdup."

Erma snorted and tucked a long, graying lock of brown hair behind her ear. "Shoot, ever'body knows it, Mercy." She set her cup on the matching saucer, then set them both down with a thud onto the tabletop. "Hell, if Bentley'd done to me what he's done to you all, I'd have robbed the bastard."

Mercy's lips thinned into a rigid line. She hated the idea that her son had become an outlaw. And the notion that two of his oldest friends were chasing him down at that very moment, was just too much to think about.

"And if Quinn wasn't the thief . . . where the hell is he lately?"

All right fine, Mercy thought. They both knew that Quinn took that money. But that didn't mean her son was a common thief.

She jumped to her feet and began to pace around the confines of the small, dusty room. "All right, let's say Quinn took the money."

"Already said so," Erma pointed out.

Mercy ignored her. "But if he did, God knows, he had good enough reason."

"True," her friend agreed. "But reason don't make it right."

"I know that, dammit!" Mercy spun around. Her braid flew over her shoulder to lay in the middle of her back. She took a half step closer to Erma and continued "Don't you think I know Quinn's done wrong?" And right at that moment, if she had her son in front of her, she'd give him a good swift kick in his backside. But she was his mother. It was all right for her to call Quinn a damned fool. Nobody else had better try it, though. "And what about Bentley?" Mercy countered quickly. "Was it right what *he* did?"

"Hell no."

Mercy jerked her a nod. "Damn right it wasn't. And ask yourself, Erma Hightower, why is it somebody like Bentley is even in Yellow Dog?"

"Huh?"

"I said, how come he moved to Texas in the first

place?" Mercy threw her arms high then let them drop helplessly to her side again. "Isn't he always talkin' about how he misses the city? How he hates livin' where 'civilization' hasn't been heard of yet?"

"Yeah, so?"

"So . . ." she walked to the settee and looked down at the other woman, "if he feels like that, why didn't he stay back east? Why'd he ever leave New York?"

"He ain't exactly the first to travel where he don't want to be, y'know."

"I know. But why Yellow Dog?" Mercy continued, asking aloud all the questions her mind had been worrying over for days. "Why not Austin? Or Houston? Why open a bank in a little town too small to do him any good?"

"Cause we didn't have one."

"Didn't need one, either. Henry Simpson down at the store's been good enough for years." Henry. It still made Mercy furious just to think of how her old friend had betrayed her. Imagine selling her note off to Bentley!

Without even telling her!

Henry must have known that Bentley wouldn't have any misgivings about foreclosing.

"True," Erma was saying, "but I figure it wasn't Henry doin' the sellin'. More'n likely, it was Adelaide behind that." The big woman sighed heavily, picked up her old china teapot and poured herself another cup. "Addy's had it in her head for years that she's too good for small town Texas. Prob'ly figured this was as good a way as any to get the money to make Henry move."

Adelaide. Of course. Mercy shook her head. If she hadn't been so damned upset, she would've realized that herself a long time ago. Henry Simpson, good man though he was, had a ring through his nose that Adelaide tugged on regularly.

Erma sighed. "But, reckon we'll see soon enough if you're right and Bentley *does* have something to hide.

You figure the New York law's gonna be answerin' you soon?"

"I hope so."

"Even if they do, won't be much you can do about it, what with Tom gone and all."

"He'll be back," Mercy answered shortly and added silently, dragging Quinn along in handcuffs, no doubt.

"He didn't just drop off the world, for God's sake!" Tom shouted and walked back to his horse. Two days of searching and they weren't any closer to finding a sign of Quinn Hawkins. Hell, Tom had always prided himself on the fact that he could tract a snake across a flat rock.

And here he was, couldn't find a footprint in fresh mud.

If he didn't know better, he'd swear Quinn was flying out of the country.

Dammit, he cursed silently as he swung aboard his horse, he *had* to find Quinn. As much as it pained him to think about arresting his old friend, he had no choice. Tom couldn't go back to Yellow Dog and tell folks that he couldn't find the man.

Nobody'd believe him. He scowled into the late afternoon sun and tugged the brim of his hat down low over his eyes. They'd all think that he'd allowed Quinn to escape him because of their friendship.

Tom leaned forward, both hands on the pommel of his saddle. Squinting off into the distance, he slowly let his gaze slide over the countryside. He'd learned long ago that the way to see something was to pretend you weren't looking for it. Maybe he'd been trying too hard. Looking too close. What he had to do was study the land casual like and if he was lucky, he'd notice something that didn't belong.

Anything.

A bent branch on a mesquite bush.

A torn piece of cloth.

A patch of land churned up by running hooves.

Dammit, he had to find something. He hated like hell to be chasing Quinn down, but it was his job. More than that, Tom admitted silently, it was who he was. He'd lived by the law and believed in it for too long to change now.

The only comforting thing in all this was, Tom knew that Quinn would understand. Quinn had always understood.

"Damn you anyway, Hawkins! Why the hell did ya have to rob *our* town?" his voice scratched against his throat in an angry mutter. "And for the love of God, if you were gonna rob the bank, why'd ya have to take that female hostage to boot?"

Thoughts of that eastern schoolteacher raced through Tom's already befuddled mind. His fingers clenched around the saddle horn as he imagined one disaster after another. No matter what Quinn's intentions were—and Tom knew that Quinn wasn't the kind to harm a woman—anything could happen. From rattlesnakes to twisters to coyotes to . . . hell. Sometimes just drawing a breath in Texas was a dangerous proposition.

If anything happened to that female, Quinn would be looking at a helluva lot more than jail time.

Damn the fool! Tom thought. Where in the devil was he?

Quinn reluctantly set Winifred back from him. Bending down, he drew the fallen branch closer to the fire and lowered her down onto it. Huddled under the rough wool blanket, he could see she was still shivering, but dammit all, he wasn't sure he could stand her sitting in his lap for much longer. This here's a fine situation, he told himself wryly. She's freezing and *he's* on fire!

He rubbed his palms along his pants legs, squatted down and fed more wood into the flames. It was the most he could do for her. If he held her again—felt her snuggling in close, he wasn't at all sure he'd be willing to let her go again.

"Thank you," she said finally and he noted with relief that her voice sounded a bit stronger. "You saved my life, *again*."

"Again?" he shot her a curious glance. Those green eyes of hers were shining like the first blades of grass in springtime. Quickly, he looked back at the fire. It was much safer that way.

"There was that snake incident, too."

"Oh, yeah."

"You must think me awfully foolish."

"No, lady. Not foolish," he said, then stopped himself. How the hell could he tell her that he was beginning to think she was some sort of jinx? A pretty, soft, sweet smelling jinx, but a jinx none the less.

"I'm glad," she said quietly and Quinn was drawn by the sound of her voice. Velvety, pleased. "I'm trying my best to be a good hostage, you know. But it's very difficult."

Quinn swallowed heavily, but let his gaze move over her pale features slowly. Being a outlaw wasn't turning out to be the easiest thing he'd ever done either, he thought. But he said only, "Yeah, must be."

"When Dastardly Dan takes a hostage you know," she went on and Quinn fought down a sigh, "the person is usually left somewhere, tied up."

"You told me. That cave."

She shuddered. "Exactly. Since the hostage never goes anywhere, it's very difficult for me to try to decide precisely what he might do if the situation presented itself. Do you see my problem?"

Yeah, Quinn thought. Her problem was, she read too

many damned books. But he didn't say that. Instead, he heard himself ask "Mind tellin' me what you were doin' at the creek in the first place?"

Winifred smiled, reached one hand up from inside her warm coccoon and scratched her nose. "I was trying to make coffee."

"By layin' down in the water?"

She laughed and it sounded almost as magical as the wind in the cottonwoods. "Oh no, that was quite by accident."

"Uh-huh." Quinn tried to push his fanciful notions out of his mind and concentrated on what she was saying.

"I was trying to get water in the coffee pot, you see and—"

Quinn stared at her, waiting.

"The water was moving very quickly." She frowned momentarily. "I wouldn't have thought that such a narrow strip of water would have such power."

"The narrower the bed, the harder the current," he said instinctively. "What happened?"

"Well, I leaned down," her brow furrowed as she tried to remember the exact course of events, "keeping of course, a firm grip on the saddlebags filled with the supplies."

"Of course," he agreed, and glanced around the campsite, looking for those saddlebags. They weren't there. And come to think of it, he told himself, he hadn't seen them anywhere near her on the creek bank, either. Quinn closed his eyes briefly, sure he wasn't going to like what she had to say.

"But when the water rushed into the coffee pot, it was so heavy it was pulled right out of my grasp."

Quinn squelched a groan. If there was one thing he would miss, it was his coffee. There wasn't any use in trying to go find the damn thing, either. The way that current was roaring, his coffee pot was probably close to Mexico by now.

"Naturally, I leaned in further, trying to retrieve it."

"Naturally," he sighed.

She cocked her head and narrowed her gaze. "Did you know that a creek's bank, when muddy, is not very stable?"

Somehow he managed to look into her wide, innocent green eyes and not shout. "What happened?"

"As I said, I leaned in further," she stretched one bare arm out of her blankets as if reliving that moment, "and the very earth beneath me began to dissolve."

Quinn's gaze followed the length of her outstretched arm back to the blanket she held clutched in one fist against her chest. The thin, white cotton straps of her chemise lay across her shoulders and made her skin look almost rosy in comparison. One side of her hair was wet and hanging down along her face, while the left side lay in abundant waves and curls.

Foolishly, he told himself she looked exactly what she was. Two people. One, his hostage, supposedly in his power. The other, a woman about to drive him 'round the bend with want. Maybe, he thought glumly, this was God's punishment for him robbing that bank. Maybe, the 'Ol Boy had decided the best way for Quinn Hawkins to pay for his mistake was to send him the one woman who would be able to destroy him.

If his own rampaging desire didn't kill him—her clumsy good intentions surely would.

"Are you all right?" she asked, reaching out to lay her hand on his arm.

Quinn flinched, but nodded. He was becoming accustomed to the flash of heat that shot through him every time she touched him. "The earth dissolved," he repeated firmly. "Then what?"

She dipped her head and he watched the firelight play in her dark red hair. He was only half-listening, so when she was finished, he had to ask her to repeat herself.

Immediately, he wished he hadn't.

"I tried to catch my balance of course," she said softly, "but it was no use. In my fright, I'm afraid somehow the saddlebag flew from my grip."

"What?"

"I *am* sorry," she added quickly. "I'm not really sure quite how it happened, but there you are." Winifred shrugged and the blanket dipped a little lower. Now, he could see the edging of lace along the top of her chemise. Blindly, he stared at it.

"Naturally, when the saddlebags fell into the water, I tried to reach them, as well." She shook her head dolefully. "Unfortunately, they were carried away much too quickly."

"Uh-huh." Not only his coffee was gone, he told himself. But the flour, bacon, cans of beans and peaches . . . *everything*.

"Quinn?" she asked, then added, "Mr. Hawkins?"

He shook his head. Unbelievable. How did one woman cause so much disaster?

Quinn pulled his hat off and ran one finger over the charred hole in the crown. The bent brim flopped over his other hand. As the blackened felt began to break off under the pressure of his touch, a bubble of laughter built in his chest.

She'd ruined a perfectly good bank robbery. Lost a horse. First broke his hat then burned it. Sent his supplies on a trip downriver. Damn near got herself drowned in the bargain. And he was going to *laugh*?

Yep, he thought and pushed himself to his feet. Swallowing back the chuckle growing even stronger inside him, Quinn walked quickly out of camp toward the creek.

"Where are you going?" she called after him.

"See if I can find any of our food," he told her and kept walking. Roughly, he rubbed one hand across his mouth. If he released the laughter strangling him, he wasn't sure he'd be able to stop. And Fred would never understand. Quinn had a feeling ol' Dastardly Dan didn't do much laughing, either.

"I got something!" Dusty yelled as his horse raced across the open land separating him from Tom Bruner.

The sheriff turned in the saddle and watched the other man ride up. Clumps of black, wet dirt flew up behind the running animal and even from a distance, Tom could see the excitement in Dusty's manner. Waving his hat in the air and shouting, it was clear that Dusty'd finally found a trail to follow.

When he pulled up alongside Tom, the other man shoved his hat back down on his head and grinned at his friend. "Found some tracks. Two horses, movin' pretty fast. One of 'em's Sadie."

"You sure?" Tom asked, even though he could see the certainty in Dusty's eyes.

"Hell yes, I'm sure!" Taking the reins in his left hand, Dusty turned his mount's head back in the direction he'd just come. "I've been shoein' that mare myself for the last two years. I reckon I'd remember the notch I make in the left corner of every damned shoe I forge."

There it was, then, Tom told himself. They had the trail. Even if they were two or three days behind Quinn and the woman, sooner or later, they'd be catching up. Then Quinn would go to jail—and he would have to be the man to send him there.

Dammit.

His jaw clenched tight, Tom spurred his horse lightly, just to get it moving. The animal leaped past Dusty's mount and Tom had to call back over his shoulder "Well come on! Ain't this what you've been waitin' for? Let's go get him and go on home."

Dusty looked after his old friend for a long moment. Torn between exultation at his own good fortune in noticing the tracks and disgust with himself for mentioning it, he urged his mount into a trot. There was no hope for it. He had to have that mare back. And to do that, they had to catch Quinn.

He didn't look happy, Winifred thought and wrapped the blanket even tighter around her. For a moment, she'd pretended that it was Quinn's arms warming her and not the old wool blanket. Probably just a reaction to her terrifying experience, she told herself.

She wrinkled her nose and stared at the pan on the fire. Quinn was stirring as though his life depended on it. Since returning from the creek, he hadn't once looked directly at her. Winifred told herself that she shouldn't blame him for being upset. But at the same time, she thought it would behoove him to adopt a more forgiving manner.

And yet, Dastardly Dan was not a forgiving man.

Still, she doubted whether Dastardly Dan would have bothered to rescue one of his hostages, either. No doubt the evildoer would have relished his helpless victim's death by drowning. Pursing her lips slightly, Winifred recalled those moments when she'd first felt Quinn's strong arms around her, dragging her back from the brink of eternity.

Immediately, she'd felt calmed. Secure. She'd known instinctively that Quinn would save her. The hero of the story is always prompt when needed for a rescue.

Hero? She studied him silently for a long moment. From his tousled blond hair, to the golden moustache covering his upper lip, to his tanned, long fingered hands. Hero.

Winifred shivered slightly and she knew it had nothing at all to do with being cold.

There was a warmth deep inside her that seemed to blossom and grow whenever she looked at Quinn Hawkins. A strange, tingling sensation gripped the most private parts of her body. She squeezed her knees tightly together, hoping to ease her sudden discomfort, but the pressure only increased it.

Shaking her head, Winifred asked herself how in heaven a man who had robbed a bank and taken her hostage could possibly be a hero. But a voice in the back of her mind argued, how could a man so gentle, so kind, be a villain?

It didn't make sense.

In her books, the heroes and villains were all defined. There were rules such men followed. Villains were evil. Heroes were good. Simple. Easy to understand.

Yet, since her arrival in the West and her untimely kidnapping, Winifred had begun to notice that not all men in the West were so easily identified. At least, she thought, Quinn Hawkins seemed to resist her every mental attempt to classify him as either villain *or* hero.

If he'd had a scar, this might have been much easier.

"Food's ready," he said and successfully interrupted her thoughts. "I only found one plate, so we'll have to share."

Quinn stood up, walked around the fire and seated himself beside her. Handing her the long handled cooking spoon, he said "Dig in."

Winifred looked from the spoon to the plate of beans he held.

"I know it ain't much," he admitted as he urged the plate toward her. "But I was lucky to find what I did. A couple of cans of beans and peaches don't make for interestin' eatin'. But at least they were too heavy to get carried downstream very far." He gave a half-laugh. "Good thing I found the saddlebags wrapped around that branch juttin' up into the water. Otherwise, we wouldn't have had a skillet either and you'd be eatin' them beans right out of the can."

"I'm so hungry," she said, "they would have tasted fine cold, too. But with only one spoon between us, perhaps we should take turns." She glanced at him. "You can go first. It's the least I can do after losing all of your supplies."

"No need," he reached into the cuff of his boot and pulled out a long, deadly looking knife.

Winifred's eyes widened.

He saw her expression and told her "It's to eat with, Fred. Relax." Then he scooped up a few of the beans with the narrow blade and carefully fed himself.

Thank heaven he was able to find one spoon, she thought. If she'd had to eat with that knife, she would surely have cut her own tongue out. Taking a bite of the beans, she chewed a moment, then smiled and said "Why, it *is* good."

He grinned briefly at her obvious surprise and took another bite. "Put some sage in for flavoring." Sighing softly, he added more to himself than to her, "Sorry we don't have any coffee to go with it, though."

Winifred swallowed and pointed out "It certainly wasn't your fault, Quinn. And again, I *am* sorry."

He flicked her a quick glance, then nodded abruptly. "Don't really matter. Won't be the first time I've done without coffee." After a few more bites, he looked at her again and said "If you don't mind me askin', Fred . . . what the devil are you doin' out here, anyway?"

"I'm your hostage," she reminded him and licked one stray bean from the corner of her mouth.

Quinn cleared his throat, shifted on the branch beside her and said "Not *here*, here. Texas here. How come you left the East?"

Winifred ran her fingertip along the line of her lips and wished momentarily that she had a napkin. "To teach school in Yellow Dog. Remember? I told you that first day."

"Yeah, I remember. But why didn't ya just teach back where ya come from?"

"The adventure, Quinn." Winifred sighed, tilted her head back and stared up at the dark sky overhead. Stars were just beginning to appear and it seemed to her that the process took longer in Texas. As if each star waited its turn to debut so that everyone could fully appreciate their beauty. "The adventure."

He grunted, took the serving spoon from her and leaned over to plop more beans on their plate.

"Haven't you ever wanted to see new places? Meet new people?"

"Nope," he replied and took another knifefull of beans. "Done enough of that when I was a boy."

"What do you mean?"

"Oh, my pa was forever draggin' me and my mother off to some new corner of this territory or the other. Always lookin' for somethin' he never found." Quinn stopped talking suddenly and stared off into the distance for a long, silent moment. Finally, he added, "That man never did find a spot he liked well enough to just set." He shook his head slowly and said as if speaking to himself, "If he hadn't up and died, we prob'ly would've left Yellow Dog, too."

"I'm sorry," she said, responding to the hint of sadness in his tone.

"Don't be." Quinn turned toward her again and his blue eyes were shuttered, unreadable. "He did things the way he wanted. Died peaceful. That's more'n some get."

Obviously, he didn't want to speak about his father. She looked into his eyes though and found herself wishing that she knew more about him. She wanted to know why a man like him had come to rob a bank. She wanted to know about his family. His hopes. His dreams. She wanted to breach the wall she saw shining in his eyes. Leaving the subject of his father for the moment, Winifred tried something else.

"Wasn't it difficult for your mother?" She took another small bite of beans, then passed the plate to him. "Raising a son alone?"

A small smile touched his features briefly as he said simply, "She's always sayin' that if somethin' comes easy, it ain't worth havin'." He shook his head in silent admiration. "She did fine. We both did."

"What does she think about your becoming a bank robber?" Even as the words left her mouth, Winifred knew it was the wrong thing to ask. His expression stiffened and she could see his jaw muscles working as he ground his teeth together. But she didn't think his anger was directed at her. As he closed up and his blue eyes became shadowed and dark, she was more certain than ever that Quinn was furious with himself.

She hadn't meant to cause him distress. It was her blasted curiosity, that was all. But was it? Was she merely curious about Quinn . . . or was there more to her desire to know him? To know his thoughts—his past—his future?

He was a criminal. He'd kidnapped her and refused to release her. He'd forced her to ride beside him until every bone in her body screamed out in protest. He'd kissed her and touched her with a gentle passion she'd never known. And he'd saved her life twice. Quinn Hawkins had quietly become important to her.

Instinctively, Winifred reached out and laid her right hand on his forearm. At that moment, a spark ignited between them. Winifred felt it and she was sure he had too.

Quinn looked down at her hand and slowly moved to cover it with one of his own. Idly, thoughtfully, he smoothed his thumb over her knuckles.

Winifred's breathing quickened. Every stroke of his thumb sent shafts of heat racing through her until she felt as though her blood was on fire. She studied their joined hands for a long minute, then raised her gaze to find him watching her.

Silence deepened and thickened around them. Winifred heard each breath she drew and listened to the thundering of her own heart. The fire snapped and hissed. The hollow thud of the horse's hooves as they stamped in place seemed to echo into the silence.

And still hostage and captor stared at each other, neither of them willing to look away.

9

She hadn't meant anything, he knew.

Quinn continued to trace small, gentle patterns on her hand with his thumb. The straight thinking part of his mind told him that she'd only reached out to him in a gesture of comfort. But the other side of his brain was in charge now. And that side of him kept arguing silently that she'd touched him because she *wanted* to. Because she enjoyed it. Because she wanted him.

It didn't make any sense at all, but Quinn could admit at least to himself, that there was nothing he'd like better than to be able to believe that little voice in his mind.

Then she did it again.

She reached for him and Quinn held himself perfectly still, afraid to move lest he break whatever spell had hold of her.

Gently, she smoothed back a scrap of hair that lay across his forehead. Her fingers slid over his skin and he felt the softness of her right down to his bones.

Without giving himself time to think, Quinn turned his face into her hand and kissed her palm. He felt her tremble and it was his undoing.

Suddenly, he didn't care that she was his captive or that he was on the run from those closest to him. He didn't want to think about what was ahead of him. He didn't want to think beyond the next moment. He only wanted to feel. He wanted to hold her close and pretend that however briefly, they belonged together.

Slowly, he pulled her to him, into the circle of his arms. She came willingly, tipping her face up to his. One hand cupped his cheek and her thumb moved to trace the line of his moustache. As her fingers slid across his lips, Quinn smiled down at her. His arms around her waist, he lifted her to meet him. Quinn's lips brushed over hers gently at first. Tenderly.

She gasped at the first contact of his mouth and that soft, tiny sound speared through him. His arms tightened around her and he deepened the kiss. Teasing her lips apart with the tip of his tongue, Quinn invaded the warmth of her mouth. She sighed and he swallowed her breath even as his tongue caressed hers in an ancient rite of passion.

Every touch, every caress, only fed his hunger. Quinn reluctantly broke the kiss and let his lips slide down her neck. She arched into him, tilting her head back to allow him easier access to her flesh. He tasted the warm scent of lilacs and when he nibbled at the base of her throat, Quinn felt her racing pulse beneath his lips.

She threaded her fingers through his hair then let her right hand slip beneath the collar of his shirt to the warm, bare flesh of his shoulders. Tiny flames shot from her fingertips down into the darkest corners of his soul and Quinn felt a warmth like he'd never known before race through him.

Alarm bells rang out in his brain. Stunned by the

force of his response to her, Quinn realized that one kiss wouldn't be enough. It wouldn't ease the hunger, it would only fan the flames of the desire he'd been fighting for days.

Reluctantly, he straightened up, sucked in a gulp of cool night air and without looking at her, tugged the edges of that wool blanket more firmly together.

"Quinn?"

Oh God, he groaned silently. Don't let her make this any harder than it is already.

"You, uh . . . better get dressed," he said as he scooted back from her. Shoving one hand through his hair, he noticed his fingers were still trembling and hoped she wouldn't see it, too.

"But," she reached for him again and Quinn braced himself for the impact of her touch. And even though he was prepared, the lightning like jolt of awareness that rippled through him was almost enough for him to forget his noble notions. Almost.

Instead, he patted her hand then moved out of her reach. "Go on," he told her. "Before you get sick or somethin'."

"You mean we're finished kissing now?"

He risked a glance at her and immediately wished he hadn't. Her hair stood out in a wild halo of color around her pale face and her lips were deep pink and still tender from his kiss. Jesus! he pleaded silently. Just this once, will Ya help her to do as I ask?

He cleared his throat, tossed another stick into the dying flames and said roughly, "Yeah, Fred. We're finished."

"Didn't you like kissing me?" Winifred asked, then reached up and smoothed her hair back from her face. She didn't understand this at all. True, she wasn't very experienced at this sort of thing, but he'd certainly seemed as though he was enjoying himself. But then, maybe he hadn't felt what she had. Maybe he hadn't experienced that feeling of coiled strength deep inside him. Maybe he wasn't suffering from the tingling, unanswered . . . *need* of some kind that was now settling low in her abdomen.

He kept staring at the flames as if he was looking for his answers there. "Oh," he said on a laugh that held no humor in it, "I liked kissin' ya fine, Fred."

"Are you sure?" She inched closer to him. It didn't seem right that she should be so affected by his touch when he was able to set her aside so easily. "Perhaps I wasn't doing it correctly."

"What?" he turned to look at her and their faces were only a breath apart.

"I, uh," she pulled in a shaky breath and said, "haven't had much practice you know. At kissing, that is."

"Uh-huh."

Why did he choose *now* to mask his feelings? Why did he have to let those shutters drop over his eyes when she most needed to know what he was thinking?

"I only thought," she went on, hoping to see the shadows in his eyes lift, "that perhaps I'd done something wrong."

"Wrong?" He rubbed one hand across his face and Winifred couldn't help remembering the teasing, ticklish feel of his moustache against her skin.

"Yes," she blurted. "You see, when you kissed me, I experienced the most marvelous sensations. Like nothing I've ever felt before."

He groaned quietly, but she went on, determined now to know if her kisses were lacking somehow.

"When you touch me, there's a feeling of tingly warmth that seems almost to ripple through me in tiny waves." She closed her eyes and relived that moment when she'd thought he was going to touch her breast. Just thinking about it brought a chill to her spine and peaked her nipples against the fabric covering them. A damp heat flooded her nether regions and she almost blushed as though he could see what thoughts of him were doing to her.

"Fred . . ." Quinn reached down, snatched up his battered hat and slammed it onto his head.

"Anyway," she interrupted, "if I did something wrong . . . if you didn't feel any of that," Winifred shrugged and one corner of her blanket slid off her right shoulder.

Quinn glanced at her, clenched his jaw, then determinedly reached over and tugged the blanket back into place.

"Let it go, will ya Fred?"

"Naturally, I'd like to do as you ask, but I feel I must know. If I didn't give you those feelings, I really do think we should try it again."

"Again?"

"Yes." She leaned in closer and thought briefly about planting a quick kiss on his lips. But first, she had to know if she was doing it right. For heaven's sake. Couldn't he understand how it would bother a person to think that they were doing something all wrong?

"No."

"No?"

"*No.*" Quinn pushed himself to his feet, then held one hand out to her to help her up.

When she was standing beside him, he bent down, scooped up her carpetbag and handed it to her. "Go get dressed."

"But Quinn, I won't be able to rest until I know—"

He grabbed her shoulders roughly, pulled her against him and ground his mouth against hers for a brief, hard kiss. Skyrockets and thunderbolts shot through her, making her knees weak and her heartbeat race double-time. When he lifted his head, he stared down at her and

Winifred had a difficult time seeing him through the haze of passion clouding her vision.

"Ya didn't do a damned thing wrong, Fred."

"You're sure?" she whispered.

"Jesus!" His head dropped until his chin hit his chest. A long moment passed before he looked at her again. Winifred held her breath as she stared into his eyes. Unshuttered, his blue eyes held such . . . *hunger,* it took her breath away.

No man ever had looked at her as though she was the very breath he needed to stay alive. A curl of pleasure spiraled through her chest and threatened to choke her with its strength. How very odd, she told herself, that she'd had to travel the length of the country to stumble across the one man who made her feel like every princess she'd ever read about.

Unconsciously, she leaned into him and for the first time, noticed his hardened flesh press against her abdomen. Her eyes widened.

"*Now* do you understand, Fred?" Muttering a curse under his breath, Quinn took one step back and waved toward the nearby trees. "Go on. Get some clothes on 'fore I change my mind and take what you've been offerin'."

Speechless for once, Winifred stared at him. *She,* Winifred Matthews, spinster schoolteacher had done *that* to a man's body! She swallowed heavily and ducked her head, suddenly embarrassed by her new knowledge. Perhaps he was right, a lone, rational voice answered from the back of her mind. Perhaps it would be best if she were clothed before attempting to continue this "discussion."

Quickly, Winifred hurried past him, both hands wrapped around the handle of her bag. As its heavy weight slapped against her knees, she glanced back over her shoulder at the tall blond man standing alone by the fire.

Well, she'd had her question answered. Now she knew for certain that Quinn Hawkins was every bit as affected by her as she was by him. One corner of her mouth lifted slowly as she studied him. Firelight played on his long, jean clad legs, narrow waist and broad shoulders. The blaze in front of him painted his shadow across the rocky earth and for a moment, she watched the dark image waver and wobble in the unsteady light.

His shadow, she thought, seemed to follow her. Reach out for her, despite the fact that Quinn himself stood with his back to her, deliberately distancing himself from her.

She smiled and kept walking.

It wasn't only his shadow stretching out to reach her, she told herself. Whether he knew it or not, a part of her outlaw was holding out his hand to her, hoping to draw her close.

As she stepped into the sheltering circle of trees, Winifred grinned. Her adventure was becoming more exciting all the time.

"Neither a borrower nor a lender be," Adelaide Simpson said and pushed her long nose into the air.

Mercy Hawkin's fingers curled into helpless fists on top of the glass merchandise case. Slowly, she counted to ten.

"You have a nerve and a half, Addy Simpson," Mercy finally ground out, her temper straining her voice. "You had no problem bein' a lender when it meant you were gettin' interest paid regularly on a loan your man made to me."

"Don't call me Addy!" Adelaide snapped and shook one finger at Mercy. "My name is Adelaide. Or, Mrs. Simpson. Whichever you prefer."

"I *prefer* not talkin' to you at all," Mercy shot back

and heard two women in the back of the general store chuckle.

Addy heard it too and fired one quelling look at the other customers. Disgusted, she looked back at Mercy. "Then for heaven's sake, go home!"

"What home would that be, *Addy?* The one you stole from me and my son and handed over to Bentley?"

A spill of dying sunlight slanted through the shop's front windows and lay across Addy's face. She winced into the light and stepped to one side.

"I did nothing of the sort." Adelaide smoothed the palm of one hand over the lace encrusted bosom of her deep blue dress. "It was business. Not stealing."

"All in the way you look at it, I guess."

"It's perfectly legal to sell a note." Adelaide stepped forward, leaning her palms on the cold glass. Almost nose to nose with Mercy, she went on, "If you were that concerned about losing your place, you shouldn't have gone into debt in the first place."

Clamping her lips together, Mercy bit back what she wanted to say. That Addy's husband Henry had talked she and Quinn into that loan. He'd told them what all they could do with ready cash—from buying up that piece of land that lay on their south border to bringing in some young breeding stock to improve their herd.

Oh, it was true. Henry *had* offered. But Mercy couldn't rightly say that it was Henry's fault. After all, she and Quinn hadn't been forced into making that loan. They'd both leaped at the chance. Of course, they'd never figured that Addy would take over their note and sell it to Bentley.

Stupid. They should have considered the possibility. Hell, everybody in town knew that Addy treated Henry like a lapdog—telling him to come, go, sit and stay.

No, it wasn't Henry's fault. It was her own. And knowing that didn't put Mercy into a better humor.

"You're right," she acknowledged, though it galled her to choke out the words.

Addy's eyes bugged out and her jaw dropped. It took her a full minute to recover long enough to snap her mouth shut. To cover her surprise, she lifted the corner of her starched white apron and began to unnecessarily shine the glass topped jewelery case.

"We never should've taken out that blasted loan," Mercy admitted and pressed her fingernails hard into her palms.

Addy smiled, nodded and dropped her apron back into place. Tugging at her cuffs, she straightened up like a queen accepting favors from her favorite peasant.

"But," Mercy added as Addy shot her a quick, sharp look, "you shouldn't have sold us out to a stranger for cash, either. You've known us too long for that. You knew damned well we'd make good on that note."

It was small satisfaction indeed to watch Addy squirm.

"Perhaps," the storekeeper's wife said on a sniff, then lovingly ran the tip of one finger across the top of her walnut money box. "But Mr. Bentley was willing to pay the note in total." Her lips turned down and for a moment, she looked as she had twenty years ago. Whiny and greedy for all the good things in life.

"Besides," the snippy woman continued, "it wasn't only you, Mercy Hawkins. I didn't set out to ruin you personally, so you can stop looking at me like you want to pull out a rifle."

Mercy inhaled slowly. Coming to the store hadn't been a good idea at all. She wasn't solving anything, she was only feeding the anger that had been eating at her for days.

"I sold *all* of the notes Henry'd taken," Adelaide said and lifted her chin defiantly. "It was perfectly legal."

"And mean spirited," Mercy added. "You sold out

your friends and neighbors for money, Addy. No fancy way of sayin' it will change things."

"True enough," one of the women in the rear of the store echoed. "Joe Hooker and his family been gone this last week. Lost everything."

Addy frowned. "It ain't . . . *isn't* my business if people want to go into debt!" She jerked her head from side to side, trying to see just who it was taking Mercy's part against her.

"No," Mercy said quietly, recapturing Addy's attention. "It's only your business to make a profit on them."

A slow flush of color spread up Addy's sharp planed features. She sucked in a slow, long, deep breath that swelled her already impressive bosom to impossible dimensions. Planting her hands on her wide hips, Addy pursed her lips and tapped the toe of her shoe against the pine plank floor.

"And just who are you to be callin' me a thief, Mercy Hawkins? Mother of a bank robbing kidnapper, that's who."

Fresh color flooded Mercy's cheeks. There wasn't any argument to that statement. Her son was a thief—blast his impatient hide. But as to the kidnapping part of things—well, Mercy knew as well as anybody that the new schoolteacher had been taken. But she also knew something else. Quinn wouldn't hurt that woman and he'd let her go the minute he could.

"That poor woman," Addy was saying, shaking her head and clucking her tongue. "Such a sweet little thing, too. You do know that Henry and me rode in on the stage with her? She seemed so small. So . . . delicate." Adelaide's eyes narrowed perceptibly. "And the poor dear's reputation is simply shattered, now. All this time? *Alone* with a man?" She clucked her tongue again and shook her head. "I wouldn't be the least bit surprised if the city fathers changed their mind about hiring her as teacher. Naturally, we have to be careful about the kind of woman we allow to teach our children. Still," Addy sighed, "such a shame, of course. No doubt, the poor woman is simply helpless against a man who ruthlessly abducted her from a public street."

"Ruthless?" Mercy leaned in closer to the other woman. Anger was forcing her to take short, uneven breaths but as she stared Addy down, Mercy's gaze was cold, calm.

Addy retreated one step and backed into the wall of shelves behind her. A bag of flour fell off and burst open on the floor at her feet, spattering her fine blue dress with a dusting of white powder.

"You want to see *ruthless*, Addy?" Mercy lifted her right hand as if preparing to take a solemn oath. "I'll *show* you ruthless if you don't keep that viperous tongue of yours off my son."

Addy blinked.

"You've done your dirt already, Addy. You leave Quinn alone or so help me Hannah, Henry'll be a widower this time next year."

Addy's gaze shot nervously from side to side, fruitlessly searching for help.

"As for that schoolteacher," Mercy went on, "you know good and well my Quinn wouldn't force himself on *anybody*. The only way her reputation will suffer is if folks pay attention to sharp-tongued, dull-witted harpies like you!"

A quickly muffled sound of applause followed Mercy's impassioned speech and told her that the women at the back of the store agreed with her. Unfortunately, that fact didn't make her feel the slightest bit better.

She wasn't accomplishing anything by screeching at Addy. Her time would be better served by going to the telegraph office. It was two days since she'd last checked in. If she was very lucky, maybe there was an answer there now, waiting for her.

Grumbling under her breath at her sense of helplessness, Mercy turned and stalked across the store's length to the front door. Grasping the doorknob, she turned it and flung the door wide, slamming it into the wall and sending the overhead bell into a frantic clatter. It was the only sound she heard as she stepped out onto the boardwalk.

Winifred leaned across Quinn's outstretched legs and smiled to herself when he flinched. She'd never known such a heady feeling. The slightest contact between them seemed to affect him. He'd spent the last two hours trying to keep his distance, but Winifred refused to let him.

After laying a fresh branch across the steadily burning fire, Winifred sat back against the tree limb and scooted just a bit closer to him. As she'd expected, he tried to inch away. Winifred moved with him.

Heavens, this is exciting, she thought. Whoever would have imagined Winifred Matthews as a tantalizing woman?

"Fred," he groaned, "why don't you go on to sleep now, huh?"

"Oh, I'm not in the least tired," she answered quickly.

"Great," he muttered.

"Isn't this cozy?" she asked and hesitantly lay her head on his shoulder.

He stiffened and Winifred bit back a smile.

"Just the two of us," she went on, "alone on the prairie, sitting beside a campfire with our trusty steeds close by."

"Trusty steeds?"

"The horses."

"Oh. Your books again, huh?"

"Yes." She nodded and thought how wonderful the worn cotton of his shirt felt against her cheek. "Do you know," she said and her voice came soft into the firelit darkness, "I've decided something about you."

He tried to shift his shoulder out from under her head. He failed.

"What's that?"

Winifred moved her head against him until she found a comfortable spot where she could listen to the quick beating of his heart. Smiling wistfully, she said "I've decided that you're not at all like Dastardly Dan. You're much more like the hero. Marshal Travis."

She felt him shake his head.

"Heroes don't rob banks, Fred."

"But villains don't save the heroine's life, either."

"Folks ain't like books, Fred," he sighed and seemed to resign himself to her closeness.

"Oh, I think you're mistaken, Quinn." She tilted her head back and stared up at the underside of his jaw. In the firelight, she could just make out the fine, golden stubble on his cheeks. Then he glanced down at her and her breath caught momentarily.

"I ain't a hero, Fred," he said simply, "and I *hope* I ain't a villain, either."

"Oh, you're not. I'm sure of it."

His lips quirked and she thought how handsome he was when he smiled.

"And why's that?"

"Because a villain couldn't possibly kiss the way you do."

His smile faded away and his gaze moved lovingly over her face. There was sadness in his eyes though when he asked, "And how would you know that? Kiss many villains, have ya?"

"No," she admitted then reached up to smooth her fingertips along his jawline. He closed his eyes and held his breath under her touch. When his eyes opened again, Winifred met his gaze squarely and told him, "But I know that I couldn't possibly feel what I feel when you kiss me if you weren't a good man."

His features softened and a wistful smile curved his lips. Quinn lifted one hand and cupped her cheek. When she turned her face into his touch, his thumb traced over her flesh tenderly. "Ah, Fred," he said softly. "Nothin's that simple."

"It could be," she told him, "if you'd let it."

10

"I can't." *Quinn watched* the disappointment flicker in her eyes and futilely wished that things were different. Maybe if they'd met after church back in Yellow Dog, maybe he and the schoolteacher might have had a chance. But as it stood now, he knew damn well that there was nothing waiting for the two of them except parting.

"Why not?" she demanded and sat up, spearing her elbow into his chest as she moved.

He grunted, rubbed the sore spot and told her "In case you forgot, I'm runnin' from the law, Fred."

"I know that, and yet I think . . ."

"Well quit it," he snapped. "All of your thinkin' and readin' hasn't done you a bit of good, far as I can see."

"On the contrary . . ."

"Fred, by all rights, you should be back in Yellow Dog gettin' ready to teach school," he pointed out. "Or even better—back East, where you belong."

Heaven knew, *his* life would've been a lot easier if she was safely tucked away somewhere.

She pushed her hair out of her eyes and he tried not to notice how thick and soft it looked. When his gaze shifted and he looked into her eyes, he saw nothing soft.

"I'm a grown woman, *Mr.* Hawkins. I believe *I* am the best judge of where I belong."

She wouldn't get an argument out of him on that score. At least not on the grown woman part.

"And," Winifred went on, "may I say that Marshal Travis would never make a woman feel so . . . unwanted."

Quinn's teeth ground together. He was getting almighty sick of hearing about how damned wonderful that pretend fella of hers was. His gaze raked over her and took note of the rigid set of her shoulders and the defiant tilt to her chin. Most hardheaded woman he'd ever met.

"Marshal Travis lives in a damn book!" Quinn argued. "Marshal Travis didn't have to worry about gettin' caught by a posse." He sucked in a deep breath, leaned forward until he was nose to nose with her and added, "And he never had some woman along, drivin' him right out of his mind neither, I'll wager."

That last part just kind of slipped out and the minute it did, Quinn wished he could call it back. Because, judging by the look on her face, that's the only part of what he'd said that Fred had listened to.

"Really?"

"Really what?" he grumbled and shifted away from her some.

"Am I really driving you out of your mind?"

"Hell yes, you are." Quinn tossed another small stick onto the fire, then stared off into the darkness outside their circle of firelight. He'd learned long ago that if a man stared too long into the light, he would be momentarily blinded when he turned to look into the darkness. That blindness could cost a man his life in a tough situation.

Besides, staring off into the growing blackness kept him from having to look into Fred's face. He knew damned well, she'd have a pleased as punch expression on her features and he simply didn't want to see it.

"Isn't that exciting?" she breathed and Quinn bit back a groan.

"No," he countered and glanced at her briefly, "it ain't. Hell, I don't know what you're gonna do from one minute to the next! Lost a horse, burned my hat, lost the supplies—for a little thing, you can surely be tryin'."

"Oh."

That one little word carried a world of hurt and disappointment. Something in Quinn turned over and despite his better judgment, he glanced at her.

Her green-eyed gaze locked on the fire, she held herself stiffly. When she spoke, her voice was so low, he had to lean in close just to hear her.

"That's how I'm driving you crazy, then?"

"Ain't that enough?" Unconsciously, his own voice dropped to match hers.

Her fingers plucked at the material of her skirt. Firelight danced on her hair, making that rich red color shine and sparkle like fireworks on the Fourth of July.

Winifred's shoulders lifted then fell in a dispirited shrug. "Actually, I had hoped," she said and Quinn was caught by the wistful note in her voice, "that your discomfort was caused by my person. Not my actions."

Oh, Lord. He rubbed one hand over his jaw, concentrating on the scrape of stubble against his palm. Her person. Huh! Oh, her "person" wasn't at all hard on the eyes, but it was more than just her gently rounded figure or her pretty face that had Quinn tied up in knots.

It was everything. Hell, he'd never met anybody who was so willing to jump in and try something without once complaining. She was good company when she wasn't comparing him to that damned Marshal Travis or

Dastardly Dan. And blast it all, kissing her was as close to Heaven as somebody like him was likely to get.

But if she knew all that, it'd be just that much harder to ignore what it was he wanted to do. She'd likely smile up at him or ask him to kiss her again and before she knew it, he'd have her stretched out on his bedroll.

Then there'd be no going back for either of them. Quinn took a deep breath and deliberately looked away from her. He might've made a few mistakes here lately, but he wasn't a damn fool. He knew the difference between a loose woman and the kind a man marries.

Winifred Matthews, sure as hell, wasn't loose—but there wasn't a chance in hell she was gonna be his wife, either.

So the only safe thing to do, he told himself, was to find somewhere he could leave her. He had to get away from her before he did something he wouldn't be able to undo. It was bad enough he'd compromised her this way, but he'd surely be lost if he actually bedded her.

His body tightened with the thought and Quinn winced, almost accustomed now to the discomfort. As he shifted uncomfortably, he told himself that whether he wanted to or not, he was going to have to find a safe place to leave Fred behind. Soon.

Quinn watched her fingers continue to smooth and tug at the folds of her black skirt until he spoke and her hands quieted.

"Get some sleep, Fred" he said. "We got a early start tomorrow."

She nodded and lay down on the blanket, her back to him. Curling up into a tight ball, Winifred closed her eyes without another word.

Silently, Quinn watched her and wished things were different.

*   *   *

"How far behind him you reckon we are?" Dusty asked and set the coffee pot back down on a flat rock near the small campfire.

"No more'n two days."

"Two days?"

"We lost a lot of time, searchin' for his tracks after the storm. And Quinn Hawkins ain't just some simpleton. He knows how to hide his tracks better than most."

"True." Dusty sighed, stretched his long legs out and crossed them at the ankles. He took a careful sip of the boiling hot liquid in his cup then commented "'Course, if you'd a listened to me, we wouldn't have wasted all that time checkin' out those little towns, either."

Tom grunted, lay his head down against his saddle and tipped his hat down over his eyes. "We had to look."

"Told you Quinn wouldn't be goin' to no town. If a posse was chasin' *you,* would you stop somewheres for a drink?"

"No, but he's got that woman with him."

"So?" Dusty frowned at the other man. What the hell did the woman have to do with Quinn not bein' dumb enough to go to a town or not? And if Tom was thinkin' about somethin' else, Dusty felt it only right to add, "You know he ain't gonna hurt her."

"Yeah," Tom agreed, his voice muffled under his hat, "but he can't keep her with him. She's slowin' him down so, he'll never get away. A few more days ridin' like today, and we've got him."

Dusty set his coffee cup aside, scooted down on his blanket and lay back against his saddle. Staring up into the night sky, he studied the bright sparkle of stars for a long moment before asking, "So you're figurin' that he'll just drop her off in one of these little bitty rat hole towns?"

"If he wants to get away from us, he will." Tom muttered. "And when he does, somebody there will notice which way he goes when he leaves. Now go to sleep, will ya?"

In seconds it seemed, Tom was asleep and snoring. Dusty though, continued staring blankly at the night sky. Everything Tom said made sense, he knew. But, he still couldn't see Quinn leaving that woman on her own in some out of the way, spot in the road town. Quinn Hawkins had always been the kind to look out for everybody else. It just didn't make sense to think that he would desert a woman whose safety was his responsibility.

Although, a voice in the back of his mind whispered as he finally closed his eyes, it didn't make sense for a posse to be chasing ol' Quinn down, either.

From a distance, Winifred wasn't entirely certain that it was a town at all. Did five or six ramshackle buildings constitute a town? Or would it more properly be called a village?

But the images brought to mind at the word "village" had nothing whatever to do with the reality facing her from just a few hundred yards away.

The buildings were the same dirt brown color as the land surrounding them. The wooden structures looked more like the ruins of a previous civilization rather than a living town. Each structure leaned against its neighbor for support and Winifred thought that it would only take a brief, hard gust of wind to shake them all into the dust.

The street, if one could call it that, looked to be no more than twenty or thirty feet long and hardly wide enough to permit a wagon passage. Several horses were tied to hitching rails on either side of the narrow road but there wasn't a soul to be seen on the boardwalks and porches.

She shivered despite the warm sun on her back and told herself she was being foolish. There was nothing sinister about the place. The unremarkable town was nothing more than a collection of disreputable structures plopped down in the middle of nowhere.

She frowned, but kept her thoughts to herself as Quinn brought their horses to a stop.

"All right," he said and leaned both hands on the pommel of his saddle as he looked at her. "Now we got to get some supplies down yonder and I'm gonna trust you not to say anything to anybody about who we are and where we're headed."

"I understand," she said and kept her gaze locked on the town in front of them. She simply couldn't bring herself to look him directly in the eyes. She'd made an utter fool of herself the night before and Winifred hadn't the slightest intention of repeating the error. Having her romantic notions so thoroughly quashed the night before had been a hard, if valuable lesson.

"No matter what I say," Quinn told her, "you just follow along. All right?"

She nodded.

"Fred," he sounded exasperated, "are you listenin' to me?"

"I've heard every word," Winifred assured him.

"Uh-huh." He leaned over, took her chin between his fingers and turned her head toward him. "You all right?"

"Certainly." Winifred pulled away from his grasp and turned her gaze back on the town.

He sighed and muttered "Fine." Tossing her the reins to her mount, he said, "Follow close behind me and don't say a thing to anybody if you can help it."

Surprised, Winifred at last turned to look at him. As her fingers curled around the leather straps, she asked, "I'm not *permitted* to speak?"

Quinn shook his head. When she opened her mouth to argue, he held up one hand. "The minute you open that pretty mouth of yours, 'Eastern School Teacher' comes pourin' out."

"I beg your pardon!" Her chin lifted and the yellow sunflower on the side of her now dilapidated hat fell off the brim and dangled on the strength of a single thread.

"Nothin' to be sorry for," he frowned at the flower, then looked at her. "You can't help it."

Winifred opened her mouth, then snapped it shut again. Really!

"The minute you start talkin'," he went on, ignoring her silence, "folks down there will pay attention. And they'll remember. Eastern ladies ridin' through one horse towns ain't all that common, ya know."

"I'll take your word for that," she finally managed to say.

"If a posse comes along askin' questions, folks in that town'd be pleased to tell 'em all about you *and* me."

It made sense. And in the logical, rational corner of her mind, Winifred admitted that fact. But, she was also forced to admit that she didn't care for being told what to do and when to do it. Not even by Quinn Hawkins.

However, memories of Dastardly Dan's exploits raced through her brain and Winifred made up her mind to do as Quinn asked. If she didn't, he just might change his mind and leave her bound and gagged somewhere he deemed "safe." Lord alone knew where that might be.

"Fine," she said quietly. "I shall be perfectly quiet. No one will know that I am there."

His gaze narrowed and he studied her thoughtfully. Several long minutes passed before he finally jerked her a nod.

As they started their horses for town, Winifred thought she heard him mutter, "This isn't gonna work," but she might have been mistaken.

*　　　*　　　*

There weren't more than five or six people in the saloon. Hell, Quinn told himself as he peered into the room over the top of the half door, probably weren't too many more than that in the whole town.

From the far corner came the unmistakable voice of Winifred Matthews. Quinn groaned quietly.

It was his own fault, he supposed. After buying what supplies he needed from the tiny general store, Quinn had relaxed his guard for a minute or two. Winifred had done just what he'd told her to while they were shopping. She'd hardly spoken a word and had spent her time in the store wandering around, inspecting everything from bolts of calico to hunting knives. Of course, the minute his back was turned, she'd disappeared on him. Quinn had finished packing the saddlebags, turned to say something and discovered her gone.

In a town that size, it hadn't taken him long to find her.

He stepped into the darkened building and paused just inside the doorway to let his eyes adjust to the dimness. Sunlight beat on the dirt encrusted windows, trying valiantly to penetrate the grime. A layer of windblown dirt covered the rough, pine plank floor and a mismatched collection of tables and chairs were scattered about the room. Directly across from the open doorway was the bar. Quinn's eyebrows lifted slightly. The bartop was a five-foot-long chunk of wood braced on either end by huge wooden barrels. His nose wrinkled. Judging from the odor, those barrels had once held pickles and no one had bothered to clean them out before putting them to work in the saloon. Behind the makeshift bar stood a man in a long, sparkling white apron drying surprisingly fine looking crystal glasses. The stub end of a cigar jutted from the corner of his mouth and the man's eyes were wary.

Dammit. He should have known that Winifred

wouldn't be able to keep her mouth shut or do what he told her to do. He should have known she wouldn't be able to keep from wandering off. If he'd had any sense at all, he would have left her behind at last night's campsite. Hell. He should've left her standing on the street in Yellow Dog and taken his chances.

At least then, he wouldn't be standing around like a fool, looking for a woman who had managed to slip out from under his watchful eye. He pushed his hat brim up, narrowed his gaze and glanced around the room until he located her.

Near the bar, a blowsy looking saloon girl stood beside Winifred, who was talking the other woman's ears off. Briefly Quinn allowed himself the pleasure of simply looking at Fred. Even after their hard days of riding—even though her black skirt was covered with trail dust and the hem was dragging from all the times she'd caught her foot in it—even with her red hair straggling free of a haphazard knot, she was the prettiest thing Quinn had ever seen. Hell, he was even getting used to that damned sunflower dangling free of her blasted hat.

In fact, he was getting far too used to Winifred altogether.

He reached up, yanked his hat off and crumpled the already ruined brim in one tightly clenched fist. Occasionally, Fred's voice would reach a note high enough for Quinn to hear what she was saying, but enough of her comments were missing to make it an interesting conversation to say the least.

"No," she said, then murmured awhile before adding, "and it *stays* up all by itself?"

Quinn squeezed his eyes shut briefly and smothered a chuckle. He wasn't sure he wanted to know what she was talking about. Quietly, he took another step into the room.

The saloon girl laughed and Winifred's delighted laughter joined in. He was surprised to realize how good it sounded to him. Quinn couldn't really remember if she'd laughed with him or not.

"It's *that* stiff?" Fred asked and bent her head toward her new friend.

Good Lord.

"Your wife?"

Quinn glanced at the speaker, a gambler by the looks of him, sprawled in a chair close by. "Huh? Oh. Oh, yeah."

The man nodded thoughtfully. "She seems a . . . friendly sort."

"She is."

"Pretty little thing."

"Hmmm." Quinn was hardly listening. Instead, he was watching Winifred. Her green eyes were wide as she listened to the other woman.

"Been married long?"

"What?" Quinn frowned at the other man. He was trying to concentrate on what Fred was up to and the gambler's constant interruptions weren't helping.

"I said, been married long?"

"Oh. No, not long." No sense in correcting the man, Quinn told himself. Besides, if folks here thought he and Fred were married, maybe a posse wouldn't find out too much information after all.

"Thought not," the gambler said and pushed himself to his feet. "She don't seem married, if you know what I mean."

"Can't say as I do," Quinn countered, his fingers tightening around the hat brim. Eyes narrowed, he gave the tall man his full attention.

"Well, she's not wearin' a ring, for one thing."

"Haven't bought one yet."

"If she was *my* wife, she'd damn well be wearin' a ring."

"She ain't your wife."

"And I wouldn't allow a woman of mine to enter a saloon, either."

Allow. Quinn almost smiled. He was willing to bet that the gambler'd never come across a woman like Winifred Matthews. But the look in the man's eyes quickly killed any thoughts of a smile. "Then it's real lucky she ain't your wife, huh?"

The gambler's jaw tightened and he flicked a quick glance at Winifred before looking back at Quinn.

"Stayin' around for long, are you?"

"Well now," Quinn gave the man a hard, unwavering stare. "I don't see how that's any of your business."

The other man shrugged a bit too casually. "I rent the rooms here. If you're going to be needing one, you'll have to talk to me."

Truth to tell, Quinn had been thinking of doing just that. Renting a room, that is. But not for he and Fred to share. For her alone. To leave her in.

Dammit, it was the only thing that made any sense. If he left her here, the posse was sure to catch up soon. They'd take care of her. His gaze shot to where she stood, still deep in conversation. It would be best for her. Even if this was the tiniest damn town he'd ever seen.

Quinn didn't know if he could stand too many more lonely nights by the campfire without giving in to the urge to hold her in his arms and kiss her senseless. Besides, a woman like her wasn't meant to be sleeping out under the stars and running from the law.

She was meant for pretty dresses and fine hotels. A Texas rancher dumb enough to rob a bank had no business at all even thinking about her the way he had been lately.

Now though, it was clear that he couldn't leave Winifred here alone. Not with *this* fella around, he told himself. Hell, she'd be safer walking into an Apache camp.

"So?" the gambler asked and interrupted Quinn's thoughts. "Will you and your *wife* be staying over?"

Irritation crawled through him. His own thoughts were giving him fits enough. He sure as hell didn't need this stranger or his barbed comments. Never a truly patient man even at the best of times, Quinn was dangerously close to his breaking point. Still though, he tried to hang on to the temper that was gradually gaining strength. When he finally trusted himself enough to speak, his voice sounded strangled.

"Why don't you just *say* what you mean, mister?"

A chair scraped along the floor somewhere in the back of the room. Winifred's voice trailed off into silence and Quinn felt the eyes of everyone in the room stabbing into him.

Dammit, he *knew* there'd be trouble. But then, hadn't he had just that since the morning Winifred had knocked him down and dragged off his bandana?

"All right, *friend*," the gambler said and bared his teeth in what was supposed to be a smile. "I don't believe she *is* your wife."

"That so?" Quinn stiffened, reached up and jammed his battered hat down onto his head. Facing the gambler squarely, Quinn kept his hands at his sides, his fingers curled into tight fists. "You're callin' me a liar, then?"

"Yeah," the man nodded. "I am. And if I'm correct, I'd like to offer the lady *my* protection."

Quinn snorted. From the corner of his eye, he saw Winifred walking toward him. He only hoped she stayed far enough back to avoid getting hit once the fists started flyin'.

"*Your* protection? Protection from what?"

"Why," the gambler gave Quinn that tight smile again and said, "from *you*, of course."

"Quinn?"

"Stay back, Fred."

"Fred?" The other man echoed. "You call this delightful creature . . . *Fred?*"

"Quinn," she asked with one dismissive glance at the gambler, "who is this person?"

"Nobody."

"Colin Tucker, madam." He bowed deeply at the waist. "At your service."

Winifred nodded distractedly, confusion clearly etched into her features.

"Is there a problem here, Mr. Tucker?" she asked.

"The problem madam, is between your *husband* and myself."

Quinn tensed. If she didn't play along with him, the game was lost.

Seconds passed. His heart near stopped, Quinn watched as Winifred's features slowly brightened. Then she gave him a small, half-smile. His breath left him in a relieved sigh. He shouldn't have worried. He should have remembered how she loved those dime novels of hers. Hell, this probably seemed like nothing more than another of her stories. Another adventure.

A moment passed, then Winifred grinned. Taking one step closer to Quinn, she told the gambler, "My husband and I have no secrets from one another sir."

The tall man smirked.

Winifred frowned at him then looked up at Quinn. "What does he want?"

"You," Quinn answered simply.

11

"Really?" she said and turned for another good look at the gambler. "Isn't that exciting!"

She heard Quinn sigh, but ignored it. This was even better than she could have hoped for when she'd first sneaked away from Quinn to explore the town saloon.

The opportunity was simply too much to resist. She'd read so much about western saloons and dance halls. And though she suspected that the small, dirty little building wasn't a fair representation of western saloons in general—it was all she had.

Winifred had ignored the stares from the men gathered inside. One could hardly blame them for being surprised at her entrance. It was the same in every single book she'd ever read about the Wild West. Everyone knew that "good" women never frequented saloons. But on the other hand, how in heaven would she be able to fully describe the place in her journal if she didn't go inside?

After making a quick turn about the room, she'd indulged her curiosity about life in a saloon by cornering one of the two women working there and peppering her with questions. Actually, Luscious Liz was most helpful, Winifred thought, and the woman had just started explaining something most intriguing when Quinn and the gambler started shouting at each other.

Winifred stared up at the gambler and hid a smile. Oh, this was going to make an incredible entry in her journal! Imagine! A tall, dark man had taken one look at her and wanted to claim her for his own!

And even better, a voice in the back of her mind whispered excitedly, Quinn was claiming her as his wife! Oh, she knew he'd done it merely to protect her. But, didn't that make him even *more* heroic?

Really, it was *so* exciting.

The very air in the saloon seemed to be charged with the kind of expectation that usually heralded a storm. Winifred inhaled sharply and looked from Quinn to the stranger and back again.

A curl of pleasure started low in the pit of her stomach and Winifred had to struggle to keep from hugging herself with the thrill of it all. The people back home would never believe it. Two men about to engage in fisticuffs over her!

At least, she told herself silently, she *hoped* it would be fisticuffs. A hint of worry began to thread its way through her excitement. She glanced at the gun on Quinn's hip and noticed just how close his right hand was to the pistol grip. Good heavens—if he and the other man were to engage in gunplay, Quinn might be killed!

She couldn't have that.

And by heaven, she wouldn't stand for it. Adventure was one thing. Watching Quinn be shot down in a dirty saloon was quite another.

"Gentlemen, please," she said and took the one small step that would place her directly between them. Sure that they would respond to simple logic, Winifred was prepared to talk them out of their foolishness.

"Fred, you step aside," Quinn told her.

"Oh no, I couldn't do that."

"Madam," the gambler said, "though I am loathe to agree with this . . . person, I must concur."

Clearly, she wasn't going to be able to reason with Quinn. Perhaps the other man would prove more receptive. Turning to the gambler, she studied him briefly. Tall and thin, with a courtly manner at odds with his surroundings, his impeccable suit looked distinctly out of place, yet he seemed completely comfortable in the little saloon. Winifred decided to try to convince him of the ridiculousness of the situation.

"Sir," she began, giving him a small, polite smile, "you have the cultured tones of an educated man. Surely you can see the folly in this."

The tall man smiled again and Winifred noticed that not a trace of warmth touched his eyes. Perhaps he wasn't quite as "civilized" as she'd thought at first. She shivered slightly but held her ground as he began to speak.

"As it happens," he said, as he shifted his narrowed gaze to Quinn, "my Harvard education is not necessary for what is about to take place."

Harvard? Winifred stared at him openmouthed. She wouldn't have believed that a Harvard man would be so eager to engage in a barroom brawl. But the gleam in his eyes told her that he was more than eager. Apparently, an education did not necessarily mean that a man would listen to reason.

For Heaven's sake.

"Fred, you go on now." Quinn told her and gave her a gentle nudge. "This'll only take a minute."

"At last, we agree," the gambler said softly.

"Isn't anyone going to stop this?" Winifred demanded from the small group of people behind her. But they were too busy scooting their chairs into more favorable positions to answer her question.

"Quinn," she said, worry creeping into her voice, "I won't have this. I *demand* that you stop this at once."

"Winifred . . ."

"Hmmph," the gambler sneered. "She *demands?* Apparently, you are less worthy of a woman like this than I at first imagined. I too enjoy a spirited female. However, there are limits to what a man should allow." He looked down at Winifred and gave her a slow smile that made her blood run cold. "She needs to be shown a woman's place."

A woman's place. The phrase seemed to echo through Winifred's brain, over and over. How many women over the course of time had been successfully strapped down by that one phrase? Her own mother had given up whatever dreams of adventure she'd nourished in her heart in order to fulfill the role society and men assigned her.

Winifred had traveled the length of the country in an attempt to dispell the very notion of taking up the role of her "place." And now, this stranger thought to tell her what she should and shouldn't be doing?

How dare he?

One would think that an educated man wouldn't hold to such outmoded thinking. One would hope that an education would open one's mind to the limitless possibilities available to one. Winifred frowned at him. Obviously though, a fine education was completely wasted on some people.

She took a step closer, tilted her chin up and said "A woman's place? And who would be teaching me that place? You?"

The gambler lowered his gaze a fraction. Just enough to spear her with his hard, dark stare. It was a look designed to intimidate.

It failed miserably.

She glared right back at him. "A woman's *place,* sir, is anywhere she chooses to make it."

A brief spatter of applause, followed by a lone woman's voice calling out, "You tell 'im, honey," filled the sudden silence.

Winifred ignored the other women. She was too busy concentrating on the stunned expression of the man in front of her.

"As to my . . . husband," she went on, hardly stumbling on the lie, "he wouldn't *think* of ordering me about—"

"Winifred," Quinn interrupted, "get out of the way!"

"Except of course," she went right on, "to ensure my safety. How dare you think to tell me what my place is!" She paused to draw a breath then and took note of what an effect her tirade was having on the man.

The gambler was furious. His tall, angular body fairly quaked with the anger glinting in his eyes. He stared down at Winifred, clearly appalled that a woman would have the temerity to chastise him.

If she'd been quicker, if she'd had the slightest idea of how the man would react, she would have leapt out of range and it might not have happened. As it was though, she wasn't expecting such a lightning like response.

With a smooth, quick motion, the gambler reached out and slapped her. Hard.

Even before tears could well up in her eyes, Quinn was pushing past her, a low snarl of rage rumbling from his throat.

Quinn's fist smashed into the gambler's jaw and a flash of satisfaction shot through him. But it wasn't enough. Not nearly enough. The other man staggered, regained his footing then swung his right fist in a roundhouse punch that Quinn ducked just before slamming his own fist into the gambler's unprotected stomach. Air rushed from the man's lungs and he doubled over.

Quinn sucked in a quick breath and blew it out again

when his opponent tackled him, slamming one shoulder into Quinn's stomach. Their momentum carried them back until they crashed into a rickety table that splintered under their combined weight.

Except for an occasional shout of encouragement from the spectators, the saloon was ominously silent but for the solid thumps of the blows being delivered. Fists and feet flew in a furious assault as each man did his best to cripple the other.

Quinn's rage gave him the upper hand, but the deceptively slim gambler was a much stronger man than he looked. When he slipped under Quinn's right and delivered an uppercut to his chin, Quinn saw stars. He shook his head, trying desperately to clear his vision and stop the ringing in his ears. Then his opponent hooked one foot around Quinn's ankle and yanked him off his feet. Quinn went down hard, slamming onto the dirty floor, smacking the back of his head against the pine planks. The gambler stood over him, right foot drawn back, preparing to kick him in the ribs.

Quinn looked up into the gambler's lean, sharp featured face and felt another powerful surge of anger shoot renewed strength into his arms and legs. Once again, Quinn saw the man slap Winifred. He saw her eyes wide with sudden pain and shock. He remembered the satisfied smile on the gambler's face after he hit her and then a blinding haze of red dropped over his eyes and all Quinn knew was that he wanted to slam that bastard into the ground.

The gambler kicked, but Quinn rolled to the left and leapt to his feet. Chairs toppled and men jumped out of the way as the fight went on.

The two men circled each other warily. Quinn's vision was blurred and he blinked furiously. A flash of color darted close and he risked a quick glance to one side. Winifred. He tried to ignore her presence and concentrate on Tucker. But from the corner of his eye, he could still see her, jumping up and down in nervous, desperate bursts. The sunflower on her hat bobbed up and down like a skinny man's Adam's apple.

Dammit, he yelled silently, why didn't she move back to safety and leave this to him?

Tucker stepped in and took a swing at him. Quinn ducked and stepped to one side. He heard Winifred muttering and knew that she'd never leave until this fight was over. Fine then, he told himself. Best to get it done with fast.

Quinn charged the other man and threw two quick, hard jabs his chin. The man's head snapped back and he staggered slightly. Reaching down, Tucker's fingers curled around a nearby slat backed chair. He lifted it high and sent it flying into Quinn.

Winifred screamed and as he raised his left arm to knock the chair aside, Quinn tried to ignore her. He had to concentrate. He had to win that fight. If he didn't, Winifred would be left to deal with Tucker on her own. He couldn't count on anyone in that tiny town coming to her defense.

Tired, blood streaming from a cut above his right eye, Quinn walked in to meet the other man. The gambler looked as beaten as Quinn felt. One of his dark eyes was swollen shut and his lip was split. His fine, dark suit was ripped and torn and blood stained the pristine white fabric of his shirt.

And still he hadn't suffered enough for striking Winifred.

Just beyond Tucker's shoulder, Quinn caught a glimpse of Winifred. Beneath the drooping brim of her hat, her green eyes were wide, frightened. And her left cheek was branded with a rose red palm print. Quinn swallowed heavily, grit his teeth and moved in to finish the man who'd hurt her.

As the two men closed in on each other, they struggled in an awkward, stumbling embrace. One after the other, they punched at each other and even as Quinn felt the gambler weaken, he knew that he too, was fading fast.

Dogged determination forced Quinn to pull his head back suddenly and slam his forehead into the other man's. The gambler's eyes rolled and he stumbled backward, dragging Quinn with him. If he hadn't been so blasted tired, Quinn would have smiled. He'd done it, he thought. One more punch and the man was finished.

Then a crashing blow came down on the back of Quinn's head and the world went black.

"Who are you?" Mercy said, her voice even despite her nervousness.

"You Mercy Hawkins?"

"Didn't ask who *I* was," she snapped and raised the double-barreled shotgun to point it at the center of the stranger's broad chest. "I asked who *you* are."

The big man standing on her front porch took a step back and lifted both hands, palms toward her. "Take it easy, lady. I don't mean you any harm."

"Not with a shotgun aimed at you, you don't." Mercy stepped through the open doorway onto the porch. Her fingers rested lightly on the twin triggers and she saw that the man had noticed exactly how ready she was to fire. She kept the barrel of her gun close enough to his chest to be intimidating, but not close enough that he could reach out and snatch her weapon from her.

The big man took another careful step back and looked away from the trigger guards to meet her gaze steadily. His eyes were gray and calm. He had a square, firm jaw and a nose that looked as if it had been broken a time or two. Short, dark brown hair peeked out from under a dirt-brown, flat-brimmed hat and his plain white shirt and black vest looked to be straining to cover the heavily muscled expanse of his chest and shoulders. There was a well cared for pistol strapped to his narrow hips and his black jeans were covered with a fine layer of trail dust.

He stood still and silent for her inspection and Mercy gave him credit for that. Most men wouldn't behave so well even with a gun trained on them. And a fine thing it was, she thought, having to answer her own front door holding a gun.

But, with her hired hands somewhere out checking the fence lines, Mercy was all alone at the house except for the cook. And he was almost blind and deaf as a post. She couldn't afford to be careless with strangers. Not since Bentley had served her a notice to get out. Even though she still had two weeks left, it would be just like the no good son-of-something-or-other to send one of his men out to the ranch to chase her off early.

But, if that was Bentley's plan, he'd have to send more than one man . . . no matter how big he was.

"I'd breathe a lot easier if you'd take your fingers off the triggers, ma'am," he said softly.

"I breathe easier this way." Mercy frowned at him. "You still haven't told me who you are, mister."

"The name's Barry. Jim Barry."

"Don't know you."

"No reason why you should."

"You work for Bentley?" she asked even though she knew it was pointless. If he did, he certainly wouldn't admit it. And if he didn't, how was she supposed to believe him?

"No ma'am." He slowly moved his right hand toward his vest. "I don't."

"Careful, mister."

He smiled. A wide, friendly smile that sent something in Mercy's chest skittering.

"Ma'am, I am always careful around a beautiful woman." He nodded. "Especially when she's holdin' a gun on me."

The creases in his sun-browned skin deepened with his grin and Mercy saw that he was a man used to smiling. Still, that didn't prove a damn thing. She'd heard that even Jesse James had a sense of humor.

"Mrs. Hawkins," Barry sighed, "if you let me get something out of my vest pocket, it'll tell you who I am and you'll see that gun ain't necessary."

Mercy's mind raced. One of two things would happen. He would show her something that would indeed tell her who he was and why he was at her ranch . . . or he would try for a small hide out gun and she'd have to kill him. Right there on her own front porch.

And it would be a damned shame to kill a man that good looking.

"All right," she finally nodded and inhaled deeply. "But before you do, you remember to be careful. My fingers are gettin' mighty tired."

He winced slightly, then smiled again. "Ma'am, like I told you, I am always careful around beautiful women."

Mercy flushed.

Reaching into his inside vest pocket, Jim Barry drew out a single sheet of paper, folded neatly. As his fingers smoothed the paper out, he said quietly, "Just take a look at this, Mrs. Hawkins. Then we'll talk."

Still wary, but more curious than she wanted to admit, Mercy stretched out her left hand for the paper. Keeping a cautious eye on the man, she glanced down at the wanted poster. As she read it, she slowly let the shotgun barrel dip until it was pointed safely at the floor.

She pulled in a deep breath and raised her gaze to meet Jim Barry's. That wide grin of his was still in place and Mercy found herself smiling back at him. Clutching the paper tightly, she shifted the shotgun to the crook of her left arm and stuck out her right hand. "Mister Barry, I am pleased as pie to meet you!"

His big hand enveloped hers and held it a bit longer than necessary before releasing it again. "Call me Jim, Mrs. Hawkins."

Mercy's hand tingled from his touch and that skittering, fluttery feeling inside her quickened until it was difficult to draw a steady breath. Somehow though, she found voice enough to say, "My name's Mercy, Jim. Why don't we step inside and have some coffee?"

"I'd like that fine . . . Mercy," he said and stepped up to open the front door for her.

Winifred let the faded, threadbare curtain drop back into place then sneezed at the resulting cloud of dust. Turning her head, she looked hopefully at the man stretched out on the bed behind her. But he hadn't moved.

It had been centuries. *Eons* since the fight downstairs and still he didn't wake. He didn't blink. He didn't even groan and mutter her name as all proper heroes did when unconscious.

For the hundredth time, Winifred paced the length of the room, counting as she went. Twenty steps from the corner to the door, ten to the bed, five more to the window and back again. If she'd been walking in a straight line, she'd have been back home in Maine by now.

Chewing at her bottom lip, Winifred kept walking until she'd reached the closed door. Quietly, she turned the knob, poked her head out into the short hallway and listened. No sound of approaching footsteps. No sound at all, but for the muted conversations drifting up the stairs from the saloon below.

Sighing, she closed the door again, turned around and leaned back against it while she stared at the man on the bed. She would have thought that the bartender would have been quicker with the water and whiskey she'd requested. How in heaven could she take proper care of Quinn if she lacked the necessary equipment?

As if in answer to her thoughts, she heard someone coming. She leapt away from the door, turned the knob and threw it wide.

The bartender jumped back a pace and when she waved him in, he walked past her cautiously, keeping as much distance between them as possible.

Winifred was right behind him though and when he set his burdens down on a small, lopsided table at the side of the bed, she was already looking over what he'd brought.

A pitcher of fresh water, two glasses and a bottle of whiskey. He plucked two clean towels off his shoulder and handed them to her wordlessly.

"And our things? On our horses?"

"One of the boys is gettin' 'em. He'll take your animals to the livery. They'll be safe there till you're ready to leave."

"Thank you very much," Winifred started and took a step forward.

The bartender skipped back a step or two.

Winifred's eyebrows shot straight up. Really, the man was very agile for someone of his size. He was already backing toward the door, his gaze locked on her when she stopped him with a question.

"What about the other man? Mr. Tucker?"

"What about him?"

"Is he all right?"

"He will be, I reckon—when he wakes up."

"Oh, good." That was a relief. Though she was happy that the gambler was in no position to cause them any further trouble, Winifred really wouldn't wish him any permanent harm. Although, she thought at almost the same instant, if he should awaken before Quinn, the man might very well be holding a grudge strong enough for him to cause trouble. "I hate to be a bother," she said quickly since the bartender was now halfway out the door, "but would you mind very much alerting me as to when the man awakens?"

"Huh?" His brow furrowed, the man looked eager to be on his way.

"Will you let me know when the man wakes up? I should hate for the trouble to begin again, you know."

The man actually shuddered.

"Don't worry about him lady," he said. "Just you get your man waked up and the hell outa here. We'll keep the other one locked up in a cell till you're outa town."

"Well," she smiled at him, "I must say, that's very thoughtful of you."

"Yeah."

"I'm quite sure Quinn, my husband that is, will appreciate your help as well." She threw the unconscious man a quick look, "When he wakes up."

"Uh-huh." He started drawing the door closed slowly.

"One more thing," she called out and heard the bartender heave a sigh.

"What?"

"How long do you suppose he will be unconscious? It seems to have lasted forever already."

"It's only been about twenty minutes or so, lady."

"Really?" She crossed her arms over her chest and hugged herself tightly. "It seems much longer than that." Letting her gaze stray to where Quinn lay, she added "He *is* all right, don't you think?"

"Breathin', ain't he?"

"Well yes, but . . ."

"Then just wait him out. Gettin' hit on the head with a whiskey bottle ain't no small thing, y'know."

She winced.

The door closed before she could say anything else and once more, Winifred was surrounded by silence. The only sound in the room was Quinn's deep, steady breathing. She watched his chest rise and fall and told herself that she should be counting her blessings. After all, that fight downstairs might have ended much worse than it had.

Determinedly, she walked to the side of the bed and perched on the edge. The ropes beneath the mattress groaned a protest, but Quinn didn't even flutter an eyelash.

He looked so pale. Except of course for the bruises blossoming into color around his eyes. Dried blood caked on his cheek and chin from small cuts and scratches and his sweat and whiskey-soaked blond hair lay across his forehead. Winifred reached out, smoothed his hair back off his face and frowned guiltily when she saw a huge knot building in the center of his forehead.

This was all her fault, she knew. If she'd stayed with Quinn as he'd asked her to, that terrible Mr. Tucker would never have seen her and Quinn wouldn't be lying here, hurt and unconscious.

She sighed, picked up one of the clean towels and clasped it tightly in her hands. Looking down at Quinn, she leaned in closer and told him "I *am* sorry, you know. I never meant for this to happen."

He gave no sign that he'd heard her. But somehow, telling him what she was feeling made Winifred feel better.

As she talked, she picked up the pitcher and splashed some fresh water into the chipped washbowl. "I was so worried about you, Quinn. You looked very tired and that dreadful man kept hitting you." She dipped the corner of the towel into the water and wrung it out. "Every time you groaned, I felt the pain with you. It was simply more than I could bear."

Carefully, she smoothed the damp towel across his battered features, wiping away the blood and grime. "I know it's hard to believe, considering how things ended," she said and blinked back the dampness filling her eyes. "But I truly thought I was helping."

Why didn't he wake up? Why didn't he open his eyes and tell her he understood? That everything was all right. That he didn't blame her.

Her hands fell to her lap and her chin dropped to her chest. Winifred sniffled, wiped her nose on the edge of the towel and looked back at Quinn, so still. So silent.

"Will you please wake up? Surely you've been insensible long enough."

She leaned over him until her lips were just a breath away from his. Gently, Winifred kissed him and almost wept at the lack of response. Shifting position slightly, she rested her head on his chest as carefully as she could and listened to the reassuring beat of his heart.

Closing her eyes, she whispered "I was aiming for Mr. Tucker. If you hadn't moved so suddenly, I never would have hit you with that liquor bottle."

12

It wasn't much. Just a small circle of stones with an even smaller pile of dead ashes lying in the center. Off about fifty feet was a narrow stand of cottonwoods and in the stillness, they could hear the rush of water over rocks from the nearby creek.

"How long ago do ya figure?" Dusty asked and kicked at the ashes with the toe of his boot.

"I don't know," Tom shrugged, squatted down and tipped his hat to the back of his head, "a day, day and a half. Hell, you're part Indian. Don't you know?"

Dusty grinned. "If I did, I'm startin' to think I wouldn't be tellin' you."

Tom looked up at his friend and frowned. "You're followin' him too. It ain't just me. Hell, you're the one who found this campsite."

"I just want Sadie back," Dusty pointed out. "I ain't the one tryin' to lock Quinn Hawkins up in jail."

Tom sighed, put his palms on his thighs and pushed himself to his feet. "Do we have to argue about this every damned day?"

"Maybe." Dusty folded his arms across his chest and squinted against the morning sunlight. "If that's what it's gonna take to make you change your mind."

Tom shook his head, pulled the brim of his hat down to shade his eyes and walked to his horse, picketed nearby. "That's not goin' to happen, Dusty. I've got a job to do and I'm goin' to do it." Rustling through his saddlebags, Tom pulled out a battered tin coffee pot, glanced over his shoulder and tossed the pot to Dusty. "Go get some water from the creek. We'll have some coffee and give the horses a breather before goin' on."

The other man caught the coffee pot one handed and half turned toward the creek. "Seems mighty strange to me," he muttered, "that you're chasin' after the very same man who helped you get the town sheriff job. Wonder if ol' Quinn's regrettin' what he did for you."

Tom's teeth ground together in helpless frustration. Squatting down again, he reached out and gathered up a few of the twigs scattered across the ground. Piling them in the center of the ashes left from Quinn's fire, Tom struck a match and held it until the tinder caught. At the first flicker of flames, Tom fed the tiny blaze until he had a strong enough fire to boil coffee and fry up some bacon.

Staring down into the flames as they danced and dipped in the wind, Tom thought about what Dusty'd said. Though it pained him to admit it, his friend was right. If it hadn't been for Quinn Hawkins, Tom might not be the sheriff of Yellow Dog.

Smiling to himself at the memory, Tom recalled how Quinn had ridden his horse damn near into the ground on election day. Him and that gray of his had stopped at every farm and ranch for miles around, telling folks to get into town to vote for Tom. Quinn had done more campaigning than a drunk politician from Washington, D.C.

And when the voting was over and Tom Bruner was the new sheriff, it was Quinn Hawkins who'd bought him the first drink to celebrate.

Dammit. Tom lifted his head and stared off into the distance. Somewhere out there, his oldest friend was running from him. And by God, Tom hoped to hell he ran fast enough to get away. Because locking Quinn up would be the hardest thing he'd ever have to do.

The first thing he noticed was the pain.

With his eyes closed, Quinn lay perfectly still and drew a long, measured breath. Yep. It hurt to breathe. But not as bad as it would if his ribs were broken. That was something. Both hands felt as though they'd been stomped and a throbbing, pulsing ache pounded in his head. Still and all, he'd been hurt a helluva lot worse than this lots of times.

His mouth and throat dry, Quinn couldn't remember wanting a drink as bad as he did at that moment. But there was a weight on his chest, successfully keeping him from moving.

Carefully, he opened one eye and for a moment, wondered why the other one wasn't cooperating. Then he remembered that it was probably swollen shut. Shifting his narrowed line of vision to his chest, Quinn saw the top of Fred's head resting just beneath his chin. She didn't stir and Quinn figured she must have fallen asleep.

Glancing from the corner of his good eye at the bedside table, he saw a pitcher, bowl . . . and a bottle of whiskey.

His lips twisted into a painful, half-smile. Now that, he thought, was right thoughtful of whoever'd brought it. He looked down again at Fred and carefully lifted his right hand. Reaching out, he tried to snag the liquor bottle, but it was just out of range.

Frustrated, a low groan rumbled from his throat.

Winifred stirred, mumbled something unintelligible and rubbed her cheek against his bare chest as if trying to fluff up a pillow.

Desire ricocheted through Quinn's body, making his heart pound, his blood race and his groin tighten. He squeezed his good eye shut and tried to ignore the feelings grabbing at him. "It ain't easy though, Lord," he whispered and was immediately sorry he'd spoken at all.

At the sound of his voice, Winifred woke and jerked up from his chest. The top of her head clipped him on the chin, snapping his teeth together and setting the ache in his head into a triple time march.

"Jesus!"

"Oh, I'm so sorry, Quinn," she said and her fingers cupped his cheek tenderly. "Did I hurt you? Oh, of course I did or you wouldn't have cried out."

"I'm all right," he managed to say and opened his good eye again to look up at her.

She leaned in over him, her hair streaming down on either side of her face, the ends of the long, red tendrils tickling his chest.

"You look dreadful."

"Thanks."

"I mean, your bruises. And your lip is split," she pointed out and touched the tip of her finger to the corner of his mouth.

Quinn's breath caught and he had to force himself to breathe again. His lip didn't hurt any, but her touch was enough to break him. When he finally felt as though he could talk without his voice shaking, he asked, "Can I have something to drink?"

"Oh!" She sat up quickly, grabbed the pitcher and poured some water into a waiting glass. Then she slid one hand under his head and held the glass to his lips.

"Careful, now," she warned him then tipped the glass up, spilling cold water down his throat and chest.

He inhaled sharply, jerked his head back and pushed himself slowly into a sitting position, his back braced against the wall behind him. Rivulets of water rolled down his flesh to soak into the sheet beneath him.

"I'm sorry," she said and grudgingly handed him the water glass. "I was only trying to help."

"I know," Quinn assured her and told himself that if he didn't get his own drink, she'd surely drown him. He winced, leaned over and poured the remaining water in the glass into the washbowl. Then his fingers curled around the neck of the whiskey bottle.

"I don't believe one is supposed to drink liquor when one has a head injury." Winifred told him, a slight frown on her face.

"I think that is when one needs liquor most." Quinn argued. Pulling the cork free with his teeth, he splashed a generous measure of the amber liquid into his glass, then set the bottle on the mattress beside him.

After his first swallow, as the whiskey's fire snaked through his bloodstream, Quinn smiled to himself. He must look a lot worse than he felt. Actually, now that he was sitting up, the world was looking quite a bit friendlier. Why he didn't even hurt as bad as he had the time he'd been thrown from Dusty's stallion.

Pushing thoughts of his friend aside, he glanced at the window across the room. Outside, the light was fading into dusk and he frowned thoughtfully. He took another quick drink, stared at Winifred and asked "How long have I been out?"

"Oh, hours," she told him and picked up the whiskey bottle. Setting it down on the far edge of the bedside table, she turned back to him and clasped her hands in her lap. "I was so worried. You didn't move. You didn't make a sound."

"Hours?" he repeated and pushed one scraped up hand through his hair.

"Yes, I was beginning to wonder if you'd ever wake up."

He shot her a quick look. She sounded as though he'd done it on purpose. Well hell, it was hardly his fault if the gambler'd gotten in a lucky swing. Although, Quinn recalled clearly the moment his opponent's eyes had rolled up in his head. Hmmph. He'd thought for sure, he'd put the man out that time.

"I guess ol' Tucker hits a good bit harder than I thought he could," he said, as much as it galled him to admit that the gambler had knocked him out.

"Yes, well . . ."

Winifred stood up, walked to the window and pulled the flimsy, nearly rotted curtains aside.

"What is it, Fred?"

What else had happened while he was unconscious? Was there a guard outside that room? Had Tom caught up to them? Or had Winifred told the townspeople about being Quinn's hostage and asked for their help?

Dammit! Supplies or no supplies, they should have never come to that blasted town.

"Well," he said and his voice scraped against his throat. He swallowed the rest of the whiskey in one long gulp and waited for her to tell him that *he* was the prisoner now. "Spit it out," he snapped. "Who's outside that door?"

She turned and gaped at him, confusion stamped on her features as clearly as the worry lines etched between her eyebrows.

"You heard me," Quinn went on, letting the anger carry him on. His ill temper fed on itself and grew in amazing proportions. Mad at everything and everybody, Quinn mostly was mad at himself, for even caring that Winifred had turned him in. "Did you get a reward? Or is that waitin' on you at Yellow Dog?"

She dropped the curtains, stepped to the foot of the bed and curled her fingers around the narrow, iron foot rail. Tilting her head to one side, she asked, "What are you talking about?"

"Hah!" Quinn leaned over, grunted when his sore body protested the sudden movement, and grabbed the whiskey bottle. As he poured more liquor into his glass, he tossed her a quick, disgusted look, took a long swallow, then said, "Shoulda known better than to take you at your word. Shoulda figured that you'd take the first chance you had to turn me in."

Twirling the glass in his hand, he stared at the golden liquid and tried not to think about how much it hurt that she had turned him in. He'd come to care for her and knowing that she'd betrayed him cut him more deeply than he'd thought possible.

Betray? He frowned at the word. Was it really a betrayal for a hostage to try to set herself free? What right did he have to ask for her loyalty? Hadn't he stolen her right off the street? Dammit, she wasn't his woman. She was his prisoner. Or rather, he added mentally, she *used* to be.

Now though, the tables were turned. Then again, he thought as he recalled the flash of rage he'd felt when that gambler had struck her, maybe things had changed awhile ago and he just hadn't noticed.

He sighed, set the glass of whiskey down on the table and rested the back of his head against the wall. Staring up at her, he finally said softly, "Hell, Fred. It ain't your fault. You just did what you had to do."

"I haven't *done* anything," she told him and tightened her grip on the iron bedstead.

He saw her knuckles whiten and nodded, "Reckon you're right. It was me who done it. First the bank . . . then you." He closed his eye and added, "Why don't you go on now and send in the sheriff?"

Long, silent minutes passed. He kept waiting to hear the heels of her shoes as she hurried across the floor to freedom. But nothing happened. In the strained silence, Quinn could hear the muted noise from the saloon downstairs and the creak of a passing wagon outside. A halfhearted breeze skirted under the partially opened window and drifted across his naked chest and Quinn idly wondered if there would be many soft winds blowing through prison.

"Have you quite finished?" Winifred finally asked and he heard the strain in her voice.

He lifted that one good eyelid again and looked at her. Her green eyes dancing with anger, her chest moved rapidly with her quick, short breaths.

"Huh?"

"Quinn Hawkins," she said stiffly, "you insult me."

"What?" He lifted his head, ignored the ache and concentrated on her.

"That you would presume that I would break my word to you is most disheartening."

He squinted at her. Either his head was hurting even more than he'd thought, or she wasn't making any sense at all.

"Did I or did I not give you my word that I would not betray you?"

"Well, yeah . . ."

"And have I yet given you reason to doubt that I am a woman of my word?"

"No, but . . ."

"And when you awakened, were there manacles on your wrists?"

"Not yet . . ."

"To think that I was worried about you!"

"Listen Fred . . ."

"No," she countered quickly, shaking one finger at him. "*You* listen!" Coming around the side of the bed,

Winifred didn't stop until she was right alongside him. Then, hands at her hips, she leaned over him until he had to tilt his head back just to meet her fire-eating gaze.

"I begged you not to fight that man, didn't I?"

"Yeah . . ."

"Then when you fought anyway, I stayed right there, didn't I?"

He remembered seeing her, just out of range, jumping up and down like a scalded cat.

"Sure, but . . ."

"And when, with my help the fight was over," she inhaled sharply. "I stayed right here with you, watching over you. Didn't I?"

"Appears that way, true . . ." Of course, he had no way of knowing that for sure. And what did she mean— her *help?*

"I hovered over you, watching and waiting for a sign, anything that would tell me you would be all right." She snorted inelegantly "And you didn't even have the decency to moan my name!"

"Moan your name?"

"Everyone knows that when a man is unconscious, he inevitably moans or whispers the name of the woman he—" she broke off suddenly, then started again. "Marshal Travis always says his beloved's name."

"Beloved?"

She flushed.

That durn Marshal Travis again. Hell, even when he was sleeping, Quinn was in trouble because of that fella.

"I cried and prayed and fretted over you until I wore myself out."

She did? A slow curl of pleasure erupted in his chest and Quinn had to fight to keep a smile off his face.

"Why, I was finally so exhausted," she pointed down at him, "I fell asleep on your chest!"

"True . . ." There went that pleasurable feeling again.

He could still recall the sensation of having her cheek resting against his naked flesh. It was something he'd like to try again.

"Then when you finally awaken, you pour whiskey down your throat and call me a Judas!"

"Now Fred . . ." he stared up into her wide, hurt-filled eyes and felt like a low down, belly-crawling, no good son-of-a-snake.

"Not so much as a thank you," she added, shaking her head furiously, "or even an 'I'm sorry I worried you Winifred'."

"Well, you didn't give me a chance, now," he said, trying to calm her down. For the life of him though, Quinn couldn't figure out how he came to be apologizing to her.

"I thought you knew me better than that, Quinn Hawkins." Tears welled up in her eyes and spilled over to run down her cheeks in tiny rivulets. She brushed them away with angry strokes. "But apparently, I was mistaken."

"Fred," he said and reached for one of her hands. She tried to pull away, but his fingers tightened around hers determinedly. His thumb moved over her fingers in soothing strokes and when he tugged gently on her hand, she sat down beside him on the bed.

She lifted her chin defiantly and Quinn felt a flash of admiration for her. Hurt, her pride stung and a fool man accusing her of all sorts of things, she still managed to look undefeatable.

Winifred Matthews was some kind of woman.

Quinn let his hand slide up her arm until he could cup her cheek with his palm. Tenderly, he rubbed away the last of her tears and said, "I'm sorry, Fred. I didn't trust you. I was wrong."

She looked into his eyes and Quinn's gaze met hers. There was so much to see in her green eyes. So much, in fact, if he had years to stare into her eyes, it wouldn't be long enough. His eyes drifted over her, from the wild red tangle of her hair, to the sprinkling of freckles across her nose to her teeth tugging at her bottom lip.

When had this woman become so important to him? And why did he have to find her at the one time in his life when he couldn't do anything about it?

She fidgeted under his thoughtful gaze and reached up to try to smooth her hair down into submission. "I know I look dreadful," she whispered and broke off when he caught her hand in his.

"No ma'am," he said and straightened up away from the wall. "You look . . . perfect."

Her tongue darted out to lick her lips and Quinn almost groaned with need. Sliding his arms around her, he pulled her across his lap and held her close. Her head cradled in the crook of his elbow, Quinn smoothed his right hand down the line of her jaw, wondering at the feel of her soft skin.

She turned her head into his hand and Quinn lost his last battle for control. Minor aches and pains forgotten, he dipped his head low and slanted his mouth across hers. Her lips parted for him and when his tongue invaded her warmth, she reached up and wrapped her arms around his neck.

Her fingers moved across his naked back and Quinn lost himself in the feel of her. Her mouth teased him and welcomed him. Her palms brushed across his skin, leaving a trail of fire that seeped into his bones and threatened to consume him.

He couldn't get enough of her. Couldn't taste her enough. Couldn't hold her closely enough.

Winifred arched against him and wordlessly told him how much she wanted his touch. His tongue darted in and out of her mouth and each warm, damp stroke seemed to slice into her soul.

The muscles in his arms and back flexed with his every movement and his flesh seemed to ripple beneath her hands. His breath brushed her cheeks and the wicked, heady scent of whiskey surrounded her. His mouth left hers and began to trail kisses along the length of her throat. His moustache scraped against her tender flesh and its bristly feel blended with the tenderness of his lips. Goosebumps marched along her spine in response.

His hand dipped down to cup her breast and Winifred gasped.

"It's all right, darlin'," he whispered and stroked her hardened nipple with the side of his thumb.

Something incredible was happening.

Winifred shifted uneasily in his grasp and squeezed her thighs together. A damp warmth centered itself between her legs and with every touch of his thumb to her nipple, the odd sensation blossomed and grew.

She felt him move to unbutton her shirtfront and knew she should say something to stop him. First one button then another sprang free under his nimble fingers and still, Winifred's mind screamed at her to stop him. But she didn't say a word. She couldn't.

Her throat was tight, clogged with too many emotions to name. Breathing was difficult and the warmth in her center was spreading up to her abdomen, making a curl of excitement dance through her body.

The rest of her buttons were soon undone and she squeezed her eyes shut in embarrassment.

He chuckled softly, left a tender kiss on her lips and then whispered, "Look at me, Winifred."

She licked her lips, swallowed heavily and forced herself to open her eyes. She stared up into his lake blue gaze and saw her own desire mirrored there.

As they stared at each other, Quinn brushed the edges of her shirt apart and laid the palm of his hand atop her breast. Through the thin cotton fabric of her chemise, she felt his warmth—and something more. Her own body's heat matched his and she felt as though she might burst into flames at any moment.

Moving the flat of his palm in a slow, sensuous circle over her nipple, he told her, "I won't touch you if you don't want me too."

There it was. Her chance.

She swallowed again and unconsciously arched her breast into his touch. It felt so good. So right. So incredibly wonderful. She had to have more.

Threading the fingers of her right hand into his hair, Winifred let her left hand slide from his shoulder to his chest. Brushing across the sprinkle of golden hairs on his skin, she smiled when his breath caught and his head fell back on his neck.

A heady, powerful feeling swept through her. It wasn't only she who was experiencing the wild sensations created by their touching. Quinn, too was moved.

She licked her lips again and hoped her voice would work as she said, "Don't stop, Quinn."

He held her tighter, lifted his head and smiled gently down at her. Then slowly, his fingers tugged her chemise aside and bared her breast to his view.

Winifred blushed and fought down the urge to cover herself.

Quinn seemed to sense what she was thinking because he shifted his gaze from her breast to look deeply into her eyes. "You're beautiful," he said and Winifred almost wept at the touch of awe in his voice.

Unable now to look away, she watched him as he bent his head and took her nipple into his mouth. She gasped again, this time with pleasure.

She'd had no idea!

Why would she? Winifred had known that a woman's nipples were a means of feeding her children. She hadn's thought that a man could suckle at them, too?

Mesmerized by the sight of Quinn Hawkins's mouth at her breast, she watched his tongue dance a slow circle around her erect nipple. He teased and toyed with the small pink nub until her thoughts fled and Winifred was twisting and writhing in his grasp. Her left hand cupped the back of his head and held him to her, hoping for something more, though she couldn't have said just what.

In response to her unspoken need, Quinn's lips closed over her nipple and he began to suckle her gently. Something deep inside her snapped and Winifred thought that it was probably what little will she had left, splintering. What was more, she didn't care.

His talented mouth tugged and pulled at her nipple while his right hand slipped down her rib cage, over her hips and down the length of her drawn-up leg. When he lifted the hem of her skirt and smoothed his palm up her calf to her thigh, Winifred sighed and arched into his mouth again.

She felt his smile against her breast and didn't care if she was being a wanton. It was all so wonderful. So good. She wanted to feel more. To experience more. She wanted the warmth in her abdomen to spread until it encompassed her entire body and the two of them burst into flames together.

Quinn lifted his head and before she could moan a protest, he had begun lavishing his attentions on her other breast. And the sensations began again.

His right hand continued on its quest and slid down her pantaloon clad thigh to the very center of her need. While his lips caressed her nipple, his hand cupped the junction of her thighs and Winifred almost shot out of his arms.

"Easy," he crooned and lifted his head again to kiss her gently.

"Quinn, I . . ." she tossed her head from side to side and lifted her hips in a most unseemly fashion. "Something is happening and I don't know . . ."

"Shhh . . ." he said softly and kissed her closed eyelids, then the tip of her nose and finally placed another quick kiss on her dry lips. "It's all right, Fred. I have you."

"But what is it?" she gasped and opened her eyes to look up at him. "What are you doing?"

His palm covered her heat and she felt her body move against him. She didn't remember moving. But once she had, she realized how good it felt and did it again.

"Something is wrong," she said breathlessly, "down . . . *there.*"

"Nothin's wrong," he assured her and bent to touch the tip of his tongue to her nipple.

She shuddered. "Yes. I've never felt like this before. It's . . ."

"Good?" he asked.

"Yes, but . . ."

"Shh," Quinn told her. "Don't talk, Fred. Don't think. Just feel."

And as he finished speaking, his thumb moved over a particularly sensitive piece of flesh and Winifred's thighs parted for him.

Her right hand clutched at his shoulder, her short, neat fingernails dug into his flesh. Something was happening to her. She felt as though she was climbing a mountain. A steep, hard climb. Everything in her stretched for the top, straining, trying to reach something she hadn't known existed until a moment ago.

Now, it was the most important thing in the world to her. She had to know. She had to find an end to this constantly escalating need.

Her hips moved of their own accord and she felt Quinn's fingers begin to move more quickly. The dampness began to spread and her thighs quivered as she strained against him.

"Quinn," she gasped, "help me. Something's happening . . ."

"Hold onto me, Fred," he said and his breath caressed her face.

He gathered her close with his left hand, cradling her against his chest. His right hand continued to intimately stroke her and Winifred buried her face in the curve of his neck.

She gave herself up with abandon. Hips moving in time with his caresses, Winifred gasped for air, clutched him tightly and rode the crest of sensation that carried her, at last, to the other side of the mountain.

Aching, throbbing release pulsed through her and Winifred heard herself shout, "Quinn!" just before her body shattered in his hands.

13

"*So how come you're* just settin' around here eatin' up my cookies?" Erma demanded. "Why ain't you over to the bank throwin' a loop over that no good?"

Mercy sighed, leaned her head back against Erma's horsehair sofa and stared up at a cobweb swinging from the ceiling. The filmy string of dust shimmied and swayed in the slight breeze from the open window and Mercy caught a whiff of rain on the wind. A storm coming soon, she told herself and wondered idly what it would be this time.

Rain? Snow? Hail?

Tornado?

Springtime in Texas meant one thing. Don't count on the weather.

Erma snorted derisively and successfully splintered Mercy's thoughts. It was just as well. Trying to think about the weather wasn't doing her any good. She wasn't fooling anyone, least of all herself.

She was worried about her son. Dammit, when did it end? When was a body able to say, "He's grown up now and on his own."? Quinn was thirty-two years old and still she wanted to race out after him. Protect him.

Hah. Mercy laughed silently. Her son hadn't let her protect him since he was a boy. He'd always been the type to succeed or fail on his own. Hell, he'd been doing a man's job on the ranch since he was twelve years old. And he'd be purely humiliated if he knew that his mother was running all over creation trying to save his hide.

It just wasn't right though, a voice in the back of her mind shouted. This shouldn't be happening. She'd had everything so well thought out. The ranch was finally making money. Soon, their debt would have been paid off and Quinn could have found himself a wife.

And she, Mercy, could have gone out and found something for herself. She'd had no intention of living at the ranch forever. Mercy wanted her son to have his own family. To make his own memories. His own children. And she wasn't about to stick around the Hawkins ranch and be an always hanging around mother-in-law.

No. She had dreams too. Dreams that had been put aside years ago so that she could provide for her child. Well now, he was a grown man and she could finally pick up the threads of her dreams and get about the business of living before it was time to die.

At least, that had been the plan until Bentley showed up and ruined everything.

Mercy blinked, lifted her head and looked across the room at the big man talking to Erma. Jim Barry stood, one elbow propped on the mantel, one foot crossed over the other, the very image of nonchalance. But there was something in his eyes that told her he was not a man to cross.

She refused to acknowledge what else she saw in his eyes. After all, she was closing in on fifty years old. And that was far too old to be thinking what she was thinking.

Wasn't it?

"Mercy!"

She jumped, looked around and settled her gaze on Erma, who was staring at her as though she'd lost her mind. "What? What is it?"

"*Where* is it, you mean?"

"Huh?"

"Your mind, woman!" Erma leaned back in her rocker and set the old chair to swinging. "Where's your mind?"

Mercy glanced at Jim Barry, saw his amused smile and quickly looked away again. Staring at her old friend, Mercy fought down the urge to throttle the older woman. Thankfully, that urge only came on her once or twice a year.

"What were you saying, Erma?"

"I was sayin' to your friend here," she jerked her thumb at Barry, "that I still don't see why he just don't get himself over to the bank and do the right thing."

Well, Mercy couldn't blame her for that. The same question had leapt to her mind too, when faced with what Jim Barry had told her. "I thought he explained all that," she said.

"Oh, I did," Jim assured her and his deep voice sent a rumble of response down the length of Mercy's spine. "But your friend here," now he jerked a thumb at Erma, "doesn't agree."

"Damn right I don't, boy!"

Mercy hid a smile. Erma couldn't be more than five or ten years older than Jim Barry. For her to call him "boy" took quite a stretch of her imagination. Lord knew there was nothing about the man that was boyish.

"What's to keep ol' Bentley from hightailin' it outa town any damn time he chooses?"

"Me." Jim met the older woman's stare evenly. There wasn't a hint of brag in his simple statement, but both women knew he meant what he said and didn't doubt him a bit. "Like I said," he continued, "it's my job to keep an eye on him until the man who hired me shows up." Jim shrugged. "If he wants to be the one to personally slap Bentley in jail, he's payin' for the privilege."

"Hmmm . . ." Erma's rocker pitched back and forth like a ship in a storm. "I s'pose, with Tom away and all, there's nothin' else we can do, but wait."

"Erma," Mercy said flatly, "don't you think I want to march over there right now, snatch that thieving bastard out of his bed and drag him to jail myself?"

Jim Barry's eyebrows lifted at her language, but Mercy ignored it. She was too old to pretend airs she didn't have and never wanted.

"Yeah," Erma allowed, her rocker slowing just a bit, "I reckon you would at that."

"But now that I know Bentley's not goin' to get away with what he's been pullin' around here," Mercy folded her hands in her lap and made a concentrated effort to calm herself, "I can wait."

"Huh!" Erma snorted, stopped her rocker and stood up. "Yeah, Mercy, it's plain to everybody that you're the soul of patience."

Mercy grimaced. "I asked Jim . . . Mr. Barry to tell you what he told me earlier because I knew you were just as worried about Quinn as I was."

"He's a good boy."

Even Erma had a hard time remembering that Quinn was a grown man. Mercy shook her head. It was truly a sign of age to look at a thirty-two year old and call him a boy. And damned if Mercy didn't feel like Methuselah at the moment.

"What she hasn't said yet," Jim picked up Mercy's story and went on, "is that you can't tell anyone about Bentley. Not a single soul. I'm takin' Mercy's . . . Mrs. Hawkins's word for it that you're trustworthy."

"Hmmph!" Erma straightened up to her formidable height and inhaled until her abundant bosom looked like a well-built shelf. "Mister, I've kept more secrets in my life than you're ever likely to know."

"Good." He pushed away from the mantel, braced his hands at his hips and looked from one woman to the other. "Because if Bentley gets wind of anything, he'll disappear again. And who knows how long it'll be before we find him next time?"

"As you say," Erma nodded and started walking toward her kitchen. "Set down mister. I made a cake today and I reckon now's as good a time as any to dig into it."

The big woman left the room muttering to herself indignantly and Mercy held her breath as Jim Barry walked to the sofa and sat down beside her. A faint scent of soap, tobacco and man wafted up to enfold her and Mercy inched away. She hadn't had a man effect her like this in she couldn't remember how long.

Not even Quinn's daddy had made her feel so . . . special.

Quinn.

Her thoughts centered on her son and she sent a brief prayer toward heaven in the hope that it would protect Quinn. Hopefully, it would also keep him from doing anything else stupid.

If Jim Barry was right . . . and she'd seen the papers herself, than maybe Quinn wouldn't end up in prison for the rest of his life after all.

"Thinking about your son?"

She turned to look at Jim. A glimmer of sympathy shone in his eyes and just for a moment, Mercy wanted him to hold her. She wanted someone to pat her shoulder and murmur nonsensical words of reassurance. She wanted someone to take care of *her* for a change.

Then she felt it.

Jim Barry's hand covering hers. His fingers curled over her own and squeezed tightly. Without words, he offered his support. His warmth.

She returned the pressure of his fingers and slowly opened her eyes to look into his. The kindness, the tenderness she saw there was like a salve to her wounded soul. And when he smiled, the gaping emptiness inside her began to close.

Winifred lay like a rag doll across Quinn's lap. It was as if every bone in her body had melted. He smiled softly to himself. He envied her her release. His own body felt as taut as an Apache bow.

But at the same time, he wouldn't change a thing. He would never forget the expression of wonder on her face when her body convulsed with pleasure. And he knew that he would always be able to dredge up the memory of her shouting his name.

Slowly, Quinn withdrew his hand from her center and smoothed her skirt down over her legs. He moved to tug her chemise back into place, then stopped. The temptation was too great to resist. Dipping his head, he kissed her nipple and flicked at it gingerly with his tongue.

She moaned and shuddered in his arms.

Quinn smiled, and winced only slightly at the accompanying pain from his split lip. He tightened his hold on her then drew the cotton chemise up over her breasts.

A brisk, hard pounding on the closed door splintered their cocoon of silence and Winifred shot straight up in his lap. Turning her face into his shoulder, she tried to burrow inside him.

His arms closed protectively around her and he shouted "Who is it?"

"The bartender," a man called and opened the door at the same time.

"Hey!" Quinn shouted and cupped the back of Winifred's head as she curled into him.

"Knew you was awake when I heard your missus," the man said in a sly, knowing tone. The door stopped moving when it was opened just a slice. The bartender poked his head around the edge of the door, took one look at Quinn's furious face and ducked back to safety. He snorted a half-laugh anyway. "Figured you was feelin' better when we heard your woman carryin' on so."

"Ohhhh . . ." Winifred groaned.

Quinn frowned at the door with enough fury that he should have scorched the man on the other side. "Say your piece and get out."

"Thought you'd wanta know," the voice was quieter now, "ol' Tucker's gettin' mighty tired settin' around the jailhouse and any time now, somebody's likely to let him loose."

"Let 'em," Quinn snarled. There's nothing he'd like better than to have another chance at the man. Even now, hours later, his blood still ran cold with rage at the thought of the gambler laying a hand on Winifred. But then again, he told himself, the kind of shape he was in now—that gambler would most likely punch his ticket for him.

The back of his head started aching again as if to remind him how the last fight had turned out. And that brought something else to mind. Quinn wanted to know how the hell that bastard had knocked him out. He was sure he'd had Tucker cold.

Winifred raised her head a bit and looked up at him. Glancing down, Quinn saw the worry in her gaze and gave her a squeeze.

"Don't fight him again," she whispered.

"Don't worry," he gave her a sheepish grin. Though he'd dearly love to push his fist through Tucker's face again, at the moment, he surely wasn't up to it.

"O'course," the bartender went on with a chuckle in his voice, "if your little woman there's gonna 'help' you again like she done before, well . . ."

Like she done before? Quinn looked down at Winifred again and saw her bite her lip before she turned her face back into his chest. Something was going on.

"So?" the man called out. "What's it to be? You gonna git, or d'ya want us to let Tucker loose?"

"No," Quinn answered, his gaze still locked on Fred. "Hang onto him. We're leavin'."

"Good enough." The bartender left, shutting the door behind him.

Once the door was closed, Winifred climbed down off Quinn's lap and began to tug her clothing into place. Her fingers fumbled a bit on the buttons and she tossed her head to whip her hair out of the way.

"Are you sure you're fit to ride now?" she asked quietly.

Apparently, he thought, they were going to ignore what had just happened between them. A pang of regret stung him but it did no good to wish things were different.

"Fit enough," he finally answered and stood up slowly. A few of his muscles screamed a protest, but he'd been in worse shape before. Probably would be again. He stepped to one side, picked up his shirt and shoved his arms into the sleeves. As he did up his own buttons, Quinn asked, "What'd he mean about my wife 'helpin'?"

Her hands stilled, then dropped to her sides. He watched her take a deep breath and refused to be distracted by the sight of her bosom straining against her shirt buttons. After several long moments, she lifted her head and looked at him.

"It was an accident," she said.

"What?"

"I hadn't planned on it happening." She shrugged helplessly and shook her head as if still trying to understand how *it* had happened at all.

"What?"

"If you hadn't moved suddenly, it wouldn't have happened in the first place."

"What?" he shouted his frustration and immediately regretted it. That was no way to try and get information from Fred.

Winifred grimaced, folded her hands together at her waist and lifted her chin. "I hit you."

"You hit me?"

"Yes, but I was aiming for Mr. Tucker."

"Oh, well," he shrugged, "that's all right then."

She winced.

"What'd you hit me with?"

Her lips twitched suspiciously.

"What was it?" Hell, the way his head was pounding, he wouldn't be surprised to hear she'd clocked him with an anvil.

She sighed heavily and blurted out, "A whiskey bottle."

"Good God."

"But if you hadn't moved so quickly," Winifred shook her index finger at him and he felt as though he was back in school. "I would have hit Mr. Tucker as I'd planned."

"Why didn't you just stay clear like I told you to?"

"He was hurting you. And it was my fault."

Oh fine. The gambler was throwing a couple of lucky punches, so Winifred steps into the fray and smashes Quinn's brains in with a bottle!

"I only wanted to help," she said and this time, Quinn heard the misery in her voice. "It was all my fault. I never should have gone into the saloon, I suppose. But how is a person supposed to find adventure if that person is always hiding in safety, I ask you?"

Quinn opened his mouth to speak and snapped it shut again.

"And actually," she went on, warming to her subject, "if I were to be completely honest, I would have to say that the whole situation could be laid at Mr. Tucker's feet." Winifred shook her head and scowled. "That *dreadful* man! You were quite right to fight him, you know." She nodded now and smiled up at him. "And it was thrilling, having you ride to my defense, just like—"

Quinn held up one hand for silence. He didn't want to hear that pretend fella's name again as long as he lived.

Winifred stared at him silently as if waiting for him to rail and shout at her. Hell, knowing the kinds of books she reads, he thought, she's probably thinking that she's about to get tied up and tossed over the backside of a horse.

Huh! He ran one hand through his hair and gingerly fingered the knot on the back of his head. Downright amazing, he told himself. But then, everything about Winifred was downright amazing. Quinn's lips curved slowly and he sighed helplessly.

A flicker of amusement quickened to life in his chest. The more he thought about the whole thing, the funnier it seemed. Before he could stop it, a bubble of laughter shot from his throat and once it was free, there was no holding the rest of it back.

Though the pain in his ribs brought tears to his eyes, Quinn couldn't stop laughing. He looked at Winifred and watched her through blurry eyes as she too gave into the urge to laugh.

Shaking his head, he told himself that he and Fred made some kind of team, all right.

In two quick steps, Quinn was beside her. He pulled her into his arms and rested his chin on top of her head.

Her palms flattened against the small of his back and for a moment, he enjoyed the feel of her hands on his body. Amusement slowly faded away as he basked in the rightness of holding her.

Jesus!

If he'd had any idea just how much trouble he'd be walking into by kidnapping her—would he have taken her anyway?

She hiccuped and her chuckles were muffled against his chest. Quinn smoothed his hands up and down her spine.

Hell yes, he would.

No matter if his head ached fair to splitting. Winifred Matthews had waded into a barfight, armed with a whiskey bottle, determined to protect him.

He chuckled softly. Maybe she was more like Marshal Travis than he ever could be.

Two hours from town and the sun was near setting. Winifred's behind ached from the continuous days of riding and she wanted nothing more than to lie down and fall asleep.

Anywhere.

But Quinn didn't show any signs of stopping.

She studied his back and found herself remembering the feel of his skin beneath her hands. She recalled the rippling muscles that shifted with her touch. She remembered everything.

Clapping one hand over her mouth, she stifled a groan and told herself that she was utterly shameless. Adventure was one thing.

Behaving like a brazen harlot was quite another.

Good Lord, what he must think of her!

A vivid mental image of herself laying across his lap, legs spread wide, leapt up before her eyes. She bit down hard on the fingers still covering her mouth. How in Heaven had things gotten so far out of hand so quickly?

Who would have thought that a kiss or two could herald such a happening? And who would have thought that Winifred Matthews would so lose control that she writhed and groaned and shouted a man's name at the top of her lungs?

Her stomach pitched and for a moment, she thought she was going to be sick. Then the feeling passed and she knew she was destined for Hell. Because instead of feeling sick—she was feeling those same stirrings again. God help her, her breasts ached for his kiss.

Even the thought of his mouth was enough to harden her nipples into rigid buds that scraped against her chemise in a teasing, irritating manner. Every breath she drew increased the pressure on her breasts and brought new life to the tingling sensations between her legs.

Her hand flew from her mouth to cover her eyes. It was pointless. She could be wearing a blanket over her head and still she would see herself, twisting in Quinn's arms, crying his name. Forever she would see him, head bent, his tongue tracing warm, damp circles around her hardened nipple.

"Oh Heavens," she muttered and gripped the saddle pommel tighter. She shifted her hips uneasily in the saddle and was rewarded—or punished—with a renewed, throbbing sense of expectation.

How was this possible?

Until a few hours ago, she'd never experienced anything remotely similar to what Quinn had shown her. Now, it was all she could think of!

Perhaps her next adventure should consist of a long visit in a convent.

She groaned and squeezed her legs together, hoping for relief.

"You all right?"

"No," she snapped without thinking. Glancing up at Quinn, she forced a smile. If she didn't, he would no doubt ask what was wrong. *Then* where would she be? "I mean, yes. Fine. I'm fine."

"You're sure?"

"Of course I'm sure. Why wouldn't I be sure?" Why couldn't she stop talking? "Whatever could be wrong?"

"All right, Fred." He shook his head and grinned at her. "I believe ya."

That grin of his was doing strange things to her as well. Oh, this entire adventure was not going at all in the proper direction.

"You see that?" He pointed in the direction off to her left. Winifred looked and strained to see whatever it was, but she didn't see a thing out of the ordinary. "There," he said again, "just above that tallest pine in the distance?"

Frowning, she stared again. Focusing her mind on anything besides what she had been thinking about was an improvement.

Then she saw it. Or thought she did. Some kind of movement. A filmy, hazy kind of movement. She looked at Quinn, her question evident.

He gave her another grin. "It's smoke from a cook fire."

Turning back, Winifred studied the wispy movement and after a few moments thought she *did* recognize it for a long finger of smoke.

"How'd ya like to spend the night in some farmer's barn?" he asked her.

"Really?"

"Yeah," he rolled one shoulder and winced. "Kinda hate to admit it, but I'm still pretty stove up and I don't care much for the idea of sleepin' on the ground tonight."

She still felt a bit guilty about his injuries, so she readily agreed. Besides, a barn meant hay. And surely a bed of straw would be more comfortable than the hard, rocky Texas earth. Strange Winifred thought, a few months ago, she would have thought that a nice hotel would be a luxury. Now, she was eager to stay in a barn.

Ah, adventures!

Even as she thought it though, she remembered the fact that a posse was somewhere behind them. "Is it safe?" she asked. "Didn't you say we were going to avoid everyone?"

"True," he rubbed one hand across his jaw then reached up to settle his battered hat more firmly on his head. "But I figure we've already been seen at that town. What more harm can happen to us by stayin' in a farmer's barn?"

Hmmm. She wished he hadn't said that.

"But just to be on the safe side," Quinn added "I'll brush out our tracks and lay down a short false trail headin' off to the mountains."

She nodded.

"So you just hang on there Fred." He reached over and gave her hands a quick squeeze. "Another hour or so and you can bed down for the night, nice and cozy."

He started their horses moving again and as she settled into the familiar rocking motion, Winifred thought about what he'd said.

An hour.

Bed down.

Nice and cozy.

The one thing he hadn't said, but that she knew to be true, was that he was going to be right alongside her.

In the hay.

All night.

She shifted as that prickly sensation started in again.

14

"Storm comin'."

Tom lifted the brim of his hat off his eyes and raised his head from the saddle. Glancing up at the star sprinkled evening sky, he frowned at his friend. "Sky's clear as glass," he argued.

Dusty shrugged and Tom could barely make out the movement in the near darkness.

"Didn't *mean* right this minute."

"Well what the hell *did* you mean?" Tom snapped. Days of travel with Dusty McDonough had taken some of the shine off their friendship. Oh, Tom knew that once things were back to normal and he only had to look at Dusty's face once every week or so, everything would be fine again.

As for now though, he was thoroughly sick of the sight of his friend.

Dusty sniffed the still, cool air, turned his head this way and that, then shrugged again. "There's a storm out there. Waitin'. Can smell it on the wind."

Tom laughed. "There *is* no wind."

"Don't make any difference to me," Dusty told him and stretched out on his bedroll. "Believe or not, as you like."

Tom sat up, sniffed a couple of times then glared at the man across from him. "I don't smell a damn thing."

"You ain't an Indian."

"Neither are you . . . hardly."

"My great-grandmothei—"

"I know," Tom interrupted and laid back down again, "she was Comanche. You've told me." Hell, he added silently, Tom'd heard about Dusty's great-grandmother, Night Wind, so often *he* could tell the stories!

Settling his hat down over his face again, Tom's mind started wandering. He'd never actually met Night Wind, since Dusty's family hadn't moved to Yellow Dog until after the old lady died. But Dusty's pa had remembered enough of his granny's stories to make the woman real to Dusty, Quinn and Tom.

He'd heard all about Night Wind's amazing predictions. She'd had some sort of special way about her. Some folks called it second sight. Most called it nonsense.

Every once in a while though, Dusty would say something—didn't matter how wild or loco it seemed—and blast if it didn't come true.

Tom called it annoying. Quinn called it pretty damned handy to have around.

Dusty called it Night Wind's gift.

Tom *snorted* into the crown of his hat and pushed aside all thoughts of mystic Indian predictions. The sky was clear. There was no wind.

There was no storm.

Tom listened to the sounds of the night around him. A coyote howled in the distance and its cry was picked up by one of its kin. Somewhere not too far off, the brush rustled gently and since his horse wasn't bothered by the noise, Tom knew it was probably a rabbit or some other little creature out scrambling for food. The dying fire crackled and spit gently and Dusty's slow, even breathing sounded suddenly—companionable.

Everything was just as it should be.

Except that it was taking too damn long to catch up to Quinn and the woman.

Another moment or two passed before Tom surrendered to the inevitable and heard himself ask, "What kind of storm?"

"Big one," Dusty returned and didn't sound the least bit surprised to hear Tom's question.

"When?"

"Too early to tell for sure." He paused, sniffed the air again and added, "Not tomorrow. But soon."

Soon. Dammit, that could be anywhere from the day after tomorrow to the end of the week. Tom squeezed his eyes closed tighter and told himself that they'd better hurry. With a storm that big coming, they had to find Quinn fast.

"Get some sleep. We ride at first light."

"'Night, Tom."

The farm was farther away than Quinn had thought.

An hour after first spotting the trail of smoke, he and Winifred rode into the overgrown yard. Even in the darkness, Quinn noted the sections of fence lying toppled on the dirt. Weeds, some nearly a foot high, sprung up from the hard packed dirt encircling the front of the cabin. As they rode closer, he saw a single light shining through the partially open front door and the broken, curtainless window panes. Quinn counted at least three rags stuffed into different holes in the glass.

The barn, not more than fifty feet away from the

house looked to be drunk. It was tilted and leaning badly to one side, its double doors standing open. From inside the structure came the unmistakable sounds of neglected animals.

By the looks of the place, nobody'd done a bit of work in some time. Hell, if it wasn't for that lamp shining, and the open door, he would've bet money that the farm was deserted.

"Oh thank heaven," Winifred muttered. "At last!" Apparently, she wasn't bothered in the least by the farm's rundown appearance.

Before Quinn could utter a word of warning, she'd slid down from her horse and practically run to the slanted boards of the small front porch.

"Fred!" Lord, it was hard to shout and whisper at the same time.

She paused, one foot across the threshold and looked back at him. Smiling, she said, "Hurry up, Quinn," just before she stepped into the house.

Quinn was halfway to the front door when he heard her horrified gasp. He caught her to him when she blindly ran outside.

"What is it?" he asked and gave her a brief squeeze before pushing her behind him and drawing his gun.

"A man," she stuttered "in . . . there . . . he . . . he . . ."

"What?"

She shook her head against his back and he felt her fingers curl into his shirt. He didn't have time to question her further. If there was trouble inside that cabin, he wanted none of it.

Slowly, carefully, he began to edge his way backward.

Winifred stumbled along, still clinging to his back. Quinn didn't take his eyes off that front door. His pistol barrel was aimed at the narrow slice of lamplight and the first damned thing that stepped outside was going to get a bullet in it.

Reb whickered and Sadie snorted at their approach.

Quinn cursed under his breath even though he knew it made little difference now. No point in trying to be quiet. Lord knew, anyone in that place had to have heard Winifred's gasp and her running footsteps.

They were almost to the horses when they heard it.

For a moment, Quinn thought he must be hearing things. Then it came again.

"It's a child," Winifred said and her words were only partially muffled by his shirt. *"Crying."*

Not just crying, Quinn amended silently. *Wailing.*

The ear splitting sound seemed to echo around them forever. Quinn frowned. He'd never been a father, but even he knew the difference between a bad-tempered cry and a cry of pain or fear.

That child was hurting. Bad.

He inhaled sharply. Dammit.

In the next instant, Winifred had let go of him and taken a few quick steps toward the door. He caught her and grabbed hold of her arm.

"Where the hell do you think you're goin'?"

She gaped at him. "In there. Of course."

"No 'of course' about it." He jerked his head in the direction of the cabin and tried to mentally shush the child.

"Anybody could be in there."

"A child is in there."

"Uh-huh," he agreed. "And whoever's makin' it cry."

Her brows drew together and she chewed at her lip for a moment. Finally, he told himself. He'd actually made her *think* before acting! Maybe there was hope for her yet. When she spoke again though, that tiny hope died.

"Then we have to take the baby away from whoever it is."

"What we have to do is get back on our horses and get the hell outa here."

Slowly, her head swiveled and she raised her gaze to his. Even in the darkness, Quinn imagined he saw the condemnation in her green eyes. For damn sure, he heard it in her tone.

"Do you mean to say that you would simply ride away and leave a child in desperate need?"

"You don't know nothin' of the kind," he whispered harshly. "For all you know, the kid just got a whippin' from his pa."

"And did you hear an adult at all?"

"No, but . . ."

She shook her head and reached out one hand to him. Laying her palm flat on his chest, she tilted her face up to his and said "You can't fool me, Quinn. You're not anything like Dastardly Dan. You couldn't possibly leave a child in distress."

His heart sank.

"I know you're concerned for my safety, but that is simply immaterial."

"What?"

"It doesn't matter."

"Oh."

"Now, would you like me to go in with you or wait out here with the horses?"

Quinn reached for her and with his left hand, stroked her hair back from her face. Hell. She was right. He'd known it all along. From the first damn minute he heard that kid cry, Quinn knew he wouldn't be able to ride away. But it had sure been worth a try.

"Stay here," he ordered. "You hear anything that sounds like trouble, you get on Sadie and ride like your seat was on fire. You understand me?"

She nodded, rose up on her toes and gave him a quick, hard kiss.

That one brief taste of her rocked him to his heels. Sucking in a great gulp of air, he patted her shoulder

absently and started for the cabin. At the door, he
turned and looked back.

She was right where he'd left her.

Amazing.

As he stepped into the dimly lit interior, Quinn
pushed all thoughts of Winifred from his mind. He
couldn't afford not to concentrate on the problem at
hand. One slip could get him killed, and then where
would Fred be?

A floorboard creaked under his weight and he grimaced. He should've just blown a bugle to announce
himself. Carefully, his gaze slid over the interior of the
cabin, noting everything.

Tattered drawings torn from books and newspapers
were affixed to the roughly hewn plank walls. A framed
daguerreotype of a young, unsmiling couple stared back
at him from across the room. The smell of old meat
hung in the air and the place was littered with dirty
clothes. An old wardrobe chest on the far wall had been
ransacked. Its drawers were scattered across the floor
and one of the doors hung crookedly from one hinge.

He took another couple of steps into the room and
that's when he saw the man that had sent Winifred flying into his arms.

On the wood floor, partially hidden behind a tall settle and half-buried under dirty clothes, a man lay dead.
Quinn didn't need to check for a pulse or to listen for a
heartbeat. A neat black hole in the center of the man's
forehead told him all he needed to know.

His jaw clenched, Quinn bent down briefly, closed
the man's wide, blankly staring eyes and at the same
time assured himself that the man had been dead for a
full day. Maybe two. The body was cold as a stone.

Another cry sliced into the room and made the hairs
on the back of Quinn's neck stand straight up. Jesus!
Some child had been left alone? With a dead man?

Keeping his gun ready, Quinn stood up and walked to the half-opened door at the corner of the main room. Laying his left hand flat on the door, he gave it a push. It swung wide slowly, begrudgingly and groaned a protest as it went.

Another lamp was lit in this small room. The wick was turned low as if to save on oil. And in the wavering, yellow glow, Quinn saw a bed. On that bed lay a woman with a child on either side of her.

And the woman didn't look to be in much better shape than the man he'd just left in the other room.

"What is it?" Winifred asked and pushed past him.

"Dammit, I told you to wait."

"I couldn't wait when you might need help," she said and walked into the room. Then disregarding Quinn completely, Winifred marched right up to the bed, lifted one of the children and crooned "Oh, you poor dears."

Still muttering vile curses under his breath, Quinn holstered his gun and walked up to stand beside Winifred. The child in Winifred's arms stopped his wailing and snuffled loudly. His breath rattled and gasped as he tried to calm down and quietly his fingers began exploring Winifred's features.

They looked down at the woman and the infant she held cradled in her left arm. After a moment, she opened her eyes and smiled.

"Praise God," she whispered.

"Ma'am?" Quinn said.

"He answered my prayers." The woman looked down at her baby, then tried to lift one hand toward her son who was perched comfortably on Winifred's hip. But she didn't have the strength and her hand dropped limply to the flowered quilt covering her.

"Please," she whispered and licked her lips tiredly.

"Let me get you some water," Winifred offered and handed the little boy over to Quinn.

Quinn took the child and smiled at him warily.

"No," the woman stopped Winifred. "No time."

"Ma'am?" Quinn asked gently. "In the other room? Your husband?"

Her eyes filled with tears and she nodded. "Two men."

"How long ago?"

"Quinn," Winifred frowned at him, "must you force her to speak now? Can't you see she's ill? Hurt?"

He saw more than that. The woman was dying. Even in the dim lamplight, Quinn saw a dark patch staining the quilt on the bed and he knew she'd been bleeding bad for quite awhile. It was a wonder how she'd managed to hold on at all.

"'Sallright," the woman whispered. "Have to talk. No time."

Quinn handed the boy back to Winifred, went down on one knee beside the bed and leaned in close to the woman.

"Came two days ago," she said in a breathless rush. "Wanted food. We fed 'em and sometime later, they shot my man."

Quinn gritted his teeth until the muscle in his jaw ached. Beside him, he heard Winifred's small gasp of outrage.

"They come after me next," the woman went on. She closed her eyes briefly and tried to turn her head away in shame. But she was simply too weak. "They stayed here 'till early this mornin'. All that time, they . . . *used* me."

Simple words that drew an ugly image. Winifred began to cry and for a moment, Quinn felt like joining her. But not all the tears in the world would be enough to help the woman lying on the bed. Now, all he could do was make sure the strangers were long gone. He didn't want to take a chance on Winifred ending up like that poor woman.

"They're gone then?"

"Yes." Her eyes rolled up toward the ceiling. "But before they left, they killed me, too."

"What?" The question flew out of Winifred's mouth but Quinn paid no attention. Judging from the spreading blood stain on the quilt, the woman'd been used so roughly, she was bleeding to death.

"Don't know why they left my children alive." She drew a ragged breath. "Must have figured with their folks dead, they wouldn't last long anyhow."

She looked into Quinn's steady gaze and tried to smile. "I prayed someone would come along. Left that lamp burnin' in the front room hopin' someone might see it. Kept a little fire goin', too." Weakly, she reached out and laid her hand on one of Quinn's. "Save my babies. Please."

"We will," Winifred blurted.

Quinn couldn't tear his gaze away from the pale features of the dying woman. No woman should be treated like that. No woman should have to lie alone in her bed waiting for her blood to finish running out of her body. No one should have to trust their children to strangers.

Helpless rage flared up in his chest and just as quickly died. Anger wouldn't do any good. Sure couldn't help her any and he knew for damn sure there was no way for him to try to find the men responsible.

Two nameless strangers wandering through Texas? No. Quinn would just have to trust in the Lord that one day, those two would stop at the wrong farm and some fella with a shotgun would send 'em to Glory.

"A town," she said and her voice was fainter now than when she'd begun talking, "fifty miles north. Fuego Cruzado." She paused, licked her dry lips and leaned a bit closer to Quinn. "Husband's brother. Decker Hale. Take kids to him. Please. Only . . . family."

Winifred bent down and soothed the woman's fears.

"Of course we will. Don't worry about your children. We'll keep them safe."

The woman's eyes closed and one corner of her mouth lifted in a tired mockery of a smile. "Safe . . . safe . . ."

Quinn frowned, straightened a bit and leaned across the woman to pick up the baby. Probably no more than a few months old, the child was soaking wet and wide awake. Avoiding touching the baby's sodden diaper, Quinn deposited the infant in Winifred's free arm and said roughly "Keep the kids in here. Stay with her. I'll go and . . ." he flashed a quick look at the little boy then looked pointedly at the open door leading into the other room.

Winifred understood immediately and she quite agreed with him. She didn't want the children leaving that room until their father's body was removed from sight. Heaven only knew what sights and sounds the poor children had already been forced to endure.

"Go on," she told him, alternately cooing at one child then the other, "we'll be fine until you return."

Quinn nodded and gave her a look that she couldn't quite read. But before she had time to question it further, he brushed past her and closed the door behind him.

Winifred glanced at the sleeping woman, then set the little boy down on the bed. He stared up at her through too long strands of night black hair. Reaching down, Winifred pushed his hair out of his eyes and asked "Do you know where your mama keeps the baby's diapers?"

He nodded, scooted himself off the mattress and ran to the corner of the room. The boy's short arms dug around in a scattered pile of clothes until he found what he was looking for. He raised one chubby fist and waved the clean diaper like a battle flag.

Winifred smiled though her heart was breaking for him. So young. And so alone. Then she stopped herself.

No. He wasn't alone and neither was his . . . she unfolded the wet diaper . . . *sister.* The two babies had her now. And Quinn.

Quinn would keep them all safe.

"Mister," Quinn said and looked down at the blanket covered body, "you and your woman surely didn't deserve what those bastards done to ya." He sighed, pulled his hat off and ran his sleeve-covered arm across his forehead. "But then, what'd I do to deserve all this, either?"

You robbed a bank, he told himself.

Shit. That couldn't be the reason. There was men out there did far worse than that on a regular basis and never had half the trouble Quinn had run into.

He left the tack room, walked the length of the rickety barn and stopped at the two occupied stalls long enough to fork the hungry horses enough hay to hold them till morning. At first light, he'd check the animals over, feed 'em good, then bury their owner.

Stopping in the archway of the open barn doors, Quinn stared at the house opposite him. *Inside,* were a dying woman, his hostage and two about to be orphaned children. His gaze slid unthinkingly toward Reb and Sadie. *Outside,* was a saddled horse, fifteen hundred dollars and a lot of open road.

If he went and climbed aboard Reb, he could be out of sight of that miserable cabin within minutes. The posse that was no doubt still hot on his back trail would eventually stumble across Winifred and the kids. Meantime, in just a day or two of riding and Quinn'd be so far from Yellow Dog, nobody'd ever find him.

He'd be free. He could find a new place. Build another ranch. See to it that his mother had a home. Reclaim his life.

Huh! Quinn shook his head, slapped his hat back on and pulled the brim down low over his eyes. Since Winifred had crushed that brim, it dipped so low, the cabin and the people inside were blocked entirely from his view. Too bad it wasn't as easy to wipe 'em from his mind.

Jesus! This whole trip had been bad enough when it was just Winifred he had to worry about. Now, he was supposed to go on the run with a woman, a little boy and a baby? Why, any *respectable* bad man would hang his head in shame.

How had this all happened? How had he lost control of everything?

Quinn shook his head. Nope, he couldn't figure it out. And it didn't really matter, either. There was no changing it now. Whether he liked it or not, he was saddled with a whole *crowd* of folks! There was just no way in hell he could run off and leave Winifred. Or those children.

Unbidden, the image of Winifred soothing those kids leapt into his mind. She'd near taken his breath away. Instinctively, she'd wrapped love around those two little mites. He remembered the smile she'd showered on that boy and how it had seemed to light up her eyes like a thousand stars.

He shook his head slowly in memory. She might think that she was an adventurous sort—moving from one exciting thing to the next. But that woman was made for loving. She should have a husband to care for and appreciate her. Children of her own to raise and nurture. She should have everything it took to make her happy.

And *he* should be that husband. The kids filling her belly should be *his . . . theirs.* Quinn blinked and swallowed heavily. Where in the name of God had that thought come from?

He scowled at the cabin and turned his gaze away, into the surrounding darkness.

It didn't help. Everywhere he looked, he saw Winifred, with her bright, curly red hair and those green eyes that looked down into his soul and found something worthwhile. Despite all the bruises he'd acquired since first meeting up with her, he could hardly remember what it was like to be without her.

Dammit, besides everything else, how could he "reclaim his life" if he left Winifred behind? Shoot, he couldn't even imagine spending a day without seeing her, talking to her, holding her. Of course, traveling with her and those kids was gonna slow him down so bad that a posse was bound to catch him.

Then, whether he could imagine it or not, he'd be spending plenty of days without seeing her. He'd be in prison and she'd be off on another "adventure." Most likely, she'd meet up with some other fella who would be able to snatch her up and hold on tight.

He'd wind up a miserable, lonely old ex-convict and she'd be a happily married grandmother.

All because he was stupid enough to rob a bank.

If he wasn't so damned tired, he'd shoot himself and save the posse the trouble.

15

Silence.

Winifred turned up the wick on the oil lamp as if more light would make the room less quiet. Leaning back in the rocking chair, she glanced down at the woman in the bed.

There was no change. The children's mother hadn't regained consciousness and in the last hour, her breathing had become more shallow. More . . . hesitant. She probably wouldn't live out the night.

It was simply astonishing to realize that the woman had somehow managed to keep a fire going in the hearth and lamps lit—despite her condition—on the chance that someone would see the light and the smoke.

Sighing deeply, Winifred's gaze shot to the door leading to the main room. Quinn had straightened up most of the mess in there and fixed a pallet by the fire for the children. Now fed, clean and warm, both of them were sound asleep, wrapped in the cocoon of a child's ability to survive.

Outside, Quinn kept guard.

Winifred laid her head against the rocker's high back and closed her eyes briefly. She wasn't sure if he was keeping watch for the posse who was following them or if he was making sure the men responsible for destroying this small family didn't come back.

Somehow, she didn't think he was sure, either.

Lifting her head, she reached for her journal, opened it on her lap and began to write.

So much has happened since I last wrote to you. In this one day, I've experienced more than most women will go through in a lifetime. Quinn and I were involved in a barroom brawl and he was hurt—really doesn't matter how. Later, in the shelter of a lonely room over the saloon, Quinn showed me a side of myself I never dreamed existed. He touched me and drove me mad with a sort of frenzied want. Embarrassing to admit, but it's true. But in these pages, I can reveal truths that I must keep hidden everywhere else. He suckled at my breast, dear journal. Even thinking about that now, brings an odd stirring to my nether regions. And what is more, because of his talented hands, I know now what that odd stirring means. And what it feels like to have that stirring satisfied. God help me, I want to feel it again. I want to watch him touch me. I want to hear him whisper words of love. I want to know the rest of the secrets men and women learn from each other. She stopped, chewed at the end of her pencil for a moment, then drew a shaky breath before continuing. *No matter how wicked it is, dear friend, I must admit to you that yes. I want to feel Quinn's body enter mine. Oh, what people would say if they only knew what bold thoughts run through my mind. Though it's true that I'm not altogether sure of the act that christens a marriage bed, judging by my experience earlier today, I can only assume that it would be wonderful. Is it wrong to admit that it is Quinn I want to initiate me?*

The woman in the bed gasped, shuddered and Winifred stopped writing. Leaning forward, she laid one hand on the woman's arm, hoping to comfort the dying woman with her presence. After a long moment, the shallow, uneven breaths resumed.

Frowning, Winifred once again began to write.

I am ashamed. Oh, not of my wants, only of the fact that I heartlessly list them here while a woman lay dying beside me. Yes, dear journal, in one day, I have experienced the joys of life and the humbling helplessness of death. My adventure has become more than I'd ever wanted it to be. In our travels, Quinn and I stumbled across a cabin where a man lay dead and his wife held on to a spark of life only through the strongest of wills. These two poor people leave behind them two small children, whom Quinn and I have promised to see to safety. Apparently, they have an uncle in a town called Fuego Cruzado. When this unfortunate woman at last leaves her battered shell to meet her Maker, we shall take her precious babies to safety. I cannot tell you, dear journal, what finding this woman and her family has done to me. I've realized something terrifying. In the blink of an eye, life can be over. With no warning. No time for prayer. No time for regrets, one's time on this earth can end. It seems to me then, that one should ensure to spend one's time in this life wisely. Doing the things most important to one. Loving, living—every moment as if it were one's last. Because it very well might be.

She stopped again, reread what she'd written and nodded in satisfaction. It was only then that Winifred noticed that she was alone in the room.

Closing her journal and setting it aside, Winifred leaned in toward the woman. Sometime in the last few moments, the children's mother had quietly lost her battle. Staring down into the woman's pale, drawn features, Winifred whispered "Be happy with your husband and don't worry about your children. Quinn and I will keep them safe."

Slowly, she lifted the sheet, drew it up over the woman's peaceful face and left the room, gently drawing the door closed after her.

Those men weren't coming back.

And the posse was at least a day or so behind them.

So, Quinn asked himself, just what is it you're looking for out here? He stared around him at the darkness and knew it was for his own peace of mind that he'd gone outside.

There was a helpless rage boiling deep within him and he wanted to be alone until he had himself under control again. Oh, not that he'd hurt Winifred or those kids. It was just that none of them needed one more thing to happen—not even if it was only him, furious because he could do nothing to change what had happened here.

He'd give a lot to have the men responsible for this in front of him for just a few minutes. What kind of man was it, he wondered, who could use a woman so hard that he left her insides so broken up that she bled to death? What kind of man could ride off leaving two babies to die slow, neglected deaths?

Quinn rubbed his face hard with both hands as if he could scrub away the thoughts flying through his brain.

His anger wouldn't help. *Nothing* could help the woman. And all he could do for those kids was get them to their uncle.

As for Winifred . . . there was quite a bit he'd like to do for her. But he didn't have the right.

Slowly, he started walking across the empty yard toward the cabin. His watchful gaze swept the area out of long standing habit. A man stayed alive in that country by being aware of what was around him.

But all was quiet. The only sounds that came to him were the ordinary, expected sounds. Night birds calling to each other, the rustle of some small critter moving through the brush at the edge of the clearing and far off, the scream of a rabbit as a hawk or owl carried it off.

Quinn squinted and stared off into the darkness. He should go on inside, make sure everything was all right. But, with the children sleeping and Winifred keeping watch over their ma, he sure as hell wasn't needed in the house. Besides, there was plenty for him to be thinking about. And he'd always done his best thinking outside.

A slight breeze dusted past him, lifting the ends of his hair off his neck. He shuddered slightly and tried not to think about old superstitions. But it was the right kind of night for it. He glanced up at the near full moon and for a moment, watched the long finger of clouds that stretched across its surface. Shadow and light. Life and death.

Quinn snorted, shook his head, and told himself he'd been talking way too much to Winifred. All those schoolteacher notions were starting to take their toll on his brain.

Winifred again. No matter what he did or how he tried to avoid it, his thoughts always circled back to Winifred Matthews. And why not? Hell, everyday, she surprised him anew. For a sheltered woman, she'd surely jumped right in today, he admitted silently.

Taking those kids over and feeding 'em like she'd been doing it for years. And the gentle way she handled their ma was enough to warm up a colder heart than his. Shaking his head, he sat down on the edge of the water trough and balanced his weight carefully on the rotting wood. A quick glance behind him at the moon's reflection shining on the water almost convinced him to move, but he was just too damned tired.

Running took a lot out of a man.

Worry took even more.

And Lord knew, thinking was downright draining.

To his right, the cabin door opened and a spill of lamplight outlined Winifred in the doorway before she stepped into the yard and closed the door behind her.

"Quinn?"

He knew she couldn't see him, coming as she'd done from a lit up room into darkness. "Over here."

She turned toward his voice and walked toward him. Stopping just a foot or two away, she folded her arms across her chest, looked down at him and said softly, "The children's mother is gone."

He sighed heavily. There would be two graves to be dug in the morning. Strange, he'd known the woman couldn't last, but hearing that she had died still bothered him.

"I'll take care of it."

She nodded and took a step closer. Letting her gaze, now accustomed to the darkness, sweep over the yard she said, "The poor woman never woke up again."

"Prob'ly just as well."

"I suppose."

He watched her silently for a long moment and felt the now familiar stirrings beginning to rumble through him. Odd that they'd been together only about a week. Logically speaking, that was no time at all. Then why was it, Quinn wondered, did he feel that he knew Winifred Matthews so well?

It was more than just being used to having her around. It was even more than being accustomed to the way she talked and her occasional bouts of clumsiness.

There was something between them that ran deeper than anything he'd ever known before. He couldn't quite put it into words, but there was something about her that reached out to him like no one else ever had. Almost as if his soul recognized hers.

"Are you all right?"

"Huh?" He blinked, looked up at her and gave himself a mental shake. "Yeah, Fred. I'm just dandy."

She frowned and he searched his tired brain for something else to say. Finally, he blurted out, "You did real good today, Winifred."

Eyes wide, she asked, "What?"

"With them kids and their ma. You handled it real good."

"Oh." Rubbing her hands up and down her arms, Winifred inhaled sharply and blew the air out in a rush. "I wish I could have done more for her."

"There was nothin' to be done."

Seconds passed and stretched into minutes. The silence between them wasn't strained, though. Quinn felt at ease with her. As though even when they weren't talking, they were still somehow—together.

"How could a man use a woman so harshly?" she asked suddenly and it sounded to him like she wasn't asking anybody in particular—just thinking out loud. At least, he hoped she wasn't asking. He didn't have the answers she needed.

When she didn't say anything else, Quinn spoke up.

"I don't know," he admitted softly. "I been askin' myself the same thing."

"I've been thinking about—"

"Yeah?"

"You know," her head dropped until her chin was on

her chest, "back at the hotel? What you uh—or rather we uh . . ."

"Oh." Quinn nodded and let the memory race through his mind. Probably bothering her, how one day could hold both wonders and horrors. She'd lived too long in a safe world. In the West, a body learned real young that absolutely anything was possible and you'd best be ready for it.

But maybe, he told himself, it was easier on her if she turned her mind to more pleasant thoughts. God knew, he'd rather think about that time in the hotel himself. "What have you been thinkin'?"

"Oh," she said and dug the toe of one shoe into the dirt and swept her leg in an arc, drawing a half circle around her "about how . . . *good* that was and exactly how that poor woman died from it?"

Quinn sighed and pushed his hat to the back of his head. Watching her in the darkness, he could see that she wasn't looking at him. Clearly, she was still a little embarrassed by what had passed between them. It struck him suddenly just how little she knew of what happened between a man and a woman. Hell, a blind man could've guessed that she was a virgin. But he'd kind of assumed that she at least knew what to expect. Apparently though, he was wrong.

Not only hadn't she been with a man. He was willing to bet that no one had ever told her a damned thing. What she must have thought when she'd heard the woman inside say how those men had used her didn't bear thinking about.

Frowning, Quinn braced his elbows on his knees, looked up at her and started thinking. Hard. He was determined she find out that making love wasn't a painful thing.

Even as he realized that it would no doubt be some other man who would claim her body with his own.

Swallowing past the knot in his throat, Quinn started talking.

"What those fellas did to her," he jerked his head back toward the cabin behind him, "didn't have a damn thing to do with love makin'."

"I realize that," she said, though she didn't sound convinced.

"Not yet you don't," a sad smile touched his lips and his gaze dropped to the pebble-strewn earth between his booted feet. "But you will. Someday. Then you'll see that the thing that passes between a man and a woman is as close to heaven as any of us can get to while we're still alive."

She drew a long, shuddering breath.

"What those men did," he forced himself to say, "had nothin' to do with pleasure. Hell, I'll bet they didn't even enjoy it." Mentally, he found himself adding a hopeful wish that their privates rotted up and fell off. Aloud, he added, "All they was interested in was hurtin' her."

"Why?"

"Who the hell knows why men like that do anything?"

"And they're going to get away with it, aren't they?"

"Not forever." His voice hardened and scraped along his throat. "Sometime, somewhere, they'll try something with the wrong folks and end up with a mountain lion by the tail."

"How can you be so sure?"

"I'm not. But most things tend to even out sooner or later."

"I hope you're right."

Well, they'd gotten off the track a bit and maybe that was just as well. Quinn shifted gingerly on the edge of the water trough. His body was hard and tight just thinking about loving Winifred. And there wasn't a damn thing he could do about it. No sense in torturing himself.

The road to Hell was stretching out in front of her and Winifred was almost positive she could see the Devil himself standing there waving her on.

She shook her head to relieve herself of the ridiculous mental image. But was it so ridiculous?

After all, what did it say about her that though there were two orphaned children sleeping inside the cabin and a woman lying cruelly dead . . . all she, Winifred wanted to do was curl up in Quinn Hawkins's lap and feel his arms slide around her?

Lord, when had she become so wanton? Had the seeds of harlotry always lain dormant inside her, needing only a man's talented hands to bring them to life? Or is this what happened when a woman gave herself to a man without the sanctity of marriage?

But perhaps she was being too hard on herself. After all, it wasn't just *any* man she wanted to hold her. It was Quinn.

Only Quinn.

Her mouth dry, Winifred tried to turn her thoughts in other directions. She tried to be strong. To tell herself that the prickly sensation beginning to blossom deep inside her would go away.

But it was simply no use.

Perhaps finding that poor woman and her children should have quelled this . . . *need* inside her. But it hadn't. Indeed, it had had the exact opposite effect. In fact, once the poor woman had gone to her reward, Winifred had felt compelled to seek Quinn out. It was as though she'd needed to be reminded that she was alive.

That *they* were alive. And together.

It was all so confusing yet at the same time, it all seemed to make some sort of strange sense.

If nothing else, finding the woman and her children

had brought home to Winifred just how fragile life really was. How quickly everything could end. And how important it was to make the most of what you were given.

Glancing at Quinn now, seated on the lip of the water trough, Winifred gave free rein to the prickly sensation beginning to weaken her knees. Heart pounding, she took a half step and stopped. Briefly, she worried over what he would say. What he might do.

What if he was appalled? What would she say if he set her aside with a stern lecture on respect for the dead?

What would she do if she didn't try?

Toss and turn all night, that's what.

She would risk his rejection. Even if for nothing else than the chance to be held by him, however briefly. For just a moment or two, she wanted to feel his strength wrapped around her. Wanted to hear his heart beating beneath her ear.

And a voice in the back of her mind admitted that she also wanted to feel his lips on hers again.

The thoughts spinning through her brain were making her crazy. This whole situation was crazy. But the more she thought about it, the worse everything seemed.

Better to just act and accept whatever consequences were the result.

Before another contrary thought could form, Winifred stepped quickly across the small space of ground separating them.

He hardly had time to look up before she'd plopped herself down on his lap. She avoided meeting his gaze by looping her arms around his neck and tucking her face into the curve of his throat and shoulder.

Quinn's arms instinctively closed around her.

"Fred?" he whispered.

Winifred heard the wood beneath them creak dangerously. She felt the muscles in his thighs tighten and flex as he fought for balance.

But it was too late.

The old wood trough creaked again, louder this time, then an ear splitting snap sounded out into the silence. He held her tighter as they dropped to the ground.

And when the icy cold water rushed over them before racing out across the dry, hard dirt, Winifred gasped with the shock and thought she heard Quinn mutter "Dammit!"

"You didn't have to see me home," Mercy said and looked up at the big man beside her. "I can take care of myself. Been doing it for a long time now."

Jim Barry shrugged and Mercy watched his shoulder muscles ripple with restrained strength.

"Just because you *can* do a thing, doesn't mean you should *have* to do it."

She didn't quite know what to say to that. And truth to tell, she'd enjoyed having a man escort her home. Oh, not for protection. She was perfectly capable of handling whatever situation presented itself. But the company had been very nice indeed.

Strange to think how long it had been since she'd even thought about being alone with a man. Still, *this* man was in Yellow Dog for one reason. And once his job was finished, he'd be leaving. She'd do well to remember that. Besides, she was too damned old for any idle, girlish fancies.

With that thought firmly in mind, she stuck her right hand out and said, "Nevertheless, you didn't have to do it. I appreciate it and goodnight."

He glanced at her outstretched hand and one corner of his well-shaped mouth lifted. Slowly, his big hand enveloped hers and Mercy almost started at the warmth tingling up the length of her arm. Squeezing her flesh gently, Jim Barry looked at her until she met his gaze.

"Think you could give me a cup of coffee before you send me on my way?"

Coffee.

The look in his eyes told her that wasn't all he had on his mind.

Still, what could happen?

She stared up at him and was thankful that her cook had left a lamp burning for her return. In the soft, dim glow of light spilling from the window on her left, Jim Barry's features looked . . . not dangerous so much as . . . alright—dangerous.

But not the kind of danger that would require a rifle to defend against. The kind of danger she'd thought herself long immune to.

Jim Barry was a danger to her heart.

She felt it. She could sense it in his very stance. In the way he looked at her. In the way he said her name.

Hell, the man brought to mind all manner of things that she hadn't let herself think about since Quinn's daddy died. And Mercy wasn't entirely sure she was ready to start thinking about 'em now.

Those kinds of thoughts and dreams were for the young.

Weren't they?

Mercy pulled her hand free of his grasp and jammed her still warm fingers into the pocket of her riding skirt. This was ridiculous. Laughable. For heaven's sake, this stranger had her stumbling for words like a schoolgirl.

Well, it couldn't go on.

She wouldn't be put in the position of blushing maiden every time she saw the man. Oh, she was damned grateful he was in town. Because of him and the man paying him, Quinn just might come out of this mess with his hide intact.

But, grateful and . . . *grateful* were two different things. Maybe, she told herself, it would be better if she simply told Jim Barry how she felt. Laid all her cards on the table, so to speak.

Then, like two rational adults, they could get past this silly flirtation and manage the business at hand.

Decision made, Mercy nodded, reached back for the door knob and turned it. As the front door swung wide, she glanced at him.

"I believe you're right, Mr. Barry. A cup of coffee would be just the thing right now."

"Thank you, Mercy."

Her throat closed at the sound of her name rumbling from deep in his chest.

Still, there was no backing down now. She stepped across the threshold and sensed, rather than heard him follow her. Struggling to keep her voice from quavering, she told him "I think you and I should have a little talk, Mr. Barry."

"Jim."

He closed the door and stepped up beside her.

"Jim," she repeated. She didn't look up at him. For the moment, she didn't dare.

"I'd like that, Mercy."

Her eyes squeezed shut briefly and she wondered frantically just what it was about the timbre of his voice that sent it ricocheting along her spine like it did.

Breathing deeply, in a futile attempt to still her racing heart, she said, "Follow me."

"Anywhere," he countered.

Mercy swallowed.

Lord help her.

Quinn groaned and Winifred shivered.

"Fred," he finally managed to say, "what the *hell* were you thinkin'?"

She looked down at the front of her and saw that her

clothing was flush against her body. Her fingers plucked at the bosom of her white shirt, but it didn't do the slightest bit of good. The moment she released the sodden material, it clung to her body like a long lost child.

After a long moment, she raised her eyes to meet his. There was really no point in lying about what she'd had in mind.

"I wanted you to kiss me again."

Stunned, he stared at her speechlessly for a long moment, then reached up, yanked off his hat and threw it as far as he could.

Winifred wasn't quite sure if he was elated or furious. His next question didn't do a thing to clear up her confusion.

"Why the hell didn't you just say so?"

"It's not something most women are taught to do, Quinn."

"Be honest, y'mean?"

"No." Really, there was no point in being rude. Wasn't it enough that the very heavens had conspired to punish her for her wantonness? Why else would a perfectly good water trough crumble to dust if not to teach Winifred Matthews a lesson in decorum?

She wiggled around on his lap in an attempt to get more comfortable, but it didn't help. Why, Quinn's body seemed suddenly as hard as the very ground beneath them.

He clapped his arms around her even tighter. Speaking through clenched teeth, he said, "Sit still."

"All right," she agreed with a note of censure in her tone. "But I'm not very comfortable. Do you have a rock in your pocket?"

16

A *short, strangled laugh* shot from Quinn's throat. "Only when I'm with you," he told her.

"I don't understand."

"I know." Grabbing hold of her waist, he lifted her off his lap and sat her down in the mud beside him with a plop. She didn't understand anything yet. But if he didn't get her the hell off him, she'd be understanding *plenty* before the night was through.

She wanted him to kiss her.

Good God, that was all he'd been thinking about for hours. But who would've guessed that a lady like her would want him, Quinn Hawkins?

At the same instant that thought entered his brain, another one rose up to knock him back down to size.

Of *course* she wanted him to kiss her. Who the hell else was around to do it? Snarling and grumbling at his own stupidity, Quinn slapped his palms down into the mud and pushed himself to his feet. Served him right for thinking about things that he had no right thinking about. Imagine him, with Winifred Matthews!

No, he told himself as he looked down at her, still sprawled in the mud, it wasn't *him* she wanted. It was only that he was the only man handy.

As he yanked her to her feet, he told her as much.

He wasn't at all prepared for the slap she gave him that set his ears to ringing.

"Of all the insulting, low minded . . ." she sucked in a breath while she mentally searched for another curse to hurl at him. Finally, she finished with two words. "You . . . *man!*"

His blond eyebrows lifted and Winifred wanted to scream at the look of astonishment on his features. Instead, the words she couldn't find a moment before filled her mind and came spilling out of her mouth.

"Are you insinuating sir, that I am the sort of woman who would lie with any passing man?"

"No ma'am," he said quickly.

"I assume that you are also insinuating that a woman of my low moral fibre is of no interest whatever to you personally."

"Huh?" He squinted at her as though she were speaking German.

"I mean, that since I am obviously nothing more than a harlot, you yourself are not interested in me at all."

"Hah!"

A short bark of laughter shot into the night and Winifred blinked. He looked at her for a long minute and then bent forward, resting his palms on his muddy thighs as wave after wave of laughter rocked him.

Clenching her jaw tight, Winifred straightened her spine, lifted her chin and squared her shoulders. Well, that certainly told her all she needed to know and more!

Brushing past him, she started for the house. Let him laugh. She needn't stand there and watch. She would simply go inside, wash up and try to get some sleep before the children woke up.

He caught her arm in a firm grip before she'd taken more than a few steps. Pulling her back to his side, Quinn dropped both hands on her shoulders before he started talking.

"Fred, I swear you're gonna kill me."

"If you insist on laughing at me, *Mr.* Hawkins, your prediction may very well come true."

"I ain't laughing at you, Fred."

The tone of his voice, more than his words convinced her to raise her gaze to his. In truth, she didn't see amusement in his eyes. There was something far more serious—more exciting—in those blue depths now.

She held her breath and waited.

He shoved one muddy hand through his hair then dropped his palm back on her shoulder.

"I wasn't laughin' at you. I was laughin' at me."

"For heaven's sake, why?"

"Because I'd just done a real good job of convincin' myself that you didn't really want me." He shook his head slowly then moved one hand to cup her cheek. "But I didn't mean it like you thought and when you slapped my face for me, it made me see something."

"Which was . . ."

"That I'm a fool."

"I wouldn't go that far, Quinn."

"Oh, I would." His thumb moved over her cheekbone gently and his gaze drifted over her face as if he was preserving a memory that would have to last him a lifetime. "'Cause what I'm thinkin' is certainly foolish."

"What is that?" Her throat was tight. Each breath that staggered in and out of her chest seemed to shake her to her bones. Knees weak, prickly sensation quickly spreading, Winifred forced herself to ask again, "What are you thinking?"

"That I'd like to kiss you." He bent down, brushed his lips along hers, then straightened.

She licked her lips as if hoping to find his taste still lingering there.

"And that I'd like to touch you again," he went on and let his right hand slide down the length of her throat and across her chest to cup her breast tenderly.

"Oh, heavens." She swayed slightly, closed her eyes and concentrated on the touch of his hand and the warm, prickly sensation setting her nether regions on fire.

"Heaven," he whispered, "yeah." His thumb stroked her nipple through the clinging, cold wet fabric of her shirt and Winifred bit down on her bottom lip to contain the moan strangling her.

He stepped in even closer to her, dropped his left hand to her bottom and pulled her tight against his hips.

The hardness of his body pressed into her and quickened a damp, warm response in her own.

"You uh . . ." she said and moved against him a bit hesitantly, "*don't* have a rock in your pocket. Do you?"

"No ma'am," his breath brushed her cheek.

"That's . . . *you,* isn't it?"

"Oh, yes ma'am," he kissed the corner of her mouth and his tongue darted out to trace the outline of her lips.

"Oh my."

"Yes ma'am."

Winifred wasn't quite sure what she should do.

Fortunately, her body seemed to know exactly what to do. Her hands lifted to the back of his neck and her fingers threaded through his wet hair. She pressed herself against him and moaned softly as he caught her to him and squeezed her tightly.

"Fred," he whispered and bent his head to nuzzle at her throat, "maybe I shouldn't, but I do want you. So bad I think I'm gonna explode if I can't have you."

"Oh yes," she agreed and let her head fall to one side, giving him greater access to her flesh.

"But I'll stop this minute," he told her and lifted his head to stare down into her eyes. "If you say so. If you want, you can go back inside with the kids and I'll go on out to the barn." He drew in a long, shuddering breath. "I already fixed me a straw bed in one of the empty stalls."

Hay?

Winifred smiled.

Just as she'd imagined earlier, before they'd arrived at this house and found . . . the children. Dare she leave them asleep in the living room?

No, her practical, logical mind argued. Her duty was clear.

And yet, the newly born wanton in her countered, the children were exhausted. Their stomachs were full, probably for the first time in days. They would no doubt sleep without stirring for several hours. The fire was carefully banked and the door to their late mother's room was barred.

They were safe. Safer than they'd been in awhile.

Safer than she was at the moment.

They wouldn't even know she was gone.

Besides, how long could this take? Why, she'd probably be back in just a few minutes.

And when she returned from the barn, she would have the answers to so many questions. And, she would have felt her body shatter again. Just the thought of experiencing that once more had her squeezing her thighs together in anticipation.

She looked up at Quinn, silently waiting for her decision. And most importantly of all, she told herself, she would learn the secrets of her body from the man she'd come to love.

Love.

A slow smile curved her lips and she felt it go deep inside her. She loved him. Her smile faltered slightly. She loved a wanted fugitive who would no doubt be going to prison. Who knew how long they might be separated? And when he was finally released from having served his sentence to society, how long might it take her to convince him that he loved her as well?

Oh, no. She couldn't possibly wait *that* long to lie with him. God forgive her, Winifred knew she didn't want to wait another minute.

A lifetime's worth of beliefs and morals flew out of her mind at the mere promise of a night spent in Quinn Hawkins's arms.

Just as it should be.

"Well Winifred?" he asked quietly. "Do you want me to go on to the barn?"

"Yes," she said and watched disappointment flare in his eyes before she added quickly, "and I want you to take me with you."

He inhaled sharply and his arms tightened around her. "Are you sure?"

"Yes," she told him and smoothed his hair back from his brow. "More sure than I've ever been of anything else in my life."

He hardly let her finish talking before his mouth came down on hers. His tongue swept between her parted lips and invaded her soul as easily as he invaded her flesh. Every warm caress sent armies of shivers racing along her spine.

She pressed herself closer to him as if trying to crawl inside his body and become one with him. Every nerve in her body was alert and sensitized. Winifred felt everything more acutely than she ever had before.

The cold, wet fabric clinging to her. The night air brushing past them in a whispered rush. Quinn's palms moving up and down her back and the hard feel of his body pushing against hers.

All at once though, he pulled away, dragged air into his lungs and caught her hand in his. He started to lead her toward the barn, but stopped beside the water barrel at the corner of the cabin. Lying alongside the barrel was an overturned, wooden bucket.

"What are you doing?"

He let go of her hand briefly, reached for the bucket, then took the top off the water barrel. Dipping the pail inside, Quinn lifted it when it was half full of fresh, clean water. Then he slapped the round wooden cover back on the barrel, grabbed her hand again and started walking.

Water sloshed over the sides of the bucket in his right hand and plopped to the hard dry ground. Her sodden skirt clung to her legs and felt as heavy as lead. Catching the toe of her shoe in the torn, ragged hem, Winifred stumbled and the already ruined fabric ripped free.

Winifred snatched up a handful of her skirt then and hurried her steps to keep up with him. It was difficult, since her knees still felt too weak to support her. The short walk to the barn would nevertheless have been enough time for her to change her mind if she'd been so inclined.

However, all she could think was that the barn seemed much further away than it had earlier in the evening.

When they entered the building, Quinn walked straight to the empty stall nearest the double doors. As she stepped around the short wooden wall, Winifred noted the fresh straw spread over the ground and the blankets laid out atop the straw.

Her breath caught. Just as she'd imagined it earlier, she and Quinn were going to lay side by side on the fresh hay. She swallowed heavily and turned to look at him.

Quinn watched her for any sign that she might be changing her mind. Hell he wouldn't blame her if she turned for the door and started running. A barn wasn't exactly the most romantic place on earth. Even with fresh hay.

But she didn't look like she was getting ready to rabbit. Instead, she was watching him with a look in her eye that could only be described as hungry.

Quinn's already tight body hardened painfully and began to throb with a need he'd never known existed.

From somewhere at the back of the barn, one of the horses stamped its feet and snorted, but he paid no attention. Hell, if she could ignore the fact that they were in a barn . . . so could he.

He stepped up close to her and reached for the top button of her shirt.

She jumped a bit, startled.

"It's all right, Fred. You can still change your mind, y'know."

"No, it's not that." She licked her lips and it was all he could do not to bend down and capture her tongue with his. "It's just that . . . uh," she shrugged helplessly "I never really thought about actually disrobing in front of you."

"Ah . . ." Embarrassed again. If he had more light to see by than just the occasional beam of moonlight poking between the slats on the roof, Quinn was willing to bet he'd be looking at a real pretty blush. Of course, if he had a lamp, he doubted that she'd let him light it. Moving his fingers from her shirt buttons, he allowed his hand to slide to the swell of her breast.

Torturing them both, his thumb brushed over her rigid nipple and he caught her gasp of pleasure with his mouth. In less than a minute, Winifred was arching into his hand and he had to force himself not to rip her shirt-front open so that he could warm himself at her flesh.

Instead, he drew his head back from her mouth and whispered, "It's better when you're undressed, Fred."

"Better than this? Are you sure?"

"Oh, yes."

Without another word, she reached up and quickly undid the row of buttons down the front of her shirt.

Quinn watched her and his throat went dry. Awed and touched by her trust in him, he had to remind himself to go slow. Her gaze fixed on the ground, she shrugged out of her shirt and stood before him. The thin, wet fabric of her chemise was all that lay between him and the warm, lush feel of her.

The sodden material clung to her body like a lover, outlining her nipples and inviting his touch. Quinn resisted the impulse to cover her breasts with his palms and told himself that they had all the time in the world. There was no rush.

He unbuttoned his own shirt and pulled it off. Then, balling it up in his hands, he dipped it into the bucket of water he'd brought with him. Wringing out the excess, Quinn held his shirt in his right hand and reached out for her hand with his left.

Winifred looked up when he lifted her arm. Her gaze widened at the sight of his naked chest and he watched that flash of hunger light up her eyes again. Slowly, carefully, he smoothed his wet shirt up and down the length of her arm, washing away all traces of mud. When he was finished, he began again on her other arm.

He knew the water was cold, yet somehow, he didn't think she was feeling it anymore than he was. Lord knew, there was a fire burning inside him hot enough to melt a mountain full of snow. Judging by the look in her eyes, Quinn thought Winifred felt the same.

He tossed his shirt into the bucket, let his hands drop to her waist and slowly unhooked the waistband of her skirt. Their gazes locked, he was spellbound by the look of trust in her eyes. It was a heavy burden for any man to bear and he only hoped he could live up to it.

Her skirt dropped to the ground and she stepped out

of the pooled material and kicked it aside. Quinn's breath staggered slightly when she bent down, grabbed up his shirt from the bucket and wrung it out.

Then it was her turn. She dragged that shirt across his chest and up and down his arms and shoulders until the brush of the shirt against his bare flesh was almost more than he could bear. She moved around him, smoothing the fabric over his back and waist and the ache in his groin became overpowering.

When she stopped in front of him again, Quinn took the shirt from her and tossed it into the bucket. He didn't care if both of them were covered in muck. He simply needed to feel her body pressed along his.

He lifted the hem of her chemise and drew it up several inches before pausing. Strangling on his own breath, he waited for Winifred's response. When it came, his breath left him in a rush.

Winifred raised her arms high over her head and tried not to gasp as Quinn drew her chemise off.

"Ah, Jesus!" he sighed and dropped the garment to the ground. He was suddenly grateful that the swelling in his eye had gone down enough to allow him to see her clearly. Gently, reverently, he lifted his right hand and cupped one breast while he bent to kiss the other.

"Oh, good heavens," Winifred muttered and swayed toward him.

He smiled against her flesh and when he began to trace his tongue around the pink circle of her nipple, Winifred's eyes squeezed shut.

So good. He was right, she thought wildly. It was much better without clothes in the way. Her own breath choking in her throat, Winifred let her head fall back in a desperate attempt to draw air into her lungs. At the same time though, she almost didn't care that she couldn't seem to breathe. Anything would be bearable as long as he didn't stop what he was doing.

Quinn eased her back a step or two until the rough wooden planks of the stall wall scratched against her back. Grateful for the support, Winifred forgot everything else except the astonishing sensations Quinn Hawkins was creating inside her.

He drew her nipple into his mouth and worked the rigid peak with the tip of his tongue. The edges of his teeth scraped at her sensitive flesh and sent jagged spears of lightning shooting through her. Her heartbeat raced until she heard the drumming of it echo in her ears. The damp, warm, prickly feeling between her thighs screamed for his attentions and she didn't know how to tell him.

Instinctively, her hips arched and he must have noticed because his right hand slipped from her breast down her rib cage over the swell of her hip and behind to cup her bottom. His fingers smoothed across the cotton covered flesh of her behind and Winifred desperately wished she'd remembered to remove her pantaloons.

Quinn lifted his head from her breast and she sighed her regret. Opening her eyes, she looked down at him. A small slice of moonlight lay across the top of his head. His blond hair looked almost silver in the pale glow of the moon. She reached for him and let her fingers trail through the too long mass of soft, shining hair.

He glanced up at her touch and smiled at her gently.

"Are we stopping now?" she asked and couldn't quite hide the note of disappointment in her voice.

Shaking his head, Quinn grinned. "Fred, we ain't hardly got started."

Oh, thank heaven, she thought but clamped her lips together to keep from saying that out loud. It certainly couldn't be proper for a woman to be so bold and shameless.

Quinn tugged at the waistband strings of her pantaloons and Winifred was so lost to the sensations wracking her body she didn't even react. Her gaze still locked on him, she watched as Quinn loosened the strings and began to push the cotton fabric down over her hips.

His hands felt wonderful on her skin. The callouses on his palms and fingertips brushed against her with the force of a Lucifer head striking its scratch pad. Every inch of flesh he touched seemed to burst into flame. She wiggled in his grasp and unconsciously spread her legs a bit further apart, hoping to steady herself.

Quinn leaned forward and placed a slow, lingering kiss on her abdomen and she felt her stomach jerk in response. Her fingers tightened in his hair as if her hold on him was the one thing keeping her on the ground.

As his hands pushed the wet cotton down the length of her legs, Quinn continued to lavish kisses on her belly, her hips, her thighs. His moustache brushed over her skin and Winifred was sure she'd never felt anything so wickedly wonderful in her life.

Then he stopped briefly. Almost before she could miss his attentions, he'd slipped her shoes off, dragged her pantaloons down and tossed them aside. All that he'd left her were her black cotton stockings and she didn't care.

His lips returned to her body and Winifred allowed herself to lean back more fully against the stall wall. Prickles of wood splinters poked at her backside but only added a different sensation to the others coursing through her.

Licking her lips, Winifred fought for breath and forced her eyes to remain open. She watched him stroke her skin. She watched him move his mouth across her abdomen, his tongue teasing at her flesh. She watched one of his hands slip around behind her and felt his fingers gently kneading her behind.

Need throbbed in her center and in a futile quest for release, Winifred rocked her hips helplessly in his grasp.

Then he moved suddenly and Winifred gasped as she watched him kiss her . . . *there.*

Unthinkingly, she yanked on his hair.

"Hey!" Quinn's gaze lifted to hers and Winifred had to battle her embarrassment to look at him.

"Quinn," she said, her voice shaking slightly, "you mustn't do . . . *that.*"

"You'll like it," he assured her wickedly. "I promise."

She was sure she would and that admission was certainly worth another paving stone on her road to Hell. Dredging up what little self control she had left, Winifred told him "Nevertheless, I must insist." She pulled in a long, ragged breath, "It simply wouldn't be proper."

Slowly, his lips curved into a grin. "You are really somethin', you know that, Fred?"

She shook her head.

"You're worried about proper while we're in a barn that's more holes than wood, layin' on a blanket-covered bed of hay with four horses watchin'?"

All right, it *did* sound silly when he said it aloud like that, but still. She just . . . couldn't let him do that.

"I'm sorry, Quinn. It's just that I—"

Quinn took her hands in his and pulled her down beside him, effectively silencing her apology. When they were both on their knees, Quinn cupped her face with his hands and told her "We'll do this your way, Winifred. Anything you don't like, you just say so and we'll quit it."

At that moment, Winifred wasn't sure she'd ever be able to speak again, but she looked deeply into his so familiar blue eyes and nodded. How had this happened? In little more than a week, she'd come to love a man she hadn't known existed a month ago. And dear Lord, how she *did* love him.

Then his lips claimed hers and she forgot everything else.

Her breasts flattened against his chest and she moved slightly to enhance the rough feel of his flesh on hers. The golden hairs dusting his chest brushed at her and she felt his heart pounding in time with her own.

He laid her down on the blanket, then quickly rose and pulled off his boots and pants. Winifred watched him, fascinated and when she saw his hardened body for the first time, she closed her eyes quickly.

Quinn stretched out alongside her and she heard his soft chuckle. "Don't be scared, Fred. I won't hurt you."

"Not intentionally, I'm sure," she answered and kept her eyes closed despite the fact that she wanted nothing more than to stare up into his face. However, that one glimpse of his . . . nakedness had been enough to convince her that perhaps they'd made a mistake. Perhaps she shouldn't have been quite so eager to be bedded. Good Heavens, she thought with a pang, this would never work. But how to tell him? Finally, she blurted out "Quinn, you look so . . . big."

"Thanks."

Her eyes snapped open and she looked up into his pleased, proud smile. Apparently, he hadn't noticed that she wasn't complimenting him.

"Don't you see?" she whispered, hoping he would understand and that she wouldn't have to explain completely. "If you're thinking of putting . . . *that,*" she hedged, "where I think you are . . ." Winifred shook her head sadly. "I don't believe *it* . . . I mean of course, *you,* will fit."

"Ah, Winifred," he sighed, leaned over her and brushed his lips across hers briefly, "you'll just have to trust me. I'll fit."

She wanted to believe him. She really did. And yet . . . Her gaze drifted down his body to the hardened length of flesh now pressing insistently against her hip. Quite frankly, she didn't see how on earth something that size would ever fit itself to her small body. Her doubts colored her voice when she asked, "Are you sure?"

"More sure than I've ever been," he said and shifted to cover her body with his. Deliberately, he moved his chest slowly against hers until she was stirring and twisting beneath him. "Darlin', we were *made* to fit each other."

"Well then," she sighed, then gasped aloud as his hand swept down her body to cup the center of the ache threatening to devour her. Lifting her hips into his touch, Winifred raised her head from the blanket and kissed him. "Show me."

"My pleasure," he whispered and dipped his fingers into her damp warmth.

Winifred nearly shot off the blanket. He soothed her with quiet whispers and gentle kisses. She forced herself to take slow, even breaths. She inhaled the scents of fresh hay and damp wool from the blanket beneath her. She opened her eyes and stared straight up through the gaps in the roof to the night sky above. Moonlight skittered in and out of the barn as clouds danced past the moon.

But she didn't need moonlight. Her body seemed to glow with the light of a thousand candles. Every inch of her flesh tingled and burned with a white hot fire.

Quinn lavished attention on her body. His mouth and tongue teased her breasts while his fingers moved gently and deliberately over the sensitive flesh between her legs.

Planting her feet flat on the straw-littered ground, Winifred's hips lifted in time with his touch. Each time his fingers entered her, she arched against him, silently pleading for more. The need she'd felt earlier in the day, when he'd touched her so intimately was intensified until it seemed as nothing compared to the overwhelming force driving her now.

She couldn't catch her breath. Her tongue darted out constantly, smoothing her parched lips and still it wasn't enough. Guttural cries from the base of her throat echoed in the stillness and she could hardly credit that it was she making such sounds.

Quinn's mouth closed over one of her nipples and she held him to her. He seemed to understand and began to suckle her harder, drawing on her flesh as if it meant his very life. Something deep inside her pulled tight as his mouth worked her nipple and when his thumb brushed a too sensitive nub of flesh at the same time, Winifred groaned aloud.

It was too much. All of it. No one could stand so much sensation at one time. She didn't know how to move. She didn't know what she wanted more of, his fingers or his mouth. Her hands moved to his shoulders and her fingers dug into the hard muscles of his back. Drawing her knees up, she offered herself to him, hoping he would see that she couldn't stand the tension any longer.

He lifted his head from her breast, moved to kiss her mouth hungrily, then shifted until he was kneeling between her thighs.

"Quinn, help me," she whispered, completely disregarding any silly notions of propriety. Nothing mattered anymore but that her need was answered. Quickly. "Please."

Smiling down at her, he shook his head slowly. "Not yet, Winifred. Not yet."

God, she wondered frantically, what was there left for him to do? Why didn't he ease the torment? Her body felt as tight as piano wire.

His fingers moved over her center and Winifred's body jerked in response. Her gaze flew to him and she watched through slitted eyes as he gently opened the folds of her body. With tender strokes of his fingertips, Quinn built the fire in her blood into a raging inferno.

Then slowly, he moved to position his hardened body at her opening. Winifred tensed, despite her desire. He looked into her eyes and whispered simply, "Trust me."

She did. She did trust him or heaven knew, she wouldn't be lying where she was at that moment. Burrowing her head back onto the blanket-covered straw, Winifred opened her thighs wider and braced herself.

She felt his flesh rub against her and she shivered. Soft and strong all at once, it was how she thought of Quinn all the time. Tender, patient, with a strength that could be depended on.

Trust him.

His thumb caressed the hard nub of her desire and he smiled as she began to move her hips eagerly. He glanced down at their joining and his breath caught. Tender, sensitive pink flesh, hidden by red curls seemed to call to him.

Inch by tantalizing inch, Quinn entered her body. It was all he could do to keep from thrusting himself home. Her warmth, her passion, the damp heat surrounding the tip of his shaft was almost enough to drive him over the edge into madness. But still, he moved slowly, giving her body time to adjust to his.

Just when he thought he couldn't bear it another moment Winifred gasped and arched her hips hard against him, drawing his body deeper into hers.

"Sweet Jesus, Winifred," he whispered as beads of sweat broke out on his forehead. "I'm tryin' to go easy here and you ain't helpin'."

Her eyes opened and fastened on him. He watched shadows of want and need move across the green depths and when she said, her voice husky, "Come inside me now, Quinn," he was lost.

Leaning forward, he laid one hand on either side of her and gave one last, hard thrust.

Her back arched, her eyes squeezed shut and she bit down hard on her bottom lip.

"It won't hurt anymore, Fred, I swear."

She nodded, but he knew she didn't believe him. Still it said something that she raised her legs and wrapped them around his hips. He buried his face in the crook of her neck and inhaled the sweet scent of her as his hips moved over hers.

In moments, the flash of pain was forgotten in a new frenzy of need. Winifred pulled his head to hers and kissed him with abandon, her tongue darting in and out of his mouth even as his flesh moved in and out of her body.

Quinn too was at his breaking point. He needed the release waiting for them every bit as badly as she did. Reluctantly, he raised up and sat back on his haunches. His flesh still a part of her, he lifted her hips slightly. Her legs fell from his waist and her feet were planted firmly on the floor.

His thumb moved over the nub of flesh at her center and he watched her climb the last peak separating her from the pleasure to come. Her hips rocked against his hand, her head tossed from side to side on the blanket and the damp heat surrounding him tightened when the first tremors shook through her. Ripples of release crashed over her and she screamed his name.

Immediately, Quinn pushed his body deep into her again. Her damp heat still quivering, he began to move in an ancient rhythm, his hips pounding against hers. Desire, pleasure and love rose up in him and threatened to strangle him.

Winifred reached out and splayed her palms on his back and buttocks. She lifted her knees and arched into his movements again and again. Quinn looked down into her eyes and saw another crashing release claim her just before his own world exploded into waves of delight.

17

"Go have a beer, will ya?"

Dusty frowned at his friend, picked up his hat and headed for the door. "Might as well. Still don't see why we have to stop at these spit in the road towns. Quinn ain't gonna be here and it's purely a waste of time."

"Jesus, will you shut up for awhile?" Tom poured some wash water into the basin, set the pitcher down, then dipped his hands into the cold liquid. Splashing the water onto his face, he gasped at the icy shock of it, wiped himself dry with a scratchy old towel then looked at Dusty again. "You know, you're worse to travel with than an old woman?"

Dusty leaned back against the hotel room door, folded his arms over his chest and crossed one booted foot over the other. "You just don't want to listen to me 'cause I'm right, is all."

"Right or wrong," Tom told him, *"I'm* in charge."

"And doin' a helluva job of it, too."

"Very funny." Tom pushed his hair straight back from his forehead with damp hands. Glaring at Dusty, he reminded him, "Nobody *asked* you to come along. Remember?"

Ignoring that, Dusty said "So tell me again. Why do we have to stay here overnight?"

Tom sighed. If this trail lasted much longer, he was goin' to end up shooting one of his oldest friends. "Because it's too damned late to ask questions around town."

"Depends on who you're askin'."

"The sheriff, maybe? A storekeeper?"

"You could ask the bartender tonight."

"Why don't *you* handle that, Dusty?"

The other man grinned and his straight, even teeth were a slash of white against his tanned skin. "Be happy to." He pushed away from the door and straightened up. "I'm too damned restless to sit still anyhow. Must be that storm that's comin'."

Tom groaned. Dusty hadn't let up about that supposed storm for *hours.*

"But how 'bout you? Don't you want a beer as long as we're here?"

"Maybe later." All he wanted that minute, Tom told himself, was some peace and quiet. He'd get that the moment he got rid of Dusty.

"Up to you," Dusty said with a shrug. As he turned the doorknob though he added, "But if ya ask me, it's you who's gettin' to be an old woman!"

Tom gritted his teeth. If he started arguing with the man, Dusty'd never leave. Nothing Dusty McDonough liked better than a good fight. Then the door opened and closed again quietly and Tom was alone.

Flopping down onto the feather mattress, Tom heaved a long sigh and stared up at the water-stained ceiling. This trip was turning into a nightmare. Hell, he'd never expected to be gone from Yellow Dog this long. Who knew what was going on back in town.

Damn Quinn anyway. If he was smart enough to make himself this hard to find, you'd think he'd have been smart enough to keep from robbing a bank. Tom's eyelids closed and he let himself enjoy the feel of a soft bed under his tired body. Jesus, he felt like he'd been nailed into that saddle.

But his peace only lasted for a few minutes. Even with the comfort of a feather bed, he couldn't keep his mind quiet. Thoughts kept chasing through his brain making it impossible to lay still.

Hell, he knew just what Dusty meant. He too, felt restless. Edgy. The only difference was, Tom wasn't blaming a coming storm on his mood. It was the constant travel. The continual watchfulness. It was staring at the ground for hours, hoping to pick up a trail. It was worry about his town.

And Quinn.

Shit. Swinging his legs off the bed. Tom rose and walked across the small room to the window overlooking the narrow street. Through the encrusted grime of at least a dozen winters, he stared at the street below and the handful of people headed for the saloon.

As he watched, Dusty stepped into his line of vision from under the hotel overhang. Took him long enough, Tom thought. Then in the next instant, he told himself that Dusty'd probably stopped in his room to get cleaned up. He was never one to pass up a chance at a woman.

And where there was a saloon, there was sure to be women.

Dusty's long, even strides carried him purposefully across the street in a straight line toward the saloon. As he watched his friend though, a frown creased Tom's features. Something was different about the other man. But what was it?

Grumbling to himself about filthy windows and shoddy innkeepers, Tom squinted as he leaned in closer to the glass.

Then it hit him.

"Goddammit!" Tom braced both hands on the window frame and pushed. "Dusty!" he shouted futilely. It was no use though. His friend couldn't hear him and the window didn't budge. Some damn fool had painted the sash shut. Pounding one fist against the wall, Tom stared helplessly as Dusty stepped up on the boardwalk and entered the brightly-lit saloon.

Too late, his brain chanted even as he turned from the window and ran around the room grabbing up his boots and hat. He'd be too late to stop the fight. But he might be in time to keep Dusty from getting his stupid head caved in.

Tom jumped up and down on one foot while he pulled his boots on, one after the other. While he was busy, his mind went over what he'd just seen as if to make sure there'd been no mistake.

But there wasn't and he knew it.

Dusty had stopped by his room to change all right.

The idiot had switched his boots for his moccasins and taken off his belt gun in favor of his long, razor-sharp Arkansas Toothpick. He also wasn't wearing his hat and he had his damned hair pulled back into a single braid.

His fighting outfit.

Dusty never fought wearing boots and a pistol. He always said he could move better in mocassins and if he had his gun it might be too damned easy to just pull a trigger instead of throwing a punch. His knife he always relied on in a fight just in case his opponent wasn't fighting fair. As for that damned hair of his, Dusty claimed one long braid was harder to catch hold of than a curtain of black hair swinging free.

"Restless," Tom muttered angrily as he jammed his hat on and raced for the door. "If we live through this, I'll show him restless."

Taking the stairs two at a time, Tom's footsteps thundered out into the silence of the old hotel. He jumped past the last three steps and hit the lobby floor running. Through the front doors, across the boardwalk and into the street, Tom had almost convinced himself that maybe this time would be different.

Then a cowboy came crashing through the saloon's wide, front window, sending a shower of glass shards in all directions.

Tom groaned. From inside the saloon, he heard a lone, Comanche war whoop.

"You make good coffee," Jim Barry said and leaned both elbows on the scrubbed, white pine table.

Her back to him, Mercy set the battered tin coffee pot down on the stove and paused before turning around. "I've had a lot of years to practice."

"Not so many, I'd bet."

Mercy laughed shortly, walked to the table and sat down directly opposite him. "You'd lose your money on that bet, mister."

One corner of his mouth lifted in a smile and Mercy tried not to look at him. He was just too handsome for his own good. And damned if he didn't know it, too. Any man with a smile like that would have to be dumb as a stump not to know the effect it had on women.

This was a mistake, she told herself. She should never have allowed him to come into the house with her. Oh, not that she was afraid of him. It's just that, hell. She took a quick glance around the sparkling clean kitchen. Hanging copper pans gleamed in the soft light of a single lantern. A fresh bouquet of bluebonnets poked up from a milk glass vase set on the wide windowsill. A cozy fire crackled in the freshly blacked, potbellied stove. The whole scene was too intimate. Too . . . *snuggled down.*

And they were the only two people in the house. Her cook surely didn't count. Sound asleep in a room down a long hall, he was so deaf, if someone shot a gun off in his room, the man wouldn't stir a hair.

No, everything here was too snug and sheltered. Too . . . *familiar* to be safe. And he looked far too comfortable. She must have been out of her mind to invite Jim Barry in for coffee.

He leaned back in his chair, lifted his coffee cup for another sip and looked at her over the rim of the thick white porcelain. "Why is it, Mercy Hawkins, that you try so hard to convince everybody that you're an old woman?"

"Don't have to try, Jim Barry. Facts are facts." She dropped her gaze from his, snatched a cookie from the plate in the center of the table and studied it. "Or did you forget I have a grown son?"

"No, I didn't forget."

"Good." Now if only she could keep reminding herself.

"But that has nothin' to do with this conversation." He set his cup down and ran one fingertip over the pine planks of the table. "I've known folks who were born old. And, I know a man who's been on this earth for ninety some years and doesn't seem a day over twenty."

She laughed again but there was no humor in the sound.

The big man across from her pushed himself to his feet and walked around the table to her side.

Mercy didn't look at him.

But he wouldn't be ignored.

He reached down, cupped her elbows in his palms and drew her up to stand in front of him.

"You're a fine looking woman, Mercy."

She swallowed heavily and tried to disregard the warmth spreading through her like a soft summer breeze after a too long winter.

"I think you'd better leave."

"You're strong, too. Oh, not the kind of strong that needs muscles to prove a point. The kind of strong that comes from a hard head and a soft heart."

She tried to back up. "It's late. You should go."

"In a minute."

She inhaled sharply. For the first time in years, she was nervous.

His fingers caught her chin and tipped her face up. Mercy stared into his gray eyes and saw something she'd thought never to see again. A man's desire. For her.

Her insides shifted.

Slowly, he bent down and tentatively brushed his lips over hers. Something powerful rocketed through her and when he drew his head back to stare at her, Mercy knew he'd felt it too. She was ready when he bent to claim her mouth again.

It seemed, she thought wildly, that *some* things, a woman didn't forget how to do.

Her arms snaked up to encircle his neck and her lips parted to allow his tongue entry. Mercy's breath caught and for one terrifying moment, she thought her heart had stopped. But in an instant, that organ was pounding out an erratic rhythm that matched exactly her strangled, ragged breaths.

Too soon, Jim lifted his head and took a half-step back from her. He rubbed one big hand across his jaw and she saw that his breathing was every bit as labored as her own.

"I'm going to leave now," he finally said and she noticed that his voice wasn't nearly as steady as it had been.

"I think that's best." She nodded, stepped away from him and quickly led the way back down the narrow hall to the front of the house. At the door, she stopped, grabbed the brass knob and yanked the oak panel wide open. A blast of cold, rain-scented air whipped into the room, ripping away the last of the cobwebs in her brain. As Jim stopped beside her, she said stiffly, "We'll just forget all about this, shall we?"

"Forget it?" His voice rumbled along her spine. "You think you can?"

"Yes, I do" she lied.

"Well, Mercy," Jim said and leaned down until he was looking her squarely in the eyes, "you're wrong. And you know how I *know* you're wrong?"

She shook her head.

"Because I'm not gonna let you forget." He pulled her into his arms one last time, gave her a hard, brief kiss and set her back again. Snatching his hat from the peg by the door, he jammed it down on his head before adding, "I've been lookin' for a woman like you—no." He corrected, "I've been lookin' for *you* too damned long to let you get away now. So you just get used to lookin' at this face, Mercy Hawkins."

Speechless, she blinked and stared at him.

"I surely hope you can stand it," he went on, "'cause you're gonna be lookin' at it every morning and every night for the rest of our lives."

"You're crazy."

"That's been said before."

Mercy forced herself to breathe and closed the door an inch or two to convince him to leave.

It worked. He took a couple of steps, but turned quickly and slapped his open palm on the door to hold it open long enough to say one more thing. "I'm gonna marry you, Mercy. And *that's* a promise."

"You are crazy!" she gasped and lifted one hand to clutch at her throat. She didn't even want to think about the flash of excitement that had briefly lit up her insides. One of them had to keep a clear head.

"Why?" he demanded. "Because I know what and who I want when I see her?"

"Because one day isn't enough to decide what to do with your life. You don't know anything about me."

"I know all I need to know. And I'll tell you something else," he added and lifted one hand to cup her cheek. "I decided to marry you the minute I clapped eyes on you."

She shook her head.

"Five minutes of knowing a person or five years. Doesn't really matter. When it's right . . . you *know* it." His thumb traced her cheekbone gently, then he reluctantly let his hand drop to his side. "If you'll be honest with yourself, Mercy girl, you'll admit *you* know it, too."

Then he turned and walked away without another word.

She slammed the door behind him and leaned back against it, her eyes wide open and her heart racing.

Quinn rolled to one side and drew Winifred into the circle of his arms. She laid her head on his chest and he stared blankly up through the roof of the barn.

Every inch of him felt more alive than he'd ever thought possible. Each breath seemed like a drink of honey and even his heart's erratic pounding seemed like the melody to a song he'd waited a lifetime to learn.

A small smile crossed his face. If he hadn't yanked his boots off earlier, Winifred would have *knocked* 'em off.

Lord! It was purely amazing that he'd had to wait thirty-two years to discover the difference between sex and making love.

She snuggled in closer to him and dragged the flat of her hand across his chest. He felt a stirring in his loins and knew that he wanted her again. And again. And again. He would never have enough of her. Like a thirst that could never be quenched, each taste was just enough to make him thirstier.

And, his brain quietly reminded him, one taste was all he was likely to get. With that numbing realization, his mind came down out of the clouds and he recognized their little love nest for what it really was.

A blanket-draped stall in a run-down barn.

Bits of hay poked through the blanket and stabbed at his skin. Clouds drifted past the moon again and closed off its light. A chill snaked through him.

Winifred Matthews deserved better. He should never have taken her like some common whore. She deserved a nice bed and clean sheets. Hell at the very least, she deserved a *roof* over her head with more wood than view.

And in the last week or so, he was pretty sure he'd come to know her well enough to guess what she was thinking now. No doubt her brain had turned to visions of churches and white satin and flowers and preachers. She was probably laying there waiting for him to propose.

As he would. If he could.

"Quinn," she mumbled and rubbed her cheek against his chest.

"What?" his voice sounded harsher than he'd meant it to.

"Is everything all right?" Winifred tipped her head back to look at him.

"Yeah. Everything's fine." Just dandy, he added mentally and allowed himself the pleasure of stroking her naked back for the last time.

"That was . . . wonderful," she said softly and her breath stirred the hairs sprinkled across his chest.

"Yeah, it was." More than wonderful, he thought. Incredible. Amazing.

"You were right, too."

"About what?"

Her fingers smoothed over his flat nipple and he caught her hand with his to still her movements.

"You *did* fit."

"Oh." Just thinking about it had him ready to fit himself to her again.

"And quite nicely, too. Just as you said, I think we *were* made to fit each other."

Shit. It figured that she'd remember hearing him say that.

"About that, Winifred . . ."

"But," she interrupted and rose up to brace herself on one elbow.

He looked up at her and noticed that her hair was half up and half down. Some of the pins were still in place and idly, Quinn reached up to pull them free. He wanted to see her hair loose and wild. He wanted to bury himself in the rich, red color and never bother to find his way out again.

She leaned her head into his touch and smiled as the pins were plucked out. Shaking her head, she set the red curls to dancing around her naked shoulders.

She was beautiful.

And he couldn't have her.

"I want you to know," she said and met his gaze squarely, "that I know things are very different in the Wild West than they are back home."

"Yeah?" Different? Different how? Where was she going with this? What was that mind of hers thinking up now?

"At home, if a man and woman had uh . . . done . . . well, *this*, they would have rushed themselves to a minister and sanctified their union."

His heart dropped to his feet. Just as he'd expected. Hymns and orange blossoms. Dammit, now he was going to have to ruin their time together by breaking her heart.

"But I realize of course, that out here, nothing like that is expected."

"Huh?" Quinn drew his head back and stared at her, speechless.

"You needn't look so surprised," Winifred assured him. "Remember, I've done a lot of reading on the West."

How the hell could he forget? He'd heard more about books in the last week or so than he'd ever wanted to know.

"And I recall Marshal Travis experiencing something along these very lines in one of his adventures."

Him again. At the mention of her fictional hero, Quinn frowned. Did he even have to share her with Travis in bed?

"Yes," she tapped one finger against her chin thoughtfully, "Yes." She nodded firmly. "The Marshal gave his heart to a lovely young woman named Prudence and—"

"Prudence?"

"Yes." Winifred grinned at the memory. "Oh, she was wonderful, too. Absolutely the perfect woman for the Marshal. But of course, not even his love for her, nor his passion was enough to sway him from his duty."

"Oh, of course not." Marshal Travis was, as Quinn had decided days ago, a damned fool.

Winifred sighed. "They had one night together, when they proclaimed their undying love for each other. He held her in his strong arms, kissed her senseless and then early the next morning, he left her."

Sounded more like Travis was the one who ended up senseless! And Winifred looked like she was proud of the idiot for walking away from a woman he'd bedded.

"What kind of man does a thing like that?" he demanded. At the moment, it was beside the point that that was precisely what Quinn had planned to do. After all, he had no choice. He was probably headed for prison. Still, it stung to know that Winifred had expected him to turn his back on her.

"An honorable one." Winifred answered then frowned slightly at Quinn's obvious agitation. "He couldn't very well give up his quest for justice or his life's work of making miscreants accountable to the law."

"Miskree . . . *what?*"

"Miscreants. Evildoers. Outlaws."

"Oh." He jerked her a nod and pushed himself up halfway to lean back on both elbows. "And what about Prudence?"

Even as he heard himself, Quinn couldn't believe that he was arguing about what a pretend man should have done. "Travis just rides off and leaves her ruined?"

Winifred sat up too. Resting on her haunches, she shook her head and her long red curls fell forward, hiding her breasts from his view. She acted as though she'd completely forgotten that she was naked. "Prudence wasn't ruined in any way."

Quinn snorted. "Then ol' Marshal Travis ain't nearly as *great* as you think he is."

"Quinn Hawkins!"

"If they spent the night together—like we just done—she was ruined. Plain and simple."

"Of course, you are a man, that would be your point of view."

"It would be anybody's point of view, Fred!" he was shouting now and made an effort to tamp down the anger that was spreading through him like a prairie fire.

"Not Prudence's." She narrowed her gaze a bit. "And not *mine.*"

"So you're sayin' you ain't ruined?"

"Of course not." She smiled and inhaled deeply. "On the contrary, I feel wonderful."

Wonderful. Holy God, didn't she care that she'd given away her virtue to a no-account bank robber? Didn't she care that she might even now be pregnant?

Shit.

He hadn't thought of that before. Frowning, he lifted one hand and pushed it through his tangled, straw-dotted hair. Christ, he'd made a mess of things.

"What if we made a baby tonight, Fred?" he demanded suddenly. "You still gonna feel wonderful? You think you'll like hearin' your child called a bastard?"

She frowned for a moment, then that blasted smile of hers was back.

"Oh, I'm sure there's no baby, Quinn."

"How can you be sure of that?"

"Well, it was only the one time. And for heaven's sake. Prudence didn't conceive!"

"Prudence ain't real!"

"Nevertheless," she said and that schoolteacher primness was back in her tone, "I'm sure everything will be fine."

She didn't want to marry him.

Stunned, Quinn stared at her. She wasn't planning a wedding. She was planning a big good-bye scene like the one she'd read about in a damned book!

Well hell. What was he expecting? That Winifred Matthews would fall in love with a bank robber? Her kidnapper? Why should she? Hell, she was worth a dozen of him!

Hadn't he told himself all along that he wasn't good enough for her? Hadn't he just a few minutes ago been trying to figure out a way to tell her he *couldn't* marry her?

He should be happy, dammit! This was working out fine.

Then why, a voice in the back of his mind asked quietly, did he feel so damned bad?

18

She was becoming entirely too adept at lying.

Winifred inhaled sharply, kept her gaze fixed on Quinn's features and tried to keep her own expression blank. If he should guess what she was really thinking . . .

Her body still tingling from his touch, it was all Winifred could do to keep from throwing herself on his chest and begging him to marry her. Oh, not that she was worried about what people might say . . . well, not *too* worried. It was mainly that she couldn't imagine going through the rest of her life without him.

Lord, to never know what it felt like to lie in his arms again. To never look into his eyes and see the different flashes of emotion she'd come to know so well. How would she face the hundreds of dawns to come knowing that Quinn Hawkins wouldn't be a part of each new day?

But how could she beg him to marry her when she knew as well as he that he was a fugitive? His life was now destined to be spent running from the law. And having a wife to worry about would only hamper him.

Winifred lifted her chin, reached for her scattered

clothing and quickly began to dress. She had to get out of that barn before she surrendered to her own selfish impulses. She had to leave while she still had the strength to let him go.

For his own good.

He didn't speak while she dressed. In fact, he didn't look her way. Winifred told herself though, that in time, Quinn would see that she had done the right thing. He would recognize her sacrifice for what it was and know that she had truly loved him.

She sniffed. Really, she was gaining a whole new respect for Prudence.

"I'm going in now, to sit with the children," she said as she stood up.

"Fine." His forearm over his eyes, Quinn still didn't look at her. "I'll take care of the kids' mama early in the mornin', so's they won't see."

She nodded, even though he wasn't watching her. Suddenly her throat was too full for speech. In the strained silence, Winifred turned and walked toward the barn doors. Before she left though, she tossed one quick glance at the stall where Quinn lay unmoving.

No matter whatever else happened in her life, she would always remember this night and the valuable lesson she'd learned.

Love hurt—and adventure was definitely not all people claimed it to be.

She'd hardly been gone ten minutes when the rain started.

Quinn opened his eyes and stared straight up into the drizzle. In seconds, the steady mist developed into a regular downpour and as the raindrops pummelled him, he closed his eyes and frowned.

"Perfect."

*   *   *

Charles Bentley tugged his vest into place over his well-fed stomach and scowled as Erma Hightower strode into the bank.

How a woman like that had become a "pillar of society" anywhere was beyond him. True, a town the size of Yellow Dog wasn't in a position to be picky, but still . . .

The woman's huge, rawboned exterior hid an interior with all the style and grace of a buffalo hunter. It was a truly appalling situation when a man of his sensibilities was forced by circumstances to treat a woman like that as an equal.

"Bentley," she announced as she marched up to the iron-barred teller cage "I want to see my money."

"I beg your pardon?"

"My money," she repeated and her voice shook the windowpanes in their sashes. "I want to see it."

"As I'm sure you're aware madam," Bentley said with as much dignity as he could manage, "the bank's funds are not always kept readily to hand."

A couple of his other customers were watching the exchange with avid eyes and he shifted position uneasily. Narrowing his gaze, he gave Erma a glare that would have intimidated most men. Erma though, leaned one muscular forearm on the counter and jutted her square chin at him.

"So you're sayin' you don't *have* my money?"

"The bank's funds are invested," he told her evenly and forced a smile on the farmer who was stepping up closer to the action, "in properties, railroads and other growing concerns." The fact that those investments had all been made in his own name was none of her business.

"Two days, Bentley."

"I beg your pardon?"

"Do that a lot, don'cha?" she shot back.

"Do what?"

"Beg folks' pardon."

"It is merely a polite turn of phrase." One he was sure she was unaware of. But then, what could one expect when one was forced to reside in the very backwaters of civilization?

"Well," Erma told him and laid both of her meaty palms flat on the polished countertop, "don't waste none of your fancy words on me, man. I ain't interested."

Heaven knew, he would have bet on *that*.

"All I'm interested in is seein' my money. *All* of it." Erma leaned in even closer and Bentley fought the urge to back away from her steely-eyed gaze and the powerful, beak of a nose jutting through the teller bars. "And I'm givin' you two days to get it here where I can count it."

"Madam, that's impossible—"

"Do it," she snapped.

"But the bank's funds are distributed among—"

"I don't give a good hang about the bank's funds. I want *my* money and I want it in two days."

"Is there somethin' wrong, Erma?" the farmer asked, looking up at the big woman.

"Don't know for sure, Joe," she said with barely a glance in his direction. "Just a hunch I got."

"Erma's hunches are enough for me, Mr. Bentley." The farmer peered through the iron bars at him. "Long as you're gettin' her money for her . . . you just get a hold of mine, too."

"Now see here . . ."

"You got your orders, Bentley." Erma cut him off again and half-turned for the door. Before she took a step though, she looked back at him. "Best get busy."

When Erma left the bank, the other customers followed her like newborn puppies after their mother.

Bentley hurried from around the counter, marched across the freshly swept floor and turned the lock on the door. Damn them all. It was *his* bank, and if he wanted to close up, he'd do it. His pudgy fingers took hold of the door shade and yanked it down over the glass. He let go too soon though and the shade flew up, rattling noisily.

He stared through the hand-lettered sign on the glass door at the hotel across the street. Silently, he watched as Erma climbed the three short steps to the boardwalk, then walked inside the small, whitewashed building. Why was she going into the hotel?

For that matter, why had she come into the bank so early? Everyone in town knew that Erma never stirred out of her house before noon. And why was she suddenly so insistent on seeing the money she had on deposit?

Something was in the air, he told himself. Something that could only bode trouble for him.

As Bentley took hold of the shade again and this time lowered it carefully, he noticed the dark, threatening sky overhead. Storm coming. By the looks of it, it was going to be a big one, too.

Once the world had been locked out, he turned around and looked at what had been the beginnings of his little empire.

He'd had such hopes for Yellow Dog. But did it really matter? he asked himself. He could find another small town with wealthy ranchers and water rights ripe for the taking. As for what he'd already accumulated, it should be easy enough to find a buyer for the properties he'd foreclosed on.

Then, he would have more than sufficient capital to lay a foundation for what would one day be the largest personal fortune in America.

Filled with renewed enthusiasm, Charles Bentley hurried across the bank to the vault. There was much to do.

*   *   *

"You shouldn't have done it, Erma," Mercy told her old friend. Carefully, she peeked at the bank from behind the curtains at the hotel's front window. "Now you've put him on his guard."

"Can't stand settin' still and not doin' a damned thing while that no account gets rich off my money." Erma pointed one long finger at the other woman for emphasis, "*And* yours, Mercy Hawkins!"

"But Jim told you it would only be another day or two."

"*Jim* is it?" Erma's bushy eyebrows lifted. "Mighty friendly, aren't you?"

Mercy dropped the curtains and glanced at the staircase leading to the rooms above. Assured that Jim Barry hadn't appeared yet, she turned back to Erma. "You said it, Erma. *Friendly.* Don't be seein' things that aren't there."

"Hmmph!" Erma snorted and brushed crumbs off her shelf-like bosom. Reaching for another slice of cold, buttered toast from Mercy's untouched breakfast plate, she glanced at the stairs and said, "Here he comes."

Mercy spun around and fought down the jangle of nerves that had suddenly leapt into life. From across the room, she met Jim Barry's gaze and was only half listening when Erma observed "Hmmm . . . he's lookin' at you the same way my man used to eye a plateful of steak and potatoes. Don't you tell *me* I'm seein' things!"

Tom's head was pounding like Satan's anvil.

He was looking at the world through slitted eyes, thanks to the swelling caused by a couple of well-thrown punches. His knee hurt from the kick he'd taken and one of his back teeth was loose.

Glancing to his right, he glared at Dusty. "Just couldn't stay out of trouble, could you?"

His old friend grinned, then winced when his split lip

pulled. Dusty's right eye was swollen and turning a vivid shade of deep purple. He had a knot on his forehead the size of a hen's egg and a fine imprint of a full set of teeth on his left forearm.

"Hell, Tom. Wasn't that bad."

"Not that bad." Tom jerked him a nod and groaned slightly at the movement. "Tore up the saloon, damn near got shot by the bartender and only escaped because some fool cowhand kicked a lantern over and started a fire . . . and that's not too bad?"

Dusty laughed and moaned at the same time. "At least we got some information, didn't we?"

"Yeah, but damned near got killed for our trouble."

"Hell, we've been in bigger fights than that." Dusty shook his head, sending his long black hair flying. "You're gettin' old. That's your problem."

"No. My problem is *you.*"

Dusty snorted and changed the subject. "You think ol' Quinn and that woman're really married?"

"No." For a moment, Tom's thoughts flew back to the night before.

After the fight and just before they'd had to run for their lives, Tom had had a chance to talk to one of the bar girls. She'd been delighted to tell him all about the handsome cowboy and his "wife" who'd been through town a few days before.

And while Tom was still pondering the idea of Quinn actually being married, the bartender had told him all about hearing Quinn's "wife" screaming his name at the top of her lungs.

Married or not, it seemed to Tom as though Quinn had gotten himself into even more trouble.

"How come?"

"How come what?"

Dusty sighed. "How come you figure they ain't really married?"

"When would they have had time?"

Dusty nodded.

"No," Tom stared at the trail ahead of him. In another day, maybe less, he'd catch up with his old friend. "They were pretending. Probably to throw us off the trail in case we happened by."

"Makes sense," Dusty said with a smile, "but you'd a thought Quinn would have had the sense to cover her mouth so she couldn't be callin' out his name."

"Shut up."

"Anything you say, Sheriff."

"If the bartender was tellin' the truth, we'll likely catch up to Quinn by tomorrow at the latest."

"Unless that storm blows in first."

Tom followed Dusty's gaze to the leaden sky overhead. It might be close.

Quinn leaned on the end of the shovel handle and stared down at the mounds of the two fresh graves. It was a shame, he told himself that all the marker he could give them was a couple of slats off the barn wall with their names crudely carved in the wood. Of course, if Winifred hadn't found their names written on the back of their wedding picture, they wouldn't have had that much.

Winifred.

It had been pure hell staying in the cabin with her all night and not touching her. But his choices had been few. It was either that or stay in the barn and drown. Of course, *she* hadn't seemed real bothered.

Just writing in that book of hers and watching over the children like nothing had happened.

But dammit, something *had* happened. At least, to him! His whole life had been changed by laying with her. Before, all he'd been interested in was getting out of Texas and finding a spot for his mother to spend her quiet years. Now, he wanted to find a place for him and Winifred, too.

He wanted a lifetime with her. He wanted to hold her, kiss her and love her through ten lifetimes.

Unfortunately, she didn't seem interested.

Quinn gave himself a shake and focused on the two fresh grave markers. Richard and Elizabeth Hale. They'd probably counted on a lifetime together too.

Sighing, Quinn tilted his head back and stared at the black, forbidding clouds overhead. He frowned and slowly turned his gaze on the surrounding countryside. Only late morning and already it was darkening up like it was full night.

There was a heavy stillness to the air, too. And it was too quiet by half. He noticed suddenly that there wasn't even the smallest birdsong to be heard.

Glancing down at the small cabin at the foot of the rise, his brain conjured up the image of the woman and children inside. Slowly, he ran one hand over the back of his neck. The small hairs there were standing on end. Almost like something in him recognized danger coming.

Maybe, he told himself, they should leave now, despite what Winifred said about needing some time to get the children's things together for the trip. Maybe they'd be better off closer to Fuego Cruzado. Immediately though, he told himself that would be foolish.

With the feeling that he had about the coming storm, Quinn didn't want to be camping out in the open tonight. Something told him that it would be a hard night to be out under the stars.

By the time she fed the children their supper, Winifred was exhausted. She'd had no idea that such small people could be so demanding. Of course, she admitted silently, if she'd had a bit of help, her first day as a substitute mother mightn't have been quite so tiring.

But Quinn had managed to stay away from both her and the children all day. She'd only caught occasional glimpses of him as he moved about the small farm, caring for the animals and readying them for the final leg of their journey. Strange, she told herself on a sigh, but if her body wasn't stiff and sore from her activities the night before, she would almost be convinced that she'd dreamed the entire episode. It was as if there was an unspoken agreement between them to simply forget about what they'd shared.

"Wi-fed," a small voice shouted. "Wi-fed!" An insistent tugging on her skirt shook Winifred from her thoughts and she looked down into the shining clean face of two-year-old Michael Hale. Or, she told herself with a smile, as the boy would say, "Mi-ko."

Not being used to speaking with children, it had taken Winifred several minutes to interpret the boy's speech when he'd told her his and his sister's names. Now, glancing over to the corner, Winifred saw that "Mana," or as she guessed, *Amanda* was happily playing with her own two feet. Looking back at Michael, Winifred said, "Yes, dear? What is it?"

"Go 'side?"

Well no wonder the child wanted to go outside. He'd been a veritable prisoner inside that cabin for days. She should have taken both children for some fresh air hours ago. But then, Winifred told herself, it was never too late. There was still time for the child to run a bit before bed.

"All right, Michael. We'll all go outside." She hurried across the cabin and picked Amanda up from the quilt spread out on the floor. Besides giving Michael a chance to run off his high spirits, it would give Winifred the opportunity to see Quinn.

The three of them had almost reached the door when the heavy oak panel swung open and crashed into the wall.

Quinn, wild eyed and breathing hard, stood in the doorway. He reached out, snatched up Michael and held him against his chest.

"What is it?" Winifred's arms tightened around the baby until Amanda began to squirm in protest. "Quinn? What's wrong?"

"Come on," he muttered, and grabbed Winifred's elbow to hurry her along.

"Where are we going?" The toe of her shoe caught in her hem and she stumbled. Only Quinn's hand on her arm kept her from falling. The wind, unlike any she'd ever seen, pushed and pulled at her. The folds of her skirt entwined around her legs and her hair was tugged from its knot to fly about her face. Quinn paid no attention to any of it. He simply dipped his hatless head into the wind, cradled Michael close and tried to hurry her steps.

Winifred's heart began to pound erratically. She'd never seen Quinn like this. No matter what had happened to them on their trip, he'd always seemed to be in perfect control.

Now, he clearly was not. And whatever it was that was so worrying him, was certain to terrify her, she was sure of it.

"Quinn, please! Tell me what's happening."

He paused briefly, glanced back over his shoulder and said simply, "Look."

Slowly, hesitatingly, Winifred turned. A long strand of red hair whipped across her eyes and she reached up to pull it away. She felt her jaw drop and instinctively, she tightened her grip on the infant in her charge. Mouth and throat dry, Winifred whispered a frantic prayer as she stared at the monstrous, violently spinning funnel cloud.

"Dear Lord . . ."

"Exactly," Quinn said, then added, "come on. We'll wait it out in the root cellar."

As she turned again, her gaze swept the barn and she grabbed at Quinn's shirt. "What about the horses?"

"I turned 'em loose," he shouted and kept walking. "They'll fare better in the open where they can run. We'll find 'em later."

Without another word, Winifred followed him, trusting him to know what to do. Trusting him not only with her own life, but with the lives of the two babies in their care. She knew he wouldn't let them down.

The tornado was still a good ways off when Dusty spotted it.

There wasn't much cover around, but he and Tom did the best they could. Dismounting, the two men lay flat in a buffalo wallow, each of them holding onto the reins of their animals.

The horses nervously pranced in place and Dusty knew just how they felt. He wanted to get up and run himself. But there was no way to outrun a tornado. Of course, maybe they should let the horses go, but then they'd be afoot in the middle of nowhere. No, they could only hope that the funnel cloud would pass them by.

"Do me a favor, will ya?"

Dusty turned his head until the right side of his face was resting on the dirt. Staring at Tom, he asked, "What?"

"Next time I don't pay attention to you and your Indian dreams," his friend said with a sheepish smile, "you remind me of today."

"I'll do it," Dusty agreed with a grin and silently added the hope that they both lived long enough to argue about it.

*   *   *

It seemed to last forever.

A loud, insistent roar filled the air as if a starving beast were right outside the cellar, trying to get in. Quinn looked up at the grassy roof of the dugout cellar and mentally blessed the late Richard Hale. Digging that root cellar right out of the earth was probably going to save the man's children.

From the sound of the cyclone, nothing much would be left standing when the storm was over.

Quinn hitched Michael a little higher on his lap and pulled Winifred and the baby into the circle of his left arm. Amazingly enough, the kids were sound asleep. Another blessing.

"Will it be all right?"

"Sure it will," he answered instinctively and pressed a quick kiss to the top of Winifred's head.

But she wouldn't be put off by easy promises. Turning to look up at him, she said "Quinn, tell me the truth, please."

He stared down into those green eyes and knew he would do whatever it took to keep her safe. Quinn told himself that he would keep them all safe if he had to go out, rope that damned tornado and tie it down to a mountain top.

Aloud though, he only said, "The cellar's strong. The kids' daddy built well. Everything'll be fine."

She nodded, cocked her head to listen to the roar of the wind for a moment, then burrowed into him. Cradling Amanda against her bosom, Winifred rested her head on Quinn's chest.

It all felt so right, he thought. Oh, not the tornado. But the rest of it. Him and Fred. Together. Children cuddled close. It was all so right and at the same time, so wrong.

At Fuego Cruzado, he would be leaving them.

The kids would go live with their uncle and Winifred would no doubt move on to another adventure. Somehow, he couldn't imagine her going back to Yellow Dog. Not after everything that had happened. Sooner or later, Quinn Hawkins would end up in prison and Banker Bentley would live happily ever after.

Tipping his head forward, Quinn rested his chin on top of Winifred's head and inhaled the familiar, sweet scent of her. Dear God, he asked himself wildly, how would he ever live without her?

"Quinn?"

"Hmmm?"

"I think there's something you should know."

Her voice was a whisper drowning in the eerie shriek of the wind. Quinn bent his head lower, determined to hear her.

"I lied."

"What?"

She leaned in closer to him and in his ear, whispered clearly, "I lied. Last night."

Quinn's heart staggered slightly, stopped, then started again.

"I wanted you to know—in case we die—that I love you."

Jesus! An incredible burst of joy lit up his insides and just as quickly fizzled away. The darkness it left behind nearly choked him.

"Did you hear me?"

"Yeah." He swallowed heavily past the knot in his throat. "Yeah, I heard you."

"Well?"

"I told you, Winifred. We're gonna be all right. We're not goin' to die."

"That's not what I meant," she said directly into his ear again.

He knew damn well what she'd meant. What she was

waiting to hear. What she wanted to hear. But he wasn't in any position to say it. Hell, he wasn't even in a position to *think* it. Quinn clenched his jaw tight and fought down all the useless yearnings swarming in his chest.

Wishing for something didn't make it so.

"Quinn?" She poked him in the chest with her elbow and stared up at him.

Her red hair stood out around her head, making her small, delicate features appear to be even more fragile. There was a streak of dirt on her cheek and baby drool on the bodice of her dress and Quinn thought she was the most beautiful woman he'd ever seen.

He wanted nothing more than to hold her to him for the rest of his life. He wanted to hold her so tightly, no one could ever pull them apart. But wants were little more than wishes.

Though it cost him more than he could have said, Quinn looked down into her slightly upturned, forest green eyes and told her, "I'm sorry, Fred. I can't give you what you want."

A sheen of tears filled her eyes, but she blinked them back. When she lifted her chin defiantly, he was proud of her.

"Can't?" she repeated. "Or won't?"

"Does it matter?"

"Of course."

He shook his head. "Can't or won't . . . nothin' changes either way."

The house was almost gone and the barn was nothing more than a scattered pile of twisted lumber.

Amanda propped on her hip, Winifred gingerly stepped through the mess that had been the cabin's main room. Broken furniture, rain-soaked clothing and ruined foodstuffs littered the area. The baby hummed delightedly and blew bubbles with her drool. Winifred sighed heavily and poked through the jumble looking for the children's clothes that she'd packed so carefully just a few hours before.

Finally, under an upended table, she spied her now bedraggled carpetbag. Squatting down beside it, Winifred used her free hand to undo the leather clasp. Frowning slightly, she rummaged through the wet clothing inside and reassured herself that the few items she'd packed for the children were still there. Sodden and dirty, but there.

Amanda's little fists beat down on Winifred's shoulder and the baby rocked back and forth as if she was astride a child's hobby horse. Winifred smiled into the milky blue eyes staring at her. Strange, how quickly she'd become accustomed to having this child on her hip. Amanda laughed, scrunched up her nose and garbled a long string of unintelligible sounds.

"What is it you're telling me, little one?" Winifred whispered and tickled the baby's chin with her forefinger. "Are you happy that the storm's over? Are you wondering where your brother and Quinn are?" Closing up the carpetbag again, Winifred grasped the handles tightly and stood up. Letting her gaze wander over the surrounding landscape, she mumbled, "Well so am I. To both questions."

Quinn had left right after the storm, taking Michael with him, to search for the horses. They'd been gone for nearly an hour and quite frankly, Winifred wouldn't relax until the two of them were back, safe and sound.

Of course, when they returned, everything would be finished.

Winifred's left arm tightened a bit under the baby's well-padded behind, holding her closer. The adventure was over. Oh, there was still the ride to Fuego Cruzado to be dealt with. And they had to see that the children were turned over to their uncle.

But the adventure she and Quinn had begun together what seemed months ago, was effectively at an end now.

He'd turned her aside. He didn't want her love and had made it quite clear that he had no intention of loving her.

Drawing in a long, deep breath, Winifred stepped out of the rubble and began to walk. A hollowness filled her chest and she thought that she might never feel completely whole again.

Once the children were taken care of, Quinn would be leaving her behind. He hadn't said so yet, but she knew it. Fuego Cruzado was the end of their journey together. And when he rode on, what would she do?

Go back to Yellow Dog as if nothing had happened? Leave Texas behind and go in search of a new adventure? Europe, perhaps?

And then what?

Winifred tilted her head to one side and rested her cheek on Amanda's silky black hair. Slowly, she continued walking until she'd reached the entrance to the root cellar. There, she dropped her carpetbag to the muddy ground and plopped down on the heavy, wooden doors set into the earth.

With Amanda on her lap, Winifred stared out at the distance. Patches of deep blue sky peeked from behind the lingering gray clouds. A soft wind, carrying the scent of rain washed over her.

She'd found so much more in Texas than she'd ever thought to find. No. No more adventures. Winifred reached out and stroked the baby's cheek gently. What adventure could possibly compare to her time in Texas? What more could she hope to find, when she'd already found love?

The memory of Quinn's arms around her in the darkness rushed into her brain and Winifred closed her eyes. Yes, she'd found love—only to lose it again on the very same day.

19

Charles Bentley pulled his bowler hat down firmly on his head, buttoned up his great coat and picked up the bag standing on the desk beside him. His sausage-like fingers curled around the leather grips and a sense of well being filled him.

In the dim light of a single lantern, he allowed himself one last look around the Bank of Yellow Dog. A small flicker of disappointment fluttered in his chest, then was gone. It really didn't matter that he must leave, he told himself. What mattered was that he was now a bit further along on the path he'd chosen.

The money he'd acquired in Yellow Dog would be more than ample to set him up in some other small ranching community in need of a bank. A satisfied smile curved his lips as he lifted the heavy satchel to his chest and wrapped both arms around it like a lover. He could almost smell the distinctive, rich scent of the banded greenbacks inside the bag. The banker sighed. A heady aroma, indeed.

But there was time enough later to enjoy the fruits of his labor. For now, it was time to leave.

He crossed the small room, lifted one edge of the shade and glanced outside. A howling wind drove sheets of rain down the length of Main Street and kept the citizens of Yellow Dog clustered around their fires. He smiled again. By the time the storm cleared, Charles Bentley would have disappeared without a trace.

Humming to himself, Bentley opened the door, slipped outside and paused only long enough to lock the bank behind him. In seconds, he was drenched, but it was a small price to pay for the cover of the storm.

Spinning about, he took a single step and was brought up short by a deep voice.

"Goin' somewhere, Bentley?"

Swiveling his head, the banker looked over his left shoulder and saw a stranger. A tall, powerfully built stranger with a flat brimmed hat shielding his steely gray eyes.

"Yes," Bentley said a little too quickly, "to the hotel. For a bite to eat."

"Good idea," the stranger said and stepped away from the building to come up directly behind the banker. "I believe I'll go with you."

"Now see here," Bentley sputtered, "I am not in the habit of speaking to strangers on the street. Nor am I in the habit of breaking bread with them."

"I'm not a stranger," the big man said, a half smile touching his lips briefly. "I'm a friend of a friend, you might say."

Suspicion and a touch of fear boiled inside Bentley. The cold, piercing rain stabbed at him like thousands of knives wielded by the righteous and the banker fought to remain calm.

The man seemed to tower over him and the portly banker felt beads of sweat roll down his back despite the cold.

"Who?"

"Richard Tankersly of Boston?"

Oh Lord. Bentley's shoulders slumped and the heavy bag he carried seemed suddenly lighter. All it held now was money. His well thought out schemes and carefully laid plans were flying from the satchel to be carried away by the storm.

It was over. All of it.

His meaty hands caressed the leather and he let himself think fondly of the hard won cash inside. What he might have done. What he might have been.

If not for the stranger standing much too closely behind him.

Briefly, the overfed banker considered fighting the big man. There was a pistol in his satchel. If he could get to it, he might be able to squeeze off one shot before being killed.

The clear mental image of himself, lying in the mud, his life's blood slowly draining away, rose up before his eyes and successfully quelled the reckless urge.

No. There was something to be said for knowing when to quit. After all, a true gentleman never dirtied himself in a brawl.

"Let's get out of this rain, shall we Bentley?" the man said.

Beaten, Charles Bentley nodded and stepped off the boardwalk into the muck.

"*My* horsie," Michael crowed and stared down from Reb's broad back to the foal walking along beside them. Quinn chuckled. Couldn't hardly blame the boy for laying claim to the newborn. Probably looked like a boy-sized horse to him. Keeping the fingers of one hand clenched around the waistband of Michael's pants, Quinn held the rope around the foal's neck with a gentle touch.

Glancing at Dusty's mare, Quinn grinned. The old girl looked proud of herself. As well she should be. Not only had she found a safe place to ride out the tornado, she'd managed to deliver her baby all on her own without a bit of trouble.

Won't Dusty be pleased, he thought absently and immediately discounted the notion. For Dusty to see that newborn, the posse would have to catch up to Quinn and Winifred. And dammit, he wasn't ready for that yet.

He had to get to Fuego Cruzado and see that the kids were all right. And dammit, he wanted a little more time with Winifred. Hell, he knew there was no future in it, but couldn't he just have a few more days with her?

In his mind, he heard again Winifred's voice, coming to him out of the darkness in the root cellar, saying "I love you." What he would have given to have been able to tell her the truth. To be able to shout out his love for her. To ask her to marry him and live with him on his ranch.

But the ranch wasn't his any longer. And he didn't have the right to lay claim to Winifred's heart. A man headed for prison wasn't exactly prime husband material.

In a heartbeat, he remembered the look on her face when they'd stumbled out of the root cellar to face the devastation left behind by the tornado. It was as if everything around them had crumbled to the dust her dreams had become. And for the first time since meeting her, Quinn had seen shadows in her eyes.

Knowing that he was responsible for those shadows only made him feel worse.

"Me ride Mi-ko's horsie," Michael announced and threw one short leg over Reb's bare back in an attempt to slide off.

Quinn caught him. Pushing his thoughts aside, he looked at the child entrusted to him. Sturdily built,

Michael Hale already showed the signs of being a big man one day. The boy was strong and stubborn, too. Quinn smiled sadly as a flash of envy ripped through him.

Somebody else would watch Michael and his sister grow up. Winifred would leave Texas and no doubt marry one day. And someone else would give her children. A few years from now, Quinn Hawkins would only be a memory to her.

"Hold on there, kid." With one hand, he settled the boy more firmly on Reb's back. "You stay right there, huh?"

The boy's bottom lip stuck out and tears welled up in his big blue eyes. Ah, Jesus.

"My horsie," the boy complained again and Quinn stopped the horses.

"Now, that baby's too little for a big boy like you," he told the child, who sniffled his response. Quinn frowned and tried to think. Hell, he hated to see a kid cry. Made him feel so damn helpless.

"How 'bout if I ride up there with you?" he said as an idea came to him, "And I'll tell ya a story."

Michael sniffed again loudly, looked down at Quinn and slowly nodded.

"All right then." Quinn rubbed Reb's neck and said softly "Sorry old boy, I thought to spare you carryin' me barebacked, but it ain't much further back to the cabin now." Threading the fingers of his left hand through the gray's mane, Quinn slapped his right palm down on the horse's back and heaved himself up behind the boy. When they were settled and Michael was leaning back against him, Quinn urged the horses into a walk again.

The soothing motion of the animal's gait calmed Michael's tears and the boy demanded, "Story!"

A story. Quinn's mind raced for a moment, then he frowned. Wouldn't you know it, he told himself. The only damned story he could think of was about the one person he'd never wanted to hear about again.

Michael tilted his head back and stared up at Quinn. Those blue eyes of his looked even bigger as he said again, "Story."

Quinn sighed and dutifully began.

"Marshal Travis . . ."

"Goddammit," Tom muttered, "why didn't you hold onto the reins tighter?"

Dusty pulled his foot free of a mudhole, shook the muck from his boot and commented, "I ain't the *only* one who lost a horse, Tom."

He knew that, Tom thought. But he had to have somebody to yell at. Nothing was going right. If he didn't know better, he'd think somebody, somewhere didn't want him following Quinn Hawkins. Tom'd never had so much trouble in his life. Brawls, tornadoes and now, he and Dusty were afoot, looking for horses who might be in Montana by now for all they knew.

"We'll find 'em," Dusty said quietly.

"Is that you talkin'?" Tom asked "Or Night Wind?"

Dusty grinned. "Me."

"That's what I was afraid of."

They rode for two days, traveling slowly to accomodate both the children and Sadie's new baby.

Quinn and Winifred switched off, holding Michael and Amanda in front of them in their saddles. And at night, when they made camp, it felt as though the four of them were a real family.

But now, Quinn told himself on the morning of the third day, that was over. Their time together was ending and the pretense of belonging to each other was exposed for what it really was. A dream.

He pulled up on the reins and drew Reb to a stop.

Keeping one arm snaked around Amanda's belly, he glanced over at Winifred, trying to keep hold of a squirming Michael.

"Fuego Cruzado is ahead," he said, jerking his head toward the horizon. "Should be there in a couple more hours."

Winifred stared into the distance as if she could see the town already.

Turning his own gaze forward, Quinn tried to fight down the sense of dread building in him. But no matter how he battled it, that feeling of coming trouble wouldn't leave him. It didn't make much sense, he knew. And he sure as hell couldn't prove it, but somehow, Quinn was sure that things were goin' to come to a head in Fuego Cruzado.

He snorted an inner laugh. Hell, even the *name* of the town suggested trouble.

"What are you laughing at?" she asked.

Quinn began, "When we get to town, I'll take the kids to the sheriff. He'll know where to find their uncle."

"I thought we would . . ."

"No." He cut her off and gave her a half-hearted smile. Quinn knew she wasn't going to like what he had to say. But he'd been thinking about this for days now and knew it was the right thing to do. Taking a deep breath, he blurted out his plan. "I don't want you goin' with me. It'd be better for you if you go into town alone. Best if no one sees you with me and the kids. That way, if there's trouble, you won't be a part of it."

"Trouble?" Winifred echoed and tightened her grip on Michael. "What kind of trouble?"

"Fred," he said on a sigh, "chances are real good that somebody from Yellow Dog has sent wires out on us. Or at least, me."

"You mean that this sheriff of . . . of . . ." she waved one hand at the distant town.

"Fuego Cruzado."

"Yes. Do you mean to say that the sheriff there might very well know about you and what you did?"

He shrugged and glanced down at the baby when she slapped his arm with her fists. A tired smile raced across his features. Lord he was going to miss those children.

And Winifred.

Looking back at her, Quinn could have sworn he could see the wheels of her mind turning. But it didn't matter what she came up with. His mind was set.

"I don't know. He might. But even if he doesn't know—it's best this way. For you."

"No, Quinn," she said firmly. "I think it should be me who takes the children to the sheriff."

"Fred . . ."

Holding up one hand, she went on quickly. "It's the only thing that makes any sense at all." She lifted her chin and looked him dead in the eyes. "*You* shouldn't go into town at all. In fact," she went on, warming to her idea, "leave us now. We can find the rest of the way ourselves."

"What?"

"I mean it. If you leave this minute, you would have more than sufficient time to get far away from whatever posse might be following us still. And no one in town would have to know that you were even with me."

"You expect me to just ride off and leave you alone with two babies in the middle of nothin'?" Quinn shoved his ruined hat to the back of his head. And he'd thought she couldn't surprise him anymore! Did she really think that he would desert her and the children?

"Hardly the middle of nothing," she said with a slow shake of her head. "You said yourself, the town is just ahead. We'll be fine."

"You're damn right, you'll be fine. Because I'll be there to make sure of it."

"Quinn," she said "I think . . ."

"Dammit, Fred!" he shouted, then shushed Amanda as she started to cry. More quietly, he added, "I ain't leavin' you."

"Fine." Winifred gave him a slow smile and reached out to touch his hand gently. "Then you can understand when I say that I am not leaving you, either."

A long, silent moment passed as they stared at each other. The touch of her fingers on his wrist warmed him through. Quinn looked into those eyes of hers and knew he'd never win this fight. As far as stubborn went, he was pretty sure that Fred would take the crown.

And as much as he hated to admit it, even to himself, he was glad she'd elected to stay with him. Lord knew he was in no rush to be parted from her.

"All right then," he finally agreed. "We go together."

"As it should be," she nodded.

"But you keep your eyes open and if trouble starts, you get the kids and get out of the way."

"What makes you so sure that there will be trouble? You can't know that the sheriff has been informed of the bank robbery."

"True," he said, "but I've got a bad feelin' about this anyway. Hell, even the town name means trouble."

"Fuego Cruzado?"

"In Spanish. In English it means, Cross Fire."

"Cross fire?"

"Yeah. Like when some innocent fool gets caught in the middle between two other fools shootin' at each other?"

"Ahhh . . ."

"Uh-huh." Quinn inhaled sharply. "Just you be sure that when trouble comes, you ain't caught in the cross-fire."

*   *   *

"Sorry folks," the Sheriff said gently, "but Decker Hale was killed in a card game nearly two months ago."

Winifred patted the baby's back absently and looked up into Quinn's worried gaze.

"If you want," the Sheriff added, leaning back in his chair and propping his booted feet up on the corner of his desk, "I'll take those kids down to my sister's place. She's got five of her own, so I reckon two more won't really be a bother." He flicked a quick glance at Michael, who was running in circles around the office. "Reckon you folks must be right tired of watchin' over them two."

Instinctively, Winifred's hands tightened on the baby and Quinn must have read her mind. He dropped one arm around her shoulders and pulled her in close to him. Shaking his head, he told the older man, "If it's all the same to you, Sheriff, we'll just keep 'em with us 'till you figure out what you want done with 'em. They're used to us and . . ."

"Sure, sure," the Sheriff agreed. "I'll contact the state orphan home and let you know what they say."

Orphan home? Winifred's heartbeat quickened. She tossed a glance at Michael and smiled as the boy squatted down to pet an impossibly fat, gray cat. Then slowly, her smile faded at the thought of the sparkling little boy and his baby sister imprisoned in an asylum.

Winifred shuddered. She'd read about such places. The caretakers of those institutions were invariably greatly outnumbered by the needy youngsters and so the children didn't receive the care and attention they deserved.

No, she thought frantically, not *her* children.

"You'll be at the hotel?" the Sheriff asked, looking from one to the other.

Quinn hesitated a moment and Winifred knew what he must be thinking. He couldn't afford to stay in Fuego

Cruzado. For his own safety, he had to leave town. Soon.

"That's right Sheriff," he said softly. "The hotel." Turning slightly, he held out his hand toward Michael. "C'mon son, let's go get somethin' to eat."

Michael jumped away from the cat and curled his little fingers around Quinn's index finger as they started for the door. Winifred felt the Sheriff's gaze on her back until they were safely outside. And even then, a small chill of apprehension refused to leave her. All four of them, she felt sure, were in danger in Fuego Cruzado.

Later, after the children were tucked into beds in the adjoining room, Winifred blew out the light and pulled the connecting door to within an inch or two of closing. Her gaze flew to Quinn, sprawled in the brown leather chair beside their bed.

Their bed.

Pausing for a moment, Winifred realized that she hadn't even blinked when Quinn had registered them as man and wife. Of course, she acknowledged silently, it would have been a bit late to worry about her virtue, or start protesting damage to her reputation. Besides, if she was to be honest with herself, she had to admit that she was glad he'd lied.

Now, she would at least have one more night with him. One more night to try to convince him to admit he loved her.

And he *did* love her. Now she was sure of it.

Hadn't he refused to leave she and the children despite the risk to his own safety? If he didn't love her, he would have taken the opportunity she'd offered him to make his escape. Now all she had to do was make him admit it. To himself and to her.

Slowly, she crossed the room to his side. When he didn't speak, or even look at her, Winifred plopped herself down on his lap. This was not the time for subtlety.

"Fred," he said and tried to push her off.

"No." Winifred linked her arms around his neck, leaned forward and kissed him briefly. "Don't push me away, Quinn. And don't pretend anymore that you don't love me, either."

"Why are you doin' this?" he asked and she saw the regrct in his eyes.

"Because," she leaned into him, fitting her face into the curve of his neck, "I'm beginning to share that feeling of foreboding you spoke about earlier."

His hands smoothed up and down her back and Winifred felt the warmth of him right through her clothing.

"Something *is* going to happen, Quinn. I feel it." She kissed his neck and felt his arms tighten convulsively around her.

"Don't worry," he whispered. "You'll be safe. I'll see to it."

"And what about you?" She drew her head back a bit and stared up at him. "Will you be safe too? Can you promise me that?"

A sad smile touched his lips then disappeared. "Safe?" He shrugged. "They don't usually hang ya for robbin' a bank."

"But you *do* go to prison?"

He let his head fall back to rest against the high back of the chair. His eyes slid closed. "Yes."

"For how long?"

Quinn chuckled but Winifred saw nothing worth smiling about.

"Don't know." He finally said. "Five years? Ten?"

Ten years. Winifred's heart felt like a rock in her chest. Ten long years. Her fingers smoothed through his hair and she snuggled in closer to him. Beneath her, she felt his body stir into life. Deliberately, she wiggled against him.

"Jesus, Fred," he groaned. "Don't make this any tougher than it is already."

"It can't be more difficult than this, Quinn." Her right hand slid down the length of his neck to his chest, then she slipped her fingers beneath the fabric of his shirt.

His breath caught.

"I love you, Quinn," she whispered, "and you love me. We may only have tonight. Don't take that away from me. Away from *us.*"

He looked down at her, caught her hand in his and lifted it. Gently, he kissed her palm, then held it to his cheek. The world seemed to stand still as she watched him fight an inner battle. Shadows covered the clear, deep blue of his eyes and Winifred knew he was torn between loving her and doing what he thought was right. Didn't he understand yet that Winifred knew what was best for her? Didn't he see that she only wanted him?

At last, he seemed to reach a decision. Smoothing her hair back from her face, Quinn's gaze moved over her like a touch and Winifred knew she would always remember this moment.

His blue eyes shimmered with warmth and a hint of sadness as he admitted, "I *do* love you, Winifred Matthews. God knows it'd be better for you if I'd never spotted you in Yellow Dog—but Jesus, I love you."

Something inside her burst and dazzled her entire body with showers of light. She pulled his head down to hers and slanted her mouth across his. Eagerly, hungrily, she kissed him, slipping her tongue inside his mouth as if she needed his very breath to live.

Quinn's hands were everywhere. She felt him surround her with his love, his passion. And when he scooped her up in his arms and carried her to the bed, Winifred simply whispered, "Hurry, Quinn. Hurry."

Desperation colored their loving and in seconds their clothing was lying in scattered piles on the floor. They came together in a rush of sensation that left little time for slow deliberation.

When he entered her, a groan shot from his throat and Winifred wrapped her arms tightly around his shoulders. She lifted her hips to meet his and concentrated on the feel of him inside her. His hard strength flowed into her and when her body joined his in an explosion of mindless release, Quinn's arms were all that anchored her to the earth.

He shifted to roll to one side but she stopped him.

"No," she whispered, reluctant to lose the solid comfort of his body atop hers. "Don't leave me yet."

Quinn pulled his head back and looked down into her eyes. "If I had my way, I'd never leave you."

A single tear rolled from the corner of her eye into her hairline. He followed its trail with his fingertip.

"Don't cry, Fred."

"I won't," she said and blinked furiously to hold any other tears at bay. She refused to ruin this night with tears.

Quinn braced most of his weight on his elbows. Giving her a half-smile, he said "It's been some adventure so far, huh?"

Winifred reached up and smoothed the fall of blond hair off his forehead. Adventure. Strange, she thought. When she'd begun her journey west, that was all she'd been thinking about. Now, she would trade any future "adventures" gladly for the chance to live out the day to day risks and hazards of being in love. With Quinn.

She shifted and wrapped her legs around his waist. Locking her ankles together, Winifred closed her eyes and wiggled her hips against him. In response, she felt his body tighten inside her. He rocked his hips slightly and a tingle of awareness snaked through her already sensitized body.

"*You're* the adventure, Winifred," he whispered and lowered his mouth to hers.

Hours later, Quinn lay wide awake, Winifred tucked against his side. A small scrabble of sound reached him and Quinn looked at the door connecting their room to the children's. Slowly, the door swung open and Michael stumbled through, rubbing both eyes with his fists.

Quinn slid out of bed carefully and walked to the boy.

"Firsty," Michael said softly and Quinn smiled as he picked him up.

"Well then, let's get you a drink real quiet, so's we don't wake Amanda and Winifred, ok?"

The boy nodded and laid his head on Quinn's naked shoulder. His sturdy little arms snaked around Quinn's neck and caused a protective ripple of emotion to shake him.

After his drink of water, the boy drifted right back to sleep and Quinn stood beside the bed watching him for a long moment. It wasn't right, he told himself. Those two kids, all alone. Nobody to look out for 'em.

Hell, if he wasn't in trouble up to his neck, he'd keep 'em himself. Maybe he wasn't the perfect father type. But even Quinn Hawkins had to be better than an orphanage. Slowly, thoughtfully, he left the children's room and crossed back to the bed where Winifred lay waiting, her eyes open now, and watching him.

"Is he all right?" she asked.

"Yeah," Quinn slid back under the covers and pulled her close, "for now." Jesus! There was so much he wanted to do. He wanted to ask Winifred to marry him. He wanted to take her home to the ranch. He wanted to take care of those kids, too. But he couldn't do *any* of it.

Not as a wanted man.

She snuggled in, rubbing her cheek against his chest before asking, "Are we going to let them put those babies in an orphan asylum?"

What else could he do? The only hope for all of them was for Quinn to get his own mess straightened out as fast as he could. And the only way to do that was to give himself up. Take his chances in court. Hell, maybe he'd be lucky and the judge would go easy since the bank would be getting its money back.

Of course, he still might get ten years in prison, too.

But either way, it was the only chance any of them had. He'd been thinking about this for days. Ever since that night in the barn with Winifred. And though it would mean that they would be separated for however long he was in prison, at least they could have a life without looking over their shoulders.

But what if she didn't wait for him? his mind screamed. What if he went to prison and she forgot all about him? Quinn scowled at the notion. He didn't have the right to expect her to wait for him anyway. Besides, this was something he had to do for himself. Not just because he loved Winifred. But because it was right.

"Quinn?"

Her whisper pushed into his brain crowding out the thoughts and plans he would have to deal with in the morning.

"Don't worry about the kids," he told her. "We'll think of something."

They walked out of the hotel dining room into the cool morning air and right into trouble.

Quinn stopped dead and Winifred, looking down at Michael, crashed into him.

"What's wrong?" she asked on a laugh then felt her throat close as she followed Quinn's line of vision to the two men walking their way.

Dirty, mud splattered, with a week's worth of stubble

dotting their tired features, both men were staring at Quinn as though he was an apparition.

The taller of the two slipped his pistol from the holster on his hip and pointed it at Quinn Hawkins. It was only then that Winifred noticed the badge pinned to the man's slicker.

"'Mornin', Tom," Quinn said, his voice even and steady. "Dusty."

"Quinn, damn your hide anyway," Tom snarled. "What the hell did ya think you were doin', robbin' the bank?"

Quinn didn't say anything, just hitched Amanda a bit higher and patted her back reassuringly.

Winifred looked from the two men to Quinn and back again. Fear, anger and frustration bubbled up inside her. Not now, she pleaded with whatever gods weren't paying attention at the moment. Don't take him now, not when we've only just found each other.

Her right hand snaked out, grabbed Michael's wrist, then with her left hand, snatched the baby from Quinn. Standing between him and the two men, she shouted, "Run! Hurry Quinn. Get away!"

Amanda began to wail at the same time Tom Bruner shouted, "Hey now lady, get outa the way!"

But Winifred didn't pay them the slightest bit of notice. Her gaze was locked on Quinn's deep blue eyes as he stared down at her, a smile curving his lips. He lifted one hand, reached out and stroked Amanda's back until the baby quieted.

"Winifred, don't do this."

"You have to get away," she demanded.

"No," he shook his head. "No more runnin'." Bending down, he brushed her lips with his then told her, "I was goin' to turn myself in this mornin', anyway."

"No, Quinn."

"Yes, Fred. It's the only way."

"What's goin' on here now?" The sheriff of Fuego Cruzado marched up, demanding answers.

As Tom explained the situation, Winifred and Quinn stood locked together in an embrace that defied their coming separation. Michael hung onto Quinn's legs with both hands and Amanda fidgeted between them.

"C'mon Quinn," Tom said as he stepped up alongside his friend. "Let's go."

"Go where?" Winifred glared at Tom until the man took one hasty step back.

"To the jail, ma'am."

"Take the kids inside, Fred," Quinn suggested.

"Can't do that," the town sheriff boomed. "That's why I come over so early. Come to get the kids. Fella from the state home's comin' in this mornin' to pick 'em up."

Winifred clutched at Amanda even as the sheriff pulled the baby from her arms. His free hand wrapped around Michael's wrist and tugged until the boy started walking. All the way across the street, little Michael stared back at the two people who had become his world. His baby sister's shrieks sent cold chills down Winifred's spine.

"Winifred . . ."

"Let's go, Quinn," Tom said stiffly, still keeping a wary eye on the small redhead.

"Dammit Tom, can't you wait a minute?"

"Nope." He tugged at Quinn's elbow and dragged him toward the jailhouse.

Dusty continued on to the hotel, shouting as he passed "Where's Sadie?"

"At the livery," Quinn called back, "she's all right. So's the baby."

"Whooeee!" Dusty cheered. "What is it?"

"A boy!"

"Hot damn!"

Still grinning, Dusty stepped up onto the boardwalk and pulled his hat off as he looked down at Winifred. "Don't you worry about ol' Quinn, ma'am. Prison won't hurt him none."

Winifred slowly swiveled her head to glare at him. Lifting her skirt hem a bit, she brought back her foot then slammed the toe of her shoe into Dusty's shin.

She left him, hopping up and down, clutching his injured leg.

20

"*It was a helluva run,*" Tom admitted and drew a stool up close to the barred cell.

"Damn near killed me," Quinn chuckled, then shifted his gaze to stare at the limp, filthy hat in his hands. "But I wouldn't have missed it for anything."

"That hat of yours is a sight."

"It had a rough trip." Quinn smiled at the memories.

"You want me to get you a new one before we head back?"

"Nah." He set the disreputable hat beside him on the cot. "Believe I'll just hang on to this one. Got it broke in just right."

"Broke in?" Tom snorted. "Broke *down* is more like it."

Quinn stared at the blank wall opposite him. Even with Tom's company, being in a jail cell was no Sunday picnic.

"About the woman and those kids," Tom said suddenly.

"It's just like I told you." Quinn glanced through the

bars at his old friend. He'd already been through the story twice. Tom knew as much about it as he did.

"And you say the kids' uncle is dead."

"Yeah."

"Shame."

Quinn snorted. A shame? Yeah, a body *could* say that. Of course, he thought it was a sight more than a shame.

"They'll be all right. The state home ain't all that bad."

Tom sounded so sure of himself that for a moment, Quinn felt a rush of hope. "You've seen it?"

"Well," his friend said slowly, "no. But hell, Texas wouldn't do nothin' to hurt its kids. We take care of our own."

Quinn frowned, leaned back and propped his feet up on the cell door. Now, for the first time in his life, he knew what it was like to be completely helpless. Locked up in a cage away from Winifred and the kids when they most needed him.

Yeah, he was *great* husband and father material.

A loud crash filtered back to them from the front of the jailhouse. Quinn and Tom both glanced at the door that separated the cells from the sheriff's office.

"What was that?" Quinn muttered.

"Beats hell outta me," Tom rose and took a step toward the door, then stopped dead when it crashed open, slamming into the iron bars of another cell.

Winifred stood framed in the open doorway. Her red curls brushed into submission and held away from her face by a wide, green ribbon, she wore a pale green dress with white lace trim on the bodice and an expression of stubborn determination.

Behind her, a pale stranger in a black suit coat and pants waited, his milk-white cheeks stained with red splotches of either anger or embarrassment. Judging from his otherwise meek expression, Quinn wagered that the man was feeling more awkward than hostile. Behind him, the town Sheriff was waving his arms indignantly.

Winifred ignored everyone in the room and walked straight to Quinn. Curling her fingers around the iron bars between them, she squeezed the cold steel until her knuckles were white.

Reaching out, Quinn laid his hands over hers, bent down to look her in the eyes and asked, "What're you up to, Fred?"

"I've brought a preacher, Mr. Hawkins. He's going to marry us. Now."

"What?"

"Marry? Quinn?" Tom echoed with a laugh that died the minute Winifred turned her gaze on him.

Looking back at the man in the cell, she said hurriedly, "Quinn Hawkins, that Sheriff is going to send *our* children to that . . . *asylum* unless we do something immediately!"

"Fred, there's nothing we can . . ."

"If we're married," she cut him off, *"I'll* be able to keep the children." Leaning her forehead against the bars, she added, "I can't let them go, Quinn. I simply can't."

His fingers moved over the backs of her hands as Quinn tried unsuccessfully to soothe her. Somehow it didn't make him feel any better to know that Winifred shared his frustration and anger.

After a moment, he looked past her at the waiting preacher. He could hardly believe she'd done this. Even for Winifred, this was pretty strange. Imagine dragging a reverend down to a jailhouse to perform a wedding! A reluctant smile tugged at Quinn's lips as he turned back to study the top of Winifred's bent head. She really was something. But as much as he'd like to marry her, he simply couldn't do that to her.

"I can't get married," he said, his voice pitched low enough so that only she heard him. "I'm goin' to prison,

Fred! How the hell could you take care of those babies on your own?"

She lifted her head and looked at him through watery eyes. Her voice, shaky but strong, echoed into the small room. "I'm a teacher. I have a position in Yellow Dog waiting for me. We would be fine. Besides, you won't be in jail long. You're returning the money."

Shaking his head, he reminded her "There's still that little kidnapping charge . . ."

"There was no kidnapping."

"What?"

"I went with you of my own accord."

"No one will believe that."

"I'll swear to it."

"You'd lie?" Quinn demanded. "In court?"

She inhaled sharply, then nodded. "For the greater good."

"I don't believe *any* of this," Tom said when Winifred finished talking.

"*I* don't believe you were invited to this conversation," she snapped without sparing him a glance.

Quinn grinned and shot Tom a quick look.

"I beg your pardon," the preacher squeaked. "Is there going to be a service or isn't there?"

Winifred leaned in closer to Quinn before he could answer the other man. Whispering in his ear, she reminded him "There's something else to consider as well. You said it yourself. I might very well be pregnant, Quinn Hawkins."

He jerked his head back and stared at her.

"That's right." A triumphant smile curved her lips as she added in a hushed voice, "You don't want your son to be called a bastard, do you?"

Quinn straightened up, rubbed one hand across his face and glanced at the minister again. After a long moment, he said, "Preacher. Start the weddin'."

*   *   *

"Isn't it the most romantic thing you've ever heard?"

Mercy listened to the woman seated behind her, but didn't turn around.

"Imagine!" Another voice added, "Getting married in a jail cell in order to protect two defenseless children." The woman sighed heavily. "And all to keep his promise to a dying woman. That Quinn . . . he always was a good-hearted boy."

"And now he's married to the schoolteacher." The first woman said. "She seems a sweet little thing."

Mercy smiled to herself, laid money beside her plate and left the hotel dining room. Quinn and Winifred. All of Yellow Dog could talk of nothing else.

Even her own precipitate engagement to Jim Barry was now old news. As if thoughts of him had conjured him out of thin air, Jim strolled up beside her, lifted her arm and tucked it into the crook of his elbow.

"And how is my fiance this fine morning?"

"Still a little anxious," she admitted and fell into step with him. "It isn't every week that a woman finds out she's a mother-in-law *and* a grandmother."

"Prettiest grandma I ever saw."

She looked up into his gray eyes and couldn't even remember what it was like before he'd shown up in Yellow Dog.

"Thank you, *Grandpa*."

He winced, then laughed. "Nice kids, though. Aren't they?"

"Adorable." She leaned into his strength and rested her head on his shoulder. "And Winifred is perfect for Quinn. She'll lead him an interesting dance or two."

"Is that what you've got planned for me?"

"Among other things," she admitted and found it hard to believe that only a couple of weeks ago, her life was in turmoil. How quickly things could change. How good life could be. Now, all she needed to make everything as it should be, was for Quinn to be out of that jail and back on the ranch where he belonged.

"It'll work out," Jim said and she wasn't even surprised that he knew just what she was thinking.

"I hope you're right."

"I'm *always* right."

Mercy laughed gently. "I'll try to keep that in mind."

"Gimme another piece of that chocolate cake, will ya, Quinn?"

Quinn stared at Dusty, amazed at the man's appetite. He'd eaten half the baked goods the ladies of Yellow Dog insisted on showering Quinn with, and *still* wanted more. Carving another slab of cake, Quinn pushed the plate through the slot in the cell door toward his friend.

Dusty grabbed it and dug in. Around a mouthful, he complained, "That whole time we was chasin' you, I about starved to death."

"Nobody asked you to go along," Tom said as he walked into the room.

Quinn groaned when he saw the apple pie the sheriff was carrying. "Who's that one from?"

"Erma."

Quinn's eyebrows lifted and he reached for the pie. "Always did love Erma's pies."

"You know, if the judge does decide to let you go," Tom pointed out as he leaned against the iron bars, "you're gonna be too damned fat to leave the cell."

"I'm a married man now. And a father." Quinn grinned around a forkful of pie. "Got to keep my strength up."

Husband and father. Hmmph. Those words still sounded a bit strange even to Quinn's ears. Of course, the word "prisoner" sounded a little odd, too. But at least his time in Tom Bruner's jail was almost at an end. Justice was moving along at a real good clip, too. Only a week back in Yellow Dog and everything was near settled.

By this time next week, he told himself, he'd either be a free man or sitting in a state prison.

"Hard to believe," Tom commented as he snatched a cupcake off a nearby plate and sat down just outside Quinn's cell, "you bein' married, I mean."

"You were there."

"Yeah." He chuckled at the memory. "That's one wedding I ain't likely to forget." Cocking his head, he looked at his friend and asked thoughtfully, "You think that wife of yours is ever gonna let up on me and Dusty?"

"Give her some time," Quinn said and mentally added, a year or two might do it.

"Ya know," Dusty spoke up as he polished off his piece of cake, "the three of us ought to leave town more often."

"Huh?"

Grinning, Dusty looked at Tom and went on, "Well, lookit what happens! Tornadoes, weddin's, adoptions, banks closin' down . . ."

"That is somethin' I wish I'd seen," Quinn muttered. "Bentley gettin' tossed in jail."

"Yeah," Tom leaned back and stretched his legs out in front of him, "guess that man of your ma's swooped down on Bentley like a dog on a bone."

Quinn frowned slightly. "Still can't believe my mother's gettin' married. Hell, she don't even know this fella . . ."

"Strange," Dusty said slowly. "I remember hearin' Addy Simpson sayin' the very same thing about you and Winifred."

Quinn scowled at him.

"Anyway," Tom interrupted, "I got a wire from Boston a while ago. Bentley, the Pinkerton and that Tankersly fella arrived and Bentley is safe in jail."

"Good." Quinn shook his head. "Imagine that ol' bastard, stealin' money back east to open a bank out here so's he could steal more."

"Right ambitious fella," Dusty commented.

"What about all the property Bentley bought up around here?" Quinn asked Tom. "What happens to it?"

"Don't know. Addy Simpson's sayin' it should revert back to her since she held the notes on the places before sellin' 'em to Bentley" Tom shrugged. "Reckon the judge'll tell us all when he's decided."

Quinn's insides stilled. The trial was almost over. Soon, that judge would be making up his mind not just about land rights, but about Quinn. Maybe, he thought, it would make a difference to the judge that Bentley was a thief. That Quinn had stolen money that had rightly belonged to him. But, then again, robbing a bank was still a crime.

Lord, he was tired.

And he missed Winifred and the kids. Oh, they came by the jail two or three times a day, but it just wasn't the same as being *with* 'em. Jesus, what he wouldn't give to be able to hold Winifred without a wall of bars between 'em.

Hell, he hadn't even been able to introduce his wife to his mother. Winifred had done that on her own, just like she'd been taking care of those kids and standing up to that judge. When she'd told her story in court, she'd almost had Quinn believing that she'd gone with him willingly.

Quick, light footsteps tapped along the floorboards and all three men turned toward the door. Winifred walked into the room and ignored Tom and Dusty deliberately.

Quinn watched his friends ease up from their chairs

and sidle soundlessly out of the room. Dusty in particular walked a real wide circle around her.

Rising, Quinn stepped up to the bars and bent down to kiss her. The cold steel bit into his cheekbone and he reluctantly broke the kiss off quickly.

"You got to get over being mad at Tom and Dusty," he told her.

She tossed a glance at the empty doorway, then looked back at him. "Your *friends?*" Winifred sniffed. "If they were truly your friends, they would have let us escape on the trip back to Yellow Dog."

"Tom couldn't do that and I wouldn't have gone anyway."

Reaching through the bars, Winifred smoothed the flat of her palms across his chest. "Dastardly Dan always escapes."

He caught one of her hands in his and kissed the palm. Smiling gently, he reminded her "And Marshal Travis always catches him again, don't he?"

"Yes." She sighed and leaned her forehead on the cold steel. "Quinn, what are we going to do?"

"We're gonna wait and see what the judge has to say."

"What if he sends you to prison?"

"Then I'll go and serve my time." His voice dropped a a bit. "Fred, I *did* rob that bank. And no matter *how* you tell the story, I *did* kidnap you."

Her lips twisted in a mockery of a smile. "I'm so glad you did."

"Me too."

"But Quinn, if you go to prison . . ."

"I've been thinkin' about that," he said, successfully cutting her off. "If I get five or ten years—"

She groaned.

"Fred, listen." He cupped her face with his hands and ran his thumbs gently over her cheekbones. "Five or ten years is a long time."

"Too long."

"And I don't want you wastin' around waitin' on me when you could be livin' your life, so . . ."

Her gaze snapped up to his and she jerked away from his touch.

"Fred . . ."

"No."

"Just listen."

"I will not listen to nonsense."

"It ain't nonsense."

"It is if you're thinking of telling me to divorce you and love someone else."

Pain stabbed at him. Just the thought of Winifred in the arms of another man was enough to kill him. But he didn't have the right to ask her to wait.

"You're a young woman," he managed to say. "You deserve to—"

"I *deserve* to have my husband beside me," she finished for him. "That's what I deserve and that's what I'm going to have." Reaching through the bars again, she grabbed his shirt front and pulled him toward her. "If I have to wait five, ten, even *twenty* years." Her hands slid up his chest until she could touch his face. "Don't you understand yet, Quinn Hawkins? I love you. You. No one else. And no matter how long it takes, the children and I will be right here in Yellow Dog, waiting for you."

The cold hard knot of his last defenses dissolved into a puddle of warmth in his chest and to his embarrassment, Quinn felt a sheen of tears fill his eyes. Quickly, he ducked his head so she wouldn't see and be ashamed of him.

Winifred smoothed her palm against his cheek and forced him to turn and look at her.

His own breath was strangling him. Tears ran down her cheeks, leaving shining silver trails across her flesh. She brushed her index finger across his face, gently wiping away the single tear that had fallen despite his best effort.

"I *love* you."

"Jesus, Winifred," he whispered and stuck his arms through the bars to hold her, "don't ever stop."

"Sit *down*, Mrs. Simpson," the judge bellowed and slammed his gavel down on the desk in front of him.

"I only wanted to tell you," Adelaide said, ignoring the man's shout.

"I heard from you already," the short, barrel-chested judge glared at Addy over the top of his spectacles. "If I hear anything else unless I *ask* for it, I'll hold you for contempt and you can go to jail."

"Well!"

Pockets of laughter rang out from the back of the schoolhouse and Adelaide spun around to glare at the crowd.

"Addy," her husband whispered and tugged at her lavender skirt, "sit *down!*"

Winifred frowned at the woman. It was hard to believe, but just three or four weeks ago, she'd actually shared a stagecoach with that woman. Now, it was all Winifred could do to remain in the same building with her.

Mercy Hawkins reached over and patted her hand and Winifred smiled at her mother-in-law. Curling her fingers around Mercy's, she glanced at her husband's profile, then turned her attention to the judge.

Everyone for miles around had crowded into the tiny schoolhouse to watch Quinn's trial. Of course, she thought with disgust, since Quinn had pled guilty, there really hadn't been much to watch. Except of course for the parade of character witnesses Tom had rounded up to speak for Quinn.

Now though, it was all over.

The judge had made his decision and they were all gathered to hear it.

Winifred's stomach flip-flopped and her toe began to tap rhythmically against the floor. She thought about the two children waiting for her back at the Hawkins' ranch. She remembered how the children and she and Quinn had been together and frantically prayed that this judge would do the right thing and send Quinn back to the family that needed him.

"What is that blamed tapping noise?" Judge Harlo Thornton shouted, glaring at the people in front of him.

Guiltily, Winifred winced and stilled her foot.

"All right now," Judge Thornton said and glanced at Quinn. "I've heard all the evidence, Mister Hawkins and I guess I'll have to go along with you. You are indeed guilty."

A hush of conversation rolled out over the crowd and Quinn sent her a sad smile over his shoulder.

Winifred's heart had plummeted to her feet but as the judge kept talking, she began to see a ray of hope after all.

"But first things first," Thornton started as he pointed his index finger at Adelaide Simpson. "You say you want the property and water rights returned to you since Charles Bentley purchased the notes with stolen money."

"That's right, your honor," Adelaide sniffed and rose stiffly. Folding her hands in front of her, she lifted her chin and announced clearly, "The people who borrowed that money from my husband haven't paid it back."

"But you sold those notes to Bentley."

"Yes, but . . ."

"And, I could add, you didn't give a hoot in hell if your friends and neighbors were goin' to lose their homes in the deal, either."

"Now, really!"

"You tell 'er, judge!" someone shouted.

"Yee-haw!"

"Quiet!" Thornton brought his gavel down in a thunderous burst of raps.

"Mrs. Simpson," he said sternly, still glaring at her over the rim of his glasses, "you sold those rights with no thought to anyone but your own greed. You didn't check on Mr. Bentley's credentials. You only cared that he had enough in his wallet to make it worth your while."

Adelaide's face blossomed a bright fiery red.

"What you didn't bother to find out was that the money in his wallet wasn't his to begin with." He folded his black clad arms on the desk before him. "Now, you want to keep that money *and* have the land rights back."

She inhaled sharply, indignantly.

"Well, you ain't gonna do it."

"What?" she shouted.

Applause shook the tiny schoolroom until the judge called out for silence again.

"You will return the money Mr. Bentley paid you. It will be sent along to Bentley's first victim in Boston. As for the land rights in Bentley's possession at the time of his arrest—they will be returned to their original owners."

Mercy squeezed Winifred's hand tightly.

This time, it took a good ten minutes for the judge to restore order. When he did, he waved that gavel at Adelaide until she paled.

"Maybe *this* will teach you a good lesson, Mrs. Simpson. Accepting stolen money for goods is a criminal offense. You could have gone to jail."

"But I didn't know . . ."

"Ignorance is not an excuse," he shot back, "though Lord knows, you're a fine example. From now on, I'm willin' to bet that you'll be a sight more careful who you do business with." Thornton glanced at Tom. "Sheriff."

"Yessir," he leaped to his feet.

"After court, you come and get these property rights and distribute them properly."

"Be a pleasure, judge." Tom sat down again, grinning.

"As for you, Mister Hawkins."

Tom nudged him and Quinn stood up to face the judge.

Thornton took his glasses off and rubbed the bridge of his nose tiredly.

"This whole town seems real fond of·you, Mister Hawkins. I don't believe I've ever heard so many character witnesses at one time."

Quinn stood ramrod straight and met the judge's gaze steadily. But Winifred saw that his hands were curled into tight, helpless fists. She ached to be standing beside him.

"As to the bank robbery," Thornton said, "I understand what drove you to it, son, but someone might have got shot."

"Shit," Dusty's father shouted from the back of the room, "Quinn Hawkins wouldn't shoot nobody. Not unless they needed it bad."

"Quiet!"

A corner of Quinn's mouth lifted then fell again quickly.

Frowning at the laughing crowd, Thornton went on. "Let's us deal with the kidnapping first, then."

All eyes shot to Winifred, who straightened perceptibly in her seat. Mercy's fingers tapped against hers comfortingly.

"Now, Miss Matthews—" he caught himself "I beg your pardon, *Mrs.* Hawkins, insists that she went with you on her own accord. Is that true?"

Winifred held her breath.

"No sir, it ain't."

Her breath escaped her in a rush.

"I didn't think so," the judge said softly.

"Don't hold it against her for lyin', though judge," Quinn told him. "Winifred's about the most honest person I know. She was just tryin' to help, is all."

"Hmmm . . ." Thornton shifted his gaze to Winifred who glared right back at him.

"And the children?" the judge asked, looking back at Quinn. "You and your wife adopted them?"

"Seemed the only right thing to do, sir." Quinn's voice was sure and steady. "They was all alone and we," he glanced at Winifred long enough to smile at her before turning back to face the judge, "well, we love 'em, your honor. We'll do right by 'em."

"You could have left them behind," Thornton reminded him, "and made your escape."

"No sir, I couldn't do that. I promised their ma that we'd see they were safe."

"I see."

Several long minutes passed and the tension in the little schoolroom was thick enough to choke a lesser woman. Winifred bit down hard on the inside of her cheek and tried to concentrate every prayer she'd ever learned on Quinn.

"Mister Hawkins," Thornton said abruptly, "I'm going to offer you a deal."

"A deal?"

"Yes. If you give me your word that you will leave Texas and never see either the children or the former Miss Matthews again, I will set you free."

"What?" Winifred jumped to her feet.

Quinn looked at her solemnly for a long moment, then turned back to the judge.

"No sir. You'll just have to send me to jail, I reckon." He took a long breath and finished in a rush. "Y'see, I gave my word to that dyin' woman to see to her children and I'm goin' to do just that. As for Winifred, well." He paused for another look at her. "It started out a kidnap-pin', your honor. But it ended up somethin' altogether different. I love my wife and if I have to go to jail for ten or twenty years, then I'll do it just so I can come back to her." He swiveled his head and met the judge's steely gaze. "The one thing I *won't* do is promise to stay away from her. That'd kill me."

"That's all I need to hear," Thornton said and stood up. "I just wanted to see for myself what kind of man you were, Hawkins. And you're all right."

Gathering up his papers and shoving them into a satchel, Thornton said in a loud, deep voice "Your sen-tence is this. For the next year, three days out of every week, you'll be workin' for Sheriff Bruner, to make up for his wasted time in chasin' you down. You will do any job required of you. Understood?"

"Yessir," Quinn said, his surprise evident in his tone.

"In addition, you will build this town a new school-house." He glanced around at the peeling paint and the one broken windowpane. "A growin' town is going to need a bigger school. And when you've finished with that, you can put a new roof on the church."

Quinn nodded.

Snatching up his hat, the judge shook a finger at Quinn. "And while you're on that roof, you might give thanks to the Lord for your friends and that family of yours. Maybe that'll keep you from doin' anything else foolish in this life."

"Yessir."

"Because Mister," the judge lowered his voice a bit, "if you're ever standin' in front of me in court again, you'll be too old to walk by the time you leave prison!"

Quinn nodded, but couldn't keep a slow grin from blossoming on his face.

Straightening up, the judge finished, "I'll be back from time to time, to see that your sentence is carried out." Then, letting his gaze stray over the gathered crowd, Thornton yelled, "Court's over! Somebody gonna buy me a drink?"

Tears blinded Winifred. She heard Mercy laughing and crying in Jim's arms. She knew Quinn was free, but somehow, she couldn't make her legs work well enough to carry her to his side.

Then he was there, holding her and all she had to do was hold him, too. She tipped her face up to his and received his kiss as the blessing it was. When he pulled back, and whispered, "Let's go home," her tears finally began to fall.

Epilogue

"Fred!"

Running bootsteps echoed along the hallway and reached Winifred just seconds before Quinn himself charged into the bedroom.

He stopped dead in the doorway and she watched his jaw drop.

Winifred hitched her newborn son a little higher in her arms and looked from him to his father. "You're late," she said.

"Why didn't you send for me sooner?" He snatched his hat off and crossed the room like he was walking on eggs.

"I sent for you as soon as the pains started," she said with a smile. "Your son was in a hurry to get here."

"My son?" He kneeled down beside the bed and stretched out one hand toward the blanket-wrapped bundle in her arms. "We have a boy?"

Winifred pulled the edge of the blanket back so Quinn could see his son's angry red features. "Isn't he beautiful?"

Quinn ran the tip of his finger across the baby's scalp gingerly. "Beautiful?" He shook his head slightly. "Handsome, yes. Won't Michael be pleased?"

Their little boy would indeed be happy. He'd been hoping for a baby brother. And Winifred knew Mercy would be delighted with her latest grandchild.

"You'll have to send a wire to Austin. Let your mother and Jim know so they can bring the children home."

"Can I hold him?"

"Of course. He's your son."

Quinn eased himself down on the mattress and carefully took the baby from Winifred. Shaking his head, he stared down into the tiny features and whispered, "Imagine that. A son." Blinking suddenly, he turned toward Winifred. "What're we gonna call him?"

"I've already decided, if it's all right with you." Winifred inched herself up and leaned into her husband's side. "I'd like to call him Travis."

"Oh, no you don't."

"It's only fair, Quinn Hawkins."

"How do you figure?"

"Why, if it wasn't for Marshal Travis's books, I never would have come west and we never would have met and we never would have been so happy." She paused for breath and smiled up at him. "Would we?"

Quinn grinned and kissed the top of her nose. "You got me there," he finally agreed. "But I'm tellin' you right now, Fred. If the next one's a boy too, you ain't callin' him Dastardly Dan."

Let HarperMonogram Sweep You Away!

Simply Heaven by Patricia Hagan
New York Times bestselling author with over ten million copies in print. Steve Maddox is determined to bring his friend's estranged daughter Raven home to Alabama. But after setting eyes on the tempestuous half-Tonkawa Indian, Steve yearns to tame the wild beauty and make Raven his.

Home Fires by Susan Kay Law
Golden Heart Award-Winning Author. Escaping with her young son from an unhappy marriage, lovely Amanda Sellington finds peace in a small Minnesota town—and the handsome Jakob Hall. Amanda longs to give in to happiness, but the past threatens to destroy the love she has so recently found.

The Bandit's Lady by Maureen Child
Schoolmarm Winifred Matthews is delighted when bank robber Quinn Hawkins takes her on a flight of fancy across Texas. They're running from the law, but already captured in love's sweet embrace.

When Midnight Comes by Robin Burcell
Time Travel Romance. A boating accident sends detective Kendra Browning sailing back to the year 1830, and into the arms of Captain Brice Montgomery. The ecstasy she feels at his touch beckons to Kendra like a siren's song, but murder threatens to steer their love off course.

And in case you missed last month's selections . . .

Touched by Angels by Debbie Macomber
From the bestselling author of *A Season of Angels* and *The Trouble with Angels.* The much-loved angelic trio—Shirley, Goodness, and Mercy—are spending this Christmas in New York City. And three deserving souls are about to have their wishes granted by this dizzy, though divinely inspired, crew.

Harper
Monogram